The Ruler of the Earth

Shanon Ngampiyaskul

Table of Contents

Prologue

The tables around the hall were covered up with perfectly white cloths for the 30th anniversary of the old people's home. Although the party had been the same every year, this year, the people were making a big deal out of it. With a full day of preparation in advance, the managers ordered their employees to clean the stinky old place up. The carpets were turned over, the bushes outside were trimmed, the service was filled with even more smiles than ever and everyone was happy.

They even pulled out their stashed-away money to buy a new flat-screen television just for us so we would spend the rest of our lives (which would not be very long) entertained by fake crap on the screen. Now that it was finally the grand lunchtime, the rest home was decorated with little colored balloons of red and black that floated against the ceiling. They looked pitiful since they were unable to go anywhere, and they drifted aimlessly a few inches at a time before they stopped and collided with other balloons.

"I can walk by myself," I said to the young assistant.

"But ...madam," he said, but I brushed him away. With my cane to support my weight, I did not need aid. Although the arthritis was getting worse every day, my pride did not allow me to be the one who needed help.

I sat down very slowly on a hard wooden chair which I had always despised. On the table laid a tray of hors d'oeuvres consisting of nuts, crackers, and dips of various sauces. I tried some but did not like them very much. My taste buds were fading quickly these days, such that I could not remember when was the last time I tasted anything good. My neighbor, whose room was opposite mine, sat down along with a few other old girls and boys I knew pretty well from our daytime socialisation.

I joined in their conversation just to be polite. It was again about family. It was always about family in this place: daughters getting married, sons getting married, granddaughters ran away from home, and grandsons going off to war. I could not blame them, since the young

4

people were the ones making a difference while we, the broken objects from the past, were discarded by society.

When one of them was about to start another topic—this time it was about the past—the soup came. It was a slightly better version of the usual tomato liquid we always had. There was even a basil leaf on top, which usually would not be there. Even the taste was a little better.

They've really put an effort into this, haven't they? I thought.

When the main course was served, I felt my appetite was already at rock bottom from the blandness of the food. When one of the assistants walked past us to serve the tables behind, my closest neighbor stopped him and asked what was in it.

"It's the grade-S meat." The young man showed us the plate. With a huge smile on his face, he pointed towards the half-raw chunk of meat still oozing red blood from its pores. He then continued, explaining the vegetables, saying what they were and what amazing techniques were used to cook them so beautifully.

Everything else on the dishes was irrelevant to me. All I could see was the meat, the big lump of muscle on white porcelain, and the past came back into my head. It was the ferrous smell of blood, the scream of people, and the redness covering the floor.

"Are you okay?"

I came back to reality when my acquaintance touched me. My hands were shaking uncontrollably. My breathing was heavy and rapid. I looked her in the eyes and tried to convince her to believe me.

"I'm fine," I lied, and she accepted my statement easily, since she immediately turned to stare at the meat from the other tables. All the old people's faces were the same: Their eyes brightened, their pupils dilated, and a big grin on their faces.

My neighbor was licking her lips. Her saliva was pouring out of her mouth messily. It was as if the eight-four-year-old woman had become a hungry wolf. The conversation had stopped completely by now and all focuses went to the main course. I kept telling myself that it was all reasonable. These people of my age were born during the Depression. It was natural that they so gravitated towards food.

"Sorry to keep you waiting." The same assistant came back to our table, bringing two platters, and decided to put one down in front of me.

"Someone else goes first." I quickly pushed the platter to the middle of the table, where my other neighbor took it without delay. Apart from the two people who were now ravenously digging into their food, the rest were simply staring at the platters without making a noise.

Forks and knives made clicks and clacks. They banged each other with so much ferocity, the tables were shaking; it was a sound of desperation, resonating with our very first instinct that existed within this world: eat or be eaten.

Soon the server came back again with the rest of the plates for everyone on the table. Everyone took theirs eagerly, except me, excusing myself by saying that I was not hungry. The others kept insisting that I eat, even when their eyes told me otherwise. If I did not take mine, there would be more for them. They said how delicious the meat was; even the assistant was trying to make me eat it.

"I said I don't want it!" I shouted and stormed off, suddenly ignoring my difficult mobility, and left the dining hall without looking back, knowing that people would be eyeing at me strangely. I did not care. The back door was right there in front of me, yet it seemed so far away.

Passing countless other tables with the meat and its devourers, my head spun, and I felt like vomiting. After limping across the hall for what seemed like forever, I eventually made it out alive.

There they were: the ray of sunlight, the fresh air, the gentle wind of the real outside world. I breathed in deeply once and the lingering scent of blood in my nose disappeared. As I kept walking, I left the noises of knives and forks behind as well, and soon I was better.

Sitting under a huge maple tree, I felt sunshine shine down on my face, gently touching the sunspots I had since I was a little girl. The birds were chirping the same old tune, the very same melody that remained unchanged for seventy years such that I could even sing along, and so I did until I was tired and decided to lie completely on my back. This time, I let the birds do their parts and I kept quiet.

"How can the world be this cruel when it is this beautiful?" I asked them.

No matter how much I tried, I could not forget the haunting nightmare of the past, even though I thought everything had changed. I realised that nothing had changed. I closed my eyes and drifted into the days of yore, to when I was still oblivious to the world around me.

Chapter 1: The Forest

Lying asleep beneath a tree, I felt something move across my face. When I stood up and wiped it away, a soft object landed with a thud and continued moving on the ground. My hair stood on end with disgust and the sweat poured out from my face. I stepped back—a little too far backward. To my side, staring with amused eyes and a big smile on her face, was Carla, laughing at me uncontrollably.

"What the hell is that thing?" I yelled, but there was no answer, because the laughter continued. It was no less than a minute before she could compose herself.

"You don't know?"

"No, it's so weird. What is it?"

"That's a caterpillar."

"A caterpillar? Oh! I've heard of it." I recalled my mom telling me when I was younger but never actually seen one. As soon as I was lost in thought, Carla picked the creepy creature up and came at me again. After what felt like forever, she stopped chasing me and put it on a tree.

"Sorry, I'll give you a hug," she offered, but I pushed her away.

"I'm not touching you again. Where do those things even come from anyway?" I asked, not expecting an answer.

Carla smiled, and even without her looking back or saying anything to me, I understood her perfectly. Her caramel-colored legs stood squarely pointing towards the darkness of the forest. Her large brown eyes on her tanned, perfectly rounded face were mischievous.

"Have you ever wondered what is in the forest?" she said, knowing that I knew the answer. The caterpillar came from there. Devils, murderers, disasters, sicknesses, every strange thing come from there. We were told to stay away from the forest. It was a known fact that everyone adhered to.

"No." I whispered it too quietly for Carla to hear.

"Then let's go." Carla patted me on the shoulder with her muscular right arm. I stood still in indecision.

"Come on, just for a little way and we can come back. There's nothing dangerous about the forests. Come on, Cat."

"Fine, just a little way..." I agreed and decided to follow her.

Carla's enthusiasm was unwavering and it was a little reassuring for me to have her by my side. Carla had never been afraid of anything since I had known her, and scary stories would not usually stop her from her adventure.

I looked back in the direction of Mister Sam's house for the last time. It was the closest marker of civilisation that I would fall back to if anything happened. I prayed to my faraway mother to keep me safe from harm. Then realised that I was now disobeying her, so it was no use asking.

"Hurry up, Cat!" Carla yelled when I was hesitating for the final time before I stepped into the darkness of the forest.

As soon as we were in there, Carla was already hopping from one place to another on her light feet. I was struggling to take proper footing on the slippery ground where tree roots were entwined in irregular and inconsistent undulation. Looking down as I walked, I did not notice how far I had come until I caught up to Carla.

"Sorry to hold you back," I said.

"That's okay. You are not doing half bad yourself." She just smiled at me, hinting at no impatience at all. The way we were heading was all dark. Even though it was in the middle of the day, the leaves were so thick they blocked out most of the sunlight. I looked back at where we just came from and it was nothing more than a small hole. It made me scared.

"You'll be okay." Carla grabbed my left arm gently. "We'll walk together."

It was probably half an hour further before Carla did something strange. She stopped suddenly and put an arm in front of me, her eyes staring forward, her ears listening, and her body tense. She glanced at me and put a finger to her mouth. I remained as still as possible.

Even though I noticed nothing, my friend's keen ears probably heard something. It was not until we started walking again that I noticed it. We stopped and it stopped. We listened and it made no sound, but when we walked again, it moved along with us. Carla broke off a branch of a tree and held it as a weapon.

"The curse is real, Carla. We shouldn't have come here," I whispered to her.

"No, it's not a curse. I know it's not and I'm going to find out what it is," She walked in the direction the sound came from. Without saying any more, she started sprinting and vanished behind the thick bushes. In an instant, Carla was gone and I was completely alone.

The forest remained unmoving. The ground was still. The wind was no longer blowing. Everything became completely silent and devoid of life. My eyes began to dart on their own from left to right, then above and below, then to the left and right again. I was not sure what to do.

Scared stiff and speechless, I felt my brain was devoid of any useful thought.

So I crouched down and waited, listening for danger and tried to control my breathing. Faintness came to me, and I had to resist. Just a moment ago, Carla had been right there, but now there was not even a sound of her in any direction.

"She knows where I am, so I will wait," I told myself.

But as time passed, I began to grow more afraid. I waited nervously in that spot for a long while—maybe it was ten minutes—but there was still no sign of her. I feared that she had been injured somewhere in the forest and could not come back on her own.

"She needs me!" I stood up. "If I do nothing, she will die."

Despite my nervousness getting worse, I kept walking to the direction Carla had gone while shouting her name.

The forest was getting thicker. The creeping plants and bushes were obstructing my path so much that I had to use my hands to tear them apart at times. Some of them were trampled on, so I figured out that they were the path that Carla had taken. Her footprints were everywhere; I followed them, one by one, making sure not to miss until I eventually came to a large opening where they disappeared.

There was a large amount of water on the ground flowing in one direction. The strange thing was that the liquid was constantly flowing down from the top of the hill. It was as if someone was pouring it down from a cup twenty times the size of me. The sound it made was loud, yet surprisingly calming. I expected the water to run out, but it would not stop no matter how long I waited. I simply stood there and watched it in astonishment. After all, it was the first time I had seen a waterfall. I lost myself in the moment and forgot that I had to rescue my best friend until I saw someone coming out of a hole behind the wall of a vertical torrent.

An old man with a scruffy brown beard in a cautious manner started to scan the surrounding so carefully before coming out as if he was hiding something. His face was crossed, his brows curved down in a frown, and his lips shut tight. He was angry and his massive body made him looked even more dangerous. I hated to think about what he was going to do with his captive.

Anyhow, I was too far away and he had not seen me. But not soon after, the man started walking towards my direction, so I slowly concealed into the thicker part of the bush and went into a prone position.

Holding my breath and pinching my eyelids shut, I prayed to my mother. "Do not see me, do not see me, please, do not see me." His footsteps came closer and closer, and after some time that seemed like forever, he finally went past me and disappeared into the other direction. He did not notice, but it was another thirty seconds that I kept myself hidden before emerging.

There was something behind that curtain of water, I knew from the way that man had come out before. After jumping from one slippery rock to another to avoid getting my shoes wet, I finally came to a hole where the water did not fall.

The grotto was so dark I could barely see the outline of the walls. The light cast at my back gave rise to a large looming shadow of myself on the wet floor. Even though I knew it was nothing more than a mere silhouette, a terrifying thought came into my mind: This was the place where the monsters hid, and I was stepping right into their lair. Their fangs and claws were already waiting for me. And maybe that outline of my body was not so harmless after all.

11

"Carla!" I shouted to snap out of my stupidity. I breathed in harder and used my voice to give me courage. There was still no response, so I moved inside a little further. When my eyes adjusted to the darkness, the outline of something big was blocking the path in front of me.

Two cuboidal structures, interconnected with a common passageway, with a chimney at the top that opened up to a small hole in the ceiling of the cave. I guessed it was some sort of a hut from the appearance. When I tried its wooden door, it opened easily into a room where the only source of light was from an oil lamp on a wooden table.

Taking it in as though I owned it, I started exploring. The first room was a kitchen with two wooden chairs and a table. A clay pot, still steaming hot from recent cooking, contained some food that smelt good.

When I looked closer, another disturbing thought came into my mind. I saw in there, in pieces, fingers, toes, ears, eyes, torn to bits—my body parts, chopped up by the monsters and put inside this pot, to be cooked slowly for several hours until the monsters could simply suck the meat from my bones.

It was one of many tales my mother had told me when I was naughty. Unlikely to be true, but I still hated to think that Carla could be in there. I hurriedly left the kitchen before more negative thoughts came to me. I passed through a tiny corridor to the other room.

"Carla!" I shouted, again using my voice to keep my fear at bay.

The next enclosure was just as gloomy as the first. After looking around the space, it seemed to be a bedroom. The small messy wooden bed in the center of the room had nothing underneath its smelly old blanket. The other side of the room housed a wardrobe with its doors shut tight.

When I tried to pull it open properly, something else shocked me: One of the double doors appeared to be out of place. It was shaggy, old and a much deeper brown compared to the rest of the armoire.

That particular piece of wood presented a line of letters carved into its surface. The carving was sketchy, barely done properly, as if the writer was in the biggest hurry. To top it off, they were not just any letters, but ones I recognised straight away, because it was the very

12

same sentence written on my most precious item: the locket that my mother had given me on the last day I saw her.

Suddenly, the front door of the house opened with a creak so loud my hair stood up. The man was back. I froze briefly but managed to hide in time. I went under the bed and lay still. The man's footsteps were clear as he walked around the house and talked to someone in the other room.

So, there are at least two of them in the house, I thought. As soon as I thought I could wait for them to leave, the talking stopped and something rushed in my direction. Then I realised what it was; its footsteps were light and did not sound like any living being.

I held my breath as the monster approached. It came straight to me as if it knew where I was. It made a strange loud noise that only a monster could ever make and I began to cry.

The man eventually caught up after the monster then ordered it to quiet down. He moved the bed and dragged me out. Too terrified to move even an inch, I closed my eyes so that I did not have to look at his face or the monster.

Like a prisoner truly guilty of her crime, I let myself be carried away without struggling. I never opened my eyes during the transportation but I felt the coarse hairs of his arms prick into my skin. When he put me down on the cold wet floor of the cave, I still had my eyes shut tight, and the next thing I felt was the monster sniffing me.

"Don't hurt me," I prayed. "Please…"

However, the smelling continued as the monster readied its appetite. The man shouted something I did not understand, but it immediately responded to his command by stopping and left.

"Who are you?" he asked, sounding too calm for a man who just had his house invaded. I opened my eyes. In front of me was a man with a lot of fur on his face. His skin was dark, barely contrasting to his brown beard but distinct from his blue eyes.

"I'm Cattleya," I answered honestly.

"No! Who are you exactly?" He asked again.

"My name is Cat," I answered but he was already asking me another question.

"How did you find your way in here?" His voice was getting annoyed, I could tell.

"I got lost."

"That might be right. There was another girl who looked like she was lost too. I assume you two are with each other?"

"Carla! Where did you take her? What did you do to her?" I was desperate for an answer, so I forgot my position and raised my voice.

"Nothing. She did not see me, so I let her go. She must have gone back the way she came already," he said and held his hand out. "And so should you. You have to get out of here too."

I looked at the hand and then his face, not confident that I could trust him. His hands suddenly grabbed mine and pulled me up. His palm was three times as big as mine and rough as tree bark. He dragged me with him out of the cave until we came to the space in front of the waterfall, where he released my hands.

"So you are letting me go?" I asked him, unsure.

"Yes, but you must forget about me and this place. You have to understand that you cannot come back here again," he said, staring off into the distance.

"Why?"

"Just keep going in that direction." Without acknowledging my question, he simply pointed. Not believing him fully, I looked him in the eyes for guidance, but they were expressionless. His lips were unsmiling, his brow gave no frown, and his eyes betrayed no emotion. I guessed I had to trust him after all.

"But why, sir?" I asked him again politely.

"Stop asking questions, little girl. You must forget about me. Go! And never come back." His stares were coming straight at me and his voice had that commanding tone, just like a trainer's voice, that I could never resist. So my legs began walking on their own. I kept going without looking back.

This might be a game to him. Maybe he will send his monster after me to hunt, I thought.

But the creature never came, and eventually I found myself back at the special place at the back of Mister Sam's property.

Every week when I came back to our special spot, the memory of this day would pop up in my mind. I would stare into the forest for hours. It was not a place of curses and death anymore, but a land of mystery. Although I did not want to go inside again, the experience had already been engraved into my brain, and there was no way I could ever forget about it.

However, it was not the same for Carla. After that day, she never came with me to our special place again, even though she said she came back safely a long time before me and did not even encounter the monster. It was as if she was hiding something. But whenever I asked her, she never answered, so I kept my story to myself as well. Maybe, on that day, something had changed us so much that we could not be the same ever again.

Chapter 2: Routine

I always woke up by my internal clock before the mechanical alarm even went off every morning. It was a fact that I was proud of, yet I was never too keen to get out of bed. Although I was conscious, my eyelids would often sit there lazily, and my body would lie still in bed until the actual alarm.

I waited and wondered what the day had in store for me. The hall bell finally rang loudly, its vibration was so intense that I could feel my bed move with it.

I jumped off my bed in one swoop to psych myself up. My small body made no sound as my soft feet landed on the cold stone floor. Once again, I decided to wake my best friend who was still sleeping soundly in the middle of the earth-shaking vibration of the alarm.

I had to wake her up nearly every single day ever since she became such a heavier sleeper. I was not free of fault either because I was spoiling her by helping every morning. I pulled at her feet several times and shook her shoulders violently until she opened her eyes. Then she dragged her half-conscious body to the bathroom as soon as she could walk. We started brushing our teeth first.

"We are going to the mines today," I said to her, trying to be enthusiastic about life.

"I don't care." Carla did not even look at me; her eyes were half-closed with her hands automatically brushing the teeth. She just looked too tired and always seemed like she hated life. I was glad that at least she could go to shower and brush her teeth by herself—that was enough for me—and I smiled in response.

When we were done, we went back to the locker room and stripped down to nothing. I had been using a shared shower for my entire life, but still felt awkward. Even though there were only girls, everybody was changing rapidly. Their chests were getting bigger every day, while mine did not look like it was even budding. I also had no hair growth in the pubic area like everyone else, including Carla, and I didn't have a period like everyone else either. I was the only one who had not had my turn. Other girls frequently made fun of my body and it made me very self-conscious.

We came to the bathing room. It had a huge tub of water situated exactly in the middle. Every girl was given a bowl of their own to take water out of the tub and pour it on themselves. I let the cold liquid ran down my head, which reminded me of the waterfall, so I smiled. A girl named Sowie across the room weirdly looked at me, like I was crazy, but I ignored her. I quickly washed and finished in five minutes and went out. Then I dried myself with my towel on the way out.

I dressed myself up in my T-shirt uniform—if I could call it that, because it was more like a rag. Although I remembered them being a shirt a long time ago, this particular garment was full of holes, one of them hanging around my neck where the left shoulder was split in half. I still kept it, because I often had an insufficient number of shirts to wear in the winter when they were so slow to dry. I was a clean freak who could not stand wearing the same sweaty shirt for two days in a row like some other girls. My other two shirts could not keep up, so I needed the third one. It was good that they could be cleaned fairly easily, and the grey colour hid the stains very well.

"Wash your shirt, Carla," I said when I saw her putting yesterday's shirt on without washing, even though it was summer when everybody sweated a lot.

Carla sniffed at her shirt and looked at me, puzzled.

"It smells fine to me," she said.

"That's because I washed them for you yesterday!"

"Oh! Thank you, that's nice of you."

"That's because I can't stand having you walking around the whole day with that stinky shirt last time. But you have to do it yourself next time, okay?"

"Sorry. I'll do it today."

"Don't just put it in the sun when you take it off. You need to wash it." That was what she had done yesterday.

"Hmm…sure," she promised me, but I had a feeling that she was going to forget again.

The alarm sounded once more, signaling the time to assemble for the morning in front of our building. Everyone, including me, ran outside. Some were not done dressing themselves, so they were putting their clothes on while running. Being late was not an option; it would result in punishment.

Our tall and golden-haired trainer Emmeline stood still in a perfectly squared stance. She looked at us one by one as we ran past her to form a line.

"Stop!" she shouted. We put our hands at our sides, our feet together, and stood very still. She walked in her black gumboots from the head of the line to the tail while stomping her feet each step as if to show her authority.

Her skin was reddened by sunburn, just like the rest of us, although hers was more patchy and full of freckles in every place on her skin. I could tell that she had naturally white skin like me. A pair of slanted blue eyes below the thick forehead scrutinised every one of us, looking tired but intimidating nevertheless.

We called people who were above us "Superiors," and we had to listen to everything they say. Emmeline was one of them, but she was also our trainer. A trainer's job was to make plans for our daily work along with making sure we do our jobs. I would never dare to cross her, since it had been established for the past five years that she had no mercy—only one mistake and we would be punished hard.

She stopped at me, the last girl on the line, after checking my ragged uniform. She gazed into my eyes without any expression. I needed to stand perfectly still and look in a straight line no matter what she did to me. "She's not there," I kept telling myself. Her eyes fixated on mine far too long, what felt like an eternity passed between she left me alone again.

Every girl here, including me, had an identification number that we needed to remember so that we could respond correctly to our trainer calling. Emmeline pulled out her notebook from a jacket pocket and began reading.

"Number 30, front yard, pick fruits," she said with the heavy accent of the Superior's language.

"Number 19, house kitchen, cleaning."

"Number 13, house parking, sweeping." Number 13—Carla—walked away towards her workplace and waved at me, smiling. I just smiled back.

Finally, my number showed up. "54, go to the back hill, weeding." But before I could even walk away, I heard the number after me.

"Number 1, back hill, weeding."

It was my bad luck that I had to go with Number 1. She was none other than our top bully named Beasty. The hair on my body stood up nervously at the mere thought of her. It looked like today was not a good day after all.

In the past, I had always been one of her favourite targets. There was no doubt that I was the strangest girl here. I gently grabbed some strands of my hair and looked at it. Although the roots were already lighter in brown colour than any other girls, but to make it worse, the tips were yellow. I was the only girl who had it; all the others had the uniformly thick, dark brown hair.

I quickly ran towards the area in the estate called the Back Hill, which was quite far away from the main building we lived in. I ran there to avoid Beasty as long as possible, but I knew that it was inevitable. When I arrived, I found the work that people from yesterday morning had left off and immediately resumed the task. I just hoped Beasty would not see me and would leave me alone.

"Pull! Cattleya, Pull!" It was not long before I heard the voice of the Beast.

"Hi, how are you, Beasty?" I said with a polite smile.

"You little shit. You think you are getting away by talking nice to me, huh?" The tall and muscular brown-haired girl with the build of a giant snarled at me. Her lips curved upwards in a slick smile that I saw from the corner of my eyes.

I kept on working and avoid facing her directly but keeping an eye on her arms in case she decided to physically hurt me. I steadied my breathing and smiled to show that I was not shaken by her. Even though she was my most disliked person, I never wanted to fight her. Conflict was not my cup of tea.

"So what do you want me to do, Beasty?"

"You are a smart girl, Cattleya." She said and pushed me on my shoulder to unbalance me. I fell with my face onto the ground, and it knocked the breath out of me.

"Oops, sorry," Beasty said teasingly with a happy smile, barely able to keep her laughter away.

I ignored her and stood up. I could tell that it was her intention all along to push me into the dirt. A chunk of dirt was stuck to my skin and it dripped down to my mouth so I had to wipe it away. Unable to keep her face straight anymore, Beasty laughed with her ugly voice.

"I knew it. Because your friend Carla is not here, right?"

"Yes?" I felt my face go red, and I kept quiet and went back to work. She was right. If Carla were with me this morning, she would not allow Beasty to bully me like this. I felt weak. I hated myself for being unable to stand up to her, but I did not want any trouble, so it was probably for the best.

"As you know, I have a toilet duty tonight," she said.

"Okay, I'll do it for you," I said without hesitation.

"Good," she said, and left for her work.

After our work period around the estate, the alarm sounded again to signal us to assemble at the front of our building. We were allowed to go back inside and eat some breakfast: soft potatoes mixed with a type of meat ingredients were served with various greens. All of them would be mashed together to form half-liquid, half-solid chunks.

Our trainer Emmeline had to rotate girls on kitchen duty in the morning to help her mix up the food, so I knew that the ingredients usually came in big bags that required two to three girls to lift it. We mixed the dry powder potatoes into a pot with hot water then stirred it, and simply called it a "potatoes meal."

I never ate a lot, but even I could feel the change in our breakfast. The meat had significantly decreased in the past year, as well as any fresh greens. Right now, we were only eating bulky, unchewable vegetable matter with dead insects appearing frequently within the food.

It had also gotten thinner and thinner as time went by, and right now it hardly filled me up. This morning, Emmeline told us again that we were too lazy and did not work hard enough, so the estate had no food to feed us.

The long wooden bench that ran the whole table length creaked loudly when I sat down. When I looked at Carla, who was sitting opposite me, and smiled, she started a conversation before I could.

"Do they expect us to live on this much food?" She started complaining and ravenously put a spoonful into her mouth in hunger.

I responded, "You can take some of mine," and pushed my bowl over to her side of the table. Although what I had was nowhere near enough for myself either, I felt bad looking at Carla's face. I never ate much anyway, and Carla never had enough.

"No, you need to grow too, Cat." She pushed the bowl back to me. She had never accepted my food despite almost certainly being very hungry herself.

"Thanks," I said quietly and looked down to continue with my food.

"What do you think our job is today?" Jenny, another girl who usually sat at our table, asked.

"I think we are going to the mine today," I said, knowing full well that we were going there. It was day one of the week. I knew because the cycle always repeated every seven days: day one mining, day two mining, day three orchard, day four orchard, day five bridge, day six city, and day seven Mister Sam's.

The schedule changed from time to time, but mostly stayed the same. I usually hated it the most at the mining site, because it was the type of work I was not good at. It required pure strength to lift stuff, so it was my least favourite time of the week.

Day seven was always the best since there was hardly any work to do. It was also a big bonus that the heartless and commanding dictator Emmeline had her day off then. Instead, we had Mister Sam, who usually gave us simple tasks around his house and garden. Most of the time, he fell asleep right after assigning them, so we could just work at our own pace until he woke up again. His place was a place of comfort for me. It was also where the forest was.

Carla waited after she finished her meal since I was always the last one to be done. From the corner of my eye, I saw Beasty staring at me, and winked. I looked down to avoid her gaze altogether. Even though I tried to hide it, Carla picked it up and looked behind her after she saw my submissive expression.

"What the hell was that?" she asked in a loud voice. She knew.

I swallowed my food and answered timidly, "Nothing." My body language was something I could not fake properly.

"I thought we have gone through this?" Carla's eyes locked into mine which made my guilt rise up. She knew full well what was going on.

"How can you be so weak, Cattleya? I said I will protect you no matter what. Don't you trust me? Do you even know that I'm hurt that you don't trust me?" she uttered in annoyance.

Before I could even reply, the alarm rang. The time to move out was now, and we were to assemble in front of the building.

Carla said nothing more and dragged me out of the mess hall, an angry look on her face but still grabbing my arm so gently. I knew that the tiger was about to meet the lion.

Chapter 3: The Mines

Emmeline counted our heads again before we departed, but all she said was, "We are going to the mine," and "get on the truck." When we were prepared to go, I could still feel Carla's anger radiating from her even though she was standing on the other side of our line. It was not the time to quarrel, she knew. But when the chance presented itself, I knew she would go for it.

When we arrived at the worksite, Carla was the first one to jump off. Her long and nimble legs dexterously landed on hard ground in one swift motion. Her cheeks bright red, her drops of sweats were pouring down from her forehead, she stood squarely with her arms crossed to wait for her enemy.

From how confident she looked, she had to be thinking that nobody could hurt her, not even Emmeline. Although she was only thirteen years old then, she was the strongest person I had ever known my whole life. None of the other girls could stand her stare and soon scampered past as soon as possible, but I could tell that they were curious about what was going on.

"It's not the time, Carla," I said to my best friend.

"Shut up, Cat." She dismissed me with a stroke of the arm.

"No, we will get into trouble," I cried, my voice desperate. If Carla were to fight with Beasty now, we would get into big trouble with Emmeline.

"I don't care."

"You have to stop!" I yelled. I grabbed her arm and dragged her away from the spot, but we struggled against each other and one of her hands ended up pushing me to the ground. Dust flew up from the dry sandy floor of a hot summer.

I saw the apologetic look on Carla's face. "I'm so sorry, Cat," she uttered before pulling me up.

"That's okay," I replied with a smile to make her feel better.

"I'm so sorry," she said again. I took this chance to hurry and pulled her away from the truck to avoid conflict. She gave in to me easily due to her guilt for hurting me.

The mines were called Devanta mines. The site comprised several digging grounds that ranged on six mountains. At that time, as a girl, I knew nothing about the purpose of the place, only that it was my least favourite place to work in. The precious mineral the massive operation was extracting was called "gold." With five thousand active workers in service who worked days and nights for seven days a week, the place was very important to this region. However, there were hardly any females except for some kitchen ladies in the dining hall.

Our work mainly consisted of filling wheelbarrows with dirt and rocks, pushing them forward, then dumping them into the trucks. Then we would walk back to do it all over again. Despite the simplicity, it was hard to work in such conditions, since we spent most of our time in the strong sun, with dust flowing everywhere—into our nostrils and our eyes—constantly.

Emmeline shouted "Line up!" and we arranged ourselves again into a single-file line.

"We are going to mine number 6. You know the rules—no touching the males," she directed us in her harsh, commanding tone. Everyone turned to the right at once, and suddenly I became the head of the train. Behind me were girls in reverse height order, with the freakishly tall Emmeline following after everyone else. In this way, they could always see the person in front while our trainer oversaw everyone.

It was often that I had to lead the way, yet the feeling of nervousness never went away since there was always a possibility that I could mess up the line. If I went the wrong way, or lead us down a hole, I would be punished.

"I know mine number 6," I thought. Emmeline kept shouting left or right whenever there was an intersection, but I did not need her direction. I had discovered a while ago my ability to recognise some symbols on directional signs.

Normally, girls such as us were not meant to read the language of the Superior, but I could not help but have gotten a little curious, so I

24

figured a few things on my own. Number symbols were easy, and I'd even taught Carla to read some of them. Six was a big curly thing, two was monstrously ugly and the seven was very lanky, to name a few. Once I could read them, I just followed the directional signs, and we reached our destination (mine number 6) in no time.

Our trainer strode off to have a chat with the manager of the mine. They talked in the Superior language, which I could not understand at all. Instead of listening in, I looked around and noticed a lot of brown-skinned males digging attentively nearby. Their arms were strong like steel, with sweat running down their shiny reddish-brown bodies like oil. I knew that they had no other purpose but to act as tireless machines, servicing the Superiors until the last day of their lives. They were mindless animals who knew nothing except to work, and we were told not to touch them because it would disturb their jobs.

Emmeline soon came back and led us to our worksite. As soon as we tried to get past the male workers, a lot of them turned their heads towards us. There was nothing in their completely dark eyes. Even though I expected savagery and inferno in them (as we had been told), there was not even so much as a sparkle. Those were the eye of those whose life purpose had been forsaken long ago in favour of more simple things.

Simply the workers' pausing briefly to look at us caused one of their masters to slap his whip on the floor. Suddenly, all of them turned back towards their work, and they did not dare look at us again.

All we would do for the whole day was shove the busted rocks onto the back of the trucks while we bathed in the hot bright sun. The constant flow of dust in the air caused many of us to sneeze and our eyes to water. Even though we were getting very good at working in the intensely hot conditions at that point, days one and two were still the worst two days of the week. The males, however, did not look like they minded it at all, as if they had been born to do this job. They worked about four times as fast as we did and seemed to have no limit on how much they could work. Sometimes I wondered why they even bothered hiring little teenage girls to come at all.

I remembered our first day ever at the mine. Someone fainted quickly as soon as we arrived. It was the girl named Hinda, one of the smallest girls back then. I could picture Emmeline on that day, very angry about our inability to stay conscious. She shouted that she would punish anyone who fainted.

I lost my consciousness too that day, but nobody was punished, because there were too many girls who did the same—even if some of them were fake. However, Mister Larrington, the real boss of the estate, insisted on our working at the mine.

After the incident, they put a movable shelter at our worksite and they made us stay near the nearby small pond all the time. After that day, the work became somewhat bearable. We started jumping into the pond and applying mud on ourselves, letting it dry to act as an excellent protection against the sun. Emmeline had no problem with our action and only called us "filthy pigs," whatever that meant to her, so everyone kept doing it. Today, as I walked toward the pond to get some mud, Jenny approached me.

"Hey! Was Carla going to have a scrap with Beasty again?" she whispered when Emmeline was far away. To be honest, Jenny looked kind of like Beasty herself, as most girls in our estate looked vaguely similar to each other. Only I was very different in almost every category. Carla was dissimilar because of her facial features, but she was still a typical brown-haired, brown-eyed, and muscular girl.

"No," I denied. Jenny was one of the girls who hated Beasty, but it was better to have nobody know about it.

"No? I don't believe you. She was trying to protect you again."

"No, she was just… just… Not doing well."

"What do you mean? She is sick?"

"Yeah."

"What's wrong with her?"

"Nothing. She just felt sick from the truck." I cooked up a terrible lie.

"Is that all?" Jenny said, clearly disbelieving me.

All of a sudden, I heard the strong confident voice of Carla from across the area, talking directly to us. She had to be listening in on our conversation from somewhere.

"Yep! That bitch is going down."

I turned away from Jenny in embarrassment.

"I thought you said she wasn't," Jenny said to me.

"Sorry, I lied. I don't want them to fight. It's better just to forget about it." I had nothing better to say.

"Then are you going let her bully you for the rest of your life?" Carla pointed a finger at me and looked me in the eye. I could never turn away when she did that, so I had to answer her about something.

"Carla… just forget about it, okay?" I said weakly.

"No, I will never let anyone do that to you again!"

"Calm down, girl," Jenny suddenly responded and grabbed ahold of her arm. Carla looked back at her in confusion for her involvement. It was as if she had forgotten that there were other people around us. After Carla calmed herself down, Jenny whispered in her ear, which made her nod. Both of them walked away from me without looking back. Then I had a feeling of being left out. I knew that Carla would not give up so easily.

What had Jenny said that could convince even her?

Chapter 4: The girl Who Left Home

To understand my story, I had to tell them from the very beginning. If the forest was where it changed me, the place called Larrington's Estate would be where it had shaped me to who I was in the first place.

I remembered my mother hanging on to me until the last moment. Was she crying or not, I could not clearly remember, but I could tell that she was in an agonizing state of sadness. She said not to worry and that everything would be fine, but I knew it would not be, because I would never see her again.

A massive truck was there along with other girls in a small confinement. A few at a time, the girls walked inside the dark and cramped space of the back. The massive metal door then shut from behind, and there was no escape. We did not question why they were sending us away, knowing only that we would never see our mothers again.

No matter how much I used my nails to scratch on its hard surface, the bar remained unmoved. The only thing that moved was the truck itself as it was going further and further from my homeland.

Three full days I was in the back of the vehicle. The room was full of children similar to me: abandoned and hopeless. Most of them were dropped off here and there but at the end of the journey, I was the only one who was left.

Finally, the journey came to an end, and I stepped out onto Larrington's Estate for the first time. I felt a chill. It was not just the weather but the atmosphere, windy with a dreary grey sky that looked like it was always going to rain. Cold gusts licked my bare skin and sent shivers through my body instantly. It was nothing like the mild, relatively unchanging warm climate of my homeland.

The first person I met was old Emmeline, who was rumoured to have been the sole trainer of Larrington's for the previous two hundred years—not because she appeared young, but because she looked old, and she constantly looked angry. Her face was the same no matter what day of the week you looked at her, always grumpy, always blaming, always punishing you.

The first thing she said to me was something in a strange accent which I could not hear properly. Her voice was a mumble, and it was impossible to understand. When I did not respond, she shouted and slapped my face with her massive palm.

She pulled my ear and dragged me along. The pain made me follow her, but I still could not understand what she wanted. Instead of trying to get to me, she instead shoved me on the ground in front of some bigger girls who were told to show me around the facility.

They were obviously girls who had been living in the Estate long before me. Judging from their heights, they were slightly older than me, but when I asked how old they were, I realised that they were all the same age.

That first day I arrived, I did not learn much about the Estate, and the night came soon after. I found myself lying stiffly on a hard bed while staring blankly into the plain texture of the ceiling. I could not sleep, yet there was not much room to move on the bed as we were all sleeping in one giant hall lined with only beds next to each other and no gaps.

The months that followed could very much be considered the worst time of my life. I missed home and missed my mother. I was a stranger in a strange land, where everybody was talking differently and trainers' commands were impossible to understand, which led to me getting a lot of punishment. The other girls, especially Beasty, were also picking on me for being small and for my hair colour.

On the morning of the second day, I was told to sweep the floor of "The Nest" (the name given to the main building where we lived). When I finished the task, I was getting tired because the area was so big, and the other girls in my group were slacking. Before I could even catch a breath, Emmeline told me to scrub the floor too.

"Yes, I will do it faster, Missus," I answered my Superior in a way that my mother had taught me, my head bowed down always, eyes staring to the ground and never looking them in the face. It was the only way a proper girl should speak to a Superior.

"Good," she said and left me to my work.

"Bow your head and follow orders." My mother's voice echoed in my head. It was the most important advice she had given me since I was young.

I worked as fast as I could while keeping the quality of my work up to standard, even though I saw that the other girls stopped working without finishing and started chatting with each other. Even if they did nothing, the work had got to be finished; there was nobody that I could change but myself, so I ignored them and buried my head into my work. My efforts were put even more into each stroke. I scrubbed, strong, hard, and determined.

"I will survive here just fine, mum." I thought of her again while keeping my tears at bay.

Without any warning, someone lifted me off the ground and carried me away. I panicked and struggled, but it was futile, because my feet did not even touch the ground. I was only a tiny skinny girl half the size of my abductor, it seemed. At that point, my instinct took over me. I tried to resist. Although it was like hitting an inanimate object, I nevertheless kept on pounding on my attacker. When it proved ineffective, I decided to bite her instead. My teeth sunk deep into the stranger's dark hand which caused her to yelp loudly, and let go of me.

"Missus Emmeline!" I yelled for help.

But my attacker caught up to me and grabbed me from behind by pulling the neck of my T-shirt. A slap came after which caused me to fall onto the dirt. My buttocks hit the ground and I snapped back to my senses.

The massive girl was towering over me. Her was expression unforgiving. Her hand was ready for another slap, but I reacted first.

"I'm so sorry," I hurriedly pleaded.

The girl did not hit me again; neither did she say any word. She simply came and dragged me off the ground. This time, however, I remembered not to resist and follow her like a good girl.

She led me far away from the Nest into a corner of the estate where a relatively unused patch of land was fully covered with weedy plants as tall as two meters. It was the outer edge of the property, next to a forest where nobody wanted to go. But some people were already waiting for my arrival.

"You know who I am?" the one who looked to be the leader with two heavy underlings asked me. "Answer me!" she yelled when I did not answer, then slapped my face while my initial capturer was holding me from behind. It was such a hard slap that I could still feel it a day after.

"No," I said.

"No? What?" Her face came very close to me and showed her fangs.

"No," I repeated. She smacked me again on the same spot.

"No, *Missus*," she said. "Repeat it, you stupid slut."

"No, Missus," I said.

Missus and Misters were the words used when referring or speaking to Superiors only, so it was strange to call another girl this way. Nevertheless, the big fat leader seemed satisfied and continued.

"I am Beasty." She pointed to herself, then to the girl who brought me to her. "This is Doer," and the other two were "Ewey and Ness. You better remember us all."

My memory was failing me because I was so frightened.

"Now, repeat!" she shouted.

"Beasty… Doer."

She punched me in my diaphragm and it knocked the wind out of me before I could get to the third name.

"Not Beasty… *Missus* Beasty," she said with a smile.

I repeated the names and forgot the third girl's name. This time Beasty allowed the person whose name I forgot to punch me instead. She hit me right in on the cheek with a loud noise. The pain and the surprise made me nearly forgot the fourth name but I managed to hold on to it.

"Missus Beasty, Doer, Ewey, and Nessy," I said, not realizing what I had done wrong and earned another punch in the face. This time I felt very dizzy and suddenly the world went black. I did not remember anything more after that.

I found myself awake at dusk among the tall grasses. The weather was getting very cold, and even with the two layers of T-shirts I had on could not stop the chill. It was how I dressed, because I had no other clothing. I lay there for a little while, trying to think of what had happened.

"Missus Beasty, Doer, Ewey, and Nessy." The reason I was down here was because it was Ness, not Nessy. I gathered up the strength to stand and touched my face, which I found to be puffy and sore. Then I walked back slowly to the Nest in a slightly dazed state.

Along the way, I saw nobody. Not even a single girl or Emmeline was around, not until I reached the mess hall in the Nest where all the sounds were gathered. I did not think that going in there was a good idea, but my hunger was so strong that I could not stop myself.

Everyone was indeed dining in the room. All of them turned towards me as soon as the main door creaked from my entry. At the front of the hall stood Emmeline, whose head was like a tree among children, with her emotionless eyes staring down directly at me. A shiver flashed down my spine. She hit her wooden table in front of her three times, and all the noises in the hall stopped. At another corner, Beasty's gang was giggling to themselves while pointing their fingers at me.

"Come here!" Emmeline yelled with an echo that reverberated through the entire hall. For a few seconds, my brain did not seem to realise that it was me she was calling out until she snapped again. This time I ran as fast as possible to reach her.

My heart was pumping as if it would pop out of my chest.

Calm down, Cattleya. Everything will be fine if you talk politely and tell her the truth. Remember to bow your head and be a good girl, I thought.

"Where have you been, number 54?" Emmeline spoke loud and clear this time, and I could understand everything.

"Sorry, Missus. I was working and …" I tried to explain.

But she cut me short with an absolute tone of voice.

"Liar! I haven't seen you work today. We were out there destroying our backs. And what have you been doing all day?"

"There were some people, Missus. They dragged me away. It was the…" I tried to tell her the truth, but thought better of it when I saw at the corner of my eye that Beasty's gang was staring intensely at me. Doer made a death threat sign by cutting her throat with her finger.

"Tell me who they are!" Emmeline questioned. Her eyes never let go, even for a second. I was so nervous. I wanted to collapse on the spot.

"No, I don't know them, Missus," I cried.

"What? You don't know them? Was it one of our girls here? Point me to them immediately," she insisted.

"Sorry Missus, I think it was just a monster from the forest. I really couldn't tell."

"Do not lie, number 54."

"I'm not lying, Missus."

"You will be punished accordingly, number 54. Come with me outside."

"I'm not lying, Missus," I protested again.

"I said come outside, you insolent girl. Now!" she shouted and grabbed me by the arm. Out from across the hall, I was dragged across the hall and out the exit. Emmeline turned her head towards the other girls.

"You all come too. I will show what happens to the liars." The trainer Emmeline put me next to a large fence post. The audience followed outside and surrounded me in a large circle.

"Somebody fetch me the cane," she ordered.

I was drowning in fear at that point. My body was shaking all over and my sweat was seeping from my skin despite the cold weather of the night. Emmeline also commanded the girls to strip me off my clothing down to my underwear.

One of them showed me how to stand on the spot while holding on to the post with my hands. One foot in front and the other back—I was standing diagonally to make my base strong.

Emmeline ordered me to bend forward while holding onto the post, exposing the back of my body as much as possible.

I did not even know when the first hit landed. It was so swift and so light. I was glad that it did not hurt, but the relief only lasted for a few split seconds before the real pain kicked in. Then another one came. The slender stick flew through the air with a sharp *whoosh* sounds as it went up and down on me again and again.

The sensation was so strong that my gritted teeth were opened. Emmeline was mixing it up: hitting many different places all over the back of my body, from my shoulders to my legs, but never the head. Pain was diffusing all over my body.

My strong base stance had stopped functioning a while ago, and I felt like I was melting down into the very ground. I had to be helped standing up by other girls before the hits resumed again—even though with each hit, drops of tears were seeping out of my eyes. I never cried in fear of getting more punishment. It was a common knowledge that we were not allowed to cry.

It seemed like an eternity had passed until it was all over. She told me that I was to resume the night duty as normal and also skip dinner.

Apparently, from what people told me afterward, I only received fifteen hits from her because I was a new girl. Normally, they would be much higher.

I swallowed my pain and said the words as I had been taught by my mother.

"Thank...thank you, Missus."

Immediately after, Emmeline broke up the circle and sent me to my station to sweep the floor. Even putting my clothes back on was difficult, as it was so painful. With my head held down, I walked past other girls who pointed and laughed at me. I silently gripped the broom and started sweeping despite being hungry, hurt, and ashamed.

What did I do wrong? How did it turn out this way when I was already bowing my head and following orders as my mother told me? I thought.

In my moment of self-loathing, someone managed to sneak up behind me. "Here!" she called out. I turned around and found her sheepish grin smiling at me, her hands at full extension as if she was presenting something to me.

I could not even believe my eyes when I recognised what it was. In her palms were some pieces of bread, torn in pieces, crumbly, with hardly any smell because they were old. Yet I could do nothing but to accept them.

"I hope you don't mind. I hid it in my pocket," the girl whispered shyly.

"No problem at all," I answered and quickly consumed it before anyone else could see. She too, hurried back to her station.

Despite going to bed with a half-full belly, I was kept awake by the skin on my back. I tried to sleep by lying on my chest where there was no wound, but my head was swimming with the nightmares that were the events of these last few days, so I decided to get up instead. Other girls had already fallen into deep slumber, so sneaking out was not hard. I put my shoes on and after some searching in the dark, found an old jacket in the wardrobe that fit me perfectly.

Only darkness awaited outside, but I ventured out anyway. As I walked, the night was completely silent except for the sound of my feet on grass. The only source of light was the big full moon hovering above the main building, yet I could see surprisingly well in the dark after my eyes adjusted. It was strange to know that the hour of darkness could be this bright. I could see the shape of trees around me, and even the Larringtons' house looming in the distance was clearly visible.

I walked for a long time, away from the Nest, away from everything. I did not care where I was going or even when I would be back. Passing the border of the Estate, turning right, enter a dirt road, then kept walking into the middle of nowhere. I wanted to walk away, to go back home, back to my mum, but I knew that it was not possible. It had taken three full days in the truck to get here, so there was no way I could do it. Even if I could, I still did not know the location of either Larrington's estate or my homeland.

Suddenly, I came to a dead end. Somehow, even though I wanted to run away, I managed to choose the path that ended up in a dead-end only after the first turn. I examined the area a little and found it to be a cliff overlooking a vast forest below. The woods would normally scare me, but I was too out of my mind to care about the curse that night. I realised for the first time that Larrington's estate was on the top of a mountain, with many others surrounding us. The view was quite spectacular, with several pinnacles rising in the distance, each of them dotted with trees covering everything as far as eyes could see. There was no sign of civilisation except for the dirt road I was standing on.

I sat down at the edge of the cliff and thought about what had happened. My mind was still in shock. Perhaps these few days had been too much for me to cope.

I began to think of my mother. I pictured her kind dark eyes with big smile and the time I spent with her. How she would take care of me, and sing to me as I was sleeping on her lap, and comfort me during my hard times. But it was all for nothing, because she sent me here.

I blamed her for giving up on me so easily. How she just told me that I would need to leave and everything was going to be all right. She was willing to throw me in a truck that carried me off across the country to this strange land with even stranger people.

I cried.

They all hated me: everybody here, everybody back at my homeland, even my mother. Nobody thought I was worth anything. I wanted to die so that all of this would stop. I wished it had simply been a nightmare, yet no pinching could wake me up. I was physically in pain from how heartbroken I was. I wanted it all to stop.

The cliff was right there, but I turned around and walked away.

Chapter 5: How I Met Hinda

I would not call the first year in Larrington's estate a bad experience, but rather a hell on earth. *Hell* was a word my mother taught me meant the place of absolute worst. The experience was probably unimaginable to a typical seven-year-old in modern times, but it was a fact that I went through it. Every day, there were new and ever-changing problems to add to my suffering. Yet I was too scared to end it all.

I came to know a girl named Hinda, a sweet and kind girl who had been bullied long before me, but that had changed since my arrival. Beasty's gang got rather bored when they were picking on the same girl for too long, so they needed to keep changing.

Unfortunately, that was not the case for me. I was their biggest attraction, their favourite servant and toy, for the longest time. There was not a day that they had forgotten about me.

One particular incident came to my mind. It was one of the nights around the first six months when Beasty cleverly conspired against me. That day I was running around, doing all of their laundry and all their night duty all at once. Every day was all the same. I had to do them every night while the gang sat around the building doing nothing but talking.

Emmeline would always go to dinner during that time, but she would come back at the end of the hour to check our completion. The first time I displayed an act of rebellion against the big girls which was a big mistake; I was beaten up badly again the next day. So I never resisted again.

My job was to do the cleaning duty of five people in one hour. I sprinted from one station to the next, doing each one in turn and in the quickest possible method, yet it was not possible to do them all. Fortunately, Hinda, the girl who previously gave me the bread, always offered to help me. We usually ended up sweating by the time we were about to go to bed.

After I had just finished my jobs one night, I opened the door to the bedroom and walked a few metres to my bed, and a hundred shoes flew towards me. They were only rubber sandals, but I shielded my face with my arms anyway, then less than gracefully scrambled away to the exit of the room.

I learnt from Hinda later on that Beasty had planned everything by forcing every girl to throw their shoes at me. I was hurt badly, not from the physical trauma, but from a psychological one.

Beasty was made so ecstatic by the result that she told everyone to repeat the play. It was not every night by any means, but it kept me nervous whenever I entered any room at all. Day after day, Beasty began to express herself, filling others with ideas to look down on me, to see me as a strange plaything, an alien, an immigrant, a midget, a slut, a whore, the worst kind of lowlife. Eventually, everyone turned against me. If they had already hurt me physically, why not hate me as well? It was easy to believe when these words were hammered into them every day. Shoe-throwing had become more than just bullying; it was the symbol of isolation for me.

I did not know how I managed to stay alive in that era. There were more times than I could count that I felt miserable, but there were no more suicidal thoughts. In the early days, the spot over the cliff was my point of solace. It was what kept me going in times of hardship. I would go out there alone in the dark, but eventually, Hinda managed to catch me escaping into the night.

"Where are we going?" she asked when I let her come with me.

"Shh...talk later, just keep walking." I told her to be quiet since we were too close to the Nest.

"You have your secret," she said when we were far enough and nobody could have heard us.

"Yeah, and you have to keep it that way," I said and crossed the fence to the outside of the estate.

"You do realise you are not supposed to go out there, right?" she said uncertainly. It was very dark that night, and I could tell Hinda was getting worried. Her foot was at the edge of the grass, afraid to go over to the other side.

I looked at her from the forbidden land, and for a brief moment, I felt guilt at disobeying the rule, but it was too late now. I lunged on my friend and pulled her arm. To none of my surprise, she came over without much resistance. When someone told us to do something, we did it; I know that she was as tame as me.

We kept quiet for the rest of the way while I led her in the dark with my knowledge of the land. After all, I knew this road like the back of my hand because I had been here so many times. The further I left the estate behind, the more I felt that what I was doing was not wrong.

"Hey, where are we going?" Hinda called out, her voice full of worry. Weirdly, it gave me even more confidence to lead her. I inhaled deeply the fresh outside air that blew through the darkness of the night sky darkness and announced, "It's my special place."

We arrived at the cliff-top. Assessing the whereabouts of my special spot, I walked through some bushes to find it. It was perfect spot because it hid us from any prying eyes and it had a solid, non-slippery ground surface with a lot of room that I could normally sleep on.

"Woah! That's high," Hinda uttered before her legs went weak. I had to drag her away from the edge just to be safe.

"I can't believe this place," Hinda gasped in astonishment when she recovered enough to take in the view.

"Yeah, pretty, huh? I wonder what's it like during the day."

"I've never seen anything like this before," Hinda said. "How did you find this place?"

I told her about how I ended up here on the first day, and we started gossiping about Beasty.

"You had it so tough. Sorry I was too cowardly to help you," Hinda replied. "The Beasty gang wasn't even that bad when we were younger. I guess they had gotten worse. My mother said a bully is usually a victim herself. That's why they need to vent their anger on someone," she added.

Hinda was born in another place quite close to here. Beasty, Doer, Hinda and a few others were the first batch who arrived in Larrington. The bullies formed their gang to maintain the power as the dominant females as more girls were moved in. Hinda said she hated them too.

Hinda and I became fast friends. She knew what it was like to be bullied a lot. She even said that she was forced to throw the shoes at me and that she regretted it. However, she threw them on the floor near my feet instead. Even with all the accusations Beasty had made against me, Hinda's faith in me never wavered.

"You know that she is Emmeline's favourite target?"

"No, what? I thought that was me!"

"No, Missus Emmeline doesn't like Beasty because she knows that she is avoiding work all the time. And you…you are just unlucky. Emmeline has nothing against you at all, I can tell. She is just wishing the best for you, really, by punishing you lots and lots."

"I guess…" I answered absently while recalling my punishments. They were never pleasant.

"Beasty has been getting on her nerves ever since she was really young, you know? From when she was all goody-goody and sucking up to our trainer all the time. Things went wrong and she was punished quite harsh once. After that she became like this: fat, ugly and always lazing around, telling other girls to do her jobs."

Then we gossiped more about the others at the Nest, and I was glad that I brought Hinda along. In the end, we were quiet and there was an awkward silence. I looked her in the eyes and smiled. She answered me back with the exact same expression. We kept staring at each other.

My eyes suddenly watered, from the overwhelming emotion that I had found someone whom I could trust and share the pain with. Ever since I left my mother, I had always longed for such a person. Hinda took me into her arms and let me cry. She stroked my hair and rubbed my back until I realised how much I loved her. I let it happen for a while before I eventually let go. Without a thought, I closed my eyes and we pressed our lips on each other. I savored the moment, but pulled away after some time.

For every bad day, there was a good day. For every hateful person, there was a person who I could love. No matter how bad today might be, there would always be a better future. I learnt that there were good things everywhere, but only if I persevered and never gave up hope.

Hinda taught me that night about something to hold on to. When times were rough, we could think of that person so that we would not fall into despair. I said that I had nobody to think of and that I was all alone except for her. She asked me if there was someone who I knew long before coming here, someone who could be eternally in my heart.

I knew the answer that it was my mother. I pulled out the wooden locket, the only memento that was left from her, out from my pocket. It was not well-made and did not even have a picture of my mother, but it reminded me of her since she had always been wearing it. All it had was some rough and strange writing carved inside.

I squeezed it tight in my hand and thought of her. I forgave her for everything. I knew that she did not mean for me to be in so much pain when she sent me across the country. There had to be a reason. Now, I could remember her face again. Above her assuring smile, there was sadness in her eyes. I knew now that she did not want to leave me.

Hinda and I became much closer after that night. However, I never kissed her again. It was a momentary action, a surge of emotion that completely overwhelmed my conscious thoughts. The next day our eyes met. We blushed, and it was too awkward to not talk to each other about something else instead. After that, we decided to forget about the kiss; it had been our secret ever since.

During those times, she was the only one who shared the pain with me. Despite being an extreme Beasty detractor, she tended to just accept the way things were and did as she was told. She never questioned or complained about work. Unlike me, who was stressed out from this unfairness I was put through, all she did was looking down at the job and did them.

If I could be like her, I would be very happy, I thought.

Chapter 6: Our Little Triangle

During my first two years, there was nobody brave enough to oppose the Beast herself, but this changed when a strange girl came into our lives.

The first impression of this person was her fist smashing onto Ewey's face. It sent Beasty's former underling crying and running away immediately. The lean girl with an unfamiliar face was smiling, her teeth all white, her eyes sparkling with excitement.

"You are next!" She looked Ness in the eyes and intimidated her with a jab of her finger into the bigger girl's face.

The gang was on the verge of breaking apart. Ewey and Ness had a fight with Beasty and Doer about something, I did not know what. One day, they saw me and Hinda working for their former boss, so they picked on us. No matter who we tried to help, we always ended up as punching bags for everyone. Even when it was already in my third year in Larrington's, I was still stuck in the same situation.

Ness looked left and right in panic, her big eyes looking like they were coming out of their sockets. She appeared indecisive about whether or not to fight the new girl when Ewey had lost so badly. She decided to let go of Hinda, who she'd previously held on to for her partner to torture, before running away herself.

"Is that all you got?" The strange tall girl with messy brown hair yelled after the bully. We were still too stunned by her arrival to say anything. "Are you all right?" she asked Hinda with a warm smile.

"Yes, I'm okay," Hinda responded. I was standing next to Hinda, but the girl noticed me as well.

"How did you do that?" I asked, genuinely puzzled.

"I just punch them. Flex my arm real tight and punch them right in the face," she answered briefly. She looked at me. "And why are you just standing there? Isn't she your friend?" She nodded at Hinda.

"I can't," I answered, looking down. "I don't want us to get into more trouble."

"What trouble? There's no trouble," she argued, but before I could explain, she cut me off. "You are her friend, but you did not even help. What a coward." She dismissed me and walked away.

News of the fight spread to every girl in the estate where the current head count was a whopping one hundred and seven. It was when Larringtons's Estate was rich and resources were plentiful. There was lots of food to eat, and there were plenty of newer girls coming in. The new girl's name was Carla, and she became the talk of the estate for having the guts to go up against the bullies.

The morning after the fight, I found a girl still lying on the bed when she was supposed to be getting ready for the morning roll call. It was Carla, sound asleep, and clueless to the ensuing punishment. As everybody else was leaving the room while giggling away, I knew that I had to be the one to wake her.

I shook her once, but it had no effect, so I did it again more violently. Only after a while of this did her eyes finally open, and she blinked several times.

"Hey! Wake up!" I shouted.

There was nobody else in the room. I told Hinda to move on. All the beds beside hers were empty and made up nicely, as part of our routine.

"Oh shit!" she exclaimed, and hurriedly got out of bed and pulled the sheets off.

"What are you doing?" I asked when I saw her unusual action.

"I'm making my bed."

"No! What are you doing? You are pulling everything apart. That's not how you make a bed!" I cried out.

"It's how *I* do it," she responded flatly.

"You are doing it wrong. Look!" I pointed to all the other beds around us, which were clearly different from what she had done to hers. She was folding everything in rectangular sheets while normally we had to put every layer nicely on top of the others and make everything so tight a coin could bounce off the blanket.

"Oh!" It was all she said. Then she stopped and looked at me. Her eyes suddenly had a sparkle.

43

"Teach me how," insisted Carla. I thought that she was late already, so I told her to go have a shower and get dressed. After some convincing, she reluctantly went.

I was the number-one bed maker in the Estate, so it was trivial for me. After so many times that the bullies had ordered me to do their beds, I had become a master of this work. I did it as fast as I could and finished it in a few minutes despite having to start everything from scratch.

Fortunately, I managed to finish everything, including dressing, before the morning inspection, and got away with the whole thing. Emmeline always came and inspected them every morning.

I went into the locker room and found the new girl in the main bathroom. She smiled at me. I took it as a sign that she was about to thank me.

"You okay?" I asked. I wanted to ask if she was lost or not, being a new girl and all.

"What's your name?"

"Cat... Cattleya. But just call me Cat," I answered politely.

"Cattleya? That's a nice name. I'm Carla. Thanks for the help, by the way."

Under normal circumstances, it had to be the most awkward meeting ever, since we were both fully naked, but this was normal for us. I stood half a head shorter than her.

"Hey! You are that girl who stood by and let your friend be bullied," she suddenly remarked, her eyes wide. It looked genuinely like she had not recognised me at all, even when I was talking and making her bed.

I could give her a clever comeback, but it was not like me to argue with people I did not know well. *And you are the girl who couldn't get up in the morning and had no clue how to make a bed*, was what I was thinking of saying back. Either way, I was not impressed with how she spoke to me.

"That's okay, though. A weak person shouldn't be trying to fight. Just leave it to me." She chuckled to herself.

How arrogant, I thought.

44

"We have to go. We have to line up in five minutes." I mentioned coldly, and tried to hide my anger as I walked away. I realised that I hardly did any conscious bathing at all, because I just poured water over my head three times and did nothing else. Carla seemed to panic when I mentioned the time.

Soon after, the Beasty gang was reunited when they came to recognise their biggest threat: Carla. They approached her together one day and tried to beat her, as they did to everybody else, to establish their dominance. To their surprise, she fought back valiantly and won. In fact, it was hardly a fight at all, even with four on one. Her arms and legs were flowing like water while each attack she dealt out was as strong as a log.

Despite being on a being on the leaner side, she was using their own body weight against them as she threw them all to the ground with seemingly little effort. There was a fire in her eyes, and she could not stop smiling throughout the fight. I had never seen anyone in the Estate as excited as her when it came to a fight before.

When I asked about how she did all that, she just answered "You just have to believe in yourself."

"No, what *exactly* did you do to them?" I asked. "It looked like you were just dancing."

"It's not a dance. It's called martial arts," she answered. "I learnt it from my father."

"Your father taught you stuff?" Hinda and I uttered almost at the same time. It was known to all girls that nobody supposed to have a father. They came to our mother, did their job, and left. They were not meant to stick around even if they wanted to.

"Yep, we all lived in a big happy family in a lifestyle block."

"What is a lifestyle block?" I asked.

"Well... it's a small place. It's very different from here. For example, we live in a small house instead of something like the Nest. It's only about a quarter of the size."

"Oh! That sounds terrible," Hinda stated.

"No, not at all. It's actually pretty sweet. It's all well heated and we have plenty of food all the time."

"But… how can a place that small fit a hundred people?"

"You're misunderstanding things. I live with only six other people in the house," said Carla.

"Eh?" We were in awe again. Never before had I heard of something like only seven people living in a house.

"Oh! And the Superiors like to come and play with us as well. They are really kind compared to that stingy Emmeline."

Fate was a funny thing. Despite our bad impression of each other, we slowly became friends. Carla had grown up in a very different home than mine. We had our differences—*huge* differences—but we managed to make it work after countless fights and arguments. I soon figured out how straightforward Carla was. She wanted me to say things directly to her face rather than keeping it to myself.

Indeed, I found out that she was actually very open-minded. One day, I could not take it anymore and said I hated her because she kept trying to change me. She did not punch me like I expected her to, but listened to my reasons. She said that she would only raise a hand on people who actually deserve it.

I told her my true feelings—that she was an arrogant piece of poo—and she still listened. Both Carla and I became better and more understanding towards each other as a result. Hinda, however, never had any problems with either of us. She acted as our bridge in times when we did not get along.

If Carla had not come into my life, I would probably never have changed. From the timid little girl I had been when I first arrived, I had become quite evil. When the bullies told me to do something, I would pretend to work for them, but secretly plan some sort of revenge. By sabotaging their works regularly, I often indirectly brought down the wrath of Missus Emmeline upon them. They hated me for it, but there was nothing they could do since Carla was protecting me. Not soon after, they stopped bothering me entirely.

Carla spent enough time with me to realise what my battle strategies were, and she had a word for it too. She called it "passive-aggressive." She sometimes used it as my pet name to annoy me. When she felt like it, I would often hear "passive-aggressive" from morning to night. In spite of that, my ears adapted, and I came to like it.

I could say that the time during my fourth year in Larrington was one of the best periods of my life. Hinda, Carla, and I were tight as a group. Carla's leadership, her supreme combat ability, and her fearless attitude; my intelligence and stubbornness; and Hinda's caring and adult sensibility made up a perfect friendship circle. Beasty's gang was broken up again into the two main factions. Both were constantly competing to gain the complete control of the estate. Carla could have become the dominant girl easily, but when I asked her, she would answer that she could not be bothered.

Emmeline, too, posed little threat to us. She was easy to figure out after so many years, which allowed me to avoid making mistakes in front of her. I was not punished even once in my fourth year, which made me very proud. Carla frequently had ideas for slipping out of work. With plans that were spontaneous rather than thought-out, I would make adjustments to ensure we could get away without getting caught, and when things were really getting out of hand, Hinda would stop us from doing something stupid.

Our first time, we went to peek at Mister Sam's house. Everyone was wondering what he had in his house, but none had dared to look inside. The result was disappointingly boring. Other times, we would often sneak out to see the shops while we were supposed to be cleaning rubbish from the streets. I even managed to take all of us to see the cliff-top during the day, and Carla really liked it as well.

In our free time, I would teach them the symbols of the Superiors I had figured out and gossiped about other girls around the estate. Carla insisted on teaching me and Hinda how to defend ourselves, but we always declined due to our dislike of violence, so she sort of hung out with other people as well. Hinda would sing for us, tell us funny stories, comfort us in our sad times.. We shared a lot of smiles, laughter, and tears. We were a perfect group...until Hinda suddenly disappeared.

Chapter 7: Broken

I was eight years old when I arrived at Larrington's for the first time. I met Carla at ten, Hinda was gone at twelve, and now, at fourteen, I was working hard in the mine.

"I will never do that," Carla said to me. Her face was dead serious. Her light brown eyes remain unblinking for a long time. She was staring at me until it was too uncomfortable and I had to turn away. It was never like this.

"Thank you, Carla," I replied shyly.

"Don't you want to see Beasty humiliated, Cat?" she asked. The tiredness in her voice and the creases on her face let me know that she was just stating the sentence for the sake of it. It was a rhetorical question.

"No, I don't."

"That's unlike you, passive-aggressive." She said it casually, but I was surprised to hear the nickname because she hadn't said in so many years. "Oops! I guess you didn't like it when I call you that," she said without any emotion.

I confronted her. "I'm okay, but what's wrong with you?"

"Nothing," said Carla before walking away.

In her teenage years, Carla often became distant when she had problems of her own. When she was sad, she turned a lot quieter. She was becoming an adult, I thought.

Six years had passed since I came to Larrington, and life could not be the same without Hinda. All I heard was the news of her getting sent away to another Estate. It was so sudden that I had no time to prepare for it. In the morning, she was there, but at lunch she was gone, and nobody even mentioned a thing about her. When I asked my trainer, there was no information she was willing to tell me. I knew that if I kept asking, I would be punished, so I stopped.

It was not at all uncommon for girls to be sent away from Larrington's during that time ,as it was actually the first sign that the Estate was failing. The other girls were angry that their friends were

48

gone and our living conditions deteriorated, but they did not seem to want to find out why it happened.

Either way, we moved on with our lives. Even though the perfect triangle was broken, Carla was still my best friend. We knew what we were missing in our lives, so we decided to salvage what was left so effectively. On the day we went into the forest, I knew that both of us were ecstatic. It was adventurous. It was dangerous. It was spontaneous.

It was just like the old times. Although I could see that it proved fruitless for Carla, I knew that it meant a lot more for me. The monster, the old man in the hut and the writing on my locket…there were so many answers I wanted to find out.

My only friend had become a lot quieter since Hinda was gone. The girl, now mostly a woman, would often contemplate for hours. Whenever I asked, she would just turn towards me with sad eyes, and said everything was okay. I noticed her becoming a lot more cautious with life despite the fact that the word "careful" was never in her dictionary when she was young. She often used this word in our conversations as if she were Hinda.

Another strange thing about her was that she completely stopped asking people to practice fighting with her. Maybe she was growing up to be a responsible adult. I understood that, but felt like we were drifting apart.

On that day in the mine, Jenny tried to plan a perfect place for Carla to fight Beasty and avoid getting into trouble with Emmeline. However, the plan had an opposite effect on Carla, who was already fired up. She straight-up refused and said that she would only fight for me and nobody else. Later on, Carla revealed her opinion that Jenny was just trying to use her to fight against Beasty who had been pissing her off.

Carla then ended up having a talk with Beasty, which resulted in no fight at all since the bully still remembered the humiliation on that day four years ago. So I did not have to do the bully's night duty anymore. After all, Beasty only tried her luck when she thought Carla seemed distant to me. Apparently, that was not the case.

The rest of the day at the mine was fairly normal. Carla and I worked alongside each other and talked for most of the time. We had a break in the middle of the day for lunch but hundreds of stairs had to be walked to get to the big white building on top of the hill.

Hundreds of dark-skinned males were passing in and out of the huge metal door that opened into the cafeteria. As usual, we walked together in one line to avoid taking up too much space, and lined up tidily to wait for the food.

Inside the building, tables were arranged in hundreds of rows. Most of them were occupied by the workers already, but a corner was reserved for the one hundred of us from Larrington's. There was a very low number of Superiors compared to the number of workers as with the case with our estate. I guess that the laborers knew their routines pretty well, so the masters did not have to control them much. There were so many people, yet all I heard were the sounds of them eating and walking. They could talk because they had their own language (which I could not understand), but they were not allowed to. I knew this because they would often started chatting when the Superiors were out of earshot.

We lined up behind a long queue of male workers. I was very hungry from all the work, but I knew that everyone was the same, so I never complained. Emmeline went up to a special room for Superiors on the mezzanine floor above.

Surprisingly, small pieces of minced meat were mixed within today's portion of mashed potatoes. Obviously, the luxury enticed everybody including me. It was such a blessing to have the extra flavors on the bland potatoes that provided a nice aroma that nobody could resist. I drooled more as I was approaching the kitchen. When I arrived, a few lady workers gave me a tray; they were the only female employees in the entire mine, it seemed. Their hands moved dexterously as they were scooping and dropping the portions on to my plate. Then they pushed them out without as much as a glance.

When I was done, I waited for Carla. We went to sit together then started eating our food ravenously. It was so good. All was gone within five minutes even for me.

"This is the only part I like about the mine," I commented.

"Yeah, the food is much better," agreed Carla.

We sat back for a while to enjoy the moment. I was already very tired from a half-day of work. Mud was all over our bodies, except for our hands and faces because we were forced to wash them before eating, but I felt thankful for its protection of my skin. Before we learnt to use the mud, our skin would often burn enough until it could be peeled almost all the time. Nevertheless, my legs and back were sore from standing for so long. Carla was staring into the blank space again when Emmeline came down and ordered everybody to line up.

"Hello, children," she greeted with a surprisingly kind voice. "I have news for you today. From this week onwards, we are going to come here one more day than normal."

"What do you mean, Missus?" someone asked.

"We are going to cancel the orchard the day after tomorrow and come here instead. So we are going to work here on day one, day two, and day three." She added a smile. The girls' unsatisfied chattering commenced and did not stop until she scolded them.

"Just bear with me, okay? Our estate is in need of money and the mines pay much better than the orchard."

"Why do we need money, Missus?" asked Carla.

"You see how much food we have left at the estate?" she questioned and waited for someone to answer.

"We aren't getting much, Missus."

"That's right, number 47. This is because we don't have enough money. If we get more money, we can eat more. How's everyone liking their food today?" There was generally a positive response to the question. They all smiled, except me and Carla. I looked in my friend's eyes and knew that she doubted the promise as well.

The next day went relatively normally, but the day after, I could see the girls were getting annoyed about having to go again. The orchard would normally be a much better choice for us because the work there was much more of a pleasant experience. It would just be picking fruits all day under the shade of the trees. Day three and day four would normally be two of my favorite days, apart from when we went to Mister Sam's. However, when day three, became another day in the blazing mine, everyone was visibly upset.

A few weeks passed with this new schedule, and even before we knew it, Emmeline told us to increase the mine job again, to four times a week. Everyone knew by then that we were getting used badly. There was no more food as she promised. People were getting more rebellious towards our trainer, but we knew that there was nothing we could do. There was no more smiles from our two-faced dictator until the day she wanted to increase our workload or reduce our living expenses again. If anyone tried to protest, they would be punished without mercy, and the most active girl was none other than Carla. I knew that the Larringtons' estate was falling fast.

Only half a year later, we were going to the mines five times a week. I was pretty black-skinned by then, but so were all the other girls. Even Emmeline was clearly getting darker even though every day her face was covered with a huge amount of sun cream that made her looked like a daylight ghost. When I was young, I thought that all Superiors naturally had whiter faces than us, but later found out that they used some sort of white cream to protect their faces from the environment.

They said it was beautiful, although I could hardly imagine Emmeline as anything but ugly due to her sagging face and her horrible attitude. I thought that no makeup could ever cover that up, and it was getting worse every day.

Then one day, she did the unimaginable.

"We are coming here again on day one, day two, day three, day four, day five, day six and day seven," Emmeline announced in front of everyone on the same exact spot in the mine. It was the day the history would change forever. I knew that I could not take it anymore, and I had been planning to run away with Carla for a long time, but never had a chance to tell her.

Every girl once again mumbled to each other in distaste after hearing her demand. I knew it was coming, so I had already planned a trip to the forest with Carla. In my head, I could already picture the image of us running away together. Emmeline smacked the table with her fist to silence everyone.

"What does that mean, Missus?" someone in the tall area of the line asked with a voice lacking in any true curiosity. I knew it was Carla.

"It's what I said. We are not going to work in other places anymore. We are going to work here every single day."

"But that's just outrageous. We are not getting any rest at all!" Carla expressed, raising her voice.

"Silence! You all must obey the wish of Mr. Larrington."

"What did we even do wrong anyway? We are working here every single day as you want us to do and what do we get? Nothing! I don't see more food as you promised, only shit that you have been giving us. You are a fucking liar." Carla stepped out of the line, stomped her feet on the ground and looked Emmeline in the eyes. The brave girl had just broke four or five rules in one go without hesitation.

I was afraid that Carla would be punished by death. Trembling strongly, I was filled with so much fear. I wanted to run away, but I could not. Now that Carla had drawn such immense attention onto herself, I would not be able to bring her with me.

Emmeline said nothing and stared at the girl who had said too much. Carla stared back at Emmeline without backing down, a feat that nobody, not even Beasty, dared to do. I could see in Carla's eyes the fierceness of a wild animal that could never be tamed. To my surprise, Emmeline broke the stare first. I signed in relief for a brief respite, but I was wrong.

The older woman struck my friend in the ear with her fist without any warning, but Carla blocked it easily. She immediately retaliated, but stopped midway, as if a mysterious force was holding her back. Her indecision resulted in her getting smacked fully in the face with Emmeline's other hand, which caused her nose to bleed.

Emmeline tried to kick her on the side, but with Carla's lightning reflex made her grab the leg in time. Carla did not let go, and kept moving forward while holding onto the leg. The trainer was forced to jump on one leg trying to balance herself as Carla toyed with her.

However, Carla did not strike back even once; she simply played around until she suddenly let go of the leg and the old woman fell onto the floor.

The other girls were smiling as they were watching the show. Thousands of adult workers in the hall also turned their heads and walked over to us. The other Superiors came running to Emmeline's rescue, but I could see that the male workers were intentionally blocking them. There were too many of them for the trainers to handle them all.

Carla made Emmeline fall over and over again as she rushed at her. Turned out that the sight was so hilarious, one of the girls started laughing and soon the others join in. There was nobody who had opposed a Superior before, so it was such a strange phenomenon that fascinated everyone.

After a number of tries, Emmeline appeared to be searching for something in her jacket pocket until she produced some sort of small device and aimed it at Carla. In an instant, my best friend shook violently and fell down on the ground. Her body was still shaking even when she was lying on the floor, and I realised that Emmeline was doing something to her. Carla screamed.

I stood there, watching my friend getting tortured, receiving some sort of telepathic assault from Emmeline. As the trainer's fingers dug deeper into the button of the device, I felt that I needed to do something, but I was too terrified to intervene. I knew the consequences of such a action. Carla was a doomed woman and she would not live to see tomorrow. After all, she was the one who should be ashamed of herself that she dared to disobey a trainer, let alone attack her. If I helped, I was as good as dead as well.

Why are you just standing there? Why aren't you helping your friend?

I suddenly thought of what Carla said to me when we first met.

I did not know what was wrong with me until I reached Emmeline and gave her an elbow to her face. She went down on the ground, but I kicked her once more in the abdomen with all my anger I had accumulated over the years.

I ran towards Carla and tried to lift her of the ground. I wanted to carry her and run away from all the Superiors forever. I did not think of anything else but that. As my body flooded with adrenaline, her unconscious body was surprisingly easily to carry.

Then it hit me. I had no idea what happened when I immediately felt my whole body going stiff, and my brain stopped working. All strength left me, and I fell down to the ground. On the other side of the hall, Emmeline was pushing hard on the device aiming at me. "I am a dead girl," was my final thought.

Chapter 8: The News

"Who do you reckon he is?" Carla asked me. The two of us stood together, in an area near the Larringtons' house on top of the hill overlooking the estate.

"I don't know," I replied. I had no idea myself as a completely unknown Mister approached us. I did not feel any anger or hostility, but I was still scared of any outsider I had never seen before. As I had been taught by Emmeline, I stood as straight as I possibly could despite my injuries.

Up close, I could see that he was a young Mister with a surprisingly handsome face with the typical colors of Superiors: blond hair and blue eyes. His height was also normal for them; he was very tall and lean. He smiled widely to greet us.

"You two must be number 54 and number 13." He spoke our language with a perfect accent, which startled me. His face was clearly that of a Superior, but he talked like us.

"Yes, sir," I and Carla replied simultaneously.

"Very well trained indeed," he praised. "Let's cut to the chase. I'm here to tell you that the previous Mr. Larrington and his trainer Emmeline have left the property for good."

"Pardon me, sir?" Carla asked in disbelief. I just went numb.

"I am saying to you two that those two cruel people will no longer be allowed to come back here again. You are all right now, little ones," he said, sustaining eye contact the whole time with both of us. Then he bent downward with his kind eyes and patted our heads with each hand. It was the strangest experience I had ever felt, because those smooth and soft palms of Superiors were stroking my fine hair instead of slapping me in the head. However, it was not comfortable at all. I would not mind Carla doing it to me but from a stranger. It felt weird.

"Why did they have to go, sir?" I asked.

He stopped rubbing our heads and answered. "It is a little complicated, number 54. I'm sure it is a little hard for you to understand."

"I want to know, sir."

"Okay...okay, I will tell you. To put it in the simplest terms, Emmeline is charged with a mistreatment conduct against you girls. That's why she has to leave. Mr. Larrington was the one responsible for forcing that excessive work onto all of you, so he was also charged. They are breaking the laws regarding welfare."

"What is welfare, sir?" I asked.

"It's a Superior concept that is hard to explain. As I said, it's very complicated. If I put it simply, there are certain rules about keeping you girls healthy and happy, and they did not follow that at all," he explained.

"That means...that means..." Carla stammered her words, but I could tell that she was very excited, in a happy way.

"That's right. You girls are not in trouble," announced the young Superior with a tone that matched my friend.

I looked at Carla and saw a smile welling up on her lips. Without any conscious thoughts, my lips started to do the same. We hugged each other, and there were tears of joy. I had forgotten that I had a broken rib after waking up from the incident at the mine so I told her to stop cuddling me so tightly. Emmeline was beating us hard after we fell unconscious which was her undoing. Carla too had some injuries, but none very serious. She had a few bruises and cuts all over her body with a broken arm and a purple eye.

"I'm sorry, sir. We got carried away," I said when I realised that we were acting inappropriately by celebrating in front of a Mister.

"Relax, number 54," said the younger Mister. "No! Actually, I really hate this goddamn number system. It feels like we are looking down on you girls. What are your names?"

I did not know what to say since this question was not valid. No Mister or Missus in the world would ever ask something like this. I was thinking hard and feeling the immense pressure. Carla looked me when I did not answer him.

"Don't be rude, Cat, answer the Mister," she scolded me.

"That's okay. I already know your names because your friends told me." He pointed towards each one of us. "Your name is Cat, and you are Carla. cute names."

"Oh! They're not that great, sir," Carla answered shyly.

"I think they are very beautiful." The Mister fixed his eyes on Carla for a while and gave her an obvious smile. Carla blushed and smiled back as I had never seen her done before.

"So what will happen to us now, sir?" I broke the silence.

"I hate to break the news so suddenly, but from now on, I will be your new trainer. I hope all of you can accept me."

"You'll be a great trainer, sir." Carla smiled even brighter.

"Anyway, that's all I want to tell you two today. You can go back to the Nest and get some rest now." He waved his hand and walked away. He did not go far before coming back to tell us his name.

"My name is Nathaniel, by the way," he said and disappeared towards the hill that went towards the Larringtons' house. When he was gone, Carla and I looked at each other.

"Hey! Do you think he will be better than Emmeline?" Carla spoke first.

"I guess so, but we don't really know him," I said. Carla motioned as if expecting me to say something else.

"He will be far better. How can you not like him?"

"I just don't know him yet, so I can't tell."

"See how he spoke to us? When has any Superior talked to us like that? And he called us by our real names? Oh, wow! I can't believe it!"

I could barely answer her before she cut me off.

"I want him to be our trainer so bad. I can already see the bright future of the estate. Our lives will be so much better than before."

"I don't think I am going that far yet."

"Come on, Cat. You've gotta think positive, and it will be true."

"I hope so," I told her unsurely.

Chapter 9: Improvement

It was on that same day that I had a chance to sit down on one of the most comfortable bed ever. Since the bed was extraordinarily springy, Carla and I had so much fun bouncing we did not want to stop. Carla was enjoying the same experience on her own bed. We laughed out loud because there was nobody there. All the other girls were out working while we, the injured, were staying here to rest for the whole day. It was one of the most awesome days we had in a long while together.

"It's so comfy." I smiled broadly.

"And it's so bouncy," Carla replied.

"It smells so good, too!" I said as I inhaled the spotless new white sheet fully into my lungs.

Our bedroom had been completely renewed. In just one week, this part of the old building had been scrapped out, the broken floorboards, walls, and ceiling that had been leaking cold outside air inside were replaced with fresh concrete. Modern glass windows were fit in place, so I could see the outside clearly, and most importantly, I was so glad to have our previous rock hard beds and smelly old mattresses thrown away.

That fact that we were the first who could experience the new bedroom made it all the more exciting. While other girls were out doing some jobs in town, Nathaniel told us to stay off work as long as we wanted. As directed by someone who called himself a doctor, we were forced to rest for a month to heal our broken bones.

Through the windows, I saw the girls start to come back. Even though it was only late afternoon, they finished work very early, unlike before, when we had to work until dark. Carla went outside to tell them the news, and I followed her.

"It's finished!" she shouted. I could see the girls' eyes go wild. They all tried to run in front of each other to see the result they had been waiting for. At the end of the mob was the handsome Mister who was walking casually towards us, with his hands in pockets and a smirk on his face.

59

"How are you today, Carla and Cat?" he asked.

"We are good, but the cast is a bit itchy. What about you, Nathan? I really appreciate what you did for our bedroom. I love it," Carla answered. He had asked us to call him by his name instead of *Mister* or *sir*, although only Carla dared to call him just Nathan and dropped the formality completely.

"I can't be any better, doing what you love every day, you know? And I'm glad you like the bedroom," he replied.

"I want you to be our trainer forever," Carla declared.

"That would be an honour." He smiled confidently with the answer.

We went inside together and saw the girls bouncing on their beds just like we did before.

"Hey! Girls! Can I have your attention please?" Nathaniel shouted when he entered the bedroom, yet there was no commanding, authoritative tone whatsoever. All the girls stopped and looked at him in an instant, not out of fear like with Emmeline, but with respect. Everyone was smiling and I could tell that they were liking our new trainer a lot.

"I want to say that the new owner of the estate will be meeting you girls tonight. I know you are all tired from working the whole day, but this is the chance to meet the man who has kindly put his money into changing this bedroom."

"Of course, Mister Nathaniel, we will do as you say," a girl in the back said in an admiring tone.

"Okay, thank you very much. That would make me very happy," he said with his head held down like he was truly appreciating our cooperation.

"When and where should we be, Nathaniel?" another girl asked him. They were all so eager.

"Just go to the main hall and be there at seven, okay?"

"Yes, sir," all the girls said at once.

"There's no need to say *sir*." He waved his hand to deny the honourific like he did not deserve it, but we all had been trained so well that it was impossible to change now.

The clock rang seven times to signal seven o'clock, and we all rushed to the main hall. We stood precisely as a single line with our bodies perfectly straight. Nathaniel was already there before us with his assuring smile.

"It's okay. Don't be nervous," our new trainer said in a calm voice. "Charles is not like me. He can't understand our language, but just do as you have been trained and you girls will be fine."

We remained perfectly still and silent until the arrival of a thin and tall middle-aged Mister. He stood beside Nathaniel, and they had a conversation in Superior language. Our trainer introduced him to us as Charles, the new owner of the estate.

The older man walked slowly but stiffly, like Emmeline when she was checking our line. I did not have a good look at him, because we were not meant to wander our eyes during our standing. I just looked straight ahead, but I could see him inspecting each one of us, one by one, from head to toe and without saying anything. He only murmured in his own language to himself.

When he came to me, he stared into my eyes for a very long time. I looked straight ahead but still could see him staring at my face. He assessed at all nooks and crannies of my body, which made me feel like I was naked before him, clothes stripped away by his piercing gaze. Because it was so uncomfortable, I held my breath and thought of something else, trying to imagine that I was somewhere working in the field of orchard while his eyes were undressing me.

His face came so close I could feel his breathing on my skin. He even came from behind, touched my hair and sniffed it until he was satisfied, but it was strange because he did not sniff the hair of other girls.

The encounter was something completely new. In fact, I had never seen old Mr. Larrington at all during the whole time I had been in his estate. He never came down from the house to look at us, since all his orders came through Emmeline. All we knew about him was that he lived in the house on top of the hill, and nobody even knew what he looked like. I guessed that he was not a very good owner because of how it turned out.

Anyway, this Mister's close examination gave me the creeps, and I did not want to feel that way ever again. It was better that he would stay away from us like Mr. Larrington did.

Well, my wish did not come true at all, and he was especially diligent about inspecting us twice a week. He would come down and Nathaniel would order us to line up.

I had no idea why he liked coming down so much, but all Nathaniel could say was that Charles was looking after us. He was trying to see if we were doing better after we had been so starved by the previous owner. It made sense, but my hunch was telling me that there was something more. After some time, I knew that his unusual interest in me was not just an illusion.

Chapter 10: A Lesson of How to Love

Nathaniel said that we needed to know the things he was about to teach and today was the first lesson, which was conducted in the main hall. The previous cold stone floor was now replaced with soft carpet, with a whiteboard installed in the front of the room onto which Nathaniel had taped a bunch of pictures.

"What do you think of this male?" he asked while pointing towards a photo of a very dark-skinned man with sweat all over his body. The man was digging up the ground with a shovel in hand. It was a typical picture of a male worker.

"We don't touch them," one of the girls answered.

"That's right. You girls stay away from them. You shouldn't touch them, because they are dangerous. If we Superiors don't look for one second, one of these guys will do something bad."

Before I could stop myself asking, I could already hear my own voice out loud.

"Sorry, Mr. Nathaniel, but what bad thing? We have been told all our lives that we can't touch them, but are they really that bad?"

"Yes, they are."

"But what bad thing are they going to do? I haven't seen them doing anything other than working."

"Umm…I hate to say why because they are bad. For a start, they will rape you, then kill you, then stuff you in their caves."

"…okay," I answered, unsure of what he was talking about.

"Oh, well… I guess you girls are old enough to face some dark concepts. Rape is when those males force themselves onto you without consent."

"What's consent, sir?" I asked. The questioning and answering went on for a while until I partly understood what he was trying to say. Although the idea confused me a lot, I just pretended to understand. All I got was that it was the worst thing that could happen to our lives. I let it go, because I did not want to hold everybody else up.

"So let's get back to the topic," Nathaniel said, then pointed to the next photo. This new picture showed a very muscular man with brown hair and eyes. The man was looking at us out of the photograph confidently with a smile. His chest was shirtless, and he was flexing his massive arm muscles. His skin was white, nearly as much as a Superior, but he was clearly not one of them. I immediately had an urge to step closer and kept on staring at his attractive muscles.

"This is what you'd call a man," Nathaniel announced. "You all have grown to be beautiful women, and it is time you need to know about mating."

The rest of the session was about this particular topic. He said that it was something we should do now that we were adults, so it was imperative that we had to know about it. He took us step by step, starting with drawing a picture to describe the process from what he called flirting, a delicate way of talking, touching and making actions that please the men. He told us that it was easy and every girl could do it.

Then he moved up to the next step, the sex. We were all making disgusted faces when he described the process in detail, but he assured us that it was something we should be proud of if we manage to get a man to do it to us.

"Do Superiors do this, Mister Nathaniel?" Carla put her hand up and asked.

Our trainer's demeanour changed and he answered with a cold voice. "No, young one, we have no desire for such a beastly act,"

"Yes, of course, sir. You are right," she replied.

Our trainer also repeated the point that the dark-skinned creatures we called "male workers: were completely different than the "men." The former we had to avoid. The latter we had to please, obey their wishes as if they were a Superior, and let them do whatever they wanted to us. The afternoon session went very well, and it was one of the sessions wherein all the girls were so attentive and listening for a long time. Even me. I felt such a strange feeling towards that man in the picture, like I was meant to be with him. I did not know why until I got back and thought about it that night.

As everyone was so exhilarated about their new sense of purpose, I heard from their conversations that they were attracted to the man in the picture as well. So it was not just me. In fact, I felt so stupid that I felt so strongly towards a picture of someone I had not even met. A few days after that, I had my first period.

I was fourteen years old by the time it happened. Everything about my body was changing so fast, but I knew what to expect since the changes on everybody else had begun a long time ago. It was not special at all, unlike the first time the first few girls started, when everyone was talking about it. Except for Carla who said congratulations to me, I was basically ignored, and I preferred it that way.

Our schedules were vastly improved as the work hours were drastically reduced. There was no heavy lifting anymore, only light work that was suited to our feminine bodies. We never had to go back to the mines again. Instead, we came back to stay mostly in the orchard, picking fruits or sweeping the streets of the nearby small town.

Most of the rooms in the Nest were changed so much I would not know it was the same building if I did not see them getting built. In the bathroom, an amazing invention called a water heater and plenty of new showers were installed, enough for every girl to take noe at the same time. Now we did not have to slowly boil the water during the winter anymore.

We also had much better clothing to combat the cold, although I still kept my old jacket with me since it had served me so well for so many winters. I was too nostalgic to part with it. However, all my ragged T-shirts were all thrown away and replaced with brand new sets of T-shirts, along with much warmer thermals.

Food became plentiful in a wide variety. Nathaniel would usually go into the kitchen with the girls on duty to supervise them, and he called himself a "chef." Now we were getting a new menu every day. When I was on kitchen duty, I was so surprised by how much care he put into each meal. He would use only freshest ingredients (so no more powdered potato soup) and his skills were undoubtedly masterful. The food always turned out delicious. There was no doubt in me anymore that he was the best trainer ever. However, Carla was hiding something from me.

65

One night I caught Carla walking out of the Nest at night alone.

"Where are you going?" I asked her as she was hurrying away just after our work had ended. Everybody was having free time before bed right now, but Carla was acting suspiciously by going outside. She never told me why, but I knew the reason anyway, because I had been observing her sneaking out every single night for the past few weeks.

"Nothing. Just getting some fresh air." She made an excuse.

"I wonder what you are up to," I asked while looking her in the eyes and frowning to let her know that I knew.

"You don't need to worry. I'm not doing anything bad," she said, avoiding my question. We each had our secrets, but that night I had reached my peak. I exploded on her.

"I know what you are doing, all right, Carla? Do you think you are cool for doing this?" I asked her harshly.

"Whoa…calm down, Cat. What the hell are you talking about?"

"You know what I am talking about. I just want you to stop this, but you won't ever listen to me. I'm doing this because I care about you," I yelled.

"Cat…if you care about me, then you have to let me do what I want." When she responded, I got so angry I slapped her in the face. She did not resist. I knew that because I was her best friend.

"You are a fool, Carla. I really hope you realise that. It's not right," I said and walked away, tears welling up in my eyes. I tried to get away from there as soon as possible, but I could not when she just had to have the last word.

"You are just jealous of me, aren't you?" asked Carla. I looked back at her, unable to believe what she had said. I jumped and tackled her down. The only reason I did that was that I was her best friend. If she was any other person, I would have let it go. I caught her by surprise and made her fall down. I sat on her and tried to punch her face. This time she blocked most of the blows, somehow using her body to swing me around and managed to sit on top of me instead. She locked both of my arms with her legs, and I could not even shake myself loose. My face was exposed for both of her free arms to do whatever she pleased. I was helpless and all I could do was cry shamefully.

"It's best if you leave me alone from now on," Carla said apathetically, with a face like a complete stranger to me. She did not hit me even once, but instead got up and walked away.

"Carla…" I called out. She ignored me and went to her new favourite person.

"Where were you, Carla?" Nathaniel arrived to see me lying on the ground.

"What's going on here?" He tried to help me by lifting me up from the ground, but Carla stopped him.

"Carla…Please stop this..." I said again.

"It's a bit loud here, Nathan. Can we go somewhere quieter?" Carla asked him with a weak and innocent voice, but glanced at me for the last time with cold, dead eyes. She grabbed his hand sweetly before dragging him away. At that moment, I felt the loneliest I had ever felt since my first year here.

Chapter 11: If I Were A Bird

I sat alone on the usual cliff-top with my bare legs hanging over the edge. The trees down below appeared like small bushes from the great height I was hanging on, yet I was not afraid of falling down. This was how I usually sat when I was alone.

The afternoon sun shone down on my face, but I did not feel very hot at all. In fact, it was quite pleasant with the perfect breeze gently flowing my way. I noticed a group of birds that was using it to effortlessly hover above ground. One followed the other in the perfect formation, as if written in their instincts. They did not need to flap their wings at all, simply open them and let the air current carry them. It had to be so nice to be those birds, to let go without a care in the world. Why would anyone flap against the wind when they could just do nothing and reach the destination all the same?

I let my wooden locket hang from its rope down my wrist over the edge of the cliff. Over the horizon were the countless mountains that had remained unchanged since I first saw them. The wind blew, spinning the locket. My eyes followed closely and watched its every movement. The rope spun around on itself until it stopped. Then it rolled back the other way from the tension, untangling itself, only to be entwined again in the opposite direction. It repeated the same process for a long time. Even though it slowed down, and the force was lessened each time, it never stopped completely. When another puff of air hit it, it sped up again.

The Superior's words engraved on the wood kept coming back and forth, glaring into my eyes every time the locket rolled. They asked to be noticed. No matter how much I tried to forget about getting curious about it, I would not be able to. But maybe, I could forget it all if I just let it go.

My palm was now sweaty and caused the grip on my locket to loosen. I trembled in my indecision. If I dropped the locket into the oblivion below, I would surely be a happy girl. I would go back to the Nest, forgot about this place and never came back here again. Then I would apologise to Carla and beg her to be my friend once more. I only needed to let her do what she wanted, and we both could be content with our lives. I would forgive everyone. Beasty, Emmeline, Mr. Larrington, Carla, my mother…everyone would be happy, including me. I would follow all Nathaniel's directions, become a good girl, and please as many handsome men as I could to stay happily ever after in the Larringtons' estate until the day I die along with Carla and everyone else. I would become a normal girl just as my mother wanted me to. I would be like these birds flying around the mountains, catching the wind and riding it to my destination.

The truth was, I was not a normal girl, and I just could not do that. From my strange hair colour to my weird way of thinking, I knew that I would always be an outcast.

Even if ten or twenty more years passed, I would still be wondering what the writing on the locket meant. The puff of wind would stir it up again and again. The locket would not stop spinning and neither would the inquisitions in my mind.

I stood up and patted off the dirt from my pants. I looked over the mountains, the trees, the birds, and the world beyond. I knew something was in there. I knew that even if I dropped the locket, I would somehow go down the cliff and tried to find it among the millions of trees. After all, it would be the greatest mistake to not use your wings if you were born a bird.

Chapter 12: A Lone Adventurer

Before anybody could wake up, I jumped off my bed as quietly as possible then went to my locker room and quickly put essential items in my new backpack. I put a bottle of water and stole a little bit of dry potato powder, which was now only used as extra food outside the meal time, from the kitchen.

Additional items that I had, including toilet paper, clothing, towels, and toiletries were added as well. I knew that Nathaniel had been way too busy trying to take care of girls along with his secret affair with Carla, so he would hardly notice if I went missing. After all, nobody really cared about me.

I knew that his rules and punishments were never strict to begin with, and lately, he had been getting even laxer. He had stopped roll calling girls on Sunday (the name given to day seven) ever since he was too busy hanging out with Carla. It was why I chose Sunday.

I walked in my old jacket out of the Larringtons' estate when the ambience was still dark. With its black colour, I was blending into the darkness pretty well. Down the hill from the estate to Mister Sam's house was only half an hour's walk, and it took even less time when I strode fast.

When I arrived, the orange sun was beginning to shine over the horizon, causing Mister Sam's little house to appear as a shadow of blocky shadow. I guessed that he had not woken up yet from the way that the entire place was dead quiet.

Nevertheless, I went straight to the spot where I entered the forest the previous time with Carla. It was actually our spot to hang out when we were working at Mister Sam's. Ever since she had been with Nathaniel, she had stopped coming here. She ignored me whenever I tried to talk to her and pretended that I did not even exist, so I gave her the same treatment.

However, it had basically no effect on her, since she spent all her time with her Nay Nay or whatever she called him. Every time she said his name, the word could not escape her mouth without an ample amount of honey-like sweetness and affection. It was so much that I wanted to puke.

I came back to my senses when I reached the opening of the forest.

This is it, I thought, then stepped inside the place that was full of monsters. I knew that I only had to find that hut behind the waterfall again and I would be satisfied.

"It's gonna be okay," I said out loud to psych myself up. "Yes, you can do it, Cat. Just step over that root a bit and be careful of that hole over there. That's right. You're doing fine. Let's walk very slowly here and hang on to the trees." I did not care if I seemed like an insane person, and I kept on talking to myself so that I would not get scared.

It was like there was someone with me. Maybe Hinda. I imagined her walking alongside me and it made me feel better. The forest was dark, but my eyes had always been very adjustable, so I did fine.

As the sun came up, beams of light started to come through the leaves of canopies. It was two years since I had been here, but anything had hardly changed. The trees were still as dark and big and unmoving as before, but little birds were singing to the morning sun helped me relax a little. I kept walking in a straight line just like the last time, so I knew that I would soon reach the waterfall.

An hour passed, yet I still found no hint of my destination. I kept walking until the morning was no more. Row after row of trees were preventing me from seeing anything further than a few tens of meters at a time. I thought it was strange that I did not recognise any landmark at all. After all, how could I remember what it looked like from visiting it only once two years ago?

After some time, I figured I should go back the same way. I could start again with no problem since there was still a lot of time left. From the directional point of view, I had to be walking a bit off to the angle for a long time and I managed to miss the path to the waterfall. I picked up the pace so that I would make up for lost time.

I walked straight back for another hour but the terrain kept getting even stranger. I took to avoiding going through bushes and vines

71

on the way in. Now, I regretted it, because there was no sign of the disturbance that I could follow along. I stopped and looked in front of me, and there were trees. Both to my sides and the back of me were also just trees. Everything was the same on every side. My body was dripping sweat now as I realised the full extent of trouble I had gotten myself in.

How naive of me to think that it would be a walk in a park.

Was this just a bad dream? I wished I would just wake up from this. But I knew that this was not a dream; it was real, and I had to keep going, or else I would die.

Instead of sitting down here and crying until somebody rescue me, I put my energy into figuring out the way. I found a smooth rock and sat on it. The prolonged walking had made me so tired that I even forgot to rest. The moment of reprieve really helped me cool my head and restart my brain.

It was breakfast time in the estate, so my belly was also protesting. I pulled out some bread with dried meat pieces from the inside of my bag and ate only half of what I had. There was no way to tell how long I was going to be stuck in here, so I needed to ration my food carefully.

I finally had an answer for what I did wrong. I was so dumb to think that "just keep walking straight" would be enough. The problem was, everywhere looked the same, so there was no way to tell if I was walking straight or not. The solutions were to find the landmarks and a way to truly walk straight.

I started looking for the easiest tree to climb. From my experience, some were easier to go up than others. The tree would need to be tall enough—not the tallest in the forest, but enough to be above the canopy line covering the sky. Secondly, it should be easy to climb. I tried to find one with big strong branches and preferably slightly roughened surface so that it would not be too slippery. I also excluded all the ones with spikes or thorns. Carla, Hinda, and I used to climb together a lot.

I finally found one tree that met all my conditions. I put down my backpack on the ground and started climbing. It felt so good to be

72

doing what I loved again after so long. I found that I had not lost the skill. Looking for the perfect places to put my hands and legs was easy, and it came naturally without too many thoughts. I had to jump and grab twice before I reached the top; it was a risky procedure to undertake, but necessary, since most trees had long vertical distances between each branch near the top. I thanked Emmeline for working my muscles so well.

I pushed branches at the top aside and stood up. The top of the trees was so thick it felt like it could compress my little body in the middle and hold it in place. After looking around, I realised that I had just wasted my time coming up here. The tree I was on was not tall enough, and it was nowhere near the tallest tree. My view was blocked by too many other trees to have a good view of anything.

I gritted my teeth in frustration, but refrained from making any outward movement. I could not get physically violent here where there was no room for error, as one wrong move and I could fall. I stood there for a while and thought of the next course of action. Before I could try anything, I realised that somehow I was missing the most obvious thing in view: the mountain.

There were many of them in the area, but I could tell which was which because I'd spent a lot of time staring at them over the cliff-top.

I could put my finger on the direction while I walked, but that would not work. I would probably go off at an angle again and lose it. I suddenly thought of making some cairns, but there were not many rocks around. Or I could mark the trees instead. I picked up a rock and scratched a tree with it. It worked pretty well, so I drew the Superior symbol number 1 on it. I moved around to a few trees nearby as well and marked the exact same symbol so I could see them from every angle.

The other problem remained. There was no way could know if I was walking straight, and I would probably go off at an angle and get lost again. But then I had another idea. Objects such as trees or rocks could be used as smaller, more frequent reference points in conjunction with the larger landmarks such as the mountain.

I also made some marks every so often and checked my direction by climbing up high many times. Then I began to remember another useful fact. The sun rose in the east and set in the west. How could I forget? And from my own observations from years of hanging over the clifftop, the wild fowls had been flying south in the morning and back to the northern mountains every night. Now I knew, north, east, south, and west. The sun was on my right and I knew that somewhere in the south, my estate was sitting on top of a hill. Mister Sam's place was slightly lower on that same hill. However, by the time I figured all these out, the sky was becoming orange.

When I went up a tree again for the final time, I saw some smoke coming from the direction of Mister Sam's house. Besides that, a white gush of water was pouring down from atop another tall mountain nearby. My jaw dropped open in amazement. It was the only cliff that had a waterfall. By its close location to the house, I knew that it had to be the one I was looking for, but there was no time to go there today.

Travelling at night would be a bad idea, so I decided to set up camp.

Chapter 13: The Monster

The temperature went down, and the wind made me shiver. The sun was almost gone, and the fear within me set in as what little light I had was disappearing. Monsters…nighttime… When the night arrived, they would resurface. Since I was little, the adults would tell the girls to behave themselves or the monsters would take them away, and there had been countless stories like this one.

The forest in general was the place where those things lived. Some of them were as tall as a mountain, some were smaller than us, some had fangs and claws as big as tree trunks, some were invisible, and some roamed in the sky while some resided within the ground, but all of them were very hungry for the blood of children. I told myself that it was just a myth, because I had not seen any of them with my own eyes even after living for fourteen years.

I tried to get the fear out of my head so I could focus on the real enemy of the night: the cold. Even though I had the thick waterproof jacket and a towel to cover myself with, they would hardly be enough. The ground and the air were both becoming inhospitably chilling, and I would end up frozen the next morning, so building a shelter was my priority.

I searched the area to find a place to sleep and found a patch of ground next to a fallen giant tree with a lot of covering around. I put some fallen branches on the ground as my mattress, and then made a roof so that it would trap air inside to shield me from the cold.

I cooked my dinner using the potato powder I had left to mix into water. After the solution had thickened properly, I sipped at it slowly to savour the taste and let my belly be full.

What is Carla doing? I thought, then interrupted myself when I remembered how much I hated her. I would be trying to play hard to get if she ever came back to reconcile with me. I wanted her to know that she could not get away with what she did, because I had my dignity too.

The forest was completely dark, which stirred fear within me. I tried to close my eyes, but slowly anxiety overtook me. Darting across the terrain, my eyes searched for someone that could be staring back at me. Every rustle of leaves, every wind howling in the sky, all sounds that birds and insects made became unreasonably scary all of a sudden. My ears were listening just as intently, but I soon fell asleep without intending to.

The cold woke me up sometime during the night when I found myself shivering profoundly. There was nothing I could do beside hug myself tighter. The air felt cold and there was already dew drops on the ground outside my shelter. I lay there, unable to fall asleep again due to the cold.

Despite my efforts, the night was freezing, and I found myself cowering in the corner of my makeshift shelter and trembled beneath my jacket. I thought about what everyone was doing without me, how warm and cozy they were on their soft beds and under their thick fluffy blankets. I wished I had not come here. I thought that I was going to die from the cold for real.

Suddenly, I heard something moving in the bush on the other end of the fallen log, like the ground was stepped on, and leaves parted aside. A shadow emerged and loomed in the distance among the trees. It came closer and closer. A few seconds later, I saw that it was only about my hip height, but its unnerving silhouette told me that it was not a living being from this world.

It stayed still in complete silence and stared into my soul. I nearly let out a scream but managed to cover my mouth with my palms. I held my breath and made no sound. Frozen in terror, I could not possibly escape it. All I could do was to stare back at it, afraid even to blink as I thought that if I did, I would be dead before I could open them again. I could see it more clearly now, walking on four legs with a long thick snout to smell its prey.

It moved casually like it had no care in the world. I knew that it wanted to tear me apart, limb by limb, and rip my belly open with a slice of its sharp claw, then chew on my organs and gnaw on my bones while I was still alive. The end was in sight, and there was no way that I could prevent it from happening. I would die just like the victims of those stories that my mother used to tell me.

Next came something that I never thought of doing. I stood up explosively and shouted with all my might. I then gathered stones that I had placed close to me before sleeping and threw them. The first one hit the creature right in its flank, which caused it to panic. The second one landed near its feet, but it was already going the other way. I did not care; I threw another, then another. Even when it was gone from sight, I kept on throwing until none of the stones were left.

The forest returned into its previous state as I panted from the nerve-wracking experience. I knew now that I could not sleep now that there was an actual monster roaming around trying to kill me. I told myself that I had to keep watch, yet I fell asleep soon after.

I woke to the songs of many different kinds of birds. Soon, gentle light finally came through the canopy to cast its brightness onto the ground. As I dragged myself out of the shelter, I filled my lungs with the fresh air of the morning.

I am still alive, I thought. Then I ate all the food that was left and started walking right away. My destination was Mister Sam's.

I hiked southwest. Now that I knew how to navigate, the way back was not as hard, and it was not long until I reached the familiar road connecting Mister Sam's house and the estate. Stumbling across the nearest civilisation at last, I nearly cried out in joy.

Mister Sam's house looked empty as it had always been, and as usual old Sam was out cold on his favourite rocking chair. His eyes were closed, and his expression was peaceful. I whispered "sorry" in his direction and sneaked to the back of his house. Placing my foot as quiet as possible, I managed to reach his kitchen without any problem. There was a possibility that there was somebody else in the house, although I had never seen anyone before, so I did that part very carefully, pausing and listening between each step I took.

The first thing I noticed was a piece of meat on the shelf, which made my saliva glands pump excitedly, but I decided against it. Taking any food from the house would be too obvious that someone had entered his property. Instead, I went over to the tap in the kitchen and filled my bottle. When I was done, I crawled out of the house and shut the door lightly. It creaked badly, but I guessed that old Sam was deaf anyway, so it did not matter.

Next stop was the garden we usually worked in. I picked some fruits and vegetables off the ground and stuffed them into my backpack to replenish all the food supply I was lacking, then proceeded into the woods to eat a potato. Although it was hard and smelled very earthy, I finished the entire thing. Fruits were much better, as all of them were very delicious. Nothing was better than fresh homegrown fruits, especially ones that I had been growing myself.

When I finished eating, I drank a lot of water and headed off. I knew where I was headed and in only about ten minutes of walking, I saw a stream with water gently flowing along. It was a good sign, since if water was coming from somewhere; it had to be that waterfall. Using this logic, I began to follow it.

The further I went up, the more streams appeared. They would merge with the existing one and create an even bigger stream. They became wider and faster flowing. Huge rocks also started appearing along it, and soon the way became slippery, but with my nimble feet, I was having no problem climbing them.

After a while, the sound of the waterfall became so intense that it was the only sound I heard at all. I climbed fairly high and suddenly found myself staring at a mountain with the tallest waterfall. I looked from the top to the bottom to admire it thoroughly.

I wondered what was up there on top of the mountain. How could there be so much water from nowhere? The torrent of water was mysteriously descending as if from the sky itself, creating some light mist that scattered into the air and the accompanying seven-color rainbow.

I looked down at the foot of the mountain where the fall became a large pool of water. I knew that behind the curtain of water was a hut, because I recognised the surroundings and knew that it was the same as the one from two years ago.

Out of nowhere, suddenly, something jumped at my chest and made me fall to the ground where it pinched me down with its heavy body.

Chapter 14: Inside the Cave

Instead of being afraid again, this time I decided to look in its eyes. I knew that I had to, or it would be the last of me.

Its face was long, its snout slender, its fur thick and grey, and its pair of yellow eyes were staring down at me. Its mouth parted and showed its vicious long fangs. The monster went for my neck, but I stopped it by kicking it in the belly. It flew backwards but recovered in no time. Its tenacity relentless, its anger immeasurable, it came at me again. I managed to stand up, but it launched at me in midair.

My left arm took the brunt of it as I reflexively shielded my body. The monster did not give up and dug deeper with its sharp fangs to hold tight as I tried to shake it off. I hit its face with my other hand, but it had no effect. Nothing seemed to faze the beast, and I knew that I was doomed.

Suddenly, another creature jumped into its flank which caused it to let go of my arm. The two monsters started rolling around the dirt, fighting, trying to tear each other apart, but the second emerged victorious. It chased my attacker away until it disappeared behind the bushes. It then returned to my position and stared at me.

"Sit down!" A voice shouted, and the monster stopped in its tracks.

I was in immense pain at this point, but could not bear to look at my injury. However, I was already feeling light-headed, so I had to sit back down.

The owner of the voice came running to me. I recognised him as the man who I had seen two years ago. I laid there on the ground, unable to stand. He came and sat down to assess the damage. When I accidentally glanced at my wound, I saw the damage for the first time. There were some holes with blood oozing out and a massive bruise underneath.

"Shit! It's bad." The man cursed and lifted me with surprising strength, like I weighed nothing, and I did not know what was going on after that.

I awoke in the darkness inside the bedroom of the hut as I remembered from last time. A throbbing pain presented in my left arm, which caused me to reach instinctively for the wound, but I felt some bandages in the way. I remembered the fight with the monster, but the memory of being carried inside was only vaguely there.

I nearly jumped as I finally noticed a shadow of a man sitting on the floor next to the bed, his body completely still. He appeared to be sleeping. I stepped out of bed one foot at a time, stepping light as a feather, so as not to wake him. My throat was dry, and I needed to drink some water.

My whole body was in some very loose clothing, oversized pajamas if I was not mistaken. As the pants dragged along when I walked, I decided to shorten the length by folding its legs.

"Is she hungry?" A voice came from behind and startled me.

I turned around and saw the man who had rescued me slowly standing up from the floor. As he brightened the room slightly by lighting up a small light on the table, he approached me. It was strange to see a light so dim being used this way. All we had in the Larrington estate were light bulbs, but this object seemed to be a lot different. I learned later that it was called a candle.

When the man stood in front of me, I realised that he was overwhelmingly tall, with me not even reaching his shoulder. His large blue eyes stared at me behind some dark and curly unkempt hair that was covering his face. He looked like one of those male workers, although a lot of things were off. There were plenty of creases on his face, and all the hair made him look old as well, but I really could not tell his age.

"Yes, I am hungry." I answered him simply, unsure of how to speak to this man who was not possible to be categorised. Should I call him a man? Or a male worker? Or Mister?

"I better give you some food, then." He walked past me to the kitchen. I followed him.

After putting his illumination machine on a table, he opened a cupboard and took something out. "Here, have some of this," suggested he.

I unwrapped its covering and bit into it. Even in the dark, I could smell the meat inside. In fact, it was really aromatic. Yet in spite of it smelling appetising, I could hardly stomach it.

"So deer meat is no good?" he asked without looking at me.

"No, it's…good." I was struggling. Before I could say any more, he put his hand, which was hard as tree bark, on my forehead.

"A fever. Damn…I should have known," he said, and tried to find something else in the cupboard. After a while, he found another item.

"Here, have this." He handed it over. It was some sort of powder within a plastic box. "Put some water in and it will be ready," he said to himself. At this point, I noticed that he was never addressing me directly at all, every word coming out of his mouth like when I was trying to keep myself company while walking in the forest.

"Okay…" I complied.

He told me to sit down on the chair next to the old wooden table. Then he put a bowl with some of the powder in front of me. I watched him as he turned on another light in a corner of the kitchen, only this time it was much bigger. He hung a kettle of water above it, then, after some time, that water became a steaming hot liquid that he poured into my bowl. Despite feeling sick, I was amazed of the miracle I had just witnessed. I looked back again at the crimson colour on the floor.

It was like a pile of red ribbon flying out from the ground and into the air. I felt like I could stare at it for hours, feeling its warmth and fascinating movement. Side to side, up and down, flickering back and forth, its movement was impossible to predict. It was something so unnatural. It felt like it had come from another planet.

"Never even seen a fire before, has she?" he muttered.

"Sorry?" I looked at him, confused.

"That is called a fire."

"A fire…"

When the powder was adequately stirred, it became a thick soup which he told me to blow on before each spoonful. The soup's appearance was similar to the potato powder, but it had a much better smell. The taste was also very good, slightly salty, slightly sweet, slightly herby, and generally had a bit of everything.

One spoonful at the time, I cooled the soup down with my breath and ate it all, with the old man saying nothing the whole time. When I was finished, he took the bowl away to wash it under the waterfall.

"What is your name?" I asked him as he came back.

He looked at me strangely, like the question mystified him, then said nothing, so I looked down in embarrassment as I felt that I had somehow offended him. I looked up again and told my name to him without expecting an answer.

"My name is Cattleya. You can call me Cat for short."

He still said nothing, but handed me another object from the cupboard instead. It was a tiny and rounded cylindrical object a size of a small pea.

"What do I do with it?" I asked him.

"Eat with water. Don't chew, just swallow in one go," he reluctantly answered while again averting his eyes. He handed me a glass of cold water, and I remembered what it was as soon as he told me the instructions.

During the time I and Carla were treated by the strangely knowledgeable Mister after Emmeline had beaten us up, we had to take these things every day. They were called medicine.

"That's the last one," he said to himself. I was confused as to what he was talking about but realised that he meant the pill. He looked back at me, said that he was going to go out to get more, then left without saying anything else.

It was a very dark place inside the hut, and I was alone all of a sudden. With the only sources of light being those *fire* things on the table and no windows whatsoever, there was no way to tell if it was day or night. To none of my surprise, I smelled the dampness in the air as expected of a building that stayed permanently in a cave. The waterfall outside had never stopped, and I wondered whether the water would ever run out.

The fever and headache made me felt like sleeping again, so I did, despite having a sticky body from not washing for at least a day.

There was nothing else to do, and I was afraid to go outside because of the monster.

I was woken again by a gentle touch of the old man when he told me to get to the kitchen and eat another bowl of soup. It was the morning time, he said, still using the third person pronoun to refer to me. This time, my arm was getting worse with its swelling, and I felt so anorexic I had to force myself to swallow the food before I finished the meal with one more pill.

"Don't go to sleep just yet, I need to wipe you with the towel first," he said, before telling me to pull off my loose clothing. I obeyed and let him do his job. I felt weird for taking my clothes off in front of someone other than girls, but it looked like that he was only focusing on the work. I also went to brush my teeth in the sink of the kitchen before going to bed again as well. When I came back to lie down, I was glad that the dirtiness that had been building up for a while was finally cleansed away.

I continued this cycle of waking up, eating, and sleeping for another two days before the sickness subsided, and I finally woke up to a duck quacking alarm beside my bed. His table clock was set to sound at dawn and that was how I knew it was the morning.

I jumped down from the bed. Today, I felt surprisingly energetic. Although the pain in the arm was still present, the fever was almost gone. I felt like I could do more than lying around in bed all day. My feet lightly touched the floor. As usual, as soon as it made a slight sound, the old man woke up. No matter how quiet I was, he would always be roused from his slumber instantly.

"I want to go outside today," I stated.

"Are you sure?" he asked. Finally, after a few days, he was able to somewhat talk to me directly.

"I am fine," I answered, then smiled at him before getting up fully from the bed. He had been sleeping on the floor ever since I had been here and his bed was given up solely for me. I felt bad.

"Okay, then"

We had our breakfast. He ate some of his dried meat stick he had with potatoes and fruits I had stolen from Mister Sam's. For me, I had

84

the soup and finished with some fruits. My nose was working very well this morning and found the aroma to be beautiful. I ate it all up very quickly and smiled in satisfaction.

He looked at me and laughed to himself. I frowned.

"What's so funny?" I asked.

"Nothing, I'm just happy you look so well."

When he finished his food after me, he stood up and went to get my clothes from the wardrobe with the Superior writings that I had not yet gotten a chance to ask him what it meant.

He handed me my original clothes that had been cleaned and were folded nicely in a perfect rectangle. He put it in my hand and strode away as soon as possible. I thought that he was asking me to change, so I did.

When I finished with both the food and the changing, he came back to lead me to the exit of the hut. While he was unlocking the metal bolt, the door made a loud noise as it opened. His monster that had been waiting the outside immediately sprang unto its feet and stared at me. The first thing it did was bearing its sharp fangs and growled.

"No!" the old man shouted once, and the monster instantly crouched down to the ground with its ears folded backward and looked sad. This man had made a monster his minion and did it so effortlessly. How could such a man exist? And how did he do it?

"Stay," the man ordered the monster, and it froze like a statue.

I walked past the creature while keeping an eye on it, fearing that it might jump and try to tear me apart like the other one I had encountered. In fact, they were so strikingly similar to each other that I could not stop worrying. I stayed close to the man as we walked together, using a hole between water, we slid past the waterfall without getting wet. We soon came to the outside, which was more beautiful than I had remembered. The sun was warm on my skin, and the air was so fresh I wanted to stay out here forever.

"What did you come here for?" the man asked before sitting down on a rock beside the pool of water.

I thought about his question for a while. There were so many things I wanted to ask him. Now that I had finally reached my destination, I wanted to ask about him about everything. I looked into his eyes hoping that I could project all the determination I had onto him.

"I came here to find out the truth," I declared.

Chapter 15: The True Face of the Monsters

The conversation with the old man certainly did not go as planned. All my questions were either rejected or avoided completely. I showed him my locket, but he lied to me and said that he did not know what it meant. He looked at it for ages, made no eye contact when answering me, and dismissed it like I was talking nonsense. It was obvious that he was being dishonest with me, yet he would not admit it.

"Why do you keep a monster with you?" I changed the topic.

"What monster? What are you talking about?" He seemed confused.

"That thing there, in front of your house, that vicious thing?" I pointed towards the location of the hut behind the fall which caused him to realise what I was talking about. His eyebrows pointed down, and his mouth twisted the other way.

"How dare you, calling Faolan a monster? After all she has done for you." He glared at me intensely as he unleashed his anger. I was taken aback by the response as it was the first time of the week that he'd raised his voice at me.

"Look at this!" I ripped off the bandage that was on my arm and showed him the damaged arm. Around the hole was a massive red and green from the bleeding under my skin. The holes were smaller but it was still oozing some discharge.

"What else should I call it other than a monster?"

"That's not Faolan! It was that male wolf. She was the one that chased him away," the man argued.

"I know. But isn't she the same as him? She opened her mouth and looked like she wanted to eat me this morning! What if you weren't there?"

"She won't. The girl is smart, and unless I order, she won't attack you. This is my house, little girl. And you are just a stranger, so of course, she would growl." He paused, then changed his tone. "Who are you, anyway? Are you one of those governmental spies? You sure don't look like one, but I can't trust anyone nowadays. Maybe I should have let that wolf eat you for dinner and I wouldn't have to be worrying now." He talked to himself like a madman.

I did not say anything in response, as I did not understand a lot of that, but I felt bad that I had gotten him so upset. He too went into silence, and I had a feeling that he was feeling remorse. The man walked back inside the hut without saying anything, and I followed him.

"What should I call … Fall...on...?" I asked to him.

"It's Foi-lan…damn it. She's a wolf," he replied.

"A wolf?" I asked him with a puzzled face. I sat there and thought about it for a while. After all the bantering, I still had not gotten the answers to what I needed. However, I had a feeling that if I only stayed for a little while longer, he would warm up to me eventually.

Two more weeks passed with the old man who I had been calling "you" the whole time. I did not ask him his name again due to a fear that he might be upset. His conversation skills got better the longer I stayed with him. I figured out that he had not been talking to anyone for a long time, so his reactions to things were usually awkward.

I decided to make friends with the scary monster called Faolan as well. I did not know before those monsters had gender, so it came to a surprise to me that this monster was called a girl all the time. The preconception that I had been taught about monsters was that their strength was unfathomable and their mind was incapable of reasoning with was now destroyed. They were supposed to be a representation of nothing but death, a force of nature just like storm or flood or diseases. I thought they were nothing like us at all, but after spending some time with the creature, I had to change my mind.

One day, when the old man was not looking, I opened the window of the kitchen and threw out some meat to the monster. At first, it looked at me from the other side and stared at me in suspicion, so I looked away and shut the window in fear of it jumping at me. As I peeked through the glass, I saw that it was happily chewing at the meat with a determined face.

At that moment, I thought that it looked cute, but soon had to consciously remove this idea from my head. The monsters were dangerous, and I could have ended up like that meat if I was not careful enough. I knew that its adorable look was fooling me because the monsters were the greatest deceivers of all.

The old man caught me feeding it when I did it for the second time, but instead of stopping me, he encouraged me to keep doing so. From then on, it became a part of my duties to share some meat with her at every meal.

It got boring at times since I spent a lot of time holed up in the hut, but the old man taught me how to do domestic chores. I learned to cook, clean and take care of vegetables in our back area.

The old man usually went out for a whole day with his monster to hunt in the forest. It sometimes took a long time, but he never failed to bring something back. The first time, he dragged a dead monster carcass back with him. I noticed that the monster was definitely a very different kind than Faolan. I had never seen a corpse before, but its dilated eyes, its tongue that was hanging out of its mouth, and a big gash with a massive bloodstain scared me.

Its body was covered with copper brown hair all over, except for its feet, which were composed of odd triangular extensions instead of fingers. It also had that long-nosed face, but looked nothing like Faolan, because the teeth were not at all sharp.

The wolf came, circled the carcass, and sniffed at it. "Get out," the man scolded her. At that point, she had stopped growling at me whenever I went outside the hut, but I could tell that she was still wary of me.

"What's this thing called?" I asked, pointing toward the corpse, completely avoiding the word *monster*.

"It's a young deer," he answered.

"Oh! A deer. That meat in the cupboard!" I remembered and got so excited. "So that's what they look like."

"Yes, they have very good meat."

"Can you tell if it's a he or a she?" I asked.

"Of course, this one is very easy. Just look at the back end. It has a scrotum and a penis, so it must be a male," he explained while lifting its leg to show me.

"Oh Wow…they sure look like the ones that men have," I stated, while thinking of one of the genitalia posters that Nathaniel used to educate us.

The old man looked at me strangely and said nothing. I thought that it was one of his moments where he acted strangely, but only much later that I found out what was wrong with what I said. Instead, he focused on using his large knife to tear the carcass apart.

"What are you going to do now?" I asked.

"I'm skinning it. It might be a bit hard to watch, so you can go back to the hut or if you think you can take it…" he said.

"I can take it." I looked in his eyes and smiled to assure him.

"Don't blame me if you get sick."

I watched him with fascination as he cut into the monster's skin with his overwhelmingly sharp knife. After the skin was peeled off, the deeper layer revealed some red meat which began to look like the ingredient I had handled in the kitchen before. I imagined cooking it and licked my lips unconsciously.

He said that the skin—or "hide," as he called it—could be used for clothing or as a carpet. There was a lot of meat from one monster, so all could not be eaten in a single day. He told me that he would usually dry, smoke, or salt it to prevent the meat from going bad, since there was no refrigerator like in the estate.

"How come you only kill this monster and keep the other one?" I pointed my finger at his wolf.

He stopped dead on his work and went quiet. Suddenly, I realised my mistake in voicing the word "monster."

"Sorry, I shouldn't have said the word," I apologised.

"It's…okay. You can say it."

"No…I don't want you to get upset."

"I should not have talked to you like last time," he said with sad eyes. "I should have known that all of you were taught from a very young age about monsters. I should have remembered."

I did not get exactly what he meant, but I could tell that he was sorry.

"It's all right…It's just me. I will have to stop. But, tell me…tell me the right word."

"But it will change what you have known for a fact. How can I tell you to change it?"

"I want to know. Please," I begged him.

"Animals." He spoke each syllable slowly and clearly.

"Animals…that's a much nicer name." I tried to say it as well.

"No, it's not a name, but a category of many different living things, like what you call a human."

I looked puzzled. "What's a human?"

"Humans are us. It's what we are. A girl, a man, a male worker, a Mister, a Missus. We are all humans. The same thing is with wolves, deers, lions, tigers, rabbits, dogs, cats, pigs, birds, cows, sheep and many others. They are all animals."

"Then what about monsters? Are they considered animals too?"

"The thing is, humans are also an animal, but not all animals are humans. In the same sense, the monsters are…" He paused suddenly and never continued the conversation, then went back to work the carcass.

"You can't just stop," I yelled at him.

"I'm sorry, but I have been talking nonsense."

Chapter 16: Forest Girl

Day by day, I slowly became a forest girl. It started with me complaining about being stuck in the hut with nothing to do. At first, I went out with the two hunters who brought with them their own sets of weapons.

The wolf Faolan would sniff out the trails of our prey. When she found our target, she would try to drive the rest of the herd away. Then the old man, who told me that his name was Brun, would finish it off with the almighty powerful weapon called a "gun." It was so powerful it would stop anything in its path if aimed correctly. The animals would then be finished off with a cut to the throat to ensure their death. A large amount of blood poured out every time; it made me feel faint at first, but eventually, it became just another common sight that came with killing.

If the animals were light and close enough to our hut, we would drag them back and save all their meat and internal organs for ourselves. If they were too big, we would cut only the meat up and put some in our container. The rest would be left for the hungry carnivorous or scavenging animals. There were plenty of those guys in this forest, so the meat was never wasted. We each had our backpack that we put our boxes of meat in. The way back, it would always be heavy, and I sometimes carried up to half of my body weight, but I never complained.

As we spent time together, our bond strengthened. Brun began to trust me more and more until he said one day that I could go back to the estate if I wanted to (not that he was holding me hostage in the first place), but I replied that I would rather not go back. I liked the forest and my new companions a lot. I was going as far as calling it as my new home.

When he heard that, he smiled and said that he would rather have me here as well. After that day, he began to seriously teach me the art of the forest. Starting by giving me a pocket knife as a gift, he taught me all sorts of survival skills including the use of a compass and a rifle. Soon after, I earned my place as a member of hunting party.

In the case of Faolan, the grey wolf, I found that she was the sweetest and the most loyal companion I could ever hope for. Not long after I began giving her food consistently, she let herself be touched by me.

After that, she would follow me around and sometimes put her head in my lap when I sat down. Often she would wag her tail and stare at me so that I would pat her on the head. Sometimes, she would even get down on the ground and roll around for a belly rub. Not only was she a friend when we were staying in, there were more times than I could count that she saved me during our hunts as well.

One day, when we were hanging out in the hut after a big day out, I managed to get enough courage up to ask him again.

"You must be able to read this locket of mine," I spoke to him while pulling the object out of my pocket to show him. After some inspection, he smiled, as if he had been waiting for this moment.

"It's the same as the one on my wardrobe, isn't it? That's the reason you came back here in the first place. I'm surprised you remembered it so well. Don't think I wouldn't recognise you? You are the only visitor I had in eight years." He smiled with his bright blue eyes under all the rough hair on his face.

I blushed from his complement and urged "Come on, read it, Mister."

"Stop calling me that."

"I'm just joking." I giggled, knowing well that he hated that word.

"It says… I will always be with you," he read out loud.

"Huh? That's it?"

"That's what it says. Whoever wrote it probably wants you to know that they will look out for you even if you two are apart."

"Mum…" I said to myself, thinking of her beautiful smile, and suddenly cried. Brun looked a little uncomfortable, but I hugged him anyway, then sobbed for a while until I felt better.

"Who wrote it for you? On the wardrobe?" I asked him with my broken voice, blowing out my snout several times before I was could pronounce words properly.

"She was my ex-lover. Her name was Seraphina." He paused. "She's dead."

"I'm so sorry," I told him.

"All because of me. I was the one leading the campaign, but I didn't think that they would go this far to take me down. She didn't do anything, wasn't even involved in anyway except that she was my girlfriend at that time." As Brun described the story, his voice turned very grim.

"She was just sitting at home and one day, she was gone. They shot her one leg at a time and followed her around as she crawled away while insulting her. They were playing, and having fun. I knew, because they sent me the video. The wardrobe door was the final message from her. She wrote it at her last breath."

Even when he finished recalling the tragedy, there was not a tear in his eyes. I could tell that his face was only apologetic, but nothing more. He then showed me a photograph of her.

"Wait! Your ex-lover was a Superior?" I uttered in surprise to see that the girl in the picture was a very light blond woman with a rounded face and bright blue eyes.

He looked at me and sighed. "Yes, she was, and so am I."

"No freaking way!" I let out. "You have brown hair, just like me!"

"Well…it's a long story, but…I was born blond. I changed my hair colour, you see?"

I learnt on that night that Brun's real name was Maximilian and his father was none other than old Mister Sam. He forsaken his original name a long time ago and changed his name to "Brun," which meant *brown* in Superior language. A criminal who had escaped from jail twice, a leader of an organisation that fought for the rights for the beings who have no voice of their own, he had seen too many Inferior people around the world getting abused. As part of his protest, he permanently changed his hair from bright golden to the dull brown hair, the same colour as us.

However, due to the absolute authoritarian group called the "government," he became nothing more than a mere criminal who had been hiding in the forest. He said that he ran into the forest because he used to play here as a child, and he was also worried about his father.

"How do you know he doesn't want to meet you?" I asked him.

"Because I am a shame to the family. To him, I am just an Inferior-lover. In the Superior language, 'humans' or Inferior means the girls, the men, the male workers, and anyone who is not a Superior," he explained.

"But at least you should let him know. He must think you are already dead."

"No, if I go to him, I will risk putting him in danger. It's better if he doesn't know. Let's just forget about it," he said and went quiet. I did not press him further.

I mentioned that I wanted to know more about the Superiors' language since I had been curious about it for a long time. Brun smiled and took out a massive amount of writing tied together that he called a "book" and handed it to me. It was filled with words I could not read except for the number of signs.

"There are three hundred and twenty-two pages. There are so many words in it," I said to myself, but Brun went wide eyes and stared at me strangely.

"You... can... read?" he asked.

"No, why?"

"But you just said there are three hundred and twenty-two pages."

"So? It's correct? There are so many pages. I don't know if I can finish this."

"How do you know there are three hundred and twenty-two pages?"

"I just read the numbers at the bottom. But I can't read all these words."

"That's amazing already! You just proved my theory right." He stood up and looked at the ceiling. I thought that he had gone mad. "You can read!" he shouted at nothing.

"No, I can't..." I made a face, not sure how to react to this behavior of his.

After that night, he agreed to be my teacher. He taught me to read, write, and have conversations in Superior language. At the end of the year, I had been learning very well according to him, especially in the winter when all we did was sit on our asses in the hut because it was too cold outside. The land was covered with snow and almost all animals disappeared during that time. There was nothing to hunt except occasional rabbits, but we had a lot of dried food stored.

When winter receded, summer came, and nearly one year had elapsed. I asked him one of the things that had been bothering me for a while—my feelings.

"Hey! Brun, why do you always have so much hair on your face?" I asked in my language, then added the last bit with the Superior language. *"You look like a grizzly bear."* I laughed at my joke, but he did not look too happy. We were close enough that I could say anything to him at this point.

"It's warm." He answered simply in the Superior language as well.

"Yes, I guess. But I think you will look better without it."

"Oh! Am I going on a fashion show sometime soon?" he said sarcastically.

"Yeah, everyone's waiting for you, man. Mister and Missus Cougar and the little pink oink oink. Hey! Little doggy over here too," I said and went to Faolan, holding her front legs up to wave to Brun. My little wolf sister looked very confused and uncomfortable with what I was doing to her, so I let her down and patted her on the head.

"You're making no sense, Cat." He sighed. "Grow up."

"Don't tell me to grow up, boy. You are still afraid of your dad." I teased him.

"You just went overboard again, girl." He tried to grab me and failed. My reaction had gotten far better since I had gone out hunting with him.

"Try to catch me if you can." I ran out of the hut. Faolan ran alongside me and howled in excitement. I saw that the lazy bum did not even try to get up from his chair. Instead, he just sighed more. Each day he had become more like an old man.

I ran around nearby with Faolan to release my childish energy for a while until I was tired and came back. I saw a strange face looking at me from the chair with all the facial hair gone.

"Who the hell are you?" I asked, just to annoy him. I was expected to laugh at him but instead, I was taken aback by his new face. When all the hair was gone, he was surprisingly handsome. He had the nicely curved and thick eyebrows. His blue eyes were bright and focused now instead of looking like a light behind a bush. His mouth and chin, which had been covered up by so much fur, were now sparkling clean, showing his pink lips clearly. I could see now that his creases on the skin were no creases at all and were instead battle scars from living in the wild.

"How do I look?" He asked with a smile.

"I thought you were like fifty years old or something. Do you know that I kept calling you an old man in my head when I first came here?" It was out of my mouth before I could stop myself.

"What? Seriously? I am only about to turn thirty." He was visibly upset by my comment.

"I didn't know, with all that fluff on your face..."

"They are called a beard, mustache, and sideburns. Didn't I teach you already?"

"I'm just teasing you, old man." I laughed at him.

"Hey! Truthfully, how do you think I look?" He stared at me with a serious face.

"Not that great." I lied and avoided eye contact, but my cheeks blushed heavily.

"Yeah, okay..." he answered with a disappointed look.

Our relationship had become somewhat strange. I was not too sure what males and females were supposed to do together. Because in my knowledge, they never mixed, except for the part that Nathaniel had taught us. I went red-faced whenever I thought about it, especially when Brun was around. The thought was plaguing me, even though between the two of us there was nothing at all like that. We were simply enjoying each other's company and we were happy together. It just went on so naturally.

We always went out together to hunt now, the three of us: Brun, Faolan, and me. Although it was nothing like the time I was in the Larringtons' estate, it reminded me of the perfect triangle I had with Carla and Hinda a lifetime ago. I killed animals regularly now too, and soon the shadows in the forests were no longer monsters to me.

When I spent enough time observing every one of them, I realised how predictable they were, and even pitiful in my eyes. All they did was mind their businesses and eat greens, but we shot them.

Brun taught me that it was better to kill in one shot or else they would suffer greatly. Because of this fear of hurting them, my aim became as good as Brun's. By that point, both big and small, from little rabbits to the biggest of the wild buffalos running with the herds, I could hit one of their vital spots in one shot. Even the birds I had become proficient enough to shoot them right down from the sky.

"I feel bad for killing them," I said to Brun.

"Then pray for them to go to animal heaven." He said it was a place of no evil. After they died, all animals would go to heaven, the place of infinite peace where they could eat all day long, and nobody would disturb them.

After that, I had been praying to animal heaven whenever I aimed my gun at the beasts. Although I still felt bad, I had accepted the fact that we needed to eat and they were our source of food. I followed Brun's principle "Only kill to eat and never eat more than what you need." While we ate a lot of meat since we were in the forest, we tried to keep fruits and vegetables as the main component of our meals.

There was also Brun's cousin, who sometimes delivered things to Mister Sam's house. Apparently, he was the only one who Brun could rely on to order our supplies that we could not get ourselves from town. Medicine, women's clothing, ammunitions—they all came from him. In return, we would give him game meat to sell. Despite all that, I had never seen the man in person, because he only dealt with us indirectly by taking orders and putting the supply at Mister Sam's house without the old man even being aware of it.

Two full years in the forest made me stronger both physically and mentally. The hunts were always dangerous and filled with uncertainty. Nevertheless, they were the most exhilarating thing I had ever done. I loved the feeling of having adrenaline filling my body. To be honest, the distance from surviving and certain death was usually only an inch, but that was the reason it was so exciting in the first place. However, avoiding death had become my second nature, I did not need to think. My actions were based purely on instinct and experiences. That was how I survived, but if I were to die, then so be it.

I became so good at keeping myself alive that I had proven to the other two that I could survive on my own. Once I got accidentally lost on a three-day trip on a mountain infested with mountain lions, but I managed to live through it and came back. I knew where each animal lived and hunted. I knew how they would behave in a certain situation and I knew how to use them to my advantage.

I could tell that something dangerous was coming from the sounds of birds and smaller mammals in the surroundings. I could tell apart each of the different howls and knew who they belong to. I knew what could be eaten in the forest and what to avoid. I knew the movements of the sun and the stars. I knew the ups and downs of every mountain and where all the rivers flow within a hundred kilometres around the hut. The forest had become my home range and the hut behind the waterfall, my territory.

One day, Brun said that he wanted to meet his father. It was because I had encouraged him for so long that he finally accepted. It was about the same time when I first came here two years ago. Summer had just arrived and I had just reached my sixteenth birthday. It was the time that my life would change once again.

Chapter 17: The Gold that Rusts

Brun stood still after knocking on the door of a house that belonged to his father. Shaking all over from intense emotion, he waited quietly, with eyes looking straight forward.

Footsteps echoed within the house, and Brun went stiff immediately. It looked like he might run away at any time, so I tugged at his shirt sleeve and held onto it. When he looked at me nervously, I smiled to reassure him.

"Who is knocking on my door this early in the morning?" a tired voice asked in Superior language, and I understood it perfectly. It was the first time I'd heard someone speaking in this language other than Brun, and it made me very proud.

A shadow appeared on the other side of the translucent but cloudy glass windows. After some sounds indicated that he had unlocked the door, he pushed it open slowly. An old face popped up, full of freckles and crow's feet, his body weak and fragile. Mister Sam looked even older than the last time I saw him. His head was completely white, but he never wore makeup like a normal Superior. He stared and inspected both of us.

"Who are you two?"

"It's me, Dad," Brun answered. Mister Sam blinked several times, as though he did not believe who he was seeing.

"Maximilian?" he shouted in joy and gingerly stepped down the stairs to hug Brun. *"I knew that you would still be alive. Son, I've missed you so much."*

Brun stayed still and said nothing while letting his father have his moment. I just smiled on the side.

"Come in and have some tea, Max," he invited. When he was finally done, we were led up the stairs and Brun's dad shut the door behind us. We came up to an old living room with a few couches and tables.

"Sit over here, son. I'll make some tea for you." Brun sat down on the biggest sofa and I sat beside him. When the old Mister was gone, I grabbed onto Brun's hand and found that it was icy cold.

"I'm so nervous," he said in my language.

"It's going to be all right. He will understand," I said and patted him in the back.

"I don't know about that."

The living room, although small and old, was much bigger than what we had in our hut, and all the windows were opened to let the air in. This house was the house that Brun grew up in until he was fiteen when he decided that the city life was for him, and by age eighteen, he was the leader of the movement. He said that his father never understood him why he left, but I believed that he would now if only Brun would explain to him.

The old Mister came back with two cups of tea. He put them on the table and Brun grabbed both of them, handling one of them to himself, and the other to me. I said *thank you* and took it.

"*That's for me*," Sam said, and then out of nowhere, his hand swiftly stole the cup right out of my hand and caused some hot water to spill onto my lap. I shook the liquid away but did not say anything in my surprise. Mister Sam did not meet my eyes nor said sorry to me.

"*Tell me your story,*" The old Mister asked his son while still only staring at him and everywhere else but me.

"*Where's the third cup?*" Brun finally got up enough courage to stand up for me. The old man pretended to look around the house like he was searching for someone.

"*What third cup? There's only two of us here. Now, where are we?*" He dismissed it and continued the next question as if it was nothing more than a hindrance to the conversation.

Now that I knew what he was really like, I felt guilty about my previous opinion of him. Once, I thought that he was a pitiful Mister, all alone and abandoned by his family. I used to feel sympathy for him, but only until this moment. Now I fully regretted it.

"Just bear with me a little," Brun whispered in my ear. When his father saw that, he gritted his teeth and frowned in disgust. It was obvious that he did not like his son speaking to me in the language of an Inferior.

101

Brun had to answer the questions anyway. He began the story that he had told me before, from the start when he left home to when he managed to build himself a place in the forest. I had heard the whole epic of it before, so I did not care much to listen. Instead, I looked out the windows and let the father and son have their own time.

They talked for at least an hour while completely ignoring me. At one point, the father disappeared into the kitchen for five minutes to put some fruits onto a plate and came back. This time, I knew better not to touch it.

The next thing I knew, they were talking about me.

"That thing here is a real Inferior?" Sam pointed rudely at me. His facial muscles were twitching from his distaste for me.

"No, stop calling her that! Her name is Cattleya." Brun fought back. After an hour of getting comfortable in his home again, Brun had finally ditched all of his nervousness from before. He was looking angrily at his father. He was full of courage to stand up for me.

"Oh! Is that so? I thought the bitch is your mistress with the same fashion sense as you. But this is on another level. A real human? You love them, don't you? You had a thing for them, didn't you? I thought you had changed, but now you are bringing this filthy human girl to be your bride? I won't stand for it. I won't!" he shouted.

"It's not like that, father...." Brun tried to argue but was cut off.

"You always brought shame to the family, a fucking disgrace that is. Look at that hair of yours! You have always wanted to become one of them." Mister Sam put his face in his hands, and his emotion changed after the pause.

"It was all my mistake, Max. I was such a bad father. I didn't look after you when you were young. I am so sorry, Max, but you can still turn around from the evil. If you only ditch her and return to me, I can give this house to you and find a nice Superior girl for you to marry. But for now, I want you to prove to me that you have changed. All you have to do is to return this human girl."

It was known that the Inferior beings could not understand the language of the Superior. Only trainers who had spent countless hours could learn to speak in our language, but it was impossible for low life

102

forms to grasp the sophisticated language of the Superior. Yet I understood everything.

"*She's my friend and I won't let you insult her again.*" Brun stood up and leaned over his father with his massive body.

"What are you gonna do about it? Punch your old man?"

"*Please... stop!*" I shouted and stood up to walk away.

It was supposed to be a happy reunion between father and son, but I messed it up. I felt that it was my fault that I decided to accompany Brun here. If I had not been here in the first place, this would not have happened.

"Know your place, you little human. You do not shout when the Superiors are talking. I let you step into this house because I thought you were another fucked-up Superior who decided to change their hair to that sickening colour. But I know now that I was wrong. You are a real fucking human...a real fucking thing, grimy from the top of the head to the bottom of your feet. Dripping piles of dirt everywhere you walk. Even your presence here makes this air difficult to breathe. The law says that your kind cannot come into a Superior house. Now I need to wipe all these floors and my furniture, and who will help me? I am just an old Mister and I don't have a fucking maid. Who would have thought I just let this fucking animal into my house?" he screamed at Brun as if I could not understand a word he said, then he stared at me like I had just killed his family.

I felt like crying, but I held it in because I knew that if I cry now, he would have won. In reality, I had not been hurt this much for a long time since leaving the estate.

Brun yelled back at his father, and they were still fighting when I left the room, but when I opened the door to the outside, I was stupefied. The familiar handsome young Mister stood in my way with a second, strange man. His hair, his eyes, and even his skin were blacker than I had ever seen. His body appeared to distort in proportion somehow as he was abnormally muscular.

"*So... Sam was right,*" Nathaniel muttered. I ran away into the forest immediately but suddenly, two arms came from behind and tackled me down to the ground. My chin struck the dirt, but my arms came up in time to absorb the shock. The sable-coloured man put his slimy giant hands all over me, so I kicked him in the face and slashed that big hand of his with my knife. It left a big gash on his palm.

He howled in pain, but before I could run away again, I felt a shock that caused my body to stiffen and fall down on the ground. I reclined there, stunned, unable to move but still fully conscious before seeing Nathaniel walking over to my paralyzed body with something in his hand. I recognised it as the same device Emmeline had once used against me and Carla.

"I was right to bring him along, huh?" the young Superior mentioned to his bodyguard before telling him to stop whining.

"Last time I saw you, you were just a little girl. Look at that face...oh... I'm definitely not mistaken. Those eyes...that nose...those ears... that blonde tip on the hair... You have grown to be quite a woman, haven't you?" he said as he leered at my body.

"But something is different...Somehow, you turned into a wild woman. Charles won't like this one bit. He won't." Nathaniel stayed at some distance to me even though I could move no longer. He would not come close to me until he picked my knife up and threw it away into the forest.

"Time to go home, my darling," he said in the sweetest voice, and ordered his bodyguard to lift me up even though his hand was still bleeding a lot.

"*What are you doing to her?*" I heard Brun shout, and he hurried to me.

"*I'm just getting her home,*" Nathaniel told him casually.

"*Nathaniel?*" Brun looked at him. On closer look, they appeared to be of similar age. Brun grabbed the man by the shirt. "*Stop!*" he commanded.

"It's you who has to stop, criminal," Nathaniel replied with a smile on his face. "She is my property and if you touch her, I will call the authority."

Brun slowly let go of Nathaniel. He stood there and avoided my gaze no matter how much I stared at him. After a while, he turned and went back into the house. Even though I could not speak, I cursed him from the bottom of my heart for sacrificing me to save himself.

Chapter 18: The New Larrington

While I was still in the arm of the big man, Nathaniel put metal cuffs on my wrists that linked my two hands together. The man put me down and let me walk behind them, attached by the chains linked to the handcuffs. The first thing I tried was to get the restraint off. but I knew how steel worked. It was cold, strong, and unbending no matter how much force I used.

"Be quiet, number 54," The Mister commanded. He sounded annoyed.

"Let me go!" I shrieked.

"Oh! Shut up, you" He looked at his personal manservant. "Slap!" he said, and the big black hand came across my face with such force it turned my face, but I still wanted to fight. I ran towards Nathaniel, aiming to use the chain between my handcuff to strangle the aloof Mister. Again, before I could do it, a shock went through my body, and this time it was stronger and lasted longer. My muscles were not responding no matter how much I ordered them to. They simply shook in spasm. The pain was so intense that I nearly fell unconscious, but managed to endure it.

"*Such a wild thing,*" Nathaniel muttered as he waited for me to recover.

In the end, I had no choice but to follow him back to the estate. When we arrived, the wooden "Larringtons' Estate" sign marking the entrance was now replaced with a much newer name tag, "Mr. Cotter's estate".

As I was moved through the fence line, I saw that nothing had changed much from the outside. However, there was some extraordinarily loud, high-pitched, continuous crying that could be heard as soon as I went through the gate. I thought they were some kind of animals at first, but I had never heard anything that sounded quite like them. As I got closer, I realised that there were hundreds of them, and all were coming from The Nest.

As soon as the black man opened the door to my old home, that loud noise flooded out into my ears. The girls immediately looked my way and said hello to Nathaniel with affection. Every single one of them was carrying small things in their arms, and I was sure that they were the ones who had been making the loud wailing noise. They were some sort of small animals. Some of the girls walked around with their breasts exposed and letting the little red creatures suck their nipples. One word I had heard somewhere from my past life came into my mind.

"Babies..." A product of love between a man and a woman, the beginning of life; it was how everyone started out, including me. I had seen plenty of young animals in the forest before, but never once had I seen a human infant. To be honest, they did not even look like us.

We came to the living room where there were a lot more girls, each with a baby on her chest. They made room for us when Nathaniel ordered me to sit down.

"Girls! Do you remember your friend Cattleya? I would advise you all not to come too close, because she might bite." He addressed the girls surrounding me then asked them to look after me while he went to talk to Charles. His black servant also stayed to watch me.

I was kind of angry about what he said about me hurting other girls, because I would never do that. They, too, had suffered with me. They, too, were the victims of the Superior race. It was a fact that Brun had taught me time and time when I was with him.

The girls mostly heeded their idol's warning, as they kept their distance. After all, they were good girls—unlike me. None of them dared to approach me, but only gave a fearful glance from the corner of their eye. It looked as if they did not who I was, even though we had known each other for at least eight years.

I could not help but notice that they all looked very healthy. In fact, most of them were out of shape, with larger abdomens and rounder faces; they were much fatter than when I left them. Compared to me and my athletic build, maybe even more athletic than two years ago, the contrast was clear, and I still looked like a teenager net to them.

However, there were surprisingly high numbers of their faces that I did not recognise. They had to be newer girls who were only recently imported into this estate.

I sat up but had no intention to run away yet. The black man was aiming the shocking device at me with all his concentration like it was his only job in the world. His other hand was still bleeding, but he was holding it up high while squeezing it tightly. His blood was everywhere. It was smeared all over his shirt and my shirt, still slowly dripping down from his palm. There was so much of it. I thought he was going to faint soon if it kept going. Yet Nathaniel had not done a thing to help him. It made me feel sorry for him.

"Hey! It really is Cattleya," someone in the crowd shouted. It was Jenny, a familiar face and the only girl brave enough to talk to me. When she approached me, the others followed, their eyes curious.

"I didn't recognise you, sorry." She said with an apologetic smile. She too had gotten fatter and had a sleeping baby in her arm.

"Long time no see, Jenny. How's everything?"

I asked a lot of questions to avoid having to tell my own story. I could not trust anyone. Brun, Faolan, the hut, the animals, the forest, and the true face of the monsters—nobody would understand me anyway, since I'd been away for too long and things had changed for far too much. They would think I was crazy. I lied that I was accidentally shipped to another estate but everything was all well.

The other girls were also approaching me now, following Jenny's lead. They were very keen to talk about the men they met a year ago. They told me about this guy and that guy. They described how handsome and alpha the men were and tried to top each other on their sexual achievement. There kept arguing about who had managed to be fucked the most.

Once they agreed on something, they all screamed in unison. They regretted that the men were only here a short while. Then they talked about pregnancy and babies. When it came to the last topic, they were kissing and talking to the little monsters in the arms with so much love and adoration. I did not understand any of that, and it reminded me of how much of an outcast I was before leaving the estate.

Nathaniel finally came back with his hair shoved to one side and his face wet with sweat. He looked rather upset. I thought that it had to be an argument with Charles. Before any girl noticed, he changed his demeanor and smiled wholeheartedly to them.

"Thank you all for looking after Cat," he said politely and told his manservant to clean the bloody mess he left on the floor of the living room before grabbing the shocking device back from him.

"Come with me, please, Cattleya," he ordered, and I followed him without question.

When we were outside and out of earshot of the other girls, I stood still as I tried to get myself to follow him. When he saw that I did not budge, he shouted at me to come.

"I don't wanna go," I protested. "Where the hell are you taking me?"

"It doesn't matter, all right? You are a girl, and you have to obey. Didn't old Emmeline teach you that?"

"I don't care about that old hag or you."

"Look, I really want to be nice to you but I can't, because you are so difficult. Please don't ask annoying questions again."

"But I don't want to be here! Let me go!" I yelled.

"Hey! Do you not understand? You know that you have to stay here. Even a two-year-old knows that. Now get yourself over here before I zap you again." He pulled out the device and aimed at me, so I had no choice but to walk over to him. I did not want to feel the pain again.

Soon, I realised where we were heading. The house on the hill slowly came into my sight, but it was so much newer, I nearly did not recognise it. The style had become blockier, with clear transparent windows everywhere. It was also painted anew and there were some extra sections popping up around the house. *"Property of McKenzie"* was written at the front.

Nathaniel opened the newly polished wooden door and told me to leave my shoes outside before going in. I stepped onto the floor with my bare feet and found that it was all white and smooth. There was a lot of light coming through the window to brighten the house, giving a nice and calm atmosphere. Along the corridor were some nice-smelling fresh flowers in many different shapes of vases which made the whole house smell pretty nice, although I was not in the mood to appreciate any of those at that time.

I came to what appeared to be the living room to find Charles already sitting down on one of the shiny couches. He appeared to be reading something on the table.

"*Sit her down here and tell her everything,*" he said to Nathaniel in their language, which reminded me that he could not understand my language, but I could his. We sat down across the older Mister with a balding head. The younger Mister turned to me and began to explain.

"Well… let me be direct with you, little wild girl…" He said, and paused to clear his throat like it was difficult to tell me.

I stayed dead still, listening with extreme anticipation. I could tell that it could not be good.

"Charles wants you to be his maid."

Chapter 19: A Stranger

I could tell that Nathaniel had been disagreeing with Charles about letting me becoming a maid. The older man said that he wanted me inside the house and nowhere else. It was a strange decision. I did not understand why and neither did the younger Mister.

However, Charles had more power, so Nathaniel could not argue. Nevertheless, he was able to get a condition out of the deal. I had to be wearing the handcuffs as I worked—for the first week, at least. All of these conversations were, of course, in the Superior language, and they had no clue that I could understand everything they said.

When they reached an agreement, Nathaniel turned towards me and told me in my language all the information I already knew. If I was well behaved, Charles would take the handcuffs off me next week.

"Charlotte! Bring Sebastian and Hayley out!" Charles shouted towards the other side of the house.

The first one to arrive was a boy of around eleven who was about as tall as me. His blue sparkling eyes were full of excitement and he had a big smile on his face. He wasted no time at all coming over to me. I was sitting on the couch, and felt surprise when he stroked my head. I moved away along the seat to indicate that I did not like the touching, but he kept on following me anyway. I was seriously thinking about biting his finger off, but concluded that was a horrible idea considering that I was in his house and was basically his dad's hostage. It creeped me out so much, but I could do nothing but to tolerate it.

"Stop doing that, Sebastian," Charles shouted.

"But father, she's our new 'pet.' Come have a feel, her hair is so soft and pretty. It's even a little golden too," he said to his father. '*Pet*' was a word that Brun had taught me. He told me that long ago, people everywhere used to keep a pet like Faolan, but the pets had largely been replaced by the Inferior beings. I did not get what the real meaning of it back then because Faolan was not our pet. She was one of us and our equal.

"No! You shouldn't touch a strange human you do not know. How many times have I told you? Leave her alone or I'll send you back to your room," his father said harshly, making his son clearly upset.

"I don't want to touch her anyway."

As part of his tantrum, he smacked me in the forehead in anger and stormed back the way he came from, shouting some Superior swear words I did not know.

Next to arrive was the wife and the daughter.

"This one is number 54 I was talking about," Charles said to the Missus with a little girl of about three years old standing next to her. The Missus nodded.

"Introduce them please, Nathaniel,*"* Charles said to his colleague.

"This is Charlotte. She is Charles's wife, and the little girl is called Hayley. The boy that had just run away was Sebastian. You know how to address a Superior boy?" Nathaniel asked me. I shook my head.

"You call them Master. For girls, it's Miss. Just miss, not Missus. So you call them Master Sebastian and Miss Hayley. Got it?"

I nodded.

"Remember that we are watching you, so if you want to run away again, don't. I have already activated the fence around the estate. You will die if you touch it," the trainer said to me, then continued in Superior language. *"Well... is that all, Charles?"*

"Yes. You can go now. I'll leave the rest to my wife. She can speak a little," Charles answered and went back to his reading. Nathaniel left the house and Charles's wife Charlotte came over to me.

"What do you think you are doing, Charles? An animal in our house? How is this acceptable?" the Missus asked her husband.

"We've talked about this. Now, hurry up and get out of here, and bring her with you," her husband commanded.

"I didn't ask for this. I'd rather do all housework by myself than letting a thing like this loose in our house," Charlotte argued.

Charles took his eyes off the reading on the table and turned his head towards her in slow motion. Without a single word, he stared at her face for several seconds. His wife never dared to meet his eyes and instead came to me.

"Get up! Do your work now." She addressed me directly in my language with a very strong Superior accent.

Despite her agreement with Charles, Charlotte did all the work on her own. Instead, she ordered me to pretend to do work just to make her husband see. All the while, she kept muttering under her breath that I was terribly filthy.

As soon as Charles left the living room, she ordered me to get out of the house and do some gardening instead.

I was out there in the sun for least two hours before I suddenly heard some thrashing and shouting around the house. Not long after, Charlotte came out, her hair messy and her face reddened with a handprint on it. She said nothing and grabbed me roughly to drag me back inside. I guessed that her husband had found out that she had pushed me out of the house. After that, she reluctantly let me work.

The jobs were relatively easy compared to when I was under Emmeline, but my hands were in metal cuffs, so it was so hard to do anything.

"This is how you wash clothes." "This is how you scrub floor." "This is how you do the flowers." She would often get angry for my slowness, but it was due to the handcuffs I was wearing. She would tell me to hand her over the equipment and did all the work herself.

As I worked, she would often stare at me with evil eyes that show the obvious deep hatred. She also would always carry her kitchen knife in her apron pocket whenever I was around.

My new master's appearance was atypical for one of the Superior race. She had curly and puffy golden hair. Her stature was much shorter than the other Superior as well. When I stood face to face with her, she was actually shorter than me. Her face, although extremely white from the cream, had many marks of a person who was chronically stressed, and she tended to overdo her make-up to mask it.

Apart from the immediate family, there were two other creatures that did not look like they belonged. The first was the black man who had help Nathaniel captured me. However, the second was a strange creature—I could not tell what it was at first, because it did not even look human. It was incredibly short and extremely bulky like a block and it had a surprising amount of loose brown skin which gave the appearance of melting into the ground.

On my first day at the house, our meeting was unexpected. I looked closely at the face did not resemble anything. Its legs were twisted inwards, due to the seemingly abnormal proportions of long bones, and walking seemed to be difficult. Although it could manage to walk upright, it did that in a slow and clumsy way. It was some sort of human. I was sure of it, but I could not say that it was close to our kind.

When it saw me, it started talking in a strange sound that was neither my language nor the Superior's. It was very loud and made no sense at all. Then I realised that all it could say was "mur," "maa," or anything that started with *m*. It would sometimes point a finger at me while repeating those sounds, and that was how I knew it was talking about me.

However, the only thing I could guess was that it was unhappy that I was in the house. The facial structures were also distorted so I could not even read its expression at all. When I was expecting the Missus to scold the weird human creature, she turned towards the animal and patted it on the head. The creature stopped the murmuring and looked up to her. I saw in its eyes an overwhelming affection for the Missus.

"You must be so upset that this bitch is inside our house, Lemonade. I'll get her out of here soon. I promise." She said to the creature then opened the fridge to get out some kind of sausage which she cut up on a plate to give it to the being. It readily sniffed at it then swallowed the food in a few bites.

"This is Lemonade. You call her Miss Lemonade. She is no Superior, but you should call her Miss Lemonade." Charlotte told me. The crooked human resumed making the sound and pointing at me after she had eaten.

The very dark-skinned man and Nathaniel suddenly showed up later on that day as well while we were in the kitchen. The Inferior man looked at me in the eyes and made a silent but angry face at me. I avoided his gaze at him to signal that I was submissive.

I wanted to say that I was sorry for the wound on his hand, but I was not sure if he knew our language, or the Superior language. I had never heard him utter a word, so maybe he could not even speak at all.

Nathaniel looked more tired, but this time there was a hint of happiness on his face, as though he had just finished working hard. On his cheek were a few scratch marks that seemed like someone dug their claws into his face. I could not remember exactly when I did that to him, but it had to have been when I was shocked and struggling.

"This is what she did to Cheesecake," Nathaniel said, grabbing the big man's arm over to show the Missus. He pulled the bandages off and presented my work for her to see.

"Oh no! My sweet Cheesecake..." She cried out, both hands at her mouth, then hugged the black-skinned man who was twice her size, kissed his forehead lightly, and whispered to him in a gentle voice. In response, he smiled, put his head on her shoulder, and hugged her back happily.

"This girl has been plotting to attack me for the whole day, so I always watch her with a knife in my hand, as you told me," she told Nathanial.

"I thought Charles would at least give you a remote."

"Oh my god! How could he? He didn't say a thing about her being dangerous. What about Hayley and Sebastian? How could he put our children in this? I cannot understand him, but I am glad I trust your advice."

"Here! Use mine." Nathaniel handed over the device, which the middle-aged woman took in with gratitude.

"I don't like this idea of his," Charlotte cried, referring to Charles's plan of having me around.

"I don't either, but once that man's decided on something, we can't change his mind."

"You are right."

"I'm glad you are on my side. Nathaniel. My little heart can't take this, having such a creature in my house. Would you come in and help me cook?"

"Of course, Missus. It's my pleasure."

Although they did not touch each other at all, their facial expressions and behaviors were obviously flirtatious. I sensed that Nathaniel did not like her at all, and he was simply trying to get something out of her. The married Missus seemed to have no clue about it and was simply astonished at his very existence.

I knew it because it felt just like that. It was like how Brun had used me.

Chapter 20: Dominance and Hierarchy

Once everybody was seated at the dinner table, Charlotte went somewhere to call her husband and came back with him. He sat down at the head of the table, telling everybody to close their eyes and put their hands together. I watched from afar as they started mumbling creepy words.

Everybody said the exact same thing, in the same manner. It was a song—no, more like a chant—but none of them were in sync. In the middle, a pair of blue eyes looked straight at me. Hers was the most innocent gaze that I had ever seen. They could only have come from someone who was untainted by the world. Her name was Hayley.

Sitting on the floor from afar, I could hardly understand the meaning. All I knew that it was something about values and pride as Superiors. It was filled with hard words and phrases I did not know.

When it finally ended, they opened their eyes and started eating. On the table, which was arranged nicely with a clean white cloth, each of the family members was using a golden ceramic plate with knives and forks made of pure steel. The wares were so reflective that they shone light across the dining room and straight into my eyes. At one side of the table sat Charlotte, with Hayley in a baby chair next to her. The other side hosted Sebastian and handsome Nathaniel, and at the head of the table was Charles.

Charlotte told me that we would be fed leftovers after they were done. The other two pet creatures, despite salivating heavily, seemed to know that there was an invisible barrier to prevent them from being too close to the table. We got up and sat up many times in anticipation of their food, yet they never approached closer than two or three metres from the table.

I was not sure what to do, so I simply stayed there with them and waited. I could tell that they were hungry and all their attention was on the dining table. My stomach groaned as well.

The Superiors ate in silence until the males finished eating. Nathaniel and Charles started talking while the boy's attention went into some sort of small device in his hands. Hayley seemed to have a very good appetite and she looked very happy to be eating.

It was a while until everyone was done and left the table. Nathaniel exited the house and walked away. Charlotte came out of the house after him and waved only me inside while ordering the other two to stay out. She still refused to allow me to clean the table or help with the dishes. Instead, she told me to wait and do nothing.

When she was done, she finally told me to pour the scraps together and took them back to eat in our own place. The leftover food did not look bad at all, I thought, as a lot of food was completely untouched. There were pieces of meat, potatoes, and vegetables lying around. But the most important thing was that it was Superior's food, which I had never dreamt of eating.

"This looks so good. Thank you, Missus," I complimented her.

"Better than you deserve," she said dismissively. She then left the house and I followed her with the tray of food in hand. The other two tailed closely behind me. The big black man named Cheesecake immediately came over to me. With his massive body, he loomed over my head and stared into my eyes to intimidate me.

"Cut it out," Charlotte shouted at him and the man stopped looking at me.

The Missus led us to the back of the house where there was a small building I had not seen before. She unlocked my handcuffs with the keys before telling me and the others to go inside, then shut the door behind us. In a second, I heard it being locked from the outside, which I confirmed when I tried to turn the knob.

When I turned around, I saw the black man staring at me again, this time without an escape or without a Superior to stop him. The disfigured human behind him started making a loud noise and pointed at me again.

Cheesecake walked slowly toward me like an angry bull. His hands compressed into fists, his massive chest muscles were puffed up, and everything in his body was tense. When I thought about fighting him, I knew that I had no chance without a weapon.

118

Then I realised that I was the one holding the food tray. I quickly put it down on the floor and left that spot. He immediately relaxed when he grabbed it and walked away. Then he went over to a cupboard to get two old-looking plates. He handed one over to his companion and kept one for himself. I took one out as well, although all of them were dirty and caked with grease and old food. It seemed like they had attempted to clean them, but could not do it. Fortunately, there was a tap and dishwasher liquid within the confinement, so I used them.

The muscular Cheesecake had already distributed food to be about 80/20: 80% to himself and 20% to his companion. He did not even look at me after I had let go of the food box, so I was left without anything to eat. I watched as he used his hands to stuff his mouth with pieces of meat in gravy and vegetable and swallow them whole.

Lemonade, who was given a lot less food, seemed to be satisfied with the portion and ate ravenously as well. My stomach groaned and I felt like I would faint if I did not eat anything. I stared at them and my vision started to blur.

Suddenly, my hands reached out for the pieces of meat and dug them out of the black man's dish. I did not care if my hand was dirty. It was only an instinctive action that I could not control. Immediately, I felt the eyes of the black man on me, but I did not care. I put everything in my mouth and swallowed them all before he could even react. When his massive hands reached out to me, I had already stepped far away. In his eyes, I saw a fire lusting for vengeance burning brightly.

He rushed towards me with surprising speed, but I rolled away in time. As adrenaline rushed into my body, it was as if I was a hunter once again and in front of me was an angry bear. If I did not win, I would die from hunger. It was to kill or be killed. It was the rule of nature. However, in the small room, there was nowhere to run, so I slipped from corner to corner to tire him out.

Suddenly, he shoved me down onto the ground. I did not realise that he had managed to tackle me. I tried to excuse why I was caught so easily. Maybe it was because my senses were too dull from the lack of energy. Maybe I had left the forest and the nature power within me had faded. But the truth was that he was too strong and there was no way that I could win against him.

He stood over my body and started to rain down a storm of fists onto me. I curled into a ball like a centipede to protect myself while he groaned in savagery as he let loose an anger that had been kept inside since morning. The wound on his palm had opened from the friction, but he hardly cared about that and kept on pummeling.

I could only block his attacks with my arms, but each hit was like getting hit by a big rock. Even though I had a lot of muscles in my limbs to soften the blow, that could only do so much. The blows went on forever, as if he would not stop until I died. I felt my body weaken, and my brain started to shut down. Blood was splashing everywhere on my face and on his hands and went everywhere.

Then he grabbed me under my arm with his good hand and lifted me up like I was nothing. I thought that he was going to slam me on the ground hard and that would be the end of me. He lifted me higher and higher. I felt that I was closer to heaven with each second passing by.

No, I will not go to that place, I thought. I had caused so much grief for the others, especially the animals. There would be no such place for me.

However, he stopped, and then looked into my nearly unconscious eyes for the last time before lowering me slowly to the ground. I could hear his breathing slow and finally he turned away. He went back to eating his food, but did not finish it because there was so much in there. After that, he walked into another small room that looked to be a shower.

I saw Lemonade, who was finished with his own plate as well. He seemed interested in the leftovers of the bigger man's plate. As soon as I heard the sound of water hitting the floor in the bathroom, I knew that the big man had gone into the shower. I glanced towards the ugly disfigured being that was now approaching the food. I quickly grabbed it first then stared at him.

The creature made some loud noise, but I knew that the big man would not hear his cry in the shower. I made my decision and feinted an attack on him with my kick. As soon as he saw me moving, he ran away to the corner of the room.

I started eating what was left on the big man's plate, and that was how I managed to stay alive for the days to come. From that day on, I swore that I would not let myself be at the bottom of the pack ever again.

Chapter 21: Powerless

I was woken up by Charlotte in the morning. My body ached from the fight, still dazed by the fact that I had woken up in a totally different place. The day before this, I was still sleeping with Brun and Faolan in the hut in the forest. Was I perhaps dreaming?

The events of last night came back to my mind as soon as I opened my eyes. I found myself lying on a cold hard floor. My throat was dry and my muscles were sore all over my body. I had hoped that everything was all just a bad dream, and I would wake up to the cool fresh air of the forest. However, the pain was evident enough to show that it had happened.

"Time for breakfast," Charlotte announced. She already looked fairly annoyed when I first saw her that morning. Nevertheless, she gave us some sort of compacted food as our breakfast. It was also a relief that she personally poured the food on three separate plates so I did not have to scavenge of the big man again. Nathaniel also appeared and put the handcuffs on me again and he started talking with Charlotte while we ate.

The food came in small pieces of many different colors within a bag. I tried the brown ones and found them to be salty with a meaty smell. When I tried a green one, I could taste the fibrous component that was made from vegetables. Despite that, it was much easier to chew, and the fiber basically turned into gelatin and melted in my mouth. There was a yellow color that represented corn, orange ones tasted of carrots, and the black ones felt nutty. However, the red ones smelt quite obviously of iron. I tasted it and it tasted metallic like blood. I did not like it, so I gave these ones to the subordinate animal as an apology for last night. As usual, the other two were devouring them like they were the best things ever.

"You look so tired. I wish I could help you with the housework, Alexandra." Nathaniel flirted with Charlotte in Superior language. It made the miserable Missus smile right away. Somehow, I

had a feeling that Alexandra was her preferred name.

"I don't have much choice, Nathaniel. Well... I am a mother. Even though Hayley has been really good, she is naughty sometimes. But she is nothing compared to Sebastian, who is now getting worse every day. That boy keeps arguing, my dear. He never does his homework unless I tell him to and all he does is play on his phone the whole day. I don't know what to do with him. And Charles... he's..."

Nathaniel stopped her with a touch of his hand to her lips before she could speak any more.

"You should let yourself go for a while," he said.

"But how?"

"Relax. Take some time off and let things run their course. Maybe go on a trip to a city, catch up with your female friends. Just forget about the house for a while. How about letting this Inferior girl work for you?" suggested the young man.

"I can't! You were the one who said yesterday that I shouldn't let her in the house."

"I'm sorry I scared you yesterday. You can control her, but you've got to believe me."

"Yes, of course, I believe you. Nathaniel. What should I do?"

"You use the remote I gave you yesterday. You don't have to be afraid of any Inferiors if you have that remote. Besides, I put her in handcuffs for a week. Remember to stay far away and never turn your back."

My face twisted in annoyance as they kept talking about how dangerous I was. Mostly it was Nathaniel bashing on me; Charlotte only said yes and agreed to everything he said. They knew nothing about me or Brun, who they also gossiped about. He was a criminal who stole me from the estate then turned me into some dangerous wild girl, Nathaniel said.

It was a good thing I was sitting while looking the other way to eat my breakfast when they were talking. They could not possibly see my face or else I was sure that they would sense some sort of anger radiating from me.

Then they came to demonstrating the remote.

123

"You have to try it." I heard Nathaniel remark, and a few moments later, I turned around just in time to see Charlotte pressing the button on the device. Suddenly, I felt a shock through my body which caused me to scream in surprise.

Nathaniel laughed and the unhappy married woman followed the example nervously.

"That worked!" Nathaniel said enthusiastically to Charlotte and rubbed her on the nape of the neck.

My eyes watered from the shame I was feeling. It was only yesterday that I was a proud queen of the forest, but *now* look at me! I had become a captive animal for their entertainment. Even though I thought I was strong, in front of the almighty Superiors, my fighting skills meant nothing. However, I could not show my tears to them. If I even let out a single drop, it would mean that I had lost to them.

When the breakfast was over, the other Inferiors went on their separate ways. Cheesecake was picked up by Nathaniel, who I knew that morning was the true master of the brute. Lemonade was taken with me into the house. He was to stay inside but could freely roam the place as he pleased. The only difference was that he was not given any work to do, which I thought that he would not be able to anyway with those uneven, clumsy legs and twisted hands.

Regardless of how painful it was from Cheesecake's attack last night, at least I was able to work. Charlotte followed Nathaniel's advice almost perfectly in every word he said. I saw her hand holding onto the device at all times whenever she came in to check my work. The rest of the time she was busy with Hayley, the little girl in another room. With her son going away during the day to a place called '*school*,' she was able to do quite a few things around the house, although this was going to change, as she was apparently pregnant with another child in her belly.

Even though Charles was missing for the whole day, his wife let me try the housework. It was relatively easy compared to when I was under Emmeline. The only annoying thing was the fact that my hands were tied in the metal cuffs. Still, I cleaned the ceiling, cleaned the wall, then

124

wiped all the surfaces and vacuumed the floor of every room of the house.

Sometime later, Charlotte sent me along a small hallway into an isolated corner of the house. She pointed to a nice polished wooden door with a tag saying "Mr. Charles Cotter, Manager of McKenzie Enterprise, 6th branch."

"Knock on the door first," Charlotte said, before leaving me to the door by myself.

I stopped because I was afraid of him. I remembered the times when I was younger, when he came down to the Nest to touch me in creepy ways. It made my thought race to some rumours I had heard from other girls that there was some male Superior who was into Inferior girls, although I had never believed them until recently. We were taught that Superiors were so pure and good that such a thing would not be possible.

I was afraid that it was his plan all along: to bring me here to be alone with him in a closed room. Even his wife was in on his plan as well, considering how submissive she was in front of him, and I could not run away now that she had a remote. There was also the black man Cheesecake who could probably snap my neck in two if he wanted to.

"You're still not going in?" Charlotte came back and shouted at me angrily before knocking the door for me.

"*The girl is going to clean your room, Charles,*" she shouted to her husband on the other side of the door. This time she stood behind me to see whether I would go in.

"*Come in,*" Charles said from the other side of the door.

I went in with no other choice. Still thinking of the man's breath on my hair from two years ago, I opened the door cautiously. I tried to peek a little and carefully looked around the surroundings, in case there was a trap. However, my fate was not my own. No matter what I did now, I would not escape this.

Around the periphery of the room were many wooden shelves filled with books. In the center, a single desk and chair were occupied by the middle-aged Superior man named Charles. He appeared to be writing something on paper and paid no attention to me, as if I was not there. I walked in slowly, looking up and down to see if there was anyone else who could attack me.

"*What are you standing around for? Come on! Clean the room,*" he said. My jaw dropped as I realised that he had figured out my secret. He knew that I could understand the language that I was not supposed to. Charles stood, then walked up to me. No emotion could be read from his stern and rough looking face. It was serious and intimidating, but I did not give in to him.

"*Hmm...not bad. Beautiful as always,*" he said as he approached my stiff body, frozen from the sheer fear of what was to come. I had to escape now...but I could not.

"You are definitely the same girl, Oh! Golden god helps me," he said while parting my hair with his fingers and stroking my bare arm very lightly. "How could I make the mistake of leaving you behind? You are the golden human. You are worth more than all of this dump combined," he said before he walked back and sat in his chair to start working again.

I started to doubt that he knew about my language capability. Instead of talking to me, it seemed that he was talking to himself the whole time. I was glad that I had not opened my mouth to answer him or else I would have given myself away.

There were hundreds of both old and new books on the shelves, but I had very little idea of what they were about. Most of them had a common word: 'science.' If I remembered correctly, Brun had said to me once that it was about testing things, but that was all I knew.

Charles was reading one of the books, alternating with writing up some words on his paper. He paid absolutely no attention to me whatsoever. I just did my job and he did his. We did not say anything to each other and I was glad that my assumption did not come true. I imagined myself being tied up on a bed somewhere right now if he had decided otherwise. However, it could be only a matter of time before he did it. There was no way to resist someone with a remote. If I could not fight, then I had to flee.

The day went much better than the first day. However, I decided to see if I could escape. Charles wanted me, I knew, but he had been resisting the temptation. That was why he was so insistent on keeping me in his home. At dinnertime, while everyone was busy, including the two stupid creatures, I decided to "take a walk" near the fence line of the estate.

It was already fairly dark outside, but Larrington's estate had been my home for nearly all my life, so I knew exactly where to go. I walked over to the exit, but it was shut tight with a new metal gate. I did not remember the fences bordering the estate as so tall, either. Even now, when I was much taller myself, the top of the fencewas definitely far out of my reach. There was no way I could jump over them, so the only hope was the metal gate.

When one of my feet stepped out the border, an electric jolt shot into my body. The sensation was nearly the same as the one coming from the remote, so I knew that it had to be electricity. The current was so intense I had to recover on the ground for a while. My lungs gasped for air and my face was all wet with sweat. As soon as I could stand, my legs started walking back the way I came without thinking, as if my body had already given up on escaping.

Chapter 22: The Visitor

It was not easy to suppress my true feelings. I would often think of the forest, and the companions I lived with. There was a sort of pressure that caused me never to feel comfortable here. I thought that there was no life without freedom, and I felt like a wild animal within a cage, waiting for the day I could finally break out.

I made a few more attempts of running away with no success, and my will to escape quickly vanished. As time went by, I came to accept the way my life worked around here. My old, submissive self resurfaced to protect my feelings. It was easier this way: accept, obey, and never think differently.

I had always been a very adaptable girl, and soon I became a mindless puppet again. I tried to forget that the time in the forest even existed and accepted that I was an Inferior human being destined to live forever in servitude to the Superiors.

Months—perhaps years—passed. I did not know, and I did not care. There was probably thirty years more for me to work my back off, so a little time spent here would not matter to me. My life was better than that of most other girls. I did not have to live with hundreds of other mothers and their crying babies. My work around the house was easier than theirs, and the leftover scraps of Superior food were a luxury that I got to taste every day. I was thankful for this life.

I never dared to look at myself in the mirror again for the fear of seeing what I had become. I fit into the role of a housemaid too nicely. I dressed properly and did my hair as Charlotte told me to. I was ordered by her to be as professional looking as possible while working around in the house. I had become what she wanted me to become.

"You have a visitor," stated the Missus one day. I could not guess who it could be. When I went outside, I was greeted by a man with a familiar face.

"Good morning, Cat," Brun said.

In a white shirt with a black tie under a black suit, his shiny golden hair put up in a popular Superior fashion, he smiled politely at me. His eyebrows and facial hair were very blond, as was normal for a person of high status. I thought that his face was angelic, a representation of the divine masculinity and the epitome of a proper Superior man. The only familiar feature I could see was his eyes.

"Would you prefer to come inside, Young Mister Maximilian?" I heard Charlotte's voice coming from behind me.

"I will be fine talking out here, thank you," he said and waved at her. She took the hint to leave.

We stood facing each other for some time without saying anything. I looked down at the ground awkwardly. I had decided to forget everything in the past, so there was absolutely nothing to say to him. Seeing him like this also did not help with forgetting things. From head to toe, he was a completely different person, and I could see no trace of the wild, hairy man who I had once loved.

"Will you take a walk with me?" he asked in my language. I nodded silently.

"How are you?" he asked me as we walked.

"I'm very well, thank you. And you?" I answered with a generic Superior greeting.

"I'm good. How's life?"

"There is no better place," I said, and turned my eyes away from his.

"That's good to hear. I have never seen you dress so well before." He smiled widely, then said, "You look beautiful." He grinned.

"Likewise, you look very smart, as appropriate for a high-class Superior," I said with distanced politeness, like I was talking to a stranger, and never returned his smile.

"About that day in the forest...I...I am sorry. I was...."

"That's okay. I forgive you." I cut him off with a straight face.

"Are you sure, Cat? What I did to you...was..."

"Why are you still talking about that?" I found myself suddenly raising my voice, which caused him to look taken aback.

"I want you to know that I am very sorry."

"What's the point? It's already in the past."

"But..."

129

"Shut up!"

My face reddened, not in awe of the radiance of his loveliness, but pure anger from my heart. In front of me was the person I had hated the most, more than Emmeline, or Beasty, or Carla, or the entire Superior race combined. I looked at him, tightened my fists, and gritted my teeth to control myself.

"I said I am sorry. I didn't mean for all of these to happen."

"'I didn't mean this. I didn't mean that.' Stop making excuses! You have done enough for me already. How about learning to accept the past? If you regretted it so much, why didn't you make that decision to save me when it mattered? I've already forgiven you, so now just go away."

"I was worried that you are not treated right, but I see now that I was wrong. You are doing quite well here."

"So this is what you call doing well?" I shouted in response. "Doing stupid cleaning jobs all day, every day?"

"But isn't it much better than when you left? You get to stay at a Superiors' place."

"Being ordered around by that bitchy Superiors, and I had to sleep with those weird people every single day? Working as someone's slave? This is what you call a good life?"

"Yes, it's a very good life. Normal Inferiors would give anything to be in your place."

"You can say that because you are a fucking Superior. Look at you now—you think you are so slick? Having that perfectly white face and shiny golden hair? You have it all, don't you? Your life is so fucking perfect and you are just coming here to taunt me about how successful your life has become after you got rid of me."

"I am not here to taunt you. I just want to see you."

"Yeah right, backstabber. You used me! You deceived me that night and used my body. Then you handed me over the next day. How's your father now? Like father, like son. You made him proud."

"Be quiet, Cat. Don't talk like that."

"You are here to shut my mouth, aren't you? If I speak of that night, you are dead as well. Why don't you try? It would be my pleasure to take you down with me."

"Just wait. I have one more thing for you. But just to be clear, I do not want to harm you."

"Whatever you say won't affect me one bit."

He reached inside his pocket and handed me a small rectangular package carefully wrapped with green paper.

"What's this? You think a bribe will make me forgive you?" I threw the package back to him, but he was already walking away, so it hit his back and dropped to the ground instead.

"Well, just don't let anyone else see it," he said with his back to me and continued walking away like what he said was not even that important.

"I won't, because it's gonna be buried here forever. I'm not picking it up," I shouted and walked the other way.

"I will come and rescue you one day."

"Save yourself the trouble and don't," I said, and hurried back before I could not hold myself back further.

That night I regretted leaving the present, so I went to pick it up. I sighed in relief when I found it completely intact in the grass.

.

Chapter 23: Pieces of Thoughts

Despite the anger Brun's visit had caused me, I realised that I still had it in me—that rebellious side that I thought I had thrown away months ago. After not thinking about it for a long time, I now knew that I was miserable at this place, and that made me feel good.

I decided to ignore his promise of rescue. Instead, I looked towards myself. I could do it. I could escape. After all these times, I had been trying to forget about the night before my capture. I did the vilest thing there was, so I had pretended it never happened.

In the forest, instincts were our best friends most of the time, as they were very important tools to keep ourselves alive. However, there was another instinct, suppressed by our fear from society, forbidden even to talk about in public, yet we did it.

The night before visiting Brun's dad, Brun and I had our weird moments together. I remembered when we were sitting together under the bright moonlight near the waterfall. His face was lit dimly, which made his features all the more handsome. In the darkness, the only thing I could see was a pair of light-colored eyes staring into mine.

Brun had taken me in his arms and suddenly kissed me all over. Although nervous at first, I soon found myself answering back to him, kiss for kiss and tongue for tongue. It felt so…strange. And…good. It was so…out of this world that I had forgotten about how wrong it was.

We were alone in the forest for two years, and I was surprised we had not done it before that final night. I did not resist. I wanted it. My body wanted it. My hands and mouth were moving in the same rhythm, in unison with my partner in an uncontrollable way, as if there was somebody else in my body. We took each other's clothes off and threw them carelessly onto the ground. After caressing and kissing each other over and over again, I let him inside me.

His hands were touching me gently. His mouth and mine met and parted countless times. I felt him going in and out again after breaking through my purity for the first time. His experience shone through his actions, and in no time I was feeling extremely good.

Finally, the moment came. It was the strangest yet the best experience like no other I had ever felt in my life. My head spun around in the cloud and the whole world ceased to exist for the moment.

I told him how wrong it was for him to do this to me, and we would both be killed if someone found out, but he just smiled. He then answered with confidence that nobody would, so long as we stayed in the forest together, just the two of us and Faolan.

Back when I was a young child, there was a tale regarding this act. I knew that it was the biggest of '*sins*' when a Superior has fallen in love with an Inferior. It was a crime punishable only by death. The story told that both the Superior man and Inferior girl should be burned alive in public, and a ritual should be performed to cleanse the tainted blood. It was why I was trying so hard to stop Carla from acting that way towards Nathaniel.

That night was the same night Brun finally agreed to meet his father. He never had enough courage to do so, but I thought that sex that night had empowered him greatly and given him his final push. I showed my support by going with him the next day, but that turned out to be my greatest mistake. It was exactly this act made me feel used. When Brun got what he wanted from me, he betrayed me. His motive was obviously to bargain with the authority that by turning me in, he could finally move back into to being a Superior again.

Now that he had given a message saying that he would rescue me, I swore to myself that I would never trust him again. Nor did I want his help. I never wanted to open his present, either, because I wanted to prove him wrong by finding a way to escape myself.

From that day I met with Brun at the estate, I started to pay attention to my surroundings again. I needed to know as much as I could so that one day I would be able to escape. When I was cured of hopelessness, I started to realise how much of an advantage I already had.

"Do you want some food too, Cattleya?" Charlotte put on a happy expression and offered me some food. Lemonade had been bothering her for a long while and finally got her to actually think that he was hungry. The creature was already as fat as a pig, but Charlotte could never stop feeling sorry for the man.

"Yes, please, Missus," I answered her politely. If she was offering food, I would not say no, because I knew what it was like to be hungry. She gave me a small pie full of meat and delicious gravy.

"You have quite an appetite for a girl. You might get fat soon if you keep eating like this."

"It's because your food is always delicious, Missus." I told her the truth.

"Oh! You don't have to always compliment me all the time. It's given that I feed you well when I am your Missus, after all. I am really glad that you are here. I wouldn't know how I would manage without you," she said.

"I'm fine, thank you. I am pretty full. Keep some for Cheesecake when he gets back."

"That's a good girl, just like I taught you. Sharing is important when it comes to Inferiors," she said before leaving again.

It had become clear that Charlotte was an easily impressionable person. After the countless times I had witnessed Nathaniel sweettalking her, I had learnt that this was not restricted to young Superior men, either. In a loveless home, without any appreciation from her husband, the housewife had turned into an unhappy woman desperate for love.

As her husband was interested more in reading 'scientific' books than interacting with his family, he always kept to himself within his room to read about the best ways to run his business. Not once in the two years that I'd been here had I seen him interact nicely with her. He was quiet and always serious, often absorbed completely within his problem and mumbling only to himself. The only words he would say to family were commands, complaints, or insults.

Regarding the children, Sebastian used to be the hope of the family before Hayley was born. Like a star that would shine down a bright light onto his lower-class family, Sebastian had a lot expected of him from his parents.

It seemed that his parents were never big in the society of the Superiors to begin with. Undivided attention had been given to him since the very first day of the eldest boy's life. His mother spoiled him, while his father scolded him a lot, pressing him hard, trying to get him to be a tough man. Charlotte told me that it had only sown hatred in him, made him despise the family.

When he was a little older, he was the opposite of what they wanted him to be. When his mother gave birth to Hayley, his father went into a study mania; his attention to his son suddenly disappeared. Sebastian never did his homework, never cared about school, and often went out with new friends—doubtful characters—as soon as he turned ten years old.

Most of this information was passed to me by Charlotte, plus some eavesdropping of conversations between the family members I overheard. Once the wife begun to trust me, she wasted no time in telling me her problems. I could handle her story, but she kept telling me the same thing over and over again every chance she got. I was the only other female in the house, and possibly the only friend she could talk to for miles about female problems since our estate was far from town. It was more than apparent that she was always eager for social life, but lacked the means to pursue one. However, I could hardly muster a similar feeling towards her since the most I could feel for her was pity.

It seemed that both of our worlds were the same; we were females below male counterparts. My mother and I had always been working a lot as far back as I could remember. The males only needed to eat, sleep, and play around with each other until mating.

While living in much better conditions, the Superior females had to serve the males. In addition to housework obligations every single day, the wives had orders from the husbands to be followed perfectly, and arguing was not something a good wife should do.

The other thing I learnt was that her previous name was Alexandra. When a Missus married a Mister, both her first name and last name would change. The surname would be replaced with her husband's, and the first name would become the feminine version of his name. Hence her name—Charlotte.

As soon as she married, her independence was no more. Her name, identity, and even personality all had to make way for a generic and obedient housewife caricature. Then, most of the time, she would only be known as 'Charles's wife'. It made sense now why she liked it so much when Nathaniel called her Alexandra.

Maximilian would be... Maxi? Maxime? Maxine? Maximina? Maximiliane? No... He would probably prefer to call himself Brun. So...Bruna? Brunee? Brunette? Those did not even sound like real names. Maybe I should take the Max path instead. I was daydreaming, and had to slap my own cheek to come back to the real world.

"Focus, Cat," I whispered to myself, which caused Charlotte to turn and look at me curiously. I grinned sheepishly in reply, because I knew that she would not have a problem with me acting suspiciously if she was happy with me. Even though she was a nice person to me right now, she could be extremely unreasonable if she was scolded by Charles before talking to me, which unfortunately happened quite frequently. She had nowhere to take out her anger, so it always had to be me.

This concluded some of my thoughts regarding the house of Cotter.

After we finished washing the blanket, we had to clean the rest of the floor. While Hayley was sweating profusely all over, I was relatively comfortable with my task.

"It's so much hard work," she complained, yet kept going.

"You can go take a rest if you want," I urged her.

"Phew! Thanks, sis. I didn't know how hard this work is. But my mum said that I have to learn to do this too, because when I grow up, I will have to do this for my husband," she explained.

"You are a good girl. Any other Superiors wouldn't help me, you know?" I patted her on the shoulder, causing her to grin brightly. I went on to clean Sebastian's room next. The door was very slightly open, so I peeked inside.

"*I'm going to go over there just in a bit,*" the tallish teenage boy said into his phone before coming out of his messy room, which was filled with clothing piling up on the floor. I cleaned his room every few days, but whenever I did, it was always in this state.

This morning, the boy did not even wake to see his parents off; he always slept very late which gave his mother the extra job every morning of waking him up. I was glad that Charlotte did not order me to do that job as well.

He was talking rapidly into his phone then walked out of the house without acknowledging me.

"You can't go out. It's your mum's order," I told the boy and ran after him.

"*I'm going out now, but the stupid Inferior bitch is talking to me for some reason,*" he said into his phone, which I guessed was connecting to his friends, and continued to ignore me. I knew that he could not understand a word of Inferior language, but I had to try to stop him. It was Charlotte's order not to let him go out on his own to his friend's place while the she was away.

"Hey! Stop that. You are gonna get yourself killed!" I shouted as he started his motorcycle.

The estate was at least twenty kilometers away from the nearest small town, where Sebastian and Hayley went to school. Most of his friends were in town, so he tried to go out often.

"Get lost!" he said and accelerated away.

I sighed again as he disappeared from my sight. Charlotte had asked me to do the impossible. Of course, I had no power to stop the boy, since he had never even acknowledged me as a person. After the incident on the first day when he tried to pat my head, he never interacted with me again. So, obviously, it was very awkward for me to try talking to him. Why did Charlotte ask me to stop him? It was something that she could not even do herself.

On the other hand, little Hayley had gotten a lot closer to me. When I first arrived in the house, she was only a cute and innocent baby, but time passed so fast, and she became the naughtiest girl I had ever seen. I was positive that I was nowhere near this energetic when I was the same age as her. She was one hell of a little girl to take care of. Despite that, she was lovely at times, even going as far as trying to please me and her mother when she felt like it.

"Sis, when are we going to go down?" she asked me again for the eleventh time this morning while I was still doing my routine jobs around the house. I told her to go play by herself but she kept coming back.

"We will go in the afternoon, Hayley," I answered. "Or do you want to help me with these?"

"No!" she yelled. "I'm bored." Then she stomped her feet while striding away.

The reason she called me 'sis' was that she saw her best friend at school being picked up by her big sister every day. The best friend always bragged about how her sister treated her so well. She would show off her pretty flowers and cute Inferior figurines that her big sis had purchased for her. Hayley was jealous and wanted to have a big sister as well, so she told me that I made her mother so happy and I had to be her sister.

I made some egg sandwiches filled with cheese, lettuce, and tomatoes for both of us, and two more for Cheesecake and Lemonade, who were roaming freely somewhere in the property. I left their portions on the kitchen table.

"Let's go," I said to Hayley before holding out my hand for her. She grabbed it and we walked together.

We descended towards the Nest. I had not seen any of the girls since the first day I was captured, so it was going to be awkward, but I decided to stay strong for little Hayley. I greeted a bunch of them, who were now holding the hands of their standing children, each of whom was the mirror image of me and Hayley. Except that they were abnormally big.

Some were twice as big as Hayley—although, from the way they talked, they did not seem to be very mature. I asked them some questions and they could hardly form a sentence. I managed to find my friend Jenny with her daughter.

"Two years and a bit," Jenny said when I asked her how old her daughter was.

"No way..." I was still shocked by how big they were. This girl was the same size as Hayley, who was twice her age.

"Yes, I guess Nathaniel fed us well. I love him," she answered me with a big happy smile. Nothing had changed regarding his prestige among the girls.

"So where is Carla?" I asked.

"What Carla?" she answered. There was a genuinely confused look on her face.

"There is only one Carla...what do you mean what Carla? My friend...Carla!" I cried, feeling that something had gone wrong.

"Oh! The girl that you used to hang out with? Carla...the first one who stood up against Beasty...yes, I remember."

"Yes, her," I agreed. "Where is she?"

"I don't know," she said with a dead face.

"How do you not know? Did she run away?" I almost shouted at her from my anger.

"No, she was transferred out of the estate, like many others, I guess. I can't remember how that happened exactly, sorry."

"What? You don't even know? You were her friend too. What about Nathaniel? They were…you know…"

"I have no idea."

"Argh! Do you not give a damn at all?" I went over to her, about to get physical, but stopped short.

"Sis…what's wrong?" A hand tugged at the hem of my shirt. I stopped immediately and gathered my thoughts.

"Sorry," I said to Jenny without looking at her, and pulled Hayley with me.

Hinda…now Carla? I thought. What had I been doing? I let both of them disappear. If I hadn't been so selfish and run away to the forest, none of this would have happened. I should have stayed here like a good girl. And what about Nathaniel? He was involved with her, so maybe I should ask him…but how? Would he just tell me what I wanted to know? Or would I have to force him? If I even laid a finger on him, I would get a good shock from the device.

"Hey, sis, what's this place?" The voice of the small girl led me back to my senses.

I stared at a location I had accidentally walked towards without thinking. The small wooden hut of a medium size sat on the edge of the forest behind our estate.

"Nathaniel's cabin?" I spoke out loud without thinking, in disbelief that I had come here by accident. The hut had always been here since the beginning of time. It was used by old Emmeline before Nathaniel's arrival and had always been the cabin for the trainer as long as anyone knew.

Over the years, I had learnt that trainer was possibly one of the lowest ranking possible jobs, one that only the poorest, uneducated, and dropouts of the Superior could get. Nobody in their world wanted to spend all days looking after a bunch of Inferiors doing work on the scorched earth below the sun.

The language of an Inferior was like a scratching of chalk on board to them. It was deemed to be uncultured and only spoken by barbaric people. This was why some Superior owners ordered their Inferior workers to stay silent most of the time.

The learning of the language fell mainly only to the two groups of Superiors: the trainers and estate owner's wives. The former had a direct role supervising the Inferiors so it was essential for all trainers to learn. The latter could speak it because it was a tradition. In olden days, the wives were forced to be a trainer, or at least to help with the work around the estate. In the case of Charlotte, she was lucky that there was a man such as Nathaniel.

Normally, though, trainers were the employees of the estate. The pay was usually very low, but I knew that it was not the case for the two of them. They had to make plans for job assignments along with leading the cooking, checking on girls' health and giving basic educations or "training"—hence the name "trainer." The lists went on and on. However, I thought that Nathaniel had a lot of say in the management. I once heard he and Charles called themselves partners. It was the 'modern way' of running an estate.

When Emmeline was gone, the shack was left to be Nathaniel's. On the front door hung a simple plain wooden sign: *Larrington*. It had been years since the old owner had left, but the name was somehow still on the door. Trainers not supposed to live with the family of the owner of the estate, so they had their own huts.

When I was little, I did not know how much Emmeline had to work, but now I could probably say that it was just as hard as being an Inferior. No wonder she was always mean to us. For Nathaniel, It was the opposite. It was still a mystery to me how he managed to stay positive in front of the girls all the time.

"I want to see." Hayley tried to stand up on the tips of her toes to peek over the window, but she was still far too short, so I lifted her.

Inside was unusually beautiful; even though there was just a single room, it was large enough to put at least four beds in. However, there was only a simple single bed with a golden blanket on top, as suitable for a typical Superior bed. The remaining space was fully furnished with a refrigerator, a microwave, and a washing machine. The room was much better than what I had imagined, but I guessed that Charles was really generous with his money.

Suddenly, I saw in the corner of my eye a big black blob of a monster on the floor. I recognised it straight away. I pulled Hayley down from the window sill before she could see the creature. It was the big man named Cheesecake sleeping soundly on the floor, and he did not appear to notice the two of us. I was not afraid of him, but I knew that letting him see me peeking over his master's hut would be a bad thing. Hayley bawled and protested my action, but I put a finger to my mouth to signal her to stop. She understood my body language immediately and left with me without further questions.

Chapter 25: Home Alone

A shiny school bus trotted up the hill before stopping in front of the estate. When the big metal gate opened, Hayley crossed over to the other side and smiled back at me. It was only natural that she would transcend the border without a problem. For me, if I were to walk over the same gate, somehow it would send electricity into me. I had tried running after Nathaniel in the hope that it would deactivate for the Superior and I could pass through, but I still received a big shock.

"Bye, sis!" Hayley waved at me. I could see the faces of the other children on the bus looking down at me. Some of their faces suggested confusion, as it was uncommon to have a Superior child calling someone Inferior a sister.

I walked back alone into the house. It was day one, or *Monday*, as the Superiors called it. They had a name for each day, but I learnt them all quickly. Now, I was left with the house that was completely vacant, except for Lemonade who lying happily on the couch of the living room, sound asleep without a worry about anything.

Cheesecake was nowhere to be found, as he was probably at his master's hut again. Hayley was off to school and Sebastian had not even come back after the whole night. *Monday* was his school day, but it looked like he decided to stay over at his friend's place. Not that it mattered to me. Otherwise, I had the whole house to my own.

"I could have a look at Charles's study," I said to myself. I had tried a few times before to read what he was so obsessed with, but could never understand the words. They were just muddles of words to me; very complicated terms and sentences appeared all over the books, not to mention the scientific symbols, numbers, graphs, and tables.

I got the gist of it, though—Charles was studying what type of food should be fed to the girls and their babies along to prevent diseases and such. It was understandable that Charles was so interested in this; he was the one who was managing the estate, after all.

"Perinatal mortality?" I picked up the most recent book he had left on his working desk. I could not understand the heading, so the content meant nothing to me. I went to the next book.

"Feeding regime for the 2-3 years age range meat Taurine," was another book heading. Many of the books mentioned this word *Taurine*.

That day, I went to check out the hut again. I thought about how I could lose my temper so easily when it came to Carla. Only the mention of her name had somehow evoked the emotion inside me.

Cheesecake might still be around in Nathaniel's hut, so I tramped over the grasses carefully to make as little noise as possible. Not only I was right about the big man being inside the cabin, but he was also in the exact same position as before, on the hard wooden floor of the cabin with his eyes closed. Nathaniel's bed was alongside him but appeared untouched. It was the rule that I had been told many times to not sleep or sit on a Superior bed and seemed that the black man had followed this rule strictly.

Cheesecake was the fastest person in the entire estate from my experience of fighting with him. This was also confirmed by a conversation between Charles and Nathaniel. The latter said that the real purpose of having Cheesecake was to keep disobedient girls in check. The runner could run up to twice the speed of any girls, so he would catch up to them if any were to run away. This was made me extremely careful about not getting caught by him.

After carefully observing, I noticed a shock remote on the floor next to his hand. It appeared that he had been holding it while awake, but dropped on the ground when he fell asleep. Tiptoeing quietly across the turf, I reached out for the door, then twisted the knob. It creaked loudly, causing Cheesecake to stir. Without delay, I ducked and hid on the back side of the hut. My ears listened in anticipation of his footsteps, but there was nothing even after a full minute, so I stood up again and found that the man had already fallen back asleep.

Now I had to try something else. After scouting the outside of the hut, I found an open window. I climbed inside and sneaked towards my objective. I snatched the remote and stepped back very cautiously, so as not to make any sound, then shut the window. I looked back for the last time before leaving to see the slumbering brute completely oblivious to my thievery.

I looked at the prize in my hand, a small yet powerful device that had taken me down countless times. I admired its simple design and felt its smooth plastic covering with my fingers. It reminded me of the weapon I once had, my rifle. I knew that looks could be deceiving when it came to power. *With this, maybe I could escape*, I thought.

I smiled wickedly as I turned towards the savage who was still sleeping like a hog. The opportunity was there and I was not going to waste it. The time for revenge had come.

I had no idea how to use it, but there were only two buttons on the device. I pressed the right one, because it was the natural button for my dominant right hand to run into. As an experiment, I squeezed it only lightly while watching the reaction of my victim. However, there was absolutely no response from the target. I tried again. There was still nothing and the man was still snoring. Could it be that I was simply standing too far away? Or the window was blocking the signal? I slid my hand with the device inside the building through the window and pointed directly at him. I pushed the button again, but there was still no reaction.

"Stupid machine," I murmured. This time, I thrust on it as hard as I could and kept my grip there for a good long while.

Suddenly, I heard a scream and Cheesecake immediately woke up. Even though the scream was kind of strange, I did not have time to check or close the window, since I was already sprinting away as fast as I could. Again, I waited for the strong and fast footsteps of the big man. However, there was nothing. When I looked back, he appeared to still be in the cottage. Still, I ran back to the house as fast as I could, knowing that if I was caught, it would be the end.

"I'm back, sis." Hayley ran over to me while I was arranging flowers in a vase. I knew every plant in the garden by heart—lavender, roses, hydrangea, geraniums, lilies, tulips, daffodils, irises, begonia, and many more. I knew what each vase meant to Charlotte and which combinations of flowers I was supposed to arrange into each specific vase. She said that decorations brought out the best of the rooms, enhancing the atmosphere, even bringing fortune to the house or such things, but I thought it was all superstition.

I relaxed my grip on my newfound treasure when I realised that it was Hayley who called me. I hoped that I would never have to use it on her.

"Welcome home," I said, but suddenly Hayley jumped onto my back. Her arms hit my neck a little too hard, causing me to sway and nearly stumble to the ground.

"Ouch!" I cried out. "Don't do that."

"Sorry, sis," she said and got off my back. She was quick to learn my body language.

"I can give you a piggyback ride if you want, but wait for me to finish first. Do you want to play by yourself for now?"

She nodded and ran towards a swing under the big tree that was in front of the house. I sighed. This girl would never stop playing unless she was asleep.

After I was done cleaning, I went into the garage to get some ingredients for dinner. There was plenty of meat and vegetables in the freezer that happened to be stored in the garage. Charlotte had bought enough food for at least two weeks before she went away, so there was still plenty left.

Every time I went down there, I always looked at this strange heavy metal door with rust everywhere. I was very curious about its purpose, since it looked much older than the rest of the wall and it was always locked with heavy metal chains.

The meat was chopped into many pieces. There were shoulders, ribs, thighs, and legs. I used them bit by bit to cook the meal for everyone, including Cheesecake and Lemonade. Both of them knew their dinner time up to the exact minute of the day. Whenever it was time, I would see them waiting at the windows, so I had to serve them on time every day or else they would start pestering me, just as they had done to Charlotte whenever she was late.

While I was cooking today, the little girl was watching the television the whole time. I knew she was not supposed to, but I let her off the hook.

"Have you done your homework?" I asked her, suddenly remembered that Charlotte used to do this every evening.

"I've done half of it in class," she shouted back.

"Then when's the other half going to be done?"

"After I finish."

"When is that?"

"I don't know."

I also remembered that Hayley was pretty difficult about her homework because she knew how to lie. She often begged and manipulated her mother to get what she wanted. There had been countless times when her teacher would call home the next day saying that she had not done her homework.

"How about we do it together after dinner?" I suggested.

"Yeah! Let's do it, sis. You can help me," she answered enthusiastically.

In the normal scenario, her mother would have trouble getting her involved. Often, after dinner, she would go back to the living room and started watching television again. I told her to help me clean up the table and dishes. After that, I held her school bag in my hand and looked into her eyes.

"Let's do it," I emphasized, just to make sure that she would not forget. Hayley pulled out one of her books titled 'Basics general knowledge. Book 2". She turned to the end of the book. There were a lot of pictures and some simple words that I could read.

"This page." She pointed at it, so I examined carefully and found that I had no idea how to answer the questions at all.

"Can you do these?" I asked her, trying to hide my cluelessness of the world, the basic knowledge that even Superior children of four or five years old would know.

"Of course. These are really easy," she said, drawing lines to match the words and their meanings. I looked at her in surprise. It looked like she did not even have to think. Her hands dexterously drew lines after lines to link the words and their descriptions together. It was like she already knew everything. There were only four choices to the left, but there were many descriptions on the right.

1. The main workforce of the world
2. Some have very large breasts
3. The smartest by far
4. Cute
5. Stupid
6. Strong
7. Fast
8. Delicious!
9. The Greatest

The 4 choices were Zebu, Taurine, Sanga, and Superior. When Hayley finished, the result was like this.

Zebu- 1, 5, 6

Taurine - 2, 5, 8

Sanga - 4, 6, 7

Superior - 3, 9

Obviously, I knew the word Superior but the others I had not heard them before. Nevertheless, they were strangely familiar. Zebu, Taurine, Sanga... Suddenly I remembered the word Taurine in Charles's study. "Perinatal mortality in meat Taurine," "Supplemental feeding for meat Taurine," "Babying percentage in young meat Taurine." It all came back to me. What were these words? Taurine, Zebu, and Sanga?

All my questions were answered when I had a look at the next section. It showed photographs of highly stereotypical people of each race. The first was of a male worker, dark yellowish-brown skin with squinty eyes. He was lifting a wheelbarrow filled with rocks. Under the

148

picture was a line. On it, Hayley wrote the word "*Zebu*." The next question showed a man smiling and looking at the camera with golden hair and bright blue eyes. The word "*Superior*" was written beneath him. The next was of a very black man from the top of his head to the soles of his feet, looking a lot like Cheesecake. The man was running against a few others of his own kind as a part of a sprinting race. "*Sanga,*" I guessed and Hayley wrote the same word down on the line.

"Taurine," I said as soon as I saw the last picture.

Hayley looked at me "That's you, sis. But you are too skinny!" It was a photograph of a burly white-skinned female with dark brown hair holding a baby. I thought that this person looked a lot like Beasty and her gang. Now that I thought of it, there were many faces down in the Nest that I thought were similar to each other.

The striking resemblance made me felt so strange. How could a random picture of someone in the book look so much like people that I knew? Zebus, Sanga, and Taurine were the terms used by the Superiors to classify us Inferior species. It was so scary to know that we were born so similar to each other, as if we were all created from the same blueprint. We were what they made us, nothing more and nothing less. We were the Taurine. Some have very large breasts. Stupid and delicious!

Chapter 27: A Couple and A Man

The whole week of spending time with only Hayley was finally over. The three members of the family who had gone were back on Sunday night. I did absolutely everything I could to welcome them back by preparing them a happy home-cooked meal for the night. A whole ham was ready in the oven along with roasted potatoes and vegetables. They came back pretty late at night, so I and Hayley ate our meals first.

After two hours, the car's bright headlights could finally be seen. It was driving along the driveway towards our house. I went down to the garage and bowed my head to them. The old-fashioned golden car with a loud engine that belonged to Charles arrived first in the garage, followed closely by Nathaniel's silver vehicle.

The travelers opened the doors and exited out hurriedly where Charlotte called me with a serious, emotionless voice to help her with lifting the luggage. Nobody else said anything to me or to each other. Both Charles's and Charlotte's faces had a tired look to them; Nathaniel was the only one looking unconcerned.

They went straight to the dining room while I carried the rest of the belongings into the house. I quickly came back to the table where they were sitting quietly. I served them some water as the lady of the house had taught me and tried to smile to lighten up the atmosphere, but it had no effect. They all looked exhausted in addition to Charles's somewhat tense look.

"I'll serve the food. Today, it's going to be maple honey mustard–glazed leg ham with roasted carrots, broccoli, and silver beets, and the dessert will be apple pie." In the end, even my voice became shaky. I simply could not handle the strange air Charles was giving off. It looked like he was angry and wanted to kill someone. I was glad when I had a chance to get back into the safety of the kitchen. Nathaniel broke the silence.

"It has been twelve weeks, but we only have fifty percent."

"What have you been doing with the detection then?" Charles answered, a hint of sarcasm in his voice. I knew by this point that they were discussing something I could not understand again; conversations related to management were often heard between these two men. To be honest, they rarely talked about anything else.

"I'm using everything I could, okay? It's like the last time, but it's the semen, I tell you. It's the semen that's bad."

"No…the semen is not bad. I chose them myself. They were a thousand dollars each. Those men I used were never below rank ten in the catalog. If it's bad, then I would like to see how the other estate is doing. Don't blame your technique on the semen. It's your technique that is wrong. Are you sure you were qualified for that course? Or is there something else going on?"

"Of course, why would I lie to you? I did everything perfectly."

"Why would you lie?" Charles replied sarcastically. I had never seen him so angry before. My hair stood on end and my eyes widened, even though I was all the way on the other side of the room.

"Well, I am not lying," Nathaniel answered with an unusual coldness in his voice that he had never shown in front of the girls. I could tell that he was getting serious, too.

"Shameful! How can you still call yourself a Superior? Golden god will curse you!" The middle-aged man shouted angrily. His face was red and tiny drops of sweats were visible on his forehead. His fist struck the table which caused it to flip over. The candle, white tablecloth, and wine glasses I had prepared so carefully all crashed down to the floor, and the glasses shattered. Charlotte screamed.

The candle burned into the tablecloth. Charlotte was completely in panic mode, so she was not able to do anything, but her husband took care of it by stomping the flame out with his feet. All he was looking now was the face of his subordinate. However, the still-masked face of Nathaniel showed neither fear nor surprise.

"Charles, calm down. You are making a mess," the younger man said casually, like he was simply talking to a perfectly sane man.

"Don't tell me how I should behave in my own house," Charles snapped at him.

"Of course, you are the master of the house. It is not my place to argue."

"My wife... You... two of you..." Charles's voice was stuttering as if the words were stuck in his throat. After some effort, he was finally able to muster the strength to say the words.

"You slept with my wife!" he shouted at Nathaniel, who somehow remained unfazed by the accusation.

Charles walked closer to him while keeping his eyes fixed on the other man's. I could tell that he was really thinking of punching him, but in another part of his brain, the inhibition of the Superior culture stopped him. Brun had told me that Superiors were not meant to solve problems by fighting. Such actions were considered barbaric and belonged only to Inferiors. In their world, a mere punch on the face of another Superior could land in jail time of at most ten years, so rarely would anybody fight. However, trainers who were disciplining Inferiors used physical punishment, which was considered normal as part of their routines.

Charles's muscles were tensing; his chest was puffed up and he held his arms out. It reminded me of how animals did the same thing to make themselves bigger if threatened.

"I did not do that," his employee said indifferently. This sentence tipped the angry man off.

"You lying piece of shit. Do you think I am blind? Yesterday, I saw you two walking outside and fondling each other in the damn park."

At that moment, his wife inserted herself between the two male Superiors, her small body barring the path to destruction.

"You are defending him?" The husband asked with a weak voice. His reaction told me that he was unable to believe that she would oppose him.

"Yes," she answered.

"Hmm...I thought you were forced. So...a mutual agreement, huh? I knew it."

"We didn't do that," she cried out to him.

152

At that moment, a violent slap landed on her face which sent her small body tumbling to the ground. It was not a rare sight for me, since I had seen Charles punish his wife like that many times. Nathaniel immediately jumped in and caught her before she fell.

"*I will call the police.*" Nathaniel held his phone to his head. "*Do not take a step.*"

"*Shh... Don't play with me... boy. I don't believe you will,*" Charles continued towards the younger man and his wife. Nathaniel pressed the call button.

"*You see? I am serious,*" Nathaniel told him while looking into the older man's eyes. Charles saw that he had no choice but to step back until Nathaniel canceled the call.

"*I'll let you go tonight, but you better watch your back. Or, if I fail, may the law punish you,*" Charles uttered.

"*It is not I who should be afraid of the law, Charles. It is you. Remember that I know what you do to her. There will be evidence all over her body. Well...I really don't want any trouble with you, Charles. So, if you want to accuse me of something, next time please bring proof,*" Nathaniel said and left as soon as he had his last word, leaving behind only a feeling of frustration for the most powerful man in the estate. I saw from behind that in the final moment, the corners of Nathaniel's lips were parted in a small smirk.

Chapter 28: Charles's Resolution

"I'm going to DNA test these children," Charles said while pulling Hayley and the baby with him to town.

In the past few days since their return, it was evident that he had been very stressed about this situation. Charles had tried as many ways as possible to find proof that Nathaniel's involvement with Charlotte was real, but the result of the DNA test showed that Charles was the father of every one of his children.

Calling him stupid behind his back, his wife told me that she was already pregnant with Hayley for five months when she first met the handsome trainer.

On the other hand, Nathaniel was acting even more smug than usual, as he seemed confident enough that Charles would not find anything against him. The guy still showed up for dinner at his employer's place and pretended that nothing had happened. Charles threatened to fire him, but it was not possible due to their relationship in McKenzie enterprise and the complicated law that prevented firing people without good reasons.

Charles had no ability to dismiss his trainer without sufficient reason and corresponding evidence. Instead, he stopped talking to Nathaniel and personally went down to manage the Nest by himself. Due to his inability to speak the Taurine language, he was hardly understood by the girls and they all feared him. He complained to me every day whenever I was cleaning his office that it was impossible for him to do his job now that there was a worm inside his house and that he did not trust his wife anymore.

Sebastian came back that night just before his parents' arrival and pretended to have been at home all along. He managed to fool everybody and successfully avoided the wrath of his father.

Even though Nathaniel basically never cared about the allegation, he had something else on his mind. He was mad at Cheesecake after he found out about the lost shocking device. One night, he came into our little outer housing and threw a tantrum over it. His *"dog"* was the one who suffered the consequences. The poor big man was kicked and hit repeatedly with a stick. All the while, his master insulted him with many swear words and degrading names. Nonetheless, the loyal servant did not utter a word in defiance; he received the beating without making a sound. In fact, he looked confused about what was happening to him, and it even seemed that he had forgotten about his task of protecting the device completely.

His owner left while muttering to himself in Superior language about how expensive it would be to buy a new one. Even though the punishment was undeserved, I could not help but felt happy about it, because I was the cause of it. The power was in my hand, and I intended to keep it.

That night an impulse to try the device again came to me. I felt like I had to learn to use it properly before I could be perfectly confident in its power. What better time for it to be tested than the middle of the night? My targets were perfectly still and had no way to resist. It was a good thing that the device had a digital screen that could be seen at night.

I sat up from my mattress in the far corner of the room away from where the other two were sleeping then pressed the right button as hard as I could while pointing towards Cheesecake's position. Nothing happened. Not even a sound. I tried again, but it was still nothing.

A message popped up—*cannot find target*—on the screen. I remembered getting shocked from 100 meters a long time ago, so distance was definitely not the problem here.

There was the left button, after all. I tried playing with it and finally got it working on myself with a small current that was not too painful. When that happened, it showed a thirteen-digit number on the screen. I was clearly pointing it towards Cheesecake, yet it still worked on me. That night, I could not get it to fire towards the other creatures at all, so I gave up.

One afternoon, as I was sweeping the floor of the living room, Charles started another conversation with his wife. This time he had a big leather-bound book in his hand. His face was unusually calm, unlike the other times when he talked to her.

"*What do you want with me?*" Charlotte asked when she saw him acting strange.

"*This is 'the law'.*" He held out the title of the book to her face.

"*I know.*"

"*Well…you know. But do you abide by it?*"

"*What are you trying to say, Charles? Do you want me to admit that I cheated on you?*"

"*No, I am just going to read it to you.*"

"*I've got better things to do than to listen to you reading a dusty tome,*" she said, and tried to leave, but Charles's swift hands immediately grabbed hold of hers. Clearly afraid of the consequences, he squeezed lightly but no more.

"*How dare you call 'the law' a dusty tome? Have you not read it? Study it and take it into your heart? Like all the good Superiors do?*" he asked.

"*Of course, Charles. I've read it. Everybody has.*" Charlotte answered with a bored tone and the face to go with it, but Charles ignored her.

"*Then you must know the section of marriage and love.*"

"*Yes, yes.*"

"*When a man and a woman have sworn fealty to a life of marriage, the woman must not touch, kiss, hug or displaying affections towards other men,*" he read out in a matter-of-fact voice. Charlotte remained quiet and uninterested. Her husband continued.

"*The punishment for such crimes is to kill the woman by a single stab to the heart and renounce the cheating man the status of Superior, castrating and turning him into an Inferior for the rest of his life.*"

"*Is that supposed to make me feel scared?*" she asked.

"*No, because if you do no wrong, you will not need to be scared. The golden god shall be with you.*"

"*Of course he will protect me, because I haven't done anything wrong. If that's all you have to say to me, then I'm going to tend to my garden now.*"

156

"*Yes, as you wish, my dear wife,*" he said. She started walking away, but he stopped her as if he just remembered something. "*By the way, the result came back negative.*"

"*Oh! The one that you brought me to the doctor for—to swab my vagina?*"

"*Yes.*"

"*You shouldn't even have doubted me.*"

"*I do not doubt you,*" Charles answered as if he was not affected by the result. But, in fact, his body was shaking once again. As Charlotte walked past me, she whispered to me in Taurine language.

"We used protection, my dear."

I understood it immediately. It had to be that she did not think that I would understand the context because of the rest of the conversations were in Superior.

It was the first time I had seen Charlotte display any sort of resistance towards Charles. I thought that the victory that Nathaniel had displayed against her husband had given her the courage to do so. On the other hand, I knew that Charles was getting even more disheartened than before from the consecutive failure of his quest for evidence, but I believed that he was not thinking of giving up. His face told me that he was a man who would follow his enemy to the world's end.

"Charles, number 46 is having a fit again," Nathaniel brought an issue up one day.

"Again? How bad was it?"

"Really bad. The temperature went up to 40. We have been treating her for so many weeks now, but the doctor said we should really think of another option. We can't let it go on like this."

"Yeah, I will do it. She can't even have a baby anymore, so there's no point keeping her. I think we've waited long enough."

No matter how much Charles would not like to talk to Nathaniel, he had to swallow his pride when it came to managing the estate. That evening, Charles, with an intensely serious face, approached his son at the dinner table. He talked slowly but clearly, emphasizing each word.

"Tonight, I will teach you to become a man. Come with me after dinner."

The son looked at his father with a perplexed expression on his face. It was one of the rare times that the rebellious boy did not say a word in response. He had to be wondering why his father had approached him in such a strange manner, unlike the usual bitter stare and cold treatment that he would receive. After everyone was done, the father and son ventured outside the house together into the dark.

Although something told me that they were acting strange, and I wanted to follow them, I had to my duty to attend to, so I decided to forget about it.

When I was going down to the garage that night to get some meat out from the freezer, there was a noticeable change on the mysterious old door that I had been looking at every time I came down. The lock was gone and the metal chain was hanging down loosely on the door handle.

It was the unquenchable curiosity of mine that led me to approach it. As if drawn by a mysterious force, I dropped what I was doing and took one step at a time towards it. I looked around to see if there was anybody watching me and put one of my ears against the cold metal to assess if there was anyone inside the room at all. When it turned out to be completely quiet, I could not help myself and pulled it open.

The room was dark, and I could hardly see anything. Yet I could make out some of the outlines of furniture in the light coming from behind me.

The inside was small and had no windows or openings except for the single door that I had just come in. The floor was made entirely of hard concrete that made it feel extremely cold. Not only that, the room appeared to be on a slight slope, with one end higher than the other, and the lowest part of the room was fit with a small drainage hole that went directly into the floor. It made me think it had to be some sort of washing space where all the water could be hosed throughout and would naturally flow down the drain due to gravity.

In the middle, a sturdy wooden chair was fixed permanently to the floor, which puzzled me. Why would anyone want to sit here in the middle of a cold and dark room with a chair that could be moved? I tried sitting on it, and felt that it was not even comfortable.

In one corner was a row of metal lockers. The other corner had an old wooden table, on top of which were some rusty tools, comprised of various types of knives, hammers, saws and other carpentry-related items. All of them were ancient as evidenced by thick layers of rust. On the ceiling, a strange contraption with a shape of a hook was hanging down from above.

"Are you tired already?" a voice said suddenly. It definitely belonged to Charles.

I panicked, because the voice came from just outside the garage. There was not enough time, so I rushed towards one of the metal lockers in the room and hid myself in there. I watched the event unfold through some door slats that were presented at my eye level.

"No, Dad. My arms are a bit sore," Sebastian's voice replied.

"We're nearly there. We don't need to rest," Charles told his son. As soon as he said that, they appeared in the light.

The room suddenly lit up with an old fashion dim yellow light when Charles pressed on its switch. He then went back out the room and helped his son lift something of the ground to bring it inside.

159

It was a body.

An Inferior.

A girl.

From the Nest, to be exact.

They placed her in the middle of the room with her body on the cold floor. From the looks of things, her flaccid form had no strength at all. I thought she was dead until her other hand punched Sebastian's leg with very little force. The teenage boy looked at her once with eyes full of disdain and kicked her square in the face with his boots.

"Hey! Don't do that," his father yelled.

"But...she tried to scratch me, dad,"

"We can't just go around and hurt them. Do you know how valuable they are, son?"

"But we aren't selling this one. We can do what we want, right? And I just kicked her in the face. That's not going to bruise her."

"You are right about the bruising, but it's about respect, son. As an estate owner, we have our code, and if you do not even respect your product, you will surely fail, just like the previous owner."

They tried to lift her up but were met with resistance. The girl suddenly screamed and thrashed around chaotically. Charles, who remained completely calm, simply pressed his remote, and immediately the girl went limp.

"You can still move when you were shocked that much?" Charles's voice changed from the kind tone that he used with his son to annoyed and intolerant.

"Do you want me to tie her to the chair?"

"Yes, we have to. Just to be safe in case she goes again," suggested the father.

They helped each other to lift the body off the floor and put her on the chair in the centre of the room. I did not notice at first that there were some leather straps attached to the chair, but now they were using them to tie her up tightly to it. From the arms to the legs and two straps on the neck, with one of them directly under the chin, which caused the woman's neck to be stretched out. When every strap was done in, the victim was now completely immobilised.

160

Putting her on the chair caused the angle to change and she was now facing my direction. I recognised the face of the girl in question immediately. Her name was Hene. I had talked to her a few times back when we were a lot younger, as she was generally a pretty nice girl, but we never knew each other very well.

"*Do you know why she has to die?*" Charles asked.

"*N...No,*" his son answered unsurely.

"*She has had several seizures and it has been getting worse. The doctor said that there is no way we can help her, and I have tried many drugs and none of them helped at all. We had to kill her to keep our cost low, because more Inferiors mean more food is use. In Taurine business, we have to keep the cost low and our profit high. It is the most important principle. Any humans that are not useful to us...we have to cull them,*" he explained.

"*I think I understand, Dad,*"

"*Good! Then are you ready, son?*" asked Charles quietly before turning to hand Sebastian a large knife. The son grasped it with his shaky fingers.

At that moment, I thought that she was looking at me. Passing through the the slats of the metal door and into my eyes, her gaze was pleading for me to help her.

"*Are you sure you can do it?*" his father asked him when he saw that his son had gone terribly quiet.

"*I can do it, Dad,*" the son answered. There was not a hint of confidence in his voice.

"*Then let's do it!*" Charles yelled enthusiastically.

Sebastian slowly put his knife to the bare white skin of Hene's throat and drew a line as a practice. He did it couple of times, but none of them even touched the girl's skin. His father was running out of patience and asked him to "*do it already.*"

"Let me go, you fuckers. I'll tell Nathaniel!" the girl shouted.

"*Do not listen to those last words of Inferior death. It will be only to make you weak. It was written in 'the law.' Son... you need to do it now,*" Charles yelled, urging his son again and again.

"*Yes...*" the son gave out a weak reply. At that moment, I could see it in his eyes, the realisation of he had gotten himself into. His legs shook, his arms went soft, and the excitement left his eyes, and replaced with fear.

"Please…I beg of you. Please do not hurt me. I have my baby. I have to go back to her," she begged for the last time.

"*Do it now before she screams more words of evil into your ears,*"

"*I… can't.*" Sebastian's eyes looked down towards the floor.

"*You cowardly son, do it now! I order you to. You need to prove yourself to be worthy of being an estate owner's son.*"

"*Dad… I can't.*"

At that moment, his dad grabbed the knife out of the son's weak hand.

"*Look! I am doing it now. I am showing it to you. This is not hard,*" the father told him.

"*I sacrifice thy blood in the name of golden god,*" Charles whispered in her ears and went behind her. I recognised the process straight away, since I had done it myself countless times in the wild.

With the sharp instrument tight in his hand, he swiftly pushed the knife inside her neck at the space between the two belts that held her head up. The knife was so sharp that it went through her like butter and its tip came out the other side. He then made some slicing motion anteriorly. The knife was so ridiculously sharp that the all tissues of her neck were instantly severed.

Blood gushed out of her neck in the rhythm of her heartbeat before flowing down by gravity towards the drain, which was right in front of me. In her last seconds, her mouth gasped for air but soon stopped midway between opening and closing.

I felt faint, but knew that I had to resist it, because if I did faint, my body would fall out of the locker and be discovered. Despite my knees getting weaker and my head feeling lighter, like I could not breathe, I preserved. I tried to divert my attention to the happy days of the forest and imagined that the blood flowing down the drain was nothing more than from another animal I had just killed.

162

Chapter 30: Purpose of Life

It was a good thing that I managed to keep myself conscious during the whole process while the Cotters were skinning and gutting the corpse, leaving her as a big chunk of meat and bone that hung on a ceiling hook with a horrifying creak.

They also did not lock the door when they left, because they said they would come back again the next day to put her in the freezer, so I managed to sneak away after they left.

The next day was fortunate for me since the entire house was due to go away to the nearest town to do their groceries. I did my duties as fast as I could so that I could spend the rest of the day as far away from the house as possible. I found myself cowering in the other side of the estate among the tall grasses area where Beasty used to bully me.

When I thought about it, it was obvious from the beginning that our purpose was to die so that they could satisfy their palates. But the thing was, how could I not see it sooner? The disappearance of some girls, the way they fed, grew and bred us, the and the way they kept us all in the dark, all pointed towards some dark truth. How could I not figure it out sooner?

But why did Charles bring me into his house? And he didn't kill me? Why was he so obsessed with me?

"*You are my golden girl,*" was the phrase that he often mumbled when I was alone with him. I remembered how he touched my skin and smelled my hair like he was looking forward to the day that he would bite into my flesh. I could guess that it was because of my hair. In the Superior world, the golden colour represented the greatness of their race, and that was what I had on the tips of my hair.

I thought back to the day that I had stumbled across an important book in Charles's study.

"*Dic-tion-na-ry*" I pronounced the word written on the cover page slowly. "*Dictionary*" looked interesting. I opened a random page and found so many words in tiny print written all over. After some time, I realised its true use. It was a book to find definitions for every word in the Superior language. When I figured how to work it, I look up the names I had been wondering about.

"Faolan: *Means little wolf. This name used to be popular among canine companions, generally males dogs,*" I read.

"Cattleya: *A genus of Orchid flowers. Typically have large and showy flowers.*"

So I was named after a flower. I thought my mother said I was named after a critter of some sort. Was that not the case?

"Brun: *Brown colour.*" I continued reading. "*Brown and black are colours of Inferiors because all of them have either of these hair colors. Antonym: Golden, which represents the Superiors*".

However, there were still a lot of new things I had never known about.

"*Gold is the most precious metal there is. It is one of the rarest metals on earth, so it is highly sought after. The worth of a Superior is considered proportional to the amount of gold he holds. In history, kings and queens were those who have the most gold. In modern days, gold is available for anyone to purchase, although the richest men tend to own the most.*"

I kept reading on and learnt that gold was everything in the Superiors' world. Even these pages of the book received a special treatment of full colour picture illustrations. One picture was of the gold within a piece of rock in its natural form just as I remembered from the mines. That stone in the picture looked exactly like what the Superiors told us to look for.

"*Gold is the colour of our people,*" it said at the end.

When I thought about it, it seemed that Charles was the only one in the family who constantly mentioned "gold" and the true value of the Superior from a book called "the law" where all the rules, beliefs, and traditions of Superiors were written.

Gold was a symbol of strength, money, and pride. It was everything that the Superiors wish for. I was his golden girl, a rare Taurine who happened to have a tint of gold within her hair. I imagined him showing me to the world one day; finally, his family would consume me to gain immense fame. It was something a lowly estate owner would surely hope to do.

I could see Charles in full suit and tie, with stainless knife and fork in hand, cutting up the pieces of meat along my spine in a true manner of a Superior gentleman. I saw Charlotte complaining that I was too bland while putting extra salt on me. I saw Sebastian gnawing on my ribs voraciously. My whole head would be on a plate, probably with an apple in my mouth. In front of me was the girl, Hayley, her little mouth opened wide and nibbling at my cheek. She looked into my dead eyes and gave me the usual innocent smile.

"I love you, sis, because you taste so good," she would say.

What difference would it make if it was an animal? I had done the same thing to them as Charles had done to that girl. These hands of mine were equally as remorseless as his when they slit the throats of those poor creatures. I had no right to complain if I were to end up on that plate.

Brun never told me about this. Numerous times that I had listened to him complaining about the Superiors, about how they were using us so unfairly, yet he never mentioned that we were born as food for the Superior. He probably kept it secret so that I would not freak out. All that time in the cave, to think that he planned to raise me to be fat so that one day he could eat me.

No! What was I thinking? Brun would never do that. Even though he had betrayed me, I did not believe that he was the same as them. All those times in the cave, all those romantic moments, they were real.

That made me think of Brun. His gift from last visit was still right under my pillow. It had been about a year since I last saw him, but I had never opened it after all this time, because of my stupid pride of wanting to escape this place by my own way.

When I tore its wrapping apart, two flat objects were inside. One was the familiar artifact I had forgotten a long time ago, my old wooden locket. At the back was the same old writing "*I will always be with you.*" But there was a new one as well. "*Under the tree with the swing.*" I looked at it in curiosity. Instead of being mad at him for writing on my precious locket, I knew that it was an instruction. The other was a plastic card.

The swing obviously referred to the one hanging from the large oak tree, since it was the only swing around On one side of the trunk, I saw a small subtle resemblance of an animal with pointy ears and long whiskers. It looked as if a child had drawn it, but I had a feeling it was not Hayley. The ground was already covered with some grass and there was no way to tell if it had been dug out a year ago. However, it was the only spot with any clue at all so I started shoveling up the dirt. Before long, I found a small box made of wood. My hunting knife and a letter from Brun were the two objects inside.

"Dear Cattleya,

I am sorry for everything I have done to you. I know it is not forgivable, but I am not going to ask you to forgive me. I am now a proper Superior as my father had always wanted, but only on the outside. They forced me to dye my hair back to golden, dressed me up, and asked me to read the law for the public every morning. At night, they do things to me in a dark room. No matter how much I say otherwise, I know that my heart still despises them. Those things that they are doing to you all...I can't simply ignore them. I have given up my status as a Superior a long time ago, and I never want to become one of them again.

Sorry for ranting about my problems, but please keep reading. I have been a bit stressed with keeping my public image up to standard. There is nobody, Cat, nobody but you who I can talk about my true feeling. I might not be able to see you ever again, but I want to tell you that I will continue to be your friend no matter what happens.

About Nathaniel: he and I used to be neighbors. Our fathers were friends as well. As you can guess, I lived down there with my father Samuel and Nathaniel with his father Richard, the person you know as Mr. Larrington. When we were kids, I used to go up there to play with him since we were each other's closest neighbours. He and his father had a major argument, and he left at fifteen years old. He told me that he would never come back here again. But it seems that it was not the case.

167

Before I forget about the most important thing, I must go into the details now. What I have given you is called an 'exempt' card. The gate of your estate has a detector that reads the microchip under your skin. You might not have realised it, but all Inferiors are implanted with a chip under the skin after birth. Normally, the electronic gate will identify and give a shock if you try to exit without authorization, but with this card, you will walk right through as if you were a Superior yourself.

All you have to do is to have the card on you. Just watch out not to be caught, because remotes will still work on you if fired manually.

Our hut is still intact. I hope. I don't know what happened to Faolan, but you can stay there if you want to. The guns and everything else are still inside, since I doubt that anyone has ever discovered it. I probably won't be able to visit you for a while, but I will try to come at some point. I know you can live in the forest on your own.

Love you always,

Brun

P.S. Remember, you can do anything, just believe in yourself."

I put the letter down, ripped it into the smallest pieces possible then buried it down in the same hole. This way it would decompose in the soil quickly. I also put the box back in its place and filled up the hole again. I tucked my favourite hunting knife inside my shirt.

I cried.

What a fool I was to doubt him, I thought. But now that I knew for sure that he was on my side. I knew I had to think of a way to escape fast or I would end up in a pot.

Chapter 31: Faith in Humanity

The Cotters would come back after about two hours, so the next chance to go down to the Nest was not until the same afternoon of the following week. The seven days in the interim were moving very slowly for me. While I became deeply troubled by the fact that I was living in the same house as my predators, I had to act perfectly normal in front of the others to avoid suspicion.

Every night, I was still the one who went down to the dark garage to get the ingredients out of the freezer. The new bag of carcass was always there. Even though headless, skinless, and chopped into pieces to the point that I could not even imagine that she used to be a human, the fact that I knew who it was made me feel all sorts of hallucinations.

"Help me" I heard her cry sometimes when I opened the freezer then. Other times she would ask, "Where's my baby?" Charlotte specifically told me to not use her yet, because her meat was too expensive to be used casually, so she was reserving it for a special occasion. However, I still felt nauseous every time I was cooking other animal meat. It could not be helped, because the diet of this house was generally of bodily parts.

Whenever I went to sleep, a dream of the girl's death would come to me. I relived the conversations between father and son again and again. I thought how lightly they took the death of another person as nothing. Even though Sebastian could not do it himself, I could feel that he wanted to for no other reason than to prove himself to his father. When I knew what they actually did to the Inferiors, I could never look at any of them the same way again, not even Charlotte or Hayley. The cute little girl would someday grow into a killer just like the rest of them.

In the daytime, I spent time daydreaming about escaping with everybody. I imagined the moment of true freedom, the moment when they stepped outside the gate and looked back the way they came. I wanted to see the looks of joy on their faces as they discovered the new hope. It was what kept me going in the week without breaking down. One week felt so excruciatingly long to me.

At last, the time had come for me to make it happen. The Superiors went away to town again just before a few days before my eighteenth birthday. I only knew that it was my birthday because they had marked it on the calendar. I'd never known the exact date of my birthday, but Charles seemed to have a record of it around.

I went down to the Nest. Nathaniel also went out to town in his own car, so I knew that I would be safe. Everybody was sitting and lying around. Nowadays, the girls were not very busy at all because of Charles's policy to work them much less. He told his trainer that they needed to concentrate energy on raising the babies, so he had them stopped working.

Everywhere I looked, there were big children running around while their mothers were sitting down and talking to each other in groups. At that moment, my nerve had gotten the better of me and I felt fear. Because they all looked so content with their lives, I did not know how to break this terrible news to them. How could I convince them that their whole lives were simply nothing but lies?

I climbed up to a podium on top of a raised platform in the middle of the hall and turned on a microphone.

"Hey! Everybody, listen up."

All heads in the hall turned in unison and stared at me with curiosity. There were many faces I did not even recognise, so I felt even more nervous, but I had to be strong.

"I have an announcement to make. Can I get everyone into the hall, please?" I asked. Some girls went out to other rooms and came back with many others. Finally, the room was packed tight. I never knew that the number had increased to be more than a hundred girls, plus a child or two for each of them.

"I am here to tell you all something very important," I began.

For the next ten minutes or so, I stood there, talking about my experience and the information I had obtained so far in the quickest way possible. However, many started to leave the room, like it was no business of theirs. Others fell asleep and many more looked very bored.

"What is 'death'?" a girl with a familiar face asked.

I could not answer, because I was shocked that they would not even know this word. Come to think of it, the girls had never seen any real demise in their real lives. I had not either before I went to the forest. The people around us, our friends and families, always just disappeared, but never *died*. What was death to them? There was only one scenario I could think of that could be helpful in explaining.

"It's like when monsters come and take us away," I stated. Many faces became scared. I now knew that I had gotten their attention.

"How come they can eat us?" another girl asked, when I said that Superiors killed us and then ate our corpses. That was another problem with linking the meat to dead things. They never knew where the meat comes from. Instead of coming from moving animals, they thought it was grown, like vegetables. I tried using many metaphors, but all I had in response were lost looks on their faces.

"I am telling you that you all have been deceived your whole life. They keep you here so they can eat you. They want you to have babies so that they can eat them as well. Everything here is a lie, and everyone who stays here will be doomed. You've got to come with me. I don't care whether you believe me now or not, but just come with me."

"Who gives you the right to order us around?" one girl in the back of the crowd shouted. I looked at her face and recognised her straight away.

"I am acting on my own, Jenny. But you should listen…"

"And who the hell are you anyway?" my previous acquaintance asked me.

"You don't remember me, Jenny? It's Cat—Cattleya?" I asked back, incredulous that she did not know me. Even though I had changed somewhat in my appearance over the past years, I doubted that it was that drastic. Plus, I had this weird hair that everybody used to pick on me for.

"I'm not asking what your name is. You are clearly not a Superior. You are not one of us. Then what the hell are you? I am not taking orders from a nobody like you," she yelled and pulled her little daughter up to the stage with her.

"No! I *am* one of you. I have been here since I was seven years old along with all of you. Doesn't anyone remember me?" I asked.

"Yeah, right! Stopping pretending like you are one of us," Jenny remarked. " Where is your baby? Wait! You don't even have one, do you? Look at that skinny body that's never even had a baby." She pointed at me.

I appeared like a lanky teenager in comparison to the very well-nourished Jenny, who was filled with fat deposits everywhere, including the face. Her belly also was a very prominent mound. Then I realised that she was already on her second pregnancy.

"No way, she's not one of us," the crowd roared.

"You have been holding Nathaniel for your own, haven't you?" another girl asked.

"I've seen you with him so many times. And look at that, can't you all see?" Jenny used this advantage to press me. "All these pretty fancy Superior clothes this bitch is wearing. Look at it closely, all white and spotless and everything.

"She flirted with our Nathaniel. It was she who stole him right in front of us. The other day I saw her come here holding hands with him and everything. There are so many times I have seen them together, and it makes me feel so bad for all of you. She manipulated him until now she is living like a Superior at Mr. Cotter's house." The pregnant lady pointed towards the house.

"That's not true…" I argued, but my voice was drowned out by the crowd when I had no microphone.

"Look around you! All the pieces of evidence are there." Jenny gestured with a wave of her hand. "There is plenty of good food, comfortable beds for us every single day, and the Superiors are treating us very well. Everyone, including myself, has been here for eighteen years and not a thing happened. Nobody died. Nobody was eaten. Look at the children besides us, and the one in your belly as well; they are the best things that have happened to us so far. Do you mean to throw all that away by going outside? What is out there anyway, except for monsters? This witch is obviously trying to lure us all to feed to her demon masters."

"Witch! Witch! Witch!" someone in front of the crowd started and others soon joined in.

"Witch! Get out of here!"

Then they all threw hundreds of shoes to my direction. Small and big; the children were contributing as well as the adults. I jumped down the stage and ran and ran.

Chapter 32: Plan to Escape

When I was moping quietly on the still swing of the oak tree, the most unexpected guest approached me. Her face had changed so much, I nearly did not recognise her. Although the others had gotten fuller on their cheeks, she had changed to the other direction. The baby-face of a relatively chubby girl was now gaunt, although it was still pretty masculine, as typical of a female Taurine. I could see beyond the changes, the same eyes that had stared at me and the mouth that had insulted me countless times. Next to her was a boy with the same build, like his mother.

"You came here to beat me up some more, Beasty?" I let out a pitiful sound.

"No, Cattleya. I came here to..." She paused. "Tell that I believed you,"

"You believe me?" I asked. "Why? Because you feel sorry for me?"

"No... I believe you because I think that you were telling the truth?"

"Even if I lied to you so many times?" I referred to the times I intentionally left my work incomplete so that Emmeline would punish her.

"Yes. I don't see any reason for you to lie about such a serious thing like that. There's no way you would risk your ass coming down here if you weren't sure that there wasn't a good reason for it. Everything has a consequence in this place and I never thought you were stupid. The other thing is that I don't like that Jenny, that manipulative piece of shit. As you probably can guess, I am no longer the dominant one."

Hearing these words coming from someone who had once bullied me so hard in my childhood caused me a strange feeling I could not describe. There was a possibility that she was playing me for a fool, but I knew that Beasty had never lowered herself to the same level as me. She was always straight as a ruler. In a way, she was like Charles.

"So, you want to go out the gate with me?"

174

"Yes, I would like to. But unfortunately, I probably can't. Do you know why? I have been doing a lot of thinking that we were born in this world for a reason. But I couldn't really find any. I thought that Superiors were using us to do this and that, but we had no real decision to make for ourselves. I've noticed that some who do not conceive a child had disappeared. I have seen so many of my friends gone, and it pains my heart to know that they are simply erased out of existence."

She continued. "They did exist, Cat. But we had to pretend that they didn't. And I'm so fucking tired of all these lies. But, unfortunately, I won't be following you outside, because I have my responsibility as the previous leader of these girls, to make them see sense, and that's not going to happen over an hour like you tried to do."

"Thank you, Beasty. You... I... I never know you have this side of you. "

"I never did. I was just so stupid back then, dumb and shameless. I knew about it all my life, but I chose to avoid it. You and Hinda were the ones who took on the misfortune of my denial, because I could not accept the way things were, so I threw it all on others. I am sorry for everything."

"I know. I am sorry for making it hard for you too," I said.

We smiled awkwardly at each other.

"I want to let you know that there is one person you should really take with you."

"But everyone else refuses to believe me."

"No, I don't mean the Nest," she said, then pointed towards the hill where Nathaniel's hut was.

"Your friend is there," Beasty said before going back the way she came.

It was only three more hours until the Cotters home time. There was no better chance than now unless I waited for another week. But there was still Cheesecake...without the remote, I might as well be throwing myself against a wall.

The last piece of the puzzle finally came to me when a horn sounded at the estate gate. The unknown visitor was waiting when I went over to see him. He was a very young Superior man in a red and white uniform on a motorcycle. I thought that he could not be more than sixteen years old from the look of his face. In his hands was a small package covered with brown paper. When I approached him, he spoke to me.

"*Can you get a Superior to come?*"

I remained silent.

"*Oh well...I guess I have to use sign language,*" he said to himself, then made some funny hand movements. I could understand the question from the start, so I turned my head left and right a few times. His eyes lit up from happiness when he knew that I understood him.

"*No Superior...I see. So, I'll just leave it at the front door. I hope my boss understands. This place is bloody far away, so it will be such a waste if I don't drop the package off just because there is nobody to receive it.*" He smiled a very naive smile to himself, then drove off. "*All right, see ya! Pretty Taurine girl,*" he yelled out, which made me blush.

On the package, it said '*please deliver to Nathaniel Kensington.*' I quickly picked it up and opened it inside the house. Lemonade was on the couch, sleeping again, but I knew that she was no threat to me. I could even kill a Superior in front of her and she would not be able to do a thing about it.

"*Remote for shocking Inferiors,*" I read the product name. "*Uncle Smith Brand.*" And another phase written below said "*Superior quality, warranty 3 years for a replacement.*" I unpacked everything in a nice and neat way to keep most of the package intact. I could steal it again so that I would have two shockers and Nathaniel would have none. It was a pleasant thought, but that was not my purpose.

"*Instruction leaflet,*" I read, then pulled out a small white sheet of paper from inside the box.

When I finished reading and mastering all the functions on devices, I was proud of myself. The weapon that had tormented me continuously had just now become mine to control.

First off, I learnt of the tool's function to select the target. When the left button was held down, the device would read the microchip in the direction it was pointed. The thirteen-digit number of the target would appear on the screen. If I pressed the right button, it would send the signal to fire. The harder I pressed, the more brutal electric discharge would be. The range of this device was about five hundred metres if there was no physical obstruction between the target and the device.

Secondly, I discovered about its memory. A list of the previous targets the devices had fired at was stored within, along with the stats regarding how many times the target was shocked. You could even nickname the target, since thirteen digits was just way too hard for most people to remember.

Since the new device had no history whatsoever, I decided to have a look at the old device. It seemed that Nathaniel had been using it a lot. Out of eleven Inferiors in the record, Cat was ranked 3rd at forty times. Cheesecake was second at 507 times, and the first was named 'bitch' at 3,481 times. My jaw dropped and I looked at the number in disbelief. I did not even think it was possible for someone to be alive after that many shocks.

The final useful discovery of the device was an option to block a certain number. I immediately blocked my number and number 1's number, then put a password of '*Faolan is a girl wolf*' on both devices to prevent anyone from unlocking them. I tested by holding the reading (left) button and directed it at myself. A sentence appeared on the screen "*Cannot find a target. Make you are pointing directly or unblock the number from the option.*" The instruction said that '*this function is used for preventing accidental discharges against your favourite pets.*'

I put the new shocker inside the same box after it was rigged with my Faolan password. I knew that I needed to hurry, because I could not seal the box back properly, so Nathaniel would eventually know that someone had opened it.

Finally, it was the moment of truth. After I had finished packing everything, I was ready to go. I changed to my best clothes for surviving and fighting. I carried with me the most important tools that would make this attempt a success. I had the exempt card, the old shocking device, and my knife. Then I proceeded to walk along the periphery of the estate to avoid being spotted by the girls in the Nest.

When Nathaniel's hut finally came into sight, I peeked over inside for one last time before going in. It was just as I thought. The big black man was on that very spot where he was last time. I tested the device by reading him from the outside. With the thirteen digits instantly popping up on the screen and the nickname "Cheesecake," I was sure that it would work. I stormed into the hut and pressed down the "fire" button.

The brute's body started twisting before he could even realised who I was. I let go of the button after only a brief moment. When he recovered, he looked at me with blank eyes. After a few seconds, he made an angry face at me, then sprang. I was standing far from him away as a precaution anyway, so I simply pressed the button again and his body went stiff in midair. I let him get up again, but this time he seemed to realise that I had the upper hand.

"*Get your keys out,*" I commanded in the Superior language, in which he knew some basic commands. It was because Nathaniel trained him entirely in Superior.

He looked at me with a confused face. "*Keys!*" I shouted again and eventually got him to understand me.

"*Now, leave them on the ground,*" I commanded, and he obeyed, although still looking at me with eyes full of hatred. Then I told him to get out, and he did.

Now that my adversary was gone, I could finally rescue her. I dragged the table where the creature was guarding away, threw the carpet off the floor and used the keys to unlock the underground basement.

"Carla!" I shouted with all my voice.

Chapter 33: The Sins of the Past

The gaping hole between the floorboards revealed a set of stairs. Even though my call was loud and clear, no response came back. The place below was quite dark, so I walked cautiously down the stairs so as not to trip over myself. However, up until this point, complete blackness was the only thing that greeted me. Using the sun behind me, I could see the outline of the room below. It was a well-built space, with concrete walls on all sides. A faint breathing sound could be heard from one corner of the room.

"Carla!" I said. The sound echoed off the full enclosure of the room. After a few moments of fumbling around, I found the light switch on the wall next to me.

There was a depressed-looking person on the floor. Her hair was very dark, greasy, and messy. In the typical T-shirt that was given to all the girls down at the Nest, her arms and legs were hanging loosely from her scrawny body that lacked any vigor. When I looked at her, she answered me back with a pair of dark, hollowed eyes. I could tell that although she was alive, she was not really living at all. She was a moving corpse of a person. But it had to be her.

"Carla!" I said.

"Hello." She opened her mouth and uttered a weak response.

"Carla? Is that you?"

"No... my name is bitch."

"Carla! What the hell happened to you? Did Nathaniel do this?"

"Master... I promise to love him forever," she said and looked up. There were some tears coming out, but she was smiling.

"What are you talking about?" I went down on my knees and shook her. "Get a hold of yourself, Carla. Let's get you out of here." I started checking for her restraints.

"I am bitch. Please...call me bitch," she continued.

"Stop it! Carla, this is me, Cat. Don't you remember? We were friends. The three of us, you, me, and Hinda. Remember how we all played together?"

179

"No."

"Can you remember how you pushed me into a muddy pond full of duck poop? But I dragged you in as well. Then we were itching for the whole day."

"No."

"How about the time you told me about how your father used to teach you to fight? When you fought Beasty and the gang? And when you beat them all without breaking a sweat then smiled to me as if you were the boss. You were the strongest person in the world, Carla. The strongest I had ever known. Without you, I wouldn't be able to be here. If it weren't for you, I would still be down there in the Nest like everyone else, sitting down and chatting until I get so fat I can't walk anywhere. I made some mistakes. I had been..." I found that some metal chains were connecting her left leg to the wall, which were impossible to remove by hand.   saw a large lock, so I started trying all the keys I had from Cheesecake.

While I was figuring out the system, Carla suddenly hugged me. The warmth of her body and the tears from her eyes dripping onto my shoulder were more real than any word that could be spoken.

"I messed up, Cat," she said. But I took the blame for myself.

"I left you here. I let you go with Nathaniel even though I knew how wrong it was. I should have tried harder, but instead, I ran away."

"No, Cat. I am the one who should say sorry. You tried to help me, but I didn't listen. Stupid me wanted to be the coolest girl in the estate so I fucked Nathaniel. But look at how it ended."

"Well... you can say sorry after I get you out of here." I kept trying but none of the keys seemed to fit.

"Get out of here…to where?" Carla asked.

"Anywhere but here! Probably into the forest," I said briefly and concentrated on putting the keys in.

"What are you talking about? I can't run, Cat. Look at me! I am a disgrace of a human." She meant the severely malnourished body of hers.

"Then I'll carry you on my back. You will get better one day and you will be able to run again. I'll teach you how to live in the forest. You will be much better at it than me, I think."

"Are you going to take me to the forest, Cat? The place where all the monsters are? They will kill us. We can't go out there by just two of us."

"Would you shut up for a minute, Carla? I'm trying to concentrate here." My hands were now shaking as I was near the end of the key sets, and there had not been a key that could open the cuff.

True enough, the last key tried and failed and I realised that nothing was working.

"Damn it, I must have not been careful enough," I said to myself and tried again from the beginning. Maybe I was not fitting them properly.

"What are you doing, Cat?" Carla asked, noticing me trying to unlock her leg for the first time.

"I am trying to get you out," I spoke a bit too roughly. It was frustrating that I had not got it right for a long time. My hands were all shaking from nervousness and I could hardly hold the keys properly. The more stressed I was, the worse my performance became. I felt like fainting but I couldn't. I needed to keep going to release Carla.

"Which one?" I swore then smashed all of them to the ground after going through them all the second time.

"No, Cat…There is no right key."

"What is that supposed to mean? Carla? Are you kidding?" I snapped.

"There…is no right key."

"Carla!"

"I'm telling you the truth here, Cat. There is no right key. Not on Nathaniel, not on Cheesecake, not on anyone. It's completely gone from this world. He destroyed it and said to me that if I wanted to escape, then I would have to cut my leg off."

"Carla! You should have told me that first."

I had to go upstairs and got some tools out of a shed. I used everything I could possibly think of on the chain: a hammer, a spade, an axe, a saw, but nothing worked. The chain was made of some sort of metal that resisted all the damage I tried to inflict upon it. In addition, its attachment over the wall was very strong. Since it was so well made, I thought that the room was built for especially this purpose in mind by Nathaniel. It had been half an hour when I looked at my watch, but there was still absolutely no progress.

"There is something I must tell you," she said when I was smacking the chain with a woodcutting axe. The axe got steadily duller as it repeatedly clashed with the special steel. It literally bounced off the metal every single time. After some time, I discovered that sawing tended to be the best. It was extremely slow, but steadily wore through.

"What is it?"

"It is what I have done in the past. It's about Hinda. Listen…I have been trying to say this to you for all this time, but it was so hard."

"Okay, I'm listening."

"It started because I made a plan to surprise you one day—me and Hinda. We saw a big flower fair across the street in the city. She was in love with you back then, you know? She never said to you but she told me everything. So I got her to pick up your namesake Cattleya flower from the exotic flower stand. Of course, we weren't Superiors, so we couldn't buy them. We grabbed one and ran." She paused.

"One moment, Hinda was laughing when we were escaping but when I looked at her again after I crossed the road, she was on the ground, with blood everywhere. But she was not dead yet. She looked at me one last time and cried in pain. She held onto the flower until the end, but the driver who had hit her immediately came down and stabbed a knife into her throat. Then the whole scene was immediately covered up with a big brown sheet by the nearby Superiors. Even though they were all strangers to each other, they knew what to do as if they had rehearsed it a hundred times. Not even a minute and any trace of her body had disappeared. You could not even tell because there was not even blood left on the road. Nobody said anything to each other, so I walked back to you thinking that it might have been just a dream, but whenever I looked beside me, Hinda was not there."

"But...how can that be real?"

182

"I was doubting myself if I had been sane the whole time or if maybe Hinda was someone I had imagined. But you remembered her! And kept asking for her. So I knew that she existed. After that, all I had ever felt was guilt, guilt of not remembering her anymore. Then I knew that all I had left was you. So I wanted to protect you. I had always wanted the best for you, Cat. But my stupid desire for Nathaniel took me over. So I...I abandoned you."

I remained silent and hurried up with the sawing. "Forty minutes," I mumbled to myself when I looked at my watch. The saw was almost through the first part of the first chain, but there were, in fact, two chains on Carla, with two links each. Therefore, I had not even reached the first quarter of the way.

"Cat, stop it. You will never be going to make it in time."

"Shut up, Carla. Let me do this."

But she held out a hand over mine and squeezed it tight so that I could not work.

"Let go!" I yelled at her.

"No..." She said.

"Why?" I looked at her angrily.

"Would you help someone like me?"

I let my anger loose, along with my hand, and slapped her on the face.

"If I hear that again, I'll really beat you up. Do you know that? You were my best friend and still are. It was you, Carla, that I used to look up to. The old you would never say this. You, who always believed that anything is possible." Then the first half of the first chain completely snapped. She went quiet. But someone was stomping the floor upstairs. At that moment, a shadow appeared and loomed over our only exit.

Chapter 34: Inside the Oven

The handsome man walked casually, as his face did not show any sort of feeling except for when he broke into a perfect confident smile. His presence might have been intimidating to Carla but I did not fear him, not even a little. I just felt excited. I hugged her with one arm. With the other, I reached for the little knife in my pocket.

"You want to join me and my bitch?" he said with a malevolent sneer. I did not open my mouth, because it would be a distraction to myself. If I let my guard down, I could be dead.

"I will get out of here, Nathaniel," Carla said.

"No matter how you run away, you will eventually come back to me, bitch. Because I am your master and you are forever in love with me. You and me...I have always taken care of your every need. I saved you from those dirty, obnoxious Taurine men. I feed you when you are hungry and keep you safe from the dangerous world of Superiors. Go out there and they will eat you. I can't let that happen because you are the one and only lover of mine."

Carla seemed to be shaken by his words. So I stood up for her.

"You call that love? What you did to her?"

"You stay out of this, you deceitful little Inferior," he shouted back. "Do not listen to her. I am your safety. Think about the child in your belly!"

"What? Did you impregnate her?"

"Well...the child will receive the best life it could get."

Carla finally looked up at him and asked anxiously, her voice a nervous wreck, "Like all the others that you had killed?"

"No, they are all at the Nest."

"Liar! I am getting out of here!" Carla shouted, then grabbed for the fallen hammer on the ground. I knew what to do right away. My quick reaction, built through the experience in the forest, had turned me into a swift taker of opportunity whenever one presented itself.

Since she was still tied to the wall with Nathaniel on the stairs, Carla had to lift the weapon with her feeble arms and try to throw it. It tumbled on the ground before even reaching halfway to the target. With

Nathaniel's eyes fixed on her, I rushed towards him. His shaking hands reached into his pocket and out came the remote.

He pressed the buttons, but nothing happened. I saw fear in his eyes for the first time before he threw the device at my face and ran away. Unfortunately, we were too far apart. He was being quite careful and had stayed on the stairs the whole time while talking to us, so I could not catch him.

As he was escaping upstairs, I picked up the hammer and threw it at him. It hit him hard, but only on his flank, which made him groan in pain, but he was able to keep on running.

I tried to follow, but the hatch was immediately closed and something was already on top of it. I tried a few times before I could manage to get it open by ramming my body into it. The gravity did not help, but it worked. I found him busy pouring down some strange smelling liquid from a large red can around the hut. It was slowly dripping down the stairs down to the basement. Quickly grabbing my knife, I launched my attack and managed to leave small gash on his thigh. After that, I aimed for his heart, but he blocked it at the last second with the can. The knife went through the inanimate object and its liquid came out, spilling over my clothing.

I punched him. He punched me back. I kicked him and clawed at him. It was not until one misstep from me that I did not see coming, and he managed to click a cigarette lighter and we both went up in flame.

I let go of him. The fire was spreading on my pants and creeping up on me. My skin beneath the clothing burned. I rolled away on the ground, but the flames still stuck around because of the gasoline in my fabric. It was not until I ran and jumped into the dirty pond nearby that the sweet relief came.

When I looked back the way I came, Nathaniel was nowhere to be seen, and the hut was already engulfed by flames.

However, there was no time to be sad about it. I knew that it was my final and only chance to escape while the estate was in turmoil and the Cotters had not been back. I ran and ran towards the exit.

Suddenly, a hundred people, more specifically, a hundred girls, came out of nowhere to completely block my path. I looked back and saw that there were many of them from the back as well. They surrounded me, coming closer every second with angry looks on their faces. On one side of the circle was Nathaniel with his hand pressed down on his bloody injury I had caused.

"You stole Nathaniel from us. You hurt him. You tried to kill him," the girls chanted. There were so many accusations I could not understand until the Superior man sat down, made a face full of excruciation, and cried out that it hurt so much. I could tell that he was pretending, but the girls were giving him so much love and care.

Everyone jumped on me. I was quickly pushed down on the ground and then came the stomping feet. They were the people I had never wanted to hurt, yet they were trying to kill me. I put my hands behind my head like I used to accept the whipping punishment from Emmeline. It was not so different from those times, I thought. I could not save Carla, I could not save any of them and here I was, paying for it. It was a fitting end for a monster like me who had done nothing but betrayed the people of my kind.

Hands and feet came from every single direction. I reflexively curled into a ball to protect myself from the attacks. They pulled my body open to let the new dominant girl have her alone time with me. All that time, I was conscious and felt each blow. All I wanted was for it to end.

Suddenly, I heard something from afar. It was the strongest shout coming from Charles.

"*What the hell are you all doing?*" he roared as the king of the estate. My life was spared.

Chapter 35: Cat's Dinner

Smells of roasted meat floated through from the kitchen while the yellow light from a lone candle on the table gave out a warm glow that I stared at. It was the first time I was sitting down as a Superior, at their table, and waiting to be served. Charlotte was preparing the dinner for me, while I was sitting at her place. Today was a special occasion because it was my 18th birthday so they decided to celebrate by letting me be a Superior for a day.

Hayley was sitting next to me; her round childish face looking at me in excitement. She kept talking happily to me although I had no mind to answer. I stared above her head while nodding out of politeness. My body was very sore. Under the black silky dress I wore, there were burn marks and bruises everywhere I touched. The wounds on my face were covered up with the white Superior powder layered as extensively as thick icing on a cake. Charlotte let me borrow everything and she dressed me up with the help of her daughter during the afternoon. I could be a Superior for a day, she said.

"Dinner's ready!" Charlotte, who was in her beautiful blood-red dress, called out. At that moment, there was a knock on the door. The wife went over to open the door to let the perfectly timed Nathaniel in. The man appeared to be fine, but I could tell that he was pretending the wound I had inflicted never existed.

After everybody was in place, they started reciting the poem-like chant as they had done every single day before dinner. The lyrics that I did not know when I first came were now clear after listening to it a thousand times.

"The golden palace we live in.
Broken twigs they sleep on.
Born to serve, born to sacrifice.
Born to die under our kind.
For we are their saviour.
Do not shunt their fate.
Do not feel sympathy.
They will make us weak.

Your fate too will be bleak.
If you believe in the sheep.
You and me, the Superiors.
Smart, strong and golden.
Like the sun that shines.
In this darkened world.
For we are the ones running the earth.
We are the rulers of the earth."

I only closed my eyes and put my hands together until the recital ended. When I opened my eyes again, everyone was congratulating me on the birthday. Charles made a speech.

"As you all know, we are celebrating this day to mark the day of change. Eighteen for us Superiors is the age when we leave the comfort of home and find a job in the big wide world. However, this is a special case. This is our maid, Cattleya, who had been serving us for nearly two years. Today, I officially anoint you as a servant of our home and thereby lifting your status as an Inferior."

"What? Are you crazy?" Nathaniel argued.

"No, she deserves it."

"But...nobody has ever done this before. I have never heard of anyone lifting an Inferior status."

"I will be the first."

"I thought you believed in the law, Charles. This is not permissible."

"Just because it is not said in the law does not mean it is not permissible. Now, please be quiet and let me finish. We shouldn't be arguing like this on such a good day. The meat is getting colder by a minute. Come on! Everyone, dig in." The other three people were so happy as soon as they heard the word. Many hands were rapidly reaching out into the middle of the table.

"I'll hand it all out for you. Remember to be polite, be a proper Superior. You have to wait for the older people." Charlotte blocked her son's hands from grabbing directly. Then she used the long knife to chop some pieces to put onto everyone's plate before handing them out.

188

Charles looked at Nathaniel and spoke to him in a quiet voice.

"*I will have a word with you after this is all done, my friend Nathaniel,*" he said, and Nathaniel's face turned pale.

"*Cat, give your plate to me. I'll give you the meat,*" Charlotte said. I did as she said. Even when I tried to hide it, she noticed the sadness on my face. "*Hey! Why the long face? This is supposed to be the happiest day of your life.*"

Why should it?

The plan failed miserably and the people who I tried to help turned against me in the end. They were too stupid to understand, but it was not their fault. Carla was dead. I deserved to die much more than her, yet I was still alive. With the face and body of a Superior, I had become one with the people I hated the most.

Charles had taken over the meat cutting from his wife. His face showed an extreme excitement I had not seen before. There was a pure, joyous aura radiating out of him as he was meticulously slicing the meat. Inside, the flesh was still relatively rare with clear oil oozing out from every cut surface. The outside was dark brown, all caramelised, and smelled of burnt fat, just like the perfectly cooked model Charlotte had taught me.

"Cut me up and eat me. Let me become a part of you, Cat," the girl on the table whispered inside my head.

Even Sebastian, who had been largely uninterested in the night, was salivating heavily to the point that he had to swallow several times. Hayley was excited because her mother kept telling her that it was would be the best meat she would ever eat.

Then Charles put a few slices onto my plate.

That was not Carla, I kept telling myself. It was the girl whom Charles had killed a week prior. But it was no less disturbing. Her name was Hene and she used to be a person. I had talked to her and seen her laugh and cry. It was not right. I could not take this. Not anymore. My eyes betrayed me and before I knew it, they were already hot and soaking with tears.

"Why are you crying, sis?" Hayley asked.

"She must be so happy that we are giving her a nice birthday," her mother answered for me.

"Yes, she probably likes your dress a lot," the daughter said as a compliment.

"Yes, honey. I think we have done a good job on it."

"She must like that Taurine meat. Oh! She hasn't had any?" Sebastian said with his mouth full.

Everyone urged me to eat the first piece of meat.

"Yes, delicious meat. The best you will ever have."

"If you are a Superior for a day, then you got to taste our best meat."

"That's right, sis. Please try a bite. It tastes really good." Hayley picked up my fork and stabbed a piece before handed it to me.

"Eat it, eat it, and eat it!" They were all cheering except for Nathaniel.

Giving in to the pressure, I put the meat inside my mouth, but I was afraid to bite into it. Nevertheless, the flavour of meat juice had diffused all over my tongue and touched off the back of my oral cavity. It tasted good, so good that it was disgusting.

"Where did you find that meat anyway, Charles?" Charlotte suddenly asked.

"It was Nathaniel." Her husband answered flatly.

"Oh! I thought you just killed that one."

"Charles sold that one, my darling. This is from my uncle's." Nathaniel answered, then turned to me. He smiled sardonically and looked into my eyes. "You earn it, Cattleya. It's time you swallow that meat like a good girl." His cold voice made my skin crawl.

"So good!" Charlotte made an ecstatic face. *"Smells a bit burnt, though but never mind that, she even has a foetus!"*

The table suddenly became even more lively. *"I want it! I want it!"* Sebastian shouted and the chaos ensued.

I spit the meat out of my mouth and nearly threw up on the table. Standing up while shaking heavily, I made an excuse to run into the bathroom.

190

Chapter 36: The End of Love

After I went to the toilet, I threw up hard even though there was nothing in my stomach. I washed her out of my mouth and waited outside to get some fresh air. It was getting cold, as it was already autumn and would soon be snowing in winter.

Then something strange happened. The house was a lot louder all of a sudden. Angry voices came from the inside where Charles and Nathaniel were arguing again. I thought about the way Charles was talking to his employee before. There was something in his voice that indicated malicious intent in the cool and collected voice. I went back into the garage just outside the dining room and listened through the dull glass door.

"Nathaniel, I thought you were acting suspiciously with my wife, but I have discovered something much worse."

"As I said before, if you don't have proof, then you can't charge me."

"Damn right, I don't have proof! Not right now, anyway. But I have someone who can help me. You can come in now!" Charles shouted the last sentence. From behind me, I heard the garage door open, which caused me to immediately go into my fighting stance as a reaction. A tall shadow of a man in a dark coat appeared. As he approached me, a little light from the dining room inside met his face, so I could see his white fluffy beard under a fedora hat as his features. He stopped in front of me, took his hat off, and bowed. His manner was none that I had seen of any Superior.

"Excuse me, young miss," he said respectfully.

"Oh! Sorry." I stood to the side and let him pass. It was astonishing to hear him address me as a young miss. But I did look like a Superior, after all, so I could not blame him. When he opened the door and went inside, I followed him.

As soon as I came in, I noticed a difference in the atmosphere straightaway. The husband and wife were standing opposite of Nathaniel in the living room. Charles was smirking slightly while staring at the younger man, whose face turned from surprise to anger

191

within a few seconds. He stared in my direction with total stupefaction on his face.

"*Good evening, my son,*" the old man said.

"*This is your father, remember?*" Charles added.

"*Who is this old man?*" Nathaniel pointed to him. "*Why is he calling me his son?*"

"*Well... I don't know? Because maybe... he's your father?*" Charles teased.

"*No, I have no idea who he is.*"

"*Then why did you look so surprised when he walked in. It is him, your father. Richard Larrington.*" Charles announced then he turned towards Richard. "*Is this your son? Mister Larrington?*"

"*Yes, I am positive,*" he answered simply.

"*Don't be ridiculous. I don't know this man,*" Nathaniel said. Suddenly, the old man punched him in the face.

"*If you keep pretending you don't know me, I'll keep smacking you. I have all the documents here if you want to see them. Your birth certificate and the name change paper I managed to find.*" He pulled out some papers from his suitcase to show it to everybody. He even had a picture of younger Nathaniel in his hand. There was a strong resemblance between the face of the child and the man he had become.

"*So... I've been asked by Mister Cotter over here about you. He thought that your new name and the old one were similar so he contacted me in the city. I wasn't living happily there, you know? I slept on the benches every night and begged money from people during the day. I was a beggar because of you. But that's enough about me. Let's talk about you.*" He stared into his son's eyes, paused, and then continued.

"*Mister Cotter said he was worried about you cheating with his wife, but I don't think that it was that simple. I know you don't love any Superior ever. Because all you love are the Inferiors! You and your fetish!*"

"*What happened, Mister Larrington?*" Charles asked. Charlotte was opening her mouth wide and had a terrified expression on her face.

Nathaniel kept silent, but his face was pale. The usual cockiness was all gone.

"When he was sixteen—that's fourteen years ago—I caught him red-handed with an Inferior girl on his bed, in my house. Not just hugging or kissing her, but fucking her. I saw them right in front of my eyes. Excuse my language."

"Is that true, Nathaniel?" Charlotte looked at him, and for the first time, she appeared to be wary of the man she used to be in love with, while he said nothing in return. His father continued.

"Well... I didn't want to believe it either. But when it happened, I chased him out of the house. Because... well... the punishment for bestiality is... you know what the law says. I didn't want my son to die."

"It was something that any father would do," Charles added.

"At that time, I thought that if I banished you away from the estate...I thought that living a new life in the city would rid you of your mental issue. But I was wrong. You never changed."

"Emmeline and I were charged with welfare problems. That I could not deny. But it was all according to your plan. Then you used 'McKenzie and whatever company' to take over my place. The reason that I went bankrupt was that my ledger was changed by someone and money went missing for the final six months. So I figured that it had to be you who was sneaking into my house. Unfortunately, by the time I solved the puzzle, I was already out on the streets with nothing in my pocket. It didn't help that I had no idea where you were, either."

"What are you going to say to that, Nathaniel?" Charles asked.

"Nothing. I have the right to remain silent in a false accusation of yours. It is a nice story indeed, but not a very likely one. As I said before, give me your evidence and maybe I will believe in any of those things. This man is not my father and the documents are forged. I can tell."

"It's true. We don't have all the pieces of evidence yet, but they can be gotten relatively easily. First off, the ledger: if it even has a single touch of your fingerprints, then you are busted. Secondly, we can test your DNA and this man's to determine whether you two are related.

And lastly, I am going to do it tomorrow morning..." Charles paused. He looked into Nathaniel's eyes and smiled in triumph. He continued.

"I knew that something was not right when I came back to see your hut burned down. It made me think that you had some sort of evidence in there that you did not want anyone to see. A few of the girls disappeared when I first came here, but you told me they all ran away. I believed you, because one girl did." He nodded at me. *"I'm going to turn that place upside down."*

"Nathaniel..." Charlotte said. *"Tell me that's not true...please."*

The man, who had been silent the whole time, looked up towards us. In his eyes was not even a little fear; instead, they were filled with the burning fire from hell. All of a sudden, he grabbed something out of his pocket with a swift movement. A loud bang echoed in the living room and smoke went up into the ceiling.

Charles grabbed his chest and fell backwards down to the floor with a loud thud. Charlotte screamed and closed her eyes. Nathaniel was standing there, smiling with insanity in his eyes. In his hand was a small revolver. When Charlotte went down and cried over her husband's body, Sebastian had already run away into his room and locked the door behind him.

"Who's next?" he shouted then ran up to his son.

"You cannot kill your father, Nate."

I ditched my uncomfortable high heels on the floors and decided to run. The matters of the Superiors did not concern me, but my body was unable to leave the room. I knew exactly why—because of Hayley—but more than that, I felt guilty to leave things as they were, so I ran to the kitchen and grabbed a knife. I carried Hayley, who was frozen in fear, from the table to hide behind the kitchen counter with me. Then I put a finger to my lips to tell her to be quiet. She nodded, despite her eyes brimming with tears.

"Please put the gun down. Do it for your old man."

"Pft... Always talk about yourself, but you never cared about me," he said. Another shot was fired followed by a body falling. *"You knew how lonely I was staying in this lonely place. I hated everything here and you knew it. All my life was a misery, and no matter how much*

194

I tried to tell you that, you always ignored it and wasted yourself away with your booze. When I finally found something I wanted, you chased me out of here. I hated you and Emmeline so much...."

"*Son...*"

One more shot was fired and the old man never spoke again.

"*Serves you right, father. May you rest in peace with mother,*" Nathaniel said coldly.

"*Please, Nathaniel... think of the feelings you have for me,*" Charlotte said desperately between hiccups.

"*Huh? You are joking, right?*" he asked casually.

"*Please, just do whatever with me but let me and my family go.*"

"*Oh! Lovely Alexandra... do you think I want to fuck you? An ugly yellowhead like you? I hate all the Superiors. I was just using you, my darling. I used you to cover my mistakes against Charles and that's how my secret survived for this long. Every time I had sex with you, I imagined a beautiful young Taurine in your place. The only thing I would do to a Superior is to cut them up and feed you to my girls.*"

"*Mum!*" Hayley cried quietly, so I put my palm to her mouth. I knew that I had to take action.

With the knife in my hand, I stood up, aimed at him while he was busy looking at Charlotte, and threw it in a spinning motion. Sometimes, in the forest, I used this method to kill animals, but it was not a very good method since the accuracy was low. I ducked down immediately to prevent getting shot and heard the knife enter his flesh. He screamed.

"*You bitch!*" he snapped. I heard the sound of the knife getting pulled out and I fell to the floor.

"*Don't think I have forgotten about you, meat girl. Do you think you are so smart? Just because you have that fake blond hair and flirtatious skill? There is only one reason why Charles liked you so much, and that's because he uses you for sex. A bloody hypocrite he is, trying to judge me when he is doing the same thing.*"

I kept quiet behind the counter. Long gone were the days I felt hurt from verbal abuse, and this was not true, anyway. I put Hayley inside the nearby cabinet to hide. But for me, I was sitting below the counter. A few more shots, I thought. He had wasted at least three shots within his little revolver. From the model, it looked like it contained only six bullets in total. There was no way I could fight a gun—as long as it had ammo, anyway.

In my hands were numerous kitchen tools. They were not ideal, but I had to make do. With his loud footsteps coming closer every second, I got ready to attack. It was easy to hear his location due to his non-stop talking.

"Give yourself up to me, Cattleya. You know what you did wrong. You snuck into my cabin without my permission and burned it down. Tonight, you killed the whole family of Cotters, including the visitor, Mr. Larrington. You have to answer for your sins. Nobody trusts an Inferior, but everybody will believe me."

I put the mirror up by using a reflective frying pan. Nathaniel took the bait and shot it needlessly. Two shots left to go. Even after damage, the pan with a hole in the middle still served its purpose. I threw a bag of flour towards his face, using the pan as a catapult. My arm came up briefly from the cover and I was glad that Nathaniel wasn't good enough to shoot the flying flour bag.

"What the fuck? Ah! " he shouted then tried to wipe his face to get the flour out of his eyes. I knew it was my turn and looked up briefly. I saw his eyes completely closed, but his hand was still holding the gun. I threw a rolling pin and it hit him hard in the face. As expected, he fired a random shot. One shot to go.

"*Please, come help us. There's a maniac,*" Charlotte yelled into the phone.

I took the opportunity to peek and saw Nathaniel looking towards her. He aimed the gun at her, although his face was still full of flour. I rushed towards him and cut his gun holding hand. The weapon fell to the floor. I was quicker than he was and managed to grab it. The look on his face immediately changed.

"Cattleya… my lovely girl. Do you think I will kill you, an Inferior? I love all of you. All I want to do is wish for true equality one day. We should be on the same side here. These people murder your kind every day." He spoke as if he still had the power. I did not lose my concentration. I aimed at his chest, right where the heart would be.

"Come on, an Inferior like you won't know how to use that thing. Just give it here."

I gave it to him. Straight into his heart.

He dropped down to his knees first, like he was trying to hold on to life for the last time, but soon gave out. His pretty face hit the floor hard and his eyes closed slowly and never opened again.

When I turned towards the others, Charles was still breathing, but only very slightly. However, the old man Larrington and his son were completely still. Their blood was soaking the floor.

"So Superiors' blood is red too," I thought.

That night. I finally escaped the Larrington/Cotter estate for good, and returned to the forest. Sometime afterward, the news reported the accident. Extensive research was carried out by the top teams of detectives, forensics, police force, doctors and psychologists. The experts were asked to come out from cities far away and it was not long until the truth was found.

Richard Larrington, a famous government official, had a single son named Nate. During Nate's childhood, he was a very smart boy, capable of obtaining the top grades in class almost every single year due to his mother's excellent love and care. However, when his mother died, the family changed. Richard traded the capital work life for a meat Taurine estate and hired his half-sister Emmeline as the trainer. However, the man was very depressed from the death of his beloved wife. He started drinking every day and ignored everything around him, leaving Nate and the estate in the hands of abusive Emmeline.

One day, when Nathaniel was only about seven years old, Emmeline saw him with an Inferior girl of similar age holding hands. She pulled Nathaniel away from her, then told his father of the incident. Richard punished him hard for it. Emmeline, who had complete control of the estate at that time, decided to sell the girl to other estates.

Nate started to do worse in school. The boy received no love like his mother had given him, so he became a stranger to the world outside. A simple dream had become his life goal, a dream to become a trainer so that he could spend all his time with Taurine girls. He pleaded with his father many times, but his father never accepted it as a possibility. He wanted him to become what he once was: a government official living in the city.

He began to hate his father, Emmeline, and every other child around him, except a certain boy named Max. The two had always been playmates since he moved in. However, that boy too became distant from him after Nate realised that his secrets were forbidden in the Superior world. Just as his relationships with other Superiors deteriorated, his love for Inferiors grew.

Whenever he could, he would go down to the Nest. He mastered their language and had a complete understanding of their culture. Every single girl down there was his friend and many of them were involved in secret sexual relationships with him. He was the weirdest kid around town. In school, he was teased by other teenagers. At home, he was physically abused all the time. But the Nest was the only place where he was truly accepted as a human being. It became his only home.

One day, when Nate was sixteen, he took an Inferior girl into his room. It was the day that he was caught red-handed on his very own bed. His father could not send the last remnants of his lost love to be hanged publicly, so instead, he chased him out of the house.

Eleven years later, Nate Larrington became Nathaniel Kensington. His hard-working and natural ability to converse with meat Taurines made him very successful as a trainer. He was accepted into one of the biggest estate chain 'McKenzie and Brandenburg Enterprise.' Even though the Larringtons' estate was on the verge of failing, Nathaniel wanted it to so badly.

To accelerate the process, he snuck into his old home to bankrupt his father by stealing money and changing the ledger. There was only one reason for his undoing; he wanted to come back to his only home, the Nest. Richard drank more and more every day as his business turned to a pile of ash. Meanwhile, Emmeline did all she could to earn more money by working the girls extra hard. It was only a matter of time before the estate fell, so it was not surprising when they were charged with abuse.

Nathaniel, with so much influential power in the enterprise, managed to convince them to take over this estate and appoint him as the trainer. He was home, at last, in the place where he belonged. But that came to an end quicker than he had ever expected.

Chapter 37: Homecoming

I shone a flashlight inside the hut behind the waterfall. It was this place where it was full of my precious memories. When I went in, Brun's masculine scent and the smell of Faolan's damp fur were still lingering in the air. They made me think of the old days.

Time had not been kind to this place, as most furniture was all extremely dusty and covered in cobwebs. However, I was glad that they were all still intact. Termites had also gotten into the wood which left some gaping holes.

Then I heard someone stepping within the dark. I froze.

As its face came into my flashlight, I recognised her straight away.

"Faolan!" I yelled.

The wolf seemed to recognise me after I said her name. She wagged her tail and came to me, although cautiously at first. She sniffed me probably ten times before letting me touch her.

"Have you been waiting for me this whole time?" I asked her, and she only answered with a hanging tongue and a wagging tail. I knew that this posture meant that she was smiling.

I lay down on my old mattress after pulling its old sheet out and beating the dust out of it. I was glad that instead of hearing Cheesecake and Lemonade breathing next to me, it was the familiar sound of the water hitting the rocks over and over again.

Tomorrow there would be no threat of Nathaniel trying to find faults in me, or Charlotte's nagging and Charles's creepiness. It felt like a bad dream, everything that had happened: Carla being burnt alive, Hene being killed as food, the massacre in the house, and the fact that I had killed Nathaniel with my own hands. It was all only a nightmare. I was safe now, under Brun's blanket, and with Faolan sleeping beside me. Everything was going to be all right. I told myself. Without changing my clothes, I dozed off into the night.

When my eyes opened in the morning, the familiar wooden ceiling was above me. I blinked several times to confirm the reality of what I was seeing. I jumped down and changed my awful Superior dress into something more practical.

Next, I planned to sneak around Mister Sam's house to see if Brun was there. Although his letter said that he would not be here, I wanted to believe in the smallest of chances. I washed the dress in the waterfall, as it was a habit of mine to clean all used clothes before jumping into the water as well. After that, I ate some of the emergency food powder that Brun left behind before I took off.

When I arrived at Sam's, I hid behind a thick bush so that there was no way anyone could notice me. I observed that the old Superior man was sitting outside on his balcony as usual, but he was not the only one there. Trucks and cars with yellow lights were coming down the hills from the Cotters' place. When they stopped, some people in black uniforms came out and talked to Mr. Sam.

Some of them proceeded to walk around Sam's property as if they were looking for something. Many were waving their hands around. Suddenly, a loud beep came from across the field. It came from a man who was pointing with his hand in my direction. Then they all turned towards my direction.

Then I realised that the things in their hands were the shocking devices.

The range of detection was 500 metres. It was stupid of me to be so close to them. I scrambled away as fast as I could. The shouting of those men followed closely behind, but due to my expertise with the forest, I managed to ditch them rather easily.

I went back to the hut, packed some essentials, then headed deeper into the forest with Faolan running beside me. I jogged through the easiest and quickest route, knowing that a kilometer distance was needed between me and them. Since my microchip was the only way they could ever hope to use as a pointer to find my position, I could avoid them completely if I was never in the range of the device. The forest was so big and wide that even I had no idea how far it stretched out. I doubted that some pompous Superiors would be able to find me here. So the very first few hours, I hurriedly put some distance between me and them.

I jogged for two hours without stopping, even with a small camouflage backpack on my back. The feeling of being in nature again soothed my very soul and kept me from getting tired. Every puff of air I breathed in was refreshing, and I felt that I could run forever. However, I had to stop before my false sense of power caused me to exercise too much. The journey would be long, so spending everything in the first few hours would probably be not a good idea.

Without worrying about the pursuers, I carried on deeper. Instead of finding me, they would be more likely to find themselves swallowed whole by the Mother Nature. All I had to do was survive and keep on walking.

Noon came. Luckily, I found some wild fruits and nuts to eat, but they did not give much energy. Faolan went out and brought back a rabbit for me while I rested as well, which helped a lot. I kept on looking for food as I walked.

The journey continued until dusk. At this point, there was absolutely no sign of my pursuers, so I decided to rest. I put up my special tent and fell asleep very quickly. When the morning came, I repeated the cycle for the next six days. No matter how much I walked, there was no end to it. For a few days now, the terrains had become unfamiliar; I had come far past the farthest point I used to come. The nights were harsh. It was cold and frosty, but I hugged my furry friend at night to keep warm.

One night, I was woken up by something very loud. Faolan was already standing aggressively. Her hair was puffed up, her fangs were bared. She was on full alert.

"*She's here!*" It was the voice of a Superior man.

I immediately readied my rifle and exited the tent. The sky was black, with a single hovering light that shone extremely brightly down into my eyes.

"What the hell is going on?" I thought.

Then a group of men rushed towards us. All of them wore black, just as I had seen at Mister Sam's house. At that moment, I felt the shock radiating throughout my body. This time, the current was stronger than ever and it kept going forever. Then it stopped—because Faolan savagely bit into the man who had shocked me and made him drop his device on the ground. Since every man there had a remote, another man immediately shocked me instead.

To rescue his buddy, another man shot my friend in her gut. Despite the injury, the wolf did not let go of the arm. She hung on. As more shots were fired at her, she did not even make a sound until her lifeless body hit the ground. Tears filled my eyes as I crawled along the ground to my friend. I hugged her for the last time before one of them lifted me and carried me into the machine in the sky.

Chapter 38: Execution Ground

The feeling of flying in the thin air like a bird was indescribable, but I was so struck by grief that it was impossible to enjoy. The *'helicopter'* flew for the whole night. There was nothing to be seen in the darkness until the warm sun of the morning finally lit the world up. The trees became green and the sky orange. Manmade structures slowly came into view as our transport approached a town. I could see the people that had me captured now. All of them were male Superiors in their twenties or thirties, except one middle-aged one who appeared to be the boss. Every one of them was wearing a black vest.

"You nearly died, bro," one of them said to his friend who was bitten.

"That was nothing, I could have killed that wolf by myself," he replied.

"No, you couldn't. It would have ripped your face off with those huge fangs if we didn't shoot it."

"But the girl was surprisingly easy, though. Can't believe she killed any Superior,"

"Yeah, of course, we had our remotes. It wasn't even fair, really."

We arrived at our destination when the sun was up in the sky. As the helicopter descended quickly, and the ground came closer, it felt like I was falling from a great height at first. But the touch of the pilot made it land surprisingly gently. The men dragged me out to the grass.

We landed in the middle of a green meadow surrounded by trees in every direction. On the other side of the clearing, a male Superior was already waiting for me. He appeared to be middle-aged, with messy-looking facial hair, a tile pattern shirt, and a pair of ragged jeans.

"This is the meat Taurine who murdered the estate owner and his trainer, yes?" he asked.

"Yes, she is. We saw her run but didn't catch her until day seven," one of the black vest men said.

"I never thought a meat Taurine could be that smart. Murdered three people and eluded the special force for seven days. Well... this one

we had to get permission from the satellite," another guy beside me added.

"Oh wow! Did she run off into a jungle or something?"

"That's what literally happened, Mr. Sanderman, but keep it quiet, will you?" my previous captor said, then pushed me towards my next one. The burly truck driver squeezed one of my arms very hard. When I struggled, he simply did it harder.

"Of course, she will be going in with one of the morning groups. I've got her documents signed in and everything."

"I know we can count on you, sir. Then let us be on our way."

"I am glad to be a part of your operation, as always."

"Likewise, Mr. Sanderman. Goodbye."

As soon as my previous holder finished his word, the rest of the team went back to the helicopter, and I was officially transferred to the fat, gruff man. He forcefully dragged me across the lawn at a fast pace. Due to the weariness of travelling seven days straight in the forest, it was hard to keep up, but he did not look back at me, just kept on walking, and pulled me hard if I ever fell behind.

At last, we came to the end of the treeline, where an opening to a small dirt road revealed a big silver truck with ten wheels parked in the middle. The men opened the back of it and shoved me inside before locking the door again. He went back to the driver seat and the vehicle started to move.

Other meat Taurine women and men I had never seen before filled the space. Most were sitting down, but some were standing. Due to a high density, there was barely any room to breathe at all. My head nearly touched the ceiling even though I was never a very tall person. When the truck moved, everyone had difficulty keeping themselves steady. The driver was driving so fast and turned so sharply that the momentum would often slide us around.

The ventilation holes on the sides were not very effective at all due to the sheer number of people. I had to poke out my nose near these holes from time to time to gasp for air. It was so incredibly hot that I started to sweat all over.

This trip reminded me of the day when I was seven years old, the event that had brought me outside my home for the first time. Even the designs were the same. If someone told me it was the same truck, I would have believed it. The truck changed my life completely last time; it would most likely be the case this time as well, but I had a feeling that this trip would not just land me in another Larringtons' estate.

The only thing we could do was to persevere until the end. There were mixed emotions of sadness, depression, fear, and even anger among the people. A few of them cried themselves silly. Others tried to help their friends by displaying false courage through their trembling voices. From every face I saw, I could guess that they had realised their fate. All of the above, combined with many vomit piles on the truck floor, caused the atmosphere to reek of despair.

The transporter stopped many times as more people were picked up along the way. The truck was divided into many different rooms, but each was packed full by the time we arrived at our destination. When we did, the vehicle driver Mr. Sanderman took us all out room by room. At that point, I was feeling nauseated and light-headed. It was pure agony to stay in there. If it was another ten minutes, I felt like I would surely die from the sickness. I rushed outside as soon as I heard the door unlock. With my face looking upwards, I breathed in the best air I had ever inhaled in my life.

When I came to again, I found myself in a large cage encircled by very high concrete walls which were perfectly vertical and smooth on their surfaces. A single aperture opened on the other side of the yard, but it was so small that only a single person could walk through at a time. It was the one and only exit I saw in all directions.

It looked to be about a hundred people when the truck was fully emptied. There were mostly girls, as expected. Some were very young, but most were old or sick. A few male Taurines were also present. However, nobody wanted to be the leader to venture into the unknown.

"Move!" the truck driver shouted in Taurine language, but nobody obeyed.

"I said, move!"

At that moment, an electric current was discharged from the microchip buried inside my neck and spread down over my chest to my feet.

"Walk, you stupid cows!" Mr. Sanderman shouted again. Another shock went through me. This time it was even stronger than before and I noticed that other people were getting their bodies twisted as well. I did not know how that was possible, but it was happening. The only explanation was that the remote of this truck driver was able to fire on multiple targets at once.

The punishment caused the desired effect for the Superior: to drive us forward. People started running away from the noxious stimulus and into the next room without hesitation. When the first girl took a step down into the alleyway, the others followed her. I went after them as well, but suddenly a hairy hand from behind grabbed the neck of my shirt.

"Wait," the truck driver whispered grimly. I remained in the awkward position with him standing behind me until everyone else had gone into the passageway.

He let go, then touched me on the shoulder with one finger. When I turned towards him, he gave me a full smack to the face. I fell and tried to get up, but he pressed on his remote hard causing my body to radiate with electrical current. The world vanished for a second. When I gained consciousness again, I was lying on the muddy ground that had been trampled by millions of people before me with the almighty Superior staring down from above.

"This is still too little for someone like you, murderer. Pity that I can't give you a real beating, but if your meat is not worth that much, then I would be beating you to death myself," he said.

He pulled me up by my ear and told me to move into the next room. However, his anger caused him to kick me from behind. My shaking legs gave in to the pressure because I was still weak from the previous electrocution. My face went down into the mud.

"Get up, or I'll shock you again," he threatened. I could not get up, so I crawled instead.

When I managed to go into the corridor, he swore at me for the last time and closed the metal gate behind. I was glad that he went back to his truck after that.

What's his problem? I thought, then wiped the dirt from my face. I assessed the wounds from the assault and found that my lip was bleeding. After walking for some time, I finally caught up with the people in front where we came to another box-like room. Again, there were only two paths we could take, one exit and one entrance.

Every time we came to the next room, the door behind would close on its own, so there was really only one way to go. However, this time, the way forward was not open yet and all one hundred or so people were just waiting around in the enclosure. Over our heads, a dark tinted roof was covering the sky. There was an extensive network of elevated walkways that was used by Superiors to look down from above without getting touched by us Inferiors. It was about four metres above the ground, so there was no way we could reach it.

From then on, our ways became monotonous. Every room we went through was the same in all aspects. While they were all separated, small corridors were used to connect each of them. Every time I walked through a room, a metal gate would come up from the ground to prevent going back. We went from one pen to another and repeat, only moving forward and unable to go back.

All the while, a few Superiors who were patrolling around on the aerial walkway shouted at us to move along. If anyone was a little bit slow, they would get jabbed with an electric pole. The high-class people wanted us to make us move as close as possible to the person in front to save time. However, although about 80% of the time was used to stand around waiting for the gates to open, the Superiors were not shy about using their prods.

As soon as I went into the fifth room, I saw several male Zebu workers doing something to the people in front of me. Our folks who lined up before them were all clothed, but the ones that went past them became naked. These determined workers of small statues were only busy taking off everybody clothing, looking straight at their work, focusing on doing everything right with as little time as possible.

208

Despite the nature of their work, there were no signs of embarrassment on their faces, as if they were machines.

We were told by a Superior who could speak Taurine to put our hands up for the Zebus to take off our tops. When it was my turn, two of them came to me. One male worker stripped my T-shirt away and worked on the bra while the second took off my shoes. Then the third one extracted my shorts along with my underwear in one swift movement. They threw everyone's clothing into the same bucket.

We came to the sixth pen and everyone stopped moving once again. As soon as the gate behind me closed, another surprise came as cold water poured down from the ceiling. I tried to look for cover, but there was none. It was probably five minutes under the torrent of water which soaked us down to our bones. There were no new clothes or even towels, and we were forced to shiver until the water was dry. The most I could do was hug myself.

It was another fifteen minutes until the gate to the next corridor opened and the light on top of the gate turned from red to green, which prompted the Superiors above to start shouting at us to move again. Some of the girls in front pushed through and went in first in their desperation to find a better place than this abominable showering room.

They rushed through and more people followed. This time about twenty people were moving inside another single-file walkway at a time, and then the gate would close behind them. The line was moving extremely slowly, but I could not see why.

Standing there for half an hour shivering in the queue was not a pleasant experience, but my turn eventually came. Several people were still behind me, but as soon as I stepped inside the corridor, the metal gate closed behind me. Regardless of how hard I tried to push the gate open, it was immovable; going back was not an option.

I was finally close enough to see the reason why the line was getting a lot slower. One of the girls in front was trying to climb out by using other people as platforms, so the whole crowd panicked, but there was nowhere to run. People just kept pushing back at the back of the line, pressing me against the metal gate. The looks on everyone's faces spoke of great terror.

However, they were shocked with electrical prods, and order was restored. The front girl was also chased back to her place. She dropped down to the ground below and kept running away from the pole towards the 'correct' way.

"Next one! Move to the entrance. Hurry up! " the Superior directly above us waved the pole and shouted. Although another girl directly behind the first girl looked terrified of the room ahead, she followed her with no hesitation.

"Wait here. If I say go, then go," the Superior man said when the next person tried to follow the girl. It appeared that they wanted one person to go in at a time. A light above the entrance was used to signify when to move and to stop. When the red light turned green, the man would tap the next person lightly on their back to signify that they needed to move.

The process repeated like this until it was close to my turn. As more and more people were disappearing into the next room, the more I felt fear. The mysterious next area was shielded by a rubber curtain. It was not until I got to the front of the line that I figured out what caused the girls ahead of me to panic so much. The smell infused out from the little opening was unmistakable as the smell of blood. It was so strong that I gagged.

Twenty people until my turn, fifteen people until my turn. ten people, eight people, six people, four people, two people, one person. Then it was my turn.

I knew what my fate would be, but I still shook. My breathing was so fast , and I felt like collapsing right there and then. My eyes were suddenly brimming with tears and I felt the most scared I ever had in my life. Even though I had told myself numerous times that it was coming, my body could not stop fearing it. The idea of pain and the horror of death were suffocating me.

I did not want to go in that room; I wanted to live. Without thinking, I ran back the other way. The Superior above me shouted and came after me by his platform. I banged on the metal gate and cried for the others back there to help me, but all they had for responses was silence. I tried to climb the walls, but it was no use. Four meters and its slipperiness made it impossible for me to grab on.

Pain shot through me at the side of my bare thigh, causing my legs to spring up as a reflex. "Go the other way, you dipshit," the man above shouted. Then he poked me from the other side of the gate, leading me out of the corner and chasing me from behind with it. My body could not help but ran away from the pain stimulus until I found myself on the other side of the rubber curtain without even realising it.

It was a very small, cube-like space bounded by glistening metal on every side. It had not a single opening anywhere except where I came from, but that too immediately locked as soon as I came in. Abruptly, the wall closed itself onto me from all angles. The walls came so close I thought it would crush me into a pulp.

"*No! You can't do this to me!*" I shouted in Superior language. Only the coldness of the pure metal answered my call.

A big probe sparkling with electricity came up in front of my face. It appeared to be moving on its own, without a person to control and without any feelings of any human being. It was simply a heartless machine; the only thing it knew was to put its electricity directly onto my brain. The probe leveled itself precisely to my forehead and came closer every second.

"*I curse you all to suffer the same fate as me!*" I yelled my last word before the probe touched my head and the world went black.

Chapter 39: Slaughterhouse

I suddenly found myself on a soft blue sofa. It was impossible to recall how I had gotten here. I looked down and found the body of mine to still be fully naked, but a pink towel was covering the most sensitive parts. I looked around and saw a monotonous green-coloured room with nothing but a single table with a few chairs on either side. A bright neon light was on the ceiling and an ancient electric fan on the table. A door was at one end of the room, but there were no windows at all. The only sound came from the electric fan in the corner, and it seemed to go on forever.

"So this is what heaven looks like?" I thought without emotion.

I stood up slowly from the bed but kept the thin piece of pink fabric wrapped around my body. I did not remember what happened to me.

As soon as I walked off to touch the table, the door unexpectedly opened and a man with golden hair and blue eyes came through.

"*How are you feeling?*" he asked.

"*I'm cold,*" I answered without thinking.

"*Would you like something to wear?*"

"*Yes, please.*"

He went back out again and left me alone in the deserted plain room. Then it hit me…I just spoke to a Superior in his language. He asked me, and I answered him. We had a conversation. I felt faint, but managed to hold myself up by the edge of the sofa. It might have been the biggest mistake I made without even realising it.

The man came back and handed me some clothes over. He came closer to me with his lips parted in a wicked smile. I saw him lick his lips—or was I imagining it? It was as if he was seeing all the meat under the pink towel. I pulled it tighter. It had been some time since I had looked at my own legs. Now, I was surprised at how big and meaty they were. I was afraid, so afraid of his golden features that I remembered that they were going to kill me.

"*Please…don't kill me.*" It was a pitiful plea.

His face changed; his smile disappeared and he stepped away.

"Yeah, she definitely looks a bit like a Superior," he mumbled to himself before leaving.

Cautiously, I grabbed the outfit and put it on. Still wary of anyone seeing my meat, I dressed under the cover of the towel.

I put on this oversize T-shirt that seemed to be men's clothing. When I was done, another Superior man I did not know came in.

"Please, sit down," the man, who had a thick mustache, said when he saw that I was scared of them.

"No...what are you doing? Why are there so many of you man-eating people?" I backed into a corner and crouched behind the sofa like a scared animal.

"We just want to talk. Don't be afraid. I promise that no harm will come to you," the man said with a light tone in his voice.

"Get out! Leave me alone. Get out!" I screamed and dug my fingernails into the couch.

The mustache man did not seem to notice that I was being very wary of him. Instead, he turned to the first man I met and talked to him.

"Thanks, Jackson. This is definitely my daughter," he said.

"That was a really close one, Andrew. Those Inferior Lovers, man. No offense to your daughter, but it's crazy how they will go and put misleading pictures on the internet."

"Yeah, thanks to your workers who notice that, or else..." the man said, then looked to his friend. *"Anyway, Jackson, would you mind leaving us alone? I have some parenting to do."*

"Right, I better no get in the way, huh? I've got work to do anyway. That's gonna be on the incident report as well. Make sure you give her a good spanking for me."

"Yeah of course," Andrew said, and his friend left. When he and I were the only two left in the room, I asked him.

"Why did you say that I am your daughter?"

"Well...it's just an excuse really, or else how would I get you out of here?"

"Wait! You are getting me out? Who are you?"

"My name is detective Andrew Waldegrave. I'm here to..."

"Do you have any weapons?" I cut him short.

"*No*," he said with a playful smile, then took off his long black coat, revealing nothing but a white shirt with a blue tie underneath. "*No weapon,*" he said, showing me the inner pockets of his outerwear before putting it down on a chair.

"*I want to know how you ended up in this place.*"

"*This place?*"

"*You know...the slaughterhouse.*"

"*I...*" When I heard the word that he just uttered, the memories of the horrors came flashing back into my mind.

"*You were seconds away from death,*" he told me.

"*How did I survive?*" I asked him.

"*Because you talked.*"

"*What?*"

"*They were confused that you talked in Superior. Obviously, a Superior woman mistakenly put into the system would get them sued very badly, but it has happened before. When it's wet, it's kinda hard to tell the hair colour apart, you know?*

"*But those people...*" I thought about the others in the line with me.

"*I know...it's sad,*" he replied.

"*So, what happens now?*" I asked him.

"*I am taking you out of here,*" he said.

"*To where?*"

"*Back to our home base. It's quite far away, but we will go by car,*" he said, then urged me to stand and follow him out the door.

"*Please close your eyes as you walk. It's not a pretty sight.*" He offered me one of his hands which I took. I did as he said, but realised straight away what the reason was. I knew that he was protecting me, but I had force my eyes open and see the atrocity as it was.

Rows and rows of human carcasses, possibly thousands of them, were hanging upside down by hooks through their tendons just like I had seen in Hene's video. All of them were traveling slowly through the production line with a conveyor directly below them. Zebu workers were standing in places in their stations. Each of them was given a task to chop and trim the different parts of the corpses. They did that religiously and without any emotion on their faces.

I nearly could not keep my eyes open. The sights of blood and body parts accompanied by the smell and the unending machinery noises caused me to feel light-headed.

I need to see this. This is what they are doing to us, I thought, and kept my eyes open.

After they were killed, bodies were cut open, the skin was removed entirely, and all internal organs were separated and thrown down a chute to another section. As I walked further, I came to the heads.

Those heads without skin twitched. The facial muscles were jerking rapidly as if they were alive but I knew that they were gone, because their eyes only could stare blankly into a distance. There was no Hene, or Cat, or Carla anymore; they were just meat for someone to put in their mouth.

It was fortunate that we had arrived at the exit before I threw up. On the other side, workers were loading the finished products that did not look anything like our dead brothers and sisters into a truck. I should have been in there as well, I thought as I stared at freakishly beautiful packages containing loin muscles.

When I managed to leave the place, my escort took me into his car. Andrew, the detective, looked back at me. He used a soft tone for his voice and his movement was slow and calm. To be honest, I did not trust him fully at this point, but I had nowhere else to go, so I decided to get in his car. The only thing I could hope for was for him to not betray and try to eat me later. Then a sentence from his mouth changed my mind completely.

"He's waiting for you, Cattleya."

Chapter 40: Cross Country

We sped off through the small town that was full of one-story shops. None of them had any real colour apart from the boring white which was stained with black from rain scalds. Only a few Superiors were walking along the footpath in equally dull clothing with uninspired expressions. It gave off the vibe of a ghost town. We passed a sign: '*You are now exiting the town.*"

"*As you can see, this is a little town called Haven. This place is in the very north of North Devanta and has the only large slaughterhouse in this area.*"

"*I've never been here, but I've been to Burgan city.*" I meant the closest city to the Larringtons' estate, the one that we occasionally went to do some sweeping jobs. However, it was still about a hundred kilometers away.

"*Oh good, so you are used to seeing some small cities. But I'll tell you that the place we are going is nothing like Burgan or anything around here.*"

When the car was outside of town, we became the only object on the two-lane highway. There were rarely other people, except for a few trucks carrying Taurines coming in the opposite direction. I felt sad for them every time one went past. Rows of trees stretched in all directions on both sides along the road. The playful detective sat on my left, holding the steering wheel lightly with one hand. He stared ahead and smiled to himself, so I asked him why.

"*I am happy, of course.*"

"*But why are you happy?*"

"*I'm happy because I have you.*"

"*That's…*"

"*Oh! Sorry I didn't mean to give a signal to you so don't take it the wrong way. I used to speak to my wife this way, so it kind of stuck with me.*"

"*So…what does that mean?*"

"*On that matter, you will know soon enough. But you should be happy that I got to you first before anyone else.*"

"Huh? What are you saying?"

"I can't tell you. Not yet, anyway,"

"But why are you taking me with you?"

"Can't tell you."

"Are you trying to play with me?"

"Just sit still and enjoy the ride, okay? Thinking too much won't do you any good."

"Fine," I said and turned away to the window instead.

It was the first time I had seen so much of the real world. For my whole life, the pickup trucks were always closed from the outside so I could never really see the view. This was the first time I'd ever sat in a front seat just like a Superior. The trees alongside were very tall, so any chance of me enjoying the panoramic views was out of the question, but it opened up.

The unfamiliar scenery astonished me. The lands were filled with green grasses stretching as far as the eye could see. Hills beyond hills caused undulation of the land in their natural formation. A range of mountains was so far away, yet gigantic; they became the horizon. An alp on our right stood out from the rest, perfect in its geometry, its great height covered largely by snow.

Occasionally, there would be some buildings on the sides. They were used to raise a type of animal called *'pigs,'* according to Andrew.

The sky was a bright blue color with very few clouds. The warm sunlight gently shone through the glass windows. As the car was a little too cool, I moved closer to the window to bask. It was comfortable, so nice that I wanted to sleep.

"The Devanta forest is one of the few places in the world that remained largely undisturbed. Look at how beautiful it is. Do you know that it stretches across three provinces?"

"Yeah, it's gorgeous."

"Unfortunately, the forestry laws have changed and companies have gained permission to use it freely next year." There was sadness in his eyes as he spoke.

Andrew stopped the car to get some lunch from a remote shop in the middle of a small town. He brought some pies and water back to me in the car. We ate under some trees among nature, then continued driving when we were done.

He drove for the rest of the day until the sky reddened and the sun sank below the horizon. The car stopped in a big town named Rifton in a valley between two major mountains. The detective stopped just outside the town, looked inside the luggage of his in the backseat, fumbled inside for a while, and finally pulled something out.

"What?" I was horrified by the object in his hand.

The detective glanced at me and laughed. *"Don't be scared. It's just a wig."*

"But…it's someone's hair. That's like a whole head. Did you kill her and pull out the hair?"

"Well… it's definitely from someone's head, but that person's not dead. Anyway, you're gonna have to put it on when we go into town."

"It's clear from a Superior's female. How did you strip out so much like this?"

Andrew sighed at my excessive ignorance of the world, but he took his time to explain to me anyway. I learnt that it came from a real Superior, but the person whose hair was cut off did not have to die. There was no need to skin the head at all. It was a relief to know this fact before I put it on. The man with a funny mustache also gave me another item called *sunglasses*.

He said that I needed to pretend to be his blind daughter. My name would be Hazel Danlingford, a young miss of seventeen years, the youngest daughter of George Danlingford, a divorced estate owner. They had been traveling from Farlander to Estricia by car since eight o'clock this morning after a visit with grandparents.

I was blinded by head trauma from a motor vehicle accident when I was twelve. He emphasised that I needed to wear sunglasses the whole time. Even still, I should close my eyes as well so that I would walk like a blind woman. I was to be holding hands with him at all times in a father-daughter way and I could take off my disguises only when I was alone with him.

The wig was bigger than my head, but only marginally. It should not have been noticeable by anyone who did not specifically look for it. Aside from confining my eyes to a darkened world, the sunglasses were perfect for my face. I could not even see my own eyes when I looked into the car mirror, which meant that nobody would be able to see my brown eyes either.

My 'father' drove down the road towards Rifton. The town was supposed to be exactly halfway for our four-day driving trip.

We arrived at our destination, the *Great Valley Lodge* with a big bright red *'No vacancy'* sign, but he went in and parked the car neatly on the last parking slot.

"Hey! Are we going in there? It's full."

"Shush…" Andrew looked at me and made a finger on his mouth sign. *"Don't talk. You're not supposed to be able to see."*

"What's with that hand language sign? You are not supposed to think that I can see, Andrew."

"It's Dad. Who is Andrew?"

"We are not even outside of the car, Andrew. Are we actually going in there? I said it's full."

"Umm…no reason. I just think that this place is not full after all," he said and got out of the car. *"Now, you have to pretend that you are my daughter. There will be people there to see us."* I opened my door and stood still, trying to play as if I had no idea how to walk on my own as if I was Hazel Danlington.

"Hazel, my blind daughter, just stand right there. Don't walk off or you'll fall. The terrain is rough here. Just wait for me and I'll be with you in a minute," he said. His voice seemed stiff as a log, like he was reading his line off a sheet of paper.

After some shuffling around, he managed to hide other spare blonde wigs of different sizes in the car and took out his brown luggage. *"Let's go."* He grabbed my arm and forced me to latch on.

Even though the motel was full, we went into the reception to ask anyway. The clerk behind the lobby counter immediately smiled at us. There were many other clients in the lobby area within our earshot, but I feigned unsightedness by never moving my head; only my eyes were scanning the area. It was pretty scary to be in the middle of a hall full of Superiors in their natural habitat when you knew that you were their prey. Andrew gave his fake name.

"*Mr. Danlingford, you have a reservation.*" He bowed and gave him the key. Andrew came back and took me to the room. It was so easy I was stumped. There were so many things I did not know about the world of Superiors.

We saw nobody else except the same clerk who came to deliver dinner to our hotel room half an hour later. Andrew gave him some money before he left, bowing his head excessively. Andrew proceeded to tell me some nighttime story about Superior's etiquette while I pulled myself deep inside the thick and comfy blanket that smelled of flowers. It was the perfect temperature too, and I quickly fell asleep. For the first time in my life, I felt like a Superior princess.

Chapter 41: The Center of the Earth

We traveled by day and rested by night. The ancient vehicle was constantly making a loud noise as it was going on the road and I thought it would give out many times, but Andrew seemed very confident that it would never break down.

The beautiful scenery of the first day died out quickly when it changed from all greens to all brown. The grasses dried up and gave way to shriveled, weedy plants. The ground became merely hard red sand with billions of cracks stretching as far as the eye could see. Black rocks were scattered here and there, but no trees. In addition to being hard to live in, the place was hot during the day, but surprisingly cold at night.

The road was much bigger; eight cars could run at the same time. There were four on one side and three on the other. We were one of the slower cars, so we always stayed on the outermost lane. It was a massive desert that offered a very few interesting panoramic views, but we were stuck driving through it for two whole days. Andrew described to me its history during our ride.

"*It used to be a forest,*" he said.

"*No way!*" I cried in an utmost surprise.

Hundreds of years ago it was, but not anymore, he told me. It was one of the biggest forests, yet it suffered complete annihilation at the hands of Superiors. Trees were cut down to make the new towns and cities that rapidly rose up in that era. It was the epoch of progressivism, he said, this was the time when Superiors invented much of modern-day technology.

"*You remember all the pigs? Those things that eat grasses and quickly turn into meat? We considered them to be very dirty, so Superiors don't usually touch them until they are properly cooked. We let the Zebus raise them instead. You see? All the cheap meat that you Taurine get fed every day are actually from those guys. You eat them, then Superiors eat you. It is the circle of life. Although I find you Taurines to be too closely related to us...*"

"*So you have eaten a Taurine before?*"

"Yes, sad to say. I did for more than twenty years, then I realised how wrong it was. I'm sorry, I shouldn't be talking about that in front of you."

"That's okay..." I answered, although I was not so sure about it myself.

"I haven't had any in the past thirty years, though. Anyway, my point about grasslands was that they were not natural either. Even though they were green, they were just another disguised synthetic land."

We checked into a motel every night and the fake personas proved useful after all. There were many times the other Superiors had talked to me. Most of the times they were simply casual passersby who felt sorry for the blind girl. My listener often looked confused from the way I spoke and they would ask where I was from. It was weird to have the strong North Devanta accent in this part of the country, but it could not be helped since I learned it from Brun and the Cotter family.

Andrew was a nice man. He took care of me like I was a Superior even though he knew that I was a filthy meat Taurine. He held the door open for me and would always call me *young lady*. He talked about his wife, his twin sons, and his daughter, and how they had made him so happy. He asked me a few things about myself as well. At first, I did not want to give anything away, but he never pressed me. In time, his relaxed attitude, gentlemanliness, and funny little mustache calmed me.

I slowly trusted him. One day, without realising it, I spoke about myself. After that, it just came in naturally to open up to him. Staying with a true chivalrous man of high-class manners like him made my animal ferocity vanish like it never existed. The wildlife in the forest seemed so far away now. Each hour, I felt myself ascending to a completely different world.

Otherwise, the trip went well. He assured me that nobody would be following us. The government, the people who sentenced me to death in the slaughterhouse, never knew that I survived. It was only customary that Inferiors who commit crimes would be put into execution and face death just like any other animal without much fuss.

However, for my case, which caused a major public outcry from my supposed murder of the Cotters, I was extensively hunted. On the first night in the desert motel, I saw the news while Andrew was in the bathroom.

"This is what a Superior killer looks like," a commentator said while holding up the severed head of a young Taurine woman by the hair. He tossed it into the hungry crowd of rough-looking Superiors who spit on it and kicked it around like a ball.

Andrew came out of the bathroom.

"Is that supposed to be me?"

"You better not watch that, young lady." He grabbed the remote.

"I want you to tell me now! I don't care if it hurts my feelings. Please, let me know that I can trust you."

He explained that the fact that he was there at the slaughterhouse at the right place and the right time was not an accident. He said that he was instructed to come here to fetch me by his mysterious unnamed boss. The corpse on the news was only something to satisfy the audiences who had followed the Cotter tragedy on their television for several days. Taurine all looked the same to most viewers anyway, so it was easy.

Four and a half days was the total duration of our trip. The end arrived with the presence of a large group of man-made structures in the distance. There had been a couple of cities that we passed through but none that we went in. We kept our profiles low by visiting only when needed. When Andrew said that this massive city in the distance was our destination, I was getting so excited and nervous that I was shaking all over.

"Are you scared?" Andrew asked.

"No, not at all," I lied.

"Good...then let me show you the world of the Superiors," he said as our car went past the sign: *'Welcome to Felicity, the place of paradise.'*

We slowly approached the sticks that reached out to the sky. Houses grew around everywhere like trees. Some big, some small, but all of them had many different colors and designs. The clumps of structures were packed tightly together and arranged in blocks after blocks in an orderly fashion.

One of the big shops had several Zebus holding onto pieces of cardboard signs. They waved them around to get the attention of the passing cars. I saw another shop that used female Zebus to wash cars. We kept going, passing about ten intersections, and came to a mighty big bridge. We moved on slowly, because there were so many cars around and they caused a traffic jam.

The overpass stretched about two to three kilometers in length with six lanes. I lost myself in wonderment at the power of Superiors. I simply could not comprehend how they had made structures so big. It looked too much like an architecture created by special beings rather than humans. Down below, a large body of deep blue water was encircling the main city. When I looked carefully, I saw that it had a vicious current, yet the Superiors had managed to control and use it as their city supply.

We finally reached the other side of the bridge where there were the tallest of the tall buildings. Up close, they looked even higher than I had imagined, with some of their tips impossible to see from below. Underneath constructions such as these, I could not help but feel like an ant within a forest.

The number of people walking around was astonishing. Once the car came to a major intersection, and the green light was turned for the pedestrians, a storm of people came out from every direction like bees coming out of a hive.

There was a 50/50 ratio of Superiors and Inferiors walking alongside each other. The high-class humans were of all ages and sexes, from young children to their parents and the old Superiors. The Inferiors were mostly the family pets: Sangas, Lemonade-like creatures, or Zebus. Most of them, except a few Zebus, were all on a leash of their masters.

After we came through the first few intersections, open space was found. Instead of buildings, it was some sort of grassland with trees. *"It's called a park. People come here to relax and connect themselves with nature. That's what they say, anyway,"* Andrew said.

224

Visitors were concentrating on one particular part that appeared to be a festival. When we were stuck in a traffic jam for a long time, I used this time to observe. As a bonus, Andrew was more than happy to explain everything to me.

There was a red inflatable castle in the middle with some small tents which were selling food and toys to little blonde children. All of them were manned by Zebus in each stall. Andrew told me that a big tycoon in this city often hosted such festivals.

One of the small girls piqued my interest. I stared at the girl with perfect golden hair and blue eyes. She laughed so happily as she ran around. With a balloon in her hand, her loving mother and father were both struggling to catch her. The little girl was quick on her feet and managed to slip away from her parents many times until she was eventually lifted off the ground by her father's gentle big pair of hands. Her mother then held out something to her.

It was a wooden stick with what appeared to be a dark brown lump on it. The girl bit into that lump and chewed. I had no idea what it was until the car moved further up. Then the reason for the children's aggregation became clear. A small stall was selling some meat to the children. Even though small, it had an exceptional number of customers compared to the others.

This particular seller was a Superior, as opposed to many other Zebu-manned booths. To make it even more attractive, the Superior vendor was a young Superior woman in her twenties with a pretty face. As if she truly enjoyed her work, she acted so warmly towards the young ones while handing them pieces of her product. Her face was '*perfect*' by the Superior standard, with the prominent eyebrows, playful large smiles, and pearly white teeth.

She was diligently putting the sticks on top of an open flame griller fueled by charcoal. "*Skewered Taurine. Only 500 silver per stick, money goes towards childhood cancer charity!*" she advertised to the passersby.

"*How much is 500 silver?*" I asked my rescuer.

"*500 silver pieces is a full day's work at a minimum-wage job. And the whole carcass is about three hundred times that. It does take at* least ten years to raise a Taurine until it is fully grown, so it is not cheap," he explained.

Our lives are worth only this much? I thought.

The final part of the park was quiet as only a few people were walking in between. The building, called the 'museum,' stood in the distance, but I had no idea what it meant. However, something much more eye-catching managed to overshadow the plain structure behind. It was an imitation of the planet earth, a statue made from real metal.

Brun taught me that the planet was big and round. He used to draw a picture of the earth for me. It even had colours and everything. One game we played back then was guessing our location. I first pointed at a blue part on the picture, but Brun corrected me; blue meant it was water. I thought we lived in blue parts because the sky was blue and of course, the earth was one big sky, but I was wrong. After a few more tries, which included a trip to the South Pole, I finally got it right. The forest that we lived in…I never had even a slight idea of how small it was compared to the whole world. When Brun drew it, he simply put a few trees on the map.

The globe in front of the museum was made of highly reflective metal so the land, the seas, and the snowy poles were all of the same colour, like they did not even matter in the first place. Big writing on the bottom pointed upwards to the metallic globe: "This is the ruler of the earth. This is you." The surface was so reflective I could see myself sitting in the car.

Chapter 42: Secret Base

Lower Felicity Hospital treated Inferiors exclusively. The middle-aged detective who had parked the car told me that it was our destination. When we were getting out, I resumed playing the part of the blind girl.

There were many different people of all shapes and sizes. I saw crooked creatures like Lemonade coughing very strongly and making a sound like they could not breathe. There was a Sanga who lied still in bed with countless scratches on his face and a freshly amputated leg. A Zebu was shaking uncontrollably as he walked with his stick. However, there was not a meat Taurine insight. Neither did the city had any of them.

I kept walking with my eyes hidden perfectly under my sunglasses. Many Superiors turned their heads and stared at me like I was a strange little creature, unknown to them. Those gazes belonged mostly to the owners of Inferiors as well as the staff in the waiting area. Their freakishly blue eyes with a black hole in the center stared deep into me as if they knew who I really was. It felt like they could stare into my soul and uncover my disguise. One of them called to me, a very old-looking lady with a Sanga twice her size sleeping on her lap.

"Excuse me, sir, I think you brought your daughter here to the wrong place," she said politely to my fake dad.

"Thank you, Missus, but I've come here with my daughter to visit our beloved Noodles. He had just got a big operation this morning."

"Oh! I'm so sorry. I thought...."

"That's okay. Don't worry about it. I hope your Sanga gets better soon."

"He's just in for his vaccination, so he'll be all right. Well... by the power of all the gold in the world, I hope it goes well with your Noodles." The old lady gave her blessing.

After that, we went through the '*staff only*' part of the hospital. Most of the nurses greeted Andrew as we went past. We went past the patient wards where some sad-looking people were locked up inside.

They tried to tell me to unlock the door for them using hand language, but Andrew told me to ignore them.

Finally, we came to a room that was very white, from the ceiling to the wall, to the floor and furniture. In the centre, a Superior woman in a white coat was already sitting at the opposite side of a table, waiting for us.

"Andrew!" she cried, and sprang out of the chair to hug him. They kissed on the cheeks a few times before turning towards me.

"*Is this her?*"

"*Yeah, this is Cattleya. The first meat Taurine ever that could speak Superior. And Cat...*" He looked at me. "*This is my wife, Joanna. She's a researcher and a doctor in this hospital.*"

"*Hi, nice to meet you, Cat. I hope you will enjoy your time here.*"

"*Sure...*" I did not know what to say.

"*Andrewwwww!*" She looked at her husband with disapproving eyes.

"*Did you not tell her?*"

"*Well... I did but...*" Andrew stammered.

"*A lab? I have heard about it before,*" I said.

"*Oh! It's nothing, my dear. We don't do any weird experiments on you or anything like that. Just so you know. We just do food trials, things like that. Plus, this place is not...*"

"*Shh...we never speak about it until we're inside, remember?*"

Joanna stopped short and nodded in agreement. I wondered what she was going to say next.

"*Anyway, come on in, Cattleya.*"

"*Just call me Cat, thanks.*"

She led me through to an examination room where I was told to sit on a bed. I took off the wig and the sunglasses when Andrew said I could. Then Joanna began to examine me from head to toe.

"*Brown eyes... hmmm... certainly not a Superior. Now, let me look inside a bit,*" she said, then took out a strange device from the corner of the room. It had a small circle in the middle and its light was illuminated directly into my eyes. "*Just keep them open for me, okay?*"

she said. I felt rude to be staring into a Superior's eyes, but I didn't look away, because she said not to.

"*Now... let's do a Superior eyes exam. Read these to me, will you?*" She pointed towards a sheet of posters stuck to the wall.

"*E F T P O Z L P E D.*" These were the few of the letters, but all of them, including the smallest, were easy for me to read.

"*That's 100% correct, very good. Let's go to the next step.*"

She took about 30 minutes more with her thorough clinical examination. I was poked and prodded in many places, but in the end, she announced that I was perfectly fine in every way. She even took some blood samples from my arm, which I did not resist at all, since I had been injected regularly with vaccines against diseases for as long as I could remember. She looked at my hair and shone light onto it. She said that the real colour was something between a blond and a brown—a dark blonde or a light brown, which was unheard of, she said.

"*Thank you, Cat. You are done here, so just go inside.*" As soon as she said it, she immediately went to her paperwork. Before I could ask any questions, Andrew gently tapped on my shoulder to signal that we were leaving.

We went through another door into a dark hallway, and suddenly, the light turned on by itself. One of the doors to the right opened and a female with extremely pale white skin came out. She was slightly shorter than me but older than me, maybe in her early twenties from her smart manner and the confidence in her voice. However, the most striking thing about her was her hair; it was such a bright red-orange color. I opened my mouth in awe, as I had not seen anything like it before.

"*This is Cat,*" Andrew said to her.

She looked me in the eyes and greeted me.

"*My name is Mikayla. Nice to meet you.*" She offered a hand, a smile reaching to her bright green eyes.

"*I'm Cat. Well... nice to meet you, too.*" I shook hands with her. It was the most common form of greeting in the Superior culture.

"I will leave you two to talk, okay? Please show her around, Mikayla," Andrew said and left the way he came. *"I will be back this evening."* When he was gone, I turned towards the stranger I just met.

"How can you speak Superior? I thought I was the only one."

"Andrew taught me," the girl with the flaming hair answered.

"Who are you? No! What *are you?"* I asked, still incredulous at her appearance.

"I'm a milk Taurine. So we speak what the Superior calls the milk language. Sounds ridiculous, but it is what it is."

"What's a milk Taurine?"

"If there's a meat Taurine, then there's a milk Taurine. These are the two types of Taurines in the world."

We talked about our situations. I found out that this place was a facility for keeping the weird and wonderful creatures like us. In reality, it was also a base for the 'Inferior rights group'. The group consisted of several Superiors, including Andrew and his wife, who did not agree with the long tradition of using Inferiors as they were used now. Many people from various professions also joined this renowned society, including the hospital owner, who kindly turned this facility into our housing. It was one of the secret bases for this group to keep rescued Inferiors around; in this case, it was in the guise of experimentation subjects.

"This place is not that big because the government is trying to suppress it, but they have managed to recruit some powerful people recently, which is very helpful. Although the rest of the population is still trying to deny the problem."

"Why?" I asked.

"I understand why most are still refusing to this day. It is because they don't want to know—they don't want to care—because it makes them feel bad. It destroys their beliefs, the very essence of what made them Superior in the first place. If we were to go out there and ask all the citizens in this city, I can say that almost everyone has never been to a slaughterhouse or killed an inferior by themselves, yet most of them have tasted our meat,"

"You are very smart," I complimented her.

"Someone taught me." She smiled. *"You hungry?"* She told me to follow her into a good-sized kitchen with two refrigerators, multiple stoves, and ovens for cooking. Even though the interior looked pretty bland, the cleanliness and amount of cookware made up for it. Mikayla opened the fridge and pulled out a plate of leftover spaghetti.

"If you don't mind?" she asked.

"No, no, of course not. I love leftovers," I answered. She scooped some out onto a plate and heated it in a microwave.

"You can come here and take things out to eat anytime," she told me.

"Oh! That's so nice. I never thought we Inferiors could do this."

"Everyone here wants you to think of yourself as a Superior, so don't worry about it." Her bright green eyes and her perfect smile really nailed her confidence into me. We went back to the bench in the dining room and I started eating.

"How long have you been learning the language?" I asked her.

"A while, maybe nearly two years? But it's been pretty hard. I'm not a Superior, so I don't have the talent for it. I envy that you are so fluent with it. How did you learn so well?"

"A Superior taught me as well. We constantly used the words in our daily lives, so I got them pretty quick, I guess."

"It seems so natural, though, how you talk and pronounce those hard letters. Especially the th, you know? I guess I'm a bit old to learn. I started when I was nineteen," She said.

"That means you are twenty-one? You sure don't look that old."

"I'm already an old hag by milk Taurine standard. I didn't get to milk much, so I guess that helped. How about you?"

"I'm just eighteen. Started learning at fourteen, been using it exclusively ever since,"

"That's how you get so good at it, I see, We should learn from each other from now."

"Yep! Let's do that together sometime." I grinned shyly at her.

And just like that, I felt that I had met a friend for the first time in a long time.

Chapter 43: A Freak Show

It was another day that I woke up in a completely strange environment. For the last five nights, it had been like this, waking onto the bizarre soft beds instead of the floor of the doghouse. It was unbelievable how life could be so different in such a short time.

I was put into one of the twenty shared rooms with Mikayla. I jumped out of bed and stretched. Her bed was already made, with a perfectly tidy style just like mine. I was wearing pink shorts with a flower pattern and a plain white T-shirt which I had borrowed from her, although they were all donated. The room was plain but comfortable, and it offered privacy like no other places I had ever lived.

I made the bed, had a shower, and brushed my teeth down in a bathroom down the hall. I was nervous at first about letting a lot of strangers see my body, since I heard that there were a lot of men living here as well. It was a relief when I saw that they were divided. In truth, I did not even have to reveal myself to other females, since each shower was completely separated from each other by walls. When I finished the steaming hot shower, I put a new set of clothes on and went back to the kitchen to have breakfast.

Many people from different types gathered. It was about twenty or thirty of them. There were Sangas and Zebus of both sexes sitting down and having a chat over breakfast. It seemed that my roommates and I were the only ones with white skin. Mikayla stood behind the kitchen counter where she continuously handed bowls of porridges out to people. When she saw me, she said good morning.

"Do you want a bowl? You are the last one, so I was wondering whether if I should go back to call you," she said.

"Sorry... I will get up sooner tomorrow." I felt myself turn red in embarrassment from being late and reluctantly grabbed a bowl from her.

"That's okay. You had a big trip over the last week. You earned it," she said, then followed me. "Let's sit together."

"Did you cook this?" I asked her when we sat down before stirring the porridge.

"*Yeah, I do it every day for other people. Since none of them can.*"

"*That's so nice of you.*" I put my first spoonful in my mouth. It was bland, but I could eat it. I could eat anything, but my friend insisted on putting some brown sugar in it.

"*How does that taste?*" she asked and stared at me with her hopeful smile.

"*Yeah.. it's great.*"

"*Let me introduce you to some people here,*" she said when we finished. The empty bowls were pooled into a sink where a female Sanga named Croquet was washing them scrupulously.

Mikayla told me to follow her to each table so that she could introduce me. After this, there would be no chance for introductions, since we would be stuck in lessons where Superiors would come in and teach us something.

"*This here is Hicks,*" she said while waving her hand with a smile on her face towards a huge Sanga man who ignored us completely.

"*I don't advise you to go too close to him. He prefers to stay alone most of the time and is pretty easily upset, too. I mean, he's not that bad, but I wouldn't risk it. He used to be a really good acrobat, working with a circus. I heard that one day, his master pushed him too far, so he punched his master to death with bare hands and killed three more Superiors who tried to stop him.*"

His head turned and his large black eyes caught mine. I quickly averted my gaze in nervousness.

"*Umm...*" I could not speak. I really wanted to ask why it was all right for the Superiors to keep him here, but I was afraid that the remorseless killer would be able to understand me, so I kept my mouth shut.

"*Don't worry, he can't understand us. He only knows simple commands. And you know, Sangas cannot speak.*"

"*I'm sure I can live with him,*" I lied. His presence alone in the same building would surely make me paranoid. There was no way that I would feel comfortable around someone like him.

"That's good. We don't judge anyone here. There is no hate towards anyone and I intend to keep it this way. The next person is ..."

Good thing there were not many others who had killed someone, although all of them were abused by their masters in the past. Nevertheless, I made sure to walk right behind my red-haired friend and be especially careful not to stare into anyone's eyes for too long.

She told me of many weirder but less dangerous people. There were five mini humans—
'mini' was the term used to describe Lemonade-like creatures. It was the first time I had learnt of this term. She said that it was so wrong that they even exist. She felt pity for them and often needed to look after them with extra care. Marley, Wasabi, Gorilla, Gummie, and Ticks were their names. Since they could not fight anyone, they often were the targets of bullying by their angry Superior owners, and that was the main reason why they were rescued. Even here, they were taken advantage of by their fellow residents.

They could not speak. It was one of their many abnormalities in their bodily structures. Their existence alone was the products of Superiors' arrogance and desire to control nature itself. For some reason, in their weird fashions, the great race decided to breed them to be the way they were today.

The more disfigured the minis were, the cuter they were considered to be. Their exaggerated short noses and faces could not allow for proper breathing due to the narrowing of the airway. Neither could they walk properly because of the deformed spines and twisted leg proportions. Some, such as Gorilla, had very long dark fur which covered the whole body, yet his owner kept him in a desert city such as here.

"Well... next is Kim." She introduced me.

Kim was a young female Zebu. Her face resembled a little bit those of the kitchen ladies I had seen at Devanta mine, although hers was much younger. Her dark brown, perfectly rounded eyes, pale yellowish skin, and pre-pubescent body indicated that she was about eleven years old or so compare to how I looked at that time.

"*Hi Milkshake, who is this?*" she spoke Superior with a very good central accent.

"*I'm Cattleya, nice to meet you,*" I answered.

"*Wow! A talking meat!*" she said.

"*Excuse me?*" I asked, confused by her remark.

"*I said, look at that talking meat. I can already feel the taste of you in my mouth.*" She actually salivated out of her mouth to the point she had to wipe it off.

"*But you are a Zebu. You can't be eating me!*" I cried out loud.

"*Who says I can't? Because I will. I will eat you one of these nights.*"

"*That's enough, Kim. We don't kid around about things like that.*" Mikayla banged her fist on the table. It was the first time I had seen my friend so angry.

"*Hahaha, I am just joking. You meaty girl. Who says that I will ever reduce myself down to the dirty habits of the Superiors? Well… If I am really hungry, maybe I will.*"

Something told me that she was not joking.

Mikayla told me later that Kim came from an apartment just in Felicity. She was purchased as a maid as soon as she was able to hold a broom. Unlike the Taurines, whose purposes were to give meat or milk to the Superiors, Zebus were commonly used for all sorts of tasks.

Kim was separated from her parents before she could remember them and came to live a life with a widowed Superior woman who could not have children. She treated her as if she was her child. Despite the fact that the language was sacred and could only be used by the greatest race according to 'The Law', her master taught her to read and write.

The Zebus had their own language, but she had not mingled with her own kind, so she was unable to speak it. The woman could not let it go public, so all of Kim's life, she was kept inside the apartment. It was not until she was dead that the news got out, and the Inferior rights group rescued her.

She could speak Superior. However, not only speech emerged out of her, but also the personality attached to the race.

"Why are there only people like these in here?" I pulled Mikayla away from the part of the dining room and talked with her alone.

"You don't like them?" she asked.

"Of course not? How do you even sleep at night in a place like this?"

"I just lock my room, I suppose."

"That's not the point. How can you even live here without breaking down? I mean...how can you still keep your smile on when you talk to these people?"

She looked at me and smiled again. *"I am tougher than I look."*

Then suddenly, out of nowhere, a voice interrupted us. "Aren't you going to introduce me?" It was a male voice speaking in meat Taurine language.

I turned towards him. His eyes and hair were both light brown as typical of my race. They were unmistakably the features of meat Taurine, although it was the first in my life I had actually seen a male version with my own eyes. His name was Buck.

His eyes instead fixed his eyes on my face then ran down to my chest. "Beautiful," he muttered, his glare never leaving my body. I put my hands over my chest.

I saw from the corner of my eyes that he had a confident and cocky smirk on his face. When I accidentally caught his eyes, he blinked at me with one eye. I quickly walked away, grabbing Mikayla with me and ran back to the dining hall full of people.

"Show no weakness, Cat, or else he will get to you," my friend finally told me when we were safe.

"I won't stand for this," I said and tapped Mikayla on the shoulder.

When he was out of earshot, I whispered, "Are they all like this? I mean the men."

"Yes, all Taurine men are. After all, the only thing they lived for is to breed with you."

Chapter 44: Free Will

After the eventful morning, a female Superior in a white lab coat came in and took everyone into a room.

"You can come in as well. Today, we will learn about the biology and industries of the Inferiors," the stranger with a golden ponytail said. She appeared to be a woman of early thirties.

"Hugh is a surgeon, Cat," Mikayla told me.

"Yes, I am a surgeon. But I don't cut people up without a reason, so rest assured."

Does that mean if she had a good reason, then she would?

"Anyway... just come to the lesson. You will need this knowledge to survive in the Superior world," she said.

The lesson went horribly. In a small meeting room, everyone was crammed inside. Since Mikayla invited me to sit in the front with her, her usual place, we managed to avoid the naughty and creepy people at the back.

Rather than a class, it was more like a detention centre, where kids were forced to sit still for a long time. Apart from those who obviously dozed off, others were messing around in the background, causing a ruckus. There were many times that they teased each other and often led to fights between themselves. Hugh would shout for them to get out while the troublemakers still had smiles on their faces. It had been their plan all along—it had to be—to get kicked out of the boring classroom.

The other matter that annoyed me was the stare; I could feel a pair of eyes leering on the exposed part of my neck. When I turned around, I saw the horny man named Buck blinking at me. I ignored him and concentrated on the lesson instead.

The teaching itself was about the differences in each type of Inferiors, what they look like and what their personalities were. Even with the distracting pair of eyes behind me, I concentrated.

Unlike other animals, Inferiors were domesticated because they had opposable thumbs, allowing them to take on delicate work that no other animals could. They were not only much better at receiving the commands, but could also thoroughly understand the tasks and carry them out in an efficient manner without the need for micromanagement. They could also work together in groups, communicate, and have a capability for problem-solving. All of these advantages were made possible only by the use of languages, which could be found in the both types of Taurines and Zebu humans.

With careful selective breeding over several centuries, each Inferior type had come to have distinct characteristics.

Meat Taurines grew very fast with very high muscle mass. As an aggressive race, a simple hierarchy arrangement was used to structure their social system. More often than not, they had a single alpha leader of the group, who was chosen by fighting among the members. It was quite true, I thought.

The milk Taurines, in contrast, were extremely docile and easy to handle. It was for this exact reason that Superiors had used them for milking. The hierarchy system was based on merit. Anyone who did agreeable deeds to the other members was regarded highly and dominated as the leader. In this race, kindness was the dominant trait that was most desirable among the members.

For both types of Taurines, females were the only ones that were usually kept alive. This was because the main product (babies for meat Taurine and milk for milk Taurines) could only be produced by females. Males were only used for mating. In general, only the best males with the most advanced genetics would be allowed to live to pass on the genes. Since one male could breed with many females, it was not necessary to keep many males. For the race to thrive on making babies, the race of Taurines was bred to have high fertility and libido.

I turned to my side to Mikayla, who noticed me and smiled. I smiled back and turned away in awkwardness. My face went bright red in embarrassment as I realised that it was guilt that I could not deny myself. The feeling was sometimes so strong, but there was a stigma about pleasuring oneself in the meat Taurine community. We were always told to do it with the males only.

We also learnt about other races. Zebus were tough as nails and small but powerful. They had small stature but high strength and endurance. This led to them not having to eat much while putting out considerable work. Their easily tanned skin also protected them from constant sun exposure in outdoor work. They were usually employed as slaves to do most of the low-end jobs.

Sangas was a race of extreme strength and agility. They were also loyal to the bone to whoever their masters were. As 'Superior's best friend' since the ancient times, they had been considered as higher class creatures when compared to all the other Inferiors. Most were used in sports such as running, ball games, and cage fighting. They were used historically as high-class steeds for rich Superiors, but now they were common household pets.

When the class ended, I approached our teacher while she packed up. I said I wanted to know more about how each of the races think. She appeared pleasantly surprised and lectured me about our intelligence level according to the Superiors.

At lunch, I approached my red-haired friend. "Is there anything I can help with?" I asked Mikayla, who was busy cooking lunch for everyone. She was acting as a chef who controlled a few Zebu cooks in her kitchen.

"Sure, you can help me peel the carrots."

Most others were lazing around doing nothing but sleeping, watching television, or playing around. It felt like they had nothing to do but having fun the whole day. They never did anything productive for as long as I had seen them.

I decided to focus on the cooking. When I turned to a cook beside me, I saw vegetables being washed so roughly they became all wilted, so I had to tell them.

Being a kitchen hand for Charlotte had taught me that they were doing a lot of things wrong, but I managed to make things a little bit better in some aspects. I carefully advised the petite female Zebus in the kitchen with the same smile I just copied from Mikayla, since I did not want to upset them. A little human gesture went a long way, I had found, but I tried to do only a little bit at the time, since faking it became tiring very quickly.

After lunch, we had some time to ourselves, so I pulled out the notebook I had taken in class this morning to read. I began to have some doubts about our very existence.

Was Buck so obsessed with me just because it was his nature? Did he have any choice at all or would he be forever trapped in a body with an insatiable hunger for sex?

What about me? Had all my decisions I made so far been the results of my own free will or was it genetic? Was my personality even real or was it because they built me this way?

Chapter 45: The Meeting

Many members of the Inferiors' rights group came to the first meeting since my arrival and they walked through the door one by one. Andrew and his wife Joanna came, then Hugh. There was also an old man with sparse grey hair on his head named Ted. He was the deputy mayor, I heard.

Then about fifteen more members came in. They dressed and talked just like any other Superiors on the streets and were virtually indistinguishable from any typical high-classed people, but I had learnt that they were different because they were the people who opposed the use of Inferiors.

"You are coming too." Joanna led me into the conference room with a long rectangular wooden table in the middle of the room with surrounding chairs on all sides. Mikayla came in as well, since she was the boss of the Inferiors in the facility.

We sat there, just the two shitty and worthless creatures among the council of angels. Even though I had known that these were good people, my body still remembered to respect and fear them. It was a nerve-wracking experience to be surrounded by so many of my natural predators.

"Almost everyone's here. Let's start the meeting," one of the female members in a green dress announced.

"We have to wait for the boss," Andrew said.

"He is always late. And we don't even know if he will come."

"I am sure this is not the case this time. It was his order to bring Cattleya here, so this directly concerns him. We have to wait."

It was five minutes more until 'the boss' arrived. It looked like some were even surprised that he could make it at all, although most emotions surrounding him seemed to be happy. They all went to him like he was some sort of idol. For that matter, he looked even whiter than normal Superiors, like he was radiating with aura of a leader. They asked him how he was doing and complimented him on his work. I wanted to do the same, except that when I stood up and got him to

241

notice me, he stared at me with harsh, cold, and seemingly commanding eyes that caused me to sit down again.

He was the same Brun, even with the extremely Superior appearance; there was no way I could mistake him for somebody else. Completely shaven, but the rest of his hair was all blonde including the eyebrows. His facial features were freakishly white in every single square inch from the 'Superiors make-up'.

"*So, this is Cattleya?*" Brun lifted his eyebrows.

"*Yep,*" Andrew answered.

"*Well done getting her here.*" Brun nodded. I stared at him. From the looks of his face, I knew that he had noticed me, but he only looked at me for less than a second with an unsmiling face and sat down like he did not know me. I kept glancing at him shyly, but he did not look back again for the whole meeting, even when referring to me in the third person.

"*As you know, we have gotten her as you asked. What is the whole story of the mission? Would you mind telling everyone here, Andrew?*" the old deputy mayor asked.

"*Yes, I can, of course. As you all know from the news on television, the Cotter estate accident happened thirteen days ago. The local police were sent to investigate the house after hearing a distress phone call from a woman. After arriving at the scene, they found three men dead. The first one was named...*" Andrew went through the details of the event that I knew better than anyone.

Some facts that were new to me included the news of Charlotte getting admitted to a mental hospital while her two children were now fostered with a relative. I also now knew that the police used a satellite (whatever that was) to locate the microchip within me, so they found me easily in the middle of the forest.

Brun had dispatched of Andrew to retrieve me at the slaughterhouse as soon as he had heard the news of the tragedy. He knew that I would be blamed and captured. He knew that I had no chance of escaping and even predicted where I would end up.

After all, that slaughterhouse was the only one in the area, and it was normal for the police to send Inferior wrongdoers through the normal slaughterhouse process. It was all to keep up the illusion that Inferiors were foolish, helpless, and could not possibly murder a Superior.

Brun had personally funded a large amount of money for this operation alone. It was to bribe various people in the slaughterhouse to spare me. I found out that even if I did not speak in Superior back then, I would still have been alive.

"*So...what do we do with her now?*" the deputy mayor asked.

"*We keep her safe, just like any other Inferiors in this facility,*" Brun said briefly.

"*But... we went to all these troubles to get her out of North Devanta in the first place. That was a long drive, wasn't it, Andrew?*" he said and looked at the detective, who nodded in agreement.

"*We haven't used as many resources as any other Inferiors like this before and you say we did it for nothing?*"

Before Brun could answer, Joanna stepped in.

"*All lives are equal, Ted? Isn't that our slogan?*"

"*But... we are throwing a lot of money for only a single meat Taurine? The money that could be used to rescue so many other abused Inferiors in our own region?*" Ted answered.

"*She is not useless, Mr. Deputy.*"

"*But nobody is more special than others. It's the whole point of this group. If you are treating one better than the rest, then that's not equality,*" Ted replied.

"*But...you can't say that she is not special. She can speak our language perfectly, How about you show them how good you are, Cat?*" The middle-aged woman turned to me.

"Umm...*Hi...everybody, my name is Cat.*"

The room applauded. I tucked my chin down, embarrassed.

"*Well done, Cattleya.*"

"*Congrats, that was amazing,*" Most people had a positive reaction, but Ted was still trying to argue.

"*Is that all? All they do is to repeat things like a parrot.*"

"*How about you give your opinion about this lab, Cat? How did you enjoy it so far?*" Joanna was trying to prove her point to Ted.

"*I...I guess it's good. The facility is great. The people are...nice?*" I lied when I looked at Mikayla's face.

"*You can tell the truth, Cat.*" She smiled back.

"*I don't know those people well, but I heard they are all murderers and no… they are not nice at all. Except for you, Mikayla. Why do you keep so many of them here?*" I spoke the truth this time.

Surprisingly, Brun was the one who answered my question, with emotionless professionalism and without looking at me. "*We rescued them. It's either they are dead or they are here.*"

"*But they are murderers that have killed real people. They could kill you too,*" I said.

"*Well… that's why we have cameras and our warden can shock any of them anytime things get out of hand.*"

"*So you think that if you just shock them, then they will just give in to you? How is it any different than an estate, then? Being watched and shocked whenever we don't do as you like?*" I raised my voice. This time it got his head turning towards me.

"*We are here to give them a better life. It's not right for us to judge them on their past. I know that they can be difficult, but things are getting a lot better. In fact, we haven't even had to shock them many times at all. Please do not judge people you don't know.*"

"*You are telling me that I shouldn't be assuming things with murderers? That I should ignore the fact that they have literally killed someone?*"

He lifted one of his eyebrows. "*How about yourself? Have you not killed anyone?*" It was a simple yet devastating blow. Yet I had to keep going.

"*All I did was self-defense. Nathaniel was going to kill me if I didn't kill him first. It is different from these senseless murderers.*"

Yet he countered my argument again without much difficulty. "*Do you know these people? Have you talked to them in person and thoroughly understood the circumstances that had caused them to do what they did? I doubt it, because you are being racist towards people you don't even know, little girl.*" The way he said it left

244

me stumped for answers and the whole room was left with nothing but awkward silence.

"*Thanks, Cat. That will be all for her today.*" Joanna finally broke the ice and the room applauded again. She also announced that we were having a break. Everyone started to chat with each other.

"*Wow! Such thick Northern accents. Both of you sounded like you came from the same place?*" a man in a business suit said.

"*No, never seen her before,*" Brun said.

"*So cute... she is so smart.*" A few young female Superiors came straight to me with very smiley faces. They put their hands over my light brown hair and started stroking.

"*What are you doing?*" I scowled at them, yet they refused to pull their hands away and kept on doing it. A few others even joined in. Some others were doing the same thing to Mikayla as well.

"*Give me your hand,*" one of them demanded. I failed to understand the reason for her request, so I ignored her.

"*Don't you know how to shake hands?*" she said to me. Then turned her head towards the others. "*I don't think she is that smart. She doesn't even know how to shake hands!*"

"*How about roll over? Can you do that? Come on! Roll over!*" The other one did some sort of hand movement.

"*Silly... she can't even shake hands, so how can she know how to roll over?*" The first woman rebuffed her friend.

"*Please... leave me alone,*" I said coldly.

"*Oh! She talked again. So cute, let me hug you.*" This time they violated my privacy severely by giving me vigorous rub all over my belly. I had enough when one decided to suddenly kiss me on my lips.

"*Fuck off!*" I shouted and pushed them all away. It took me by surprise, so I did not manage to back away in time. Her red lipstick-stained lips left a deep mark on mine, which I immediately wiped away in disgust.

They all immediately backed away and looked offended.

"*I guess she has a bad temper. We better leave her alone or she might bite us,*" one of them said and they all walked away.

The meeting resumed not long after and Ted continued the argument with Joanna. They concluded there was nothing to be done since it was all in the past and I was already here, so Ted gave in, but made sure to let us know that he did not approve of me being here.

"I won't claim that it was the best decision to rescue a single meat Taurine out of death row with that much money. I know her life isn't worth much and I don't think the world will even notice if she live or die in that place," he said to apologise for his mistake.

The meeting ended with Brun hurriedly exited the building without even looking back at me. All he left was the instructions that I would live here like a normal resident, learning lessons about the Superior world in the morning and helping with language teaching in the afternoon. However, everything was to be confined within. I would not be able to go to the outside world ever again.

I exited the boardroom with my head hanging down. It was a terrible feeling knowing that my life was nothing to Brun. He rescued me because he wanted to make up for when he got me captured and nothing more. Now that we were even, he would not need to care about me anymore. I felt so empty inside. I knew all along that he was the boss and was looking forward to meeting him. I wanted to hug him and thank him for caring for me.

I knew that he was the only person who would even remember me, even if we were five countries apart. Now that he had rescued me. But then what? He could not stay with me and I knew how wrong I was to even think that in the first place. I was an animal and he was my master.

Chapter 46: Forbidden Relationship

I had not seen Brun for several weeks since my first arrival, but he suddenly appeared, which caused my heart to throb uncontrollably the whole time. My palms were sweaty, and I kept looking at him, thinking about what to say to him after the conference. I did not listen to a word of the meeting at all. When it was over, he quickly stood up and left as soon as he could. I had to run to catch him and managed to grab him by his coat. He turned around.

"Can I help you?" he asked distantly, but I had no words in return. I simply stared at him like the dumb Taurine that I was and an awkward silence ensued until he gently pushed away my grip on his clothes and strode away. I could not do anything, but watched him go. I quickly ran back to my bedroom and started weeping.

"Can I come in?" The owner of the voice knocked on the door.

"Come in," I said while struggling to control my sobbing.

The girl with red hair came in and locked the door behind her. She sat down next to me, now hiding behind my blanket on my bed. She gave me a pink handkerchief, which I used to my tears away.

"So you know him before coming here?" she asked.

"No, no, no, no. We didn't."

"Was he someone important to you?" She ignored my lie.

I thought hard about it about the taboo surrounding my secret. Anyone who heard me would certainly kill me for it. I had a forbidden relationship with a Superior. Not only that, it was the boss of the Inferior rights group. But it was Mik who had been so good to me. So what was there to hide?

"Yes, he was my boyfriend," I answered her.

"Brun? Really? I figured as much." She smiled in answer and was surprisingly calm about it.

I explained it to her about our history together. I emphasised that she should not tell a soul about it and she agreed. I knew I could trust her.

"So you still feel something for him, huh? That's tough when he doesn't want you. But I think he is just keeping up appearances. After

all, it is not accepted even in the Rights group to have a cross-species relationship. I don't think he means to hurt you."

"*You might be right.*" I gave it a thought and was finally able to smile.

Chapter 47: Survival of the Strongest

A few months passed. Apart from the small patch of a garden outside, I had never had a chance to connect with nature. There were a few trees on the patches of grass, but we were otherwise surrounded in all directions with tall buildings. There was a bench where I often sat on and a fish pond I often stared at idly.

It was a quiet place for relaxation, but I was frequently upset about the state of the pond. It would often dry up. In the desert, there was not much rain at all. A Sanga who was assigned to fill the water would not do it, no matter how many times I had complained to him. It was the puzzled look on his face every time I brought the issue up that made me give up trying to reason with him and do it myself instead. I pretty much owned this place anyway, since nobody else used it.

This time, I found the pond more than a quarter empty, so I felt a little sorry for the fish. It was the only home they had, since they could not go anywhere else. They were at my complete mercy. If I turned a blind eye and never filled the pond, they would just die on the spot without being able to do anything. It was just like us, the Inferiors, who had no voice of our own.

I had forgotten it all about Brun. We were both better off this way and it was a waste of time to think about it. I was grateful to him that I was able to live in possibly the best place for an Inferior. I had Mikayla, anyway, and she was my new best friend who I could trust with my utmost secrets.

I called her Mik and she called me Cat. She was always full of life, extremely nice and kind to everyone. She was a leader who genuinely liked her job and the smile on her face never disappeared. She was the reason I enjoyed living here at all.

Living among the 'special' Inferiors was not easy at first. Most of them left you alone, but Buck and the pompous girl Kim liked to bother me especially. Buck constantly followed my tail like a little puppy hungry for love. He still walked around after me and cried for attention.

"Buck likes to fuck!" he liked to call out. I thought he was not doing any harm, so I simply ignored him. One day, I found him sitting directly behind me in the classroom, looking very suspicious. He flashed his junk to me from under the table.

When he did, I feigned ignorance, but simply hooked my legs under his desk and shoved it hard to the side. He was caught with his pants down in front of the classroom. He ran away, denying as he went and with huge laughter behind him.

A week after, he came back to take revenge on me as I was doing my night study. When Mik left our bedroom, he pulled the door open before I could close it.

"What are you doing here all alone at night?" He had done this many times in the past, waiting for my friend to leave so that he could talk to me alone, but never once that he had invaded my room directly like this.

"It's none of your business," I said coldly, but turned around on the chair to face him. I put on a brave face despite being scared.

"Well… a hard-working girl, I see. You are looking at writing and stuff. Very smart… very smart girl. I like you."

"Go away, I don't need your compliments."

"Buck has lots of love to give. Lots of big love. Do you want Buck?"

"How many times have I say that I want you? Never. Now, just shut up and go back to your room. I am busy," I said.

Out of the blue, his big hairy hand launched at me and grabbed mine. I struggled but he dragged me out of my chair like nothing. His grip was unbendingly strong. He finally pushed me up against a wall.

"You think I am stupid?" He scolded me. His face was tense with anger.

"Yes, you are. Very stupid,"

"Bitch!" He shouted and used his other hand to smack me from behind. The slap hurt only a little because he punched my upper back out of all places.

"You are a girl! A girl meat Taurine! So you must give yourself to me. You are me wife. Wife needs to obey husband. I did many things for your affection but you are ignoring your husband," he shouted as he twisted my arms around to my back.

"I am not your wife, you fucking freak!"

He pulled my pants down, but at the same time, my feet went backward and landed on his crotch. His hands let go of me immediately. He dropped down onto the floor and writhed in pain while holding onto his traumatised groin where my kick had landed with full force. I pulled my pants up and kicked him many more times just to make sure he stayed down. It wasn't until he was begging for mercy for about the fourth time that I stopped.

I only realised that there were a great number of spectators watching the show. Since he was crying so much, everyone came. The males mostly had a surprised look on their faces. Even Kim, who had tried constantly to harass me, looked scared. Hicks the circus murderer had a sardonic smile on his face. While Mikayla was running to me, she asked whether I was all right. I said yes and we got out of there. That was the night I had gained a considerable amount of respect. Strength was a universal way to show dominance.

In terms of other things, I had gained a fair bit of knowledge from regular studies. There were guest Superiors who came to teach us different topics every time. I was pressing the members of the Rights group in every meeting about changing the teaching protocol. I told them that most of the Inferiors were simply not interested in classes. So we ended up with only me, Mikayla, and Kim, all of whom were assessed to be intelligent enough to get anything out of it.

For the others, the Superiors found technical jobs such as machinery, art, gardening, cooking, and many others for them to do instead. On the subsequent meetings, the talk of the success of this new project was overwhelming. Not to be racist or anything, but it was clear that many people here were born to do these types of jobs and they did them well.

There were so many times that I had voiced an opinion in the meetings. After observing me, Mikayla was brave enough to voice all her opinions in the meetings of the Inferior rights group.

I also studied about the true history of the world. Andrew was a really good history teacher. He was very kind and patient with me. In fact, almost every lecturer was excellent. He told me that there was a war five hundred years ago between the races. The blonde hair/blue eyes race thought themselves to be the divine race, coming down from heaven, sent down by God to rule the world. With their supreme technology at that time, they won the war. After the war, they called themselves the Superiors. Before that, it was Aryan.

Everybody else fell into slavery while they made themselves the rulers of the world. I went as far as asking Andrew for more private lessons when it was busy for everybody else, including Mik. I promised to write things down and tell it to her afterward.

Superiors like to think of themselves as a different species than the other humans, even though that was never true. Although this fact was denied persistently by the government, the Superiors lied that we had been predator/prey, master/slave since the ancient times to make it more believable that it was God's intention, as if it had been like this since the beginning of the world.

Every book and writing that could potentially undermine this false fact was burned away or replaced with made-up information. Andrew said that truth would not even exist within the deepest governmental archives. It would just crash this whole system if it was to be revealed to the public. To keep up the deception, everyone, even the highest of the Superior kings, would need to have no doubt of this faulty fact.

"Then how do you know this, Andrew?" I asked him before he explained in detail about a great historian.

This man, who had travelled to many civilisations of ruins where he deciphered countless languages in different locations around the earth, once gave Andrew this particular knowledge when he was little. He was long dead, but before his demise, he was deemed a lunatic by the entire population at the time and was executed by the government. Nowadays, there was not even an acceptable theory in any place, even among the people of the Inferior rights group.

"He was my father," Andrew said.

252

Chapter 48: No More an Inferior

In the afternoon, I would spend a lot of time in the testing room with Joanna to assess my language skills. She would give me something, such as a story, to remember and tested me. Hugh came in occasionally to do the physical side of things. I was examined by her often, as she made me eat specific food for an experiment and took my blood frequently. In exchange, she gave me an offer.

"I will take that microchip out of your neck if you want," she said one day.

"But...how?" I was puzzled.

"Surgery, of course."

"So you will cut my neck? Ugh..." Imagining it was more than enough to give me goosebumps.

"I am just going to cut a really small hole at the back. It will be quick and easy."

"Are you sure I won't die?" I rubbed the side of my neck.

"Probably not. It will be just five minutes and you don't even have to go to sleep."

"Okay..." I was nervous.

"First, I'll confirm that it's there." She ran a small electric instrument along my neck. My body was feeling tingly as it anticipated a painful spasm from the device. I knew that the tiny gadget in her hand could hurt me pretty badly, or possibly even kill me if she wanted to. But nothing happened. She did not fire the button that had been keeping me and a hundred million more people enslaved.

Beep, beep. The device found the signal in a spot and displayed the thirteen-digit number. In the Superior viewpoint, our names were not important. We were not living beings, but simply numbers and statistics.

"Yes, it's there. So, will you do it?"

"What about the rules? Everyone here still has a chip, right? Why should I be the one who has the privilege?"

"Mikayla had it removed too. I think we all know you enough."

"But... I am a meat Taurine. What if I go crazy and kill someone?"

"I know that you won't. You might not think so, but you are a nicer girl than you realise. You are just as good, if not better, than most Superior girls out there, I assure you."

I blushed and nodded with a shy smile. "Thank you, Hugh."

To cut it out would mean that the last possible control over me would be gone. I would be immune to all the remotes, including the satellite from outer space that had located me in the deep forest. Since the Superiors had outlawed most older weapons, such as guns and knives, to prevent their people from killing each other, and with mass-produced electrical weapons to control the Inferiors, there would not be many things left that could stop me. If there was no microchip, could I still possibly be considered an Inferior?

"Yes, I will do it," I finally answered.

I was scheduled for the following week, but the day came faster than I had expected. I woke up extra early that morning because of my nerves and proceeded to walk back and forth in the garden outside. It was more comfortable this way.

As soon as it was eight o'clock, a few Superior nurses came in and told me to follow them. I hugged Mikayla for the last time before leaving. She smiled and assured me that I would be all right. After that, I exited the building with the nurses. They put me on a bed and told me to stay still. The surgeon soon came and injected some painful shots that numbed my skin and I could not feel a thing anymore. Then it was done in ten minutes.

"That was quick," I said to my doctor, then thanked her and walked out. She told me to keep the bandage on today and not to let it get wet until it healed.

"You made it." Mikayla, who was waiting outside hugged me.

"That wasn't so bad," I said.

"How do you feel?"

"I'm hungry," I answered truthfully.

We had a meal together in the dining hall. She brought me the food she made from the Inferior cooking lesson today and it was delicious. I was beginning to think that our little rescued Inferiors looked more like a Superior society every day.

Chapter 49: Chimera

Days later, I was called into the meeting room alone with Hugh, Joanna, and Andrew.

"I've got some news for you, a serious matter. In fact. I want you to promise not to discuss this with nobody else other than those who are present in the room." Hugh looked at the husband and wife in turn.

"*Okay*," I agreed unsurely.

"*Your turn, Jo?*" Hugh signaled to the researcher, who stepped in front. In her hand was a strand of hair. It was brown, yet reflected off bright blond colored at the tip.

"*This is your hair, Cat,*" she said. "*I've sent it to the lab for the DNA analysis.*"

"*Yes, it looks kind of like mine,*" I said. My heart was beating fast as I remembered the fact that I gave her my hair to her two weeks ago in the lab.

"*The result came back and they're not pretty.*"

"*What do you mean? My DNA is not good?*"

"*You are what we call a chimera.*" Her face remained worrisome. I had a feeling that it could not be a good word, but I let her speak. "*Chimera is the word for a mythical creature. But you are somehow one of them. You are a half meat Taurine, half Superior chimera.*" She paused.

Jo explained in detail why it was an impossibility. In the history of Superior rules, there had never been such hybrid such as me before. The common notion was that the angelic race could never have sex with mere humans. It was physically impossible and there could never be a viable offspring.

Yet, here I was, listening, talking, thinking, existing, and I shouldn't.

I left the room quietly without even saying anything to my rescuers. That night I spent the time holding myself inside the blanket and could not sleep. "It can't be right." I kept telling myself. I was just a normal girl, not a monster.

The next morning, I took the usual class during the day, but could not concentrate. *I am a meat Taurine.* My mother told me so. I kept repeating "I am a meat Taurine" to myself over and over again. Eventually, I stopped talking to anyone, because if I had to talk, it would be in the Superior language. I feared that my genetics had been leading me all these times. I was a Chimera; that was why I looked like a meat Taurine, yet I spoke in Superior.

The voice in my head persisted for who knew how long.

"You are a chimera," the voice said. "Disgusting! You are a mistake! Accept it! Acce[t that you are nothing but trash that your mother threw away!"

"No! I'm not!" I screamed out of nowhere in the night. It caused Mik to turn on the light and rush to me.

"Are you okay, Cat?" She touched my forehead to check for a fever. I refused to answer her and turned away. She remained silent until I heard her walk over to the light to turn it off.

Many nights that I had gone through this cycle of self-pity and complete refusal to utter a word to anyone apart from the indecent Buck, who I had now chosen to hang out with all the time. It was to his pleasant surprise, of course, that I would always go to his table and talked to him exclusively.

However, I never did comply with his sexual requests, despite being asked daily. He knew who the boss was, so he did not dare to try anything funny.

Despite my desire to be a good meat Taurine for once, I could not bring myself to let my dignity go and bend over like the good wife my mother had wanted me to be. That reminded me that I was still different.

My friend Mikayla never stopped trying. It was her persistence that made me begin to crack one night. She was asking one more "Are you okay?"

"Help me, Mik!" I finally opened up to her, feeling extremely nervous that I might have made the wrong move.

"Cat." She smiled so widely. I could see the utmost pleasure in her eyes. Then I wept. With my body instinctively drawn towards hers, I put my face on her chest, just as I had done with Brun.

"I am not a monster. Am I, Mik?"

"No, you are just you. You did nothing wrong. It was the fault of whoever made you."

"You mean my father? Who is he? A Superior? And my mother...I know her but ... I never knew how evil she was. She must have tempted him."

"You can't assume that, but that is beside the point. You are still you, Cattleya, and always will be you."

"Maybe, but what do you know about that? I still shouldn't exist."

" I know what it feels like to be an outcast, in fact. I thought that I shouldn't even be alive at that time. But I didn't give up. So here I am."

" Tell me..." I pleaded.

Despite having been together for months, I had not heard a full story of how Mikayla came to be yet.

She told me that in the milk industry, females were bred so much for their milk that the size of their breasts would be twice that of any other races. She, along with other milk Taurines, were forced to be pregnant every single year. Parturitions were essential to let the body know to produce milk. The milk Taurine females were the heart and soul of this industry and they were the workers who were usually driven to the extreme.

Because of their genetics, they could be milked so much that their bodies were unable to cope. Even if they wanted to stop, their bodies could not, and they would keep lactating until they ran out of nutrients. It was essential that they kept eating as much as possible to prevent this from happening, to replace the energy and minerals that were constantly leached out into the milk every single day.

In every estate, girls collapsed frequently and some never stood up again. The highest lifespan of a milking female was about eighteen years old, starting as early as eight years old. They were bred to reach puberty even earlier than the meat Taurines. Every single year, they were forced to conceive a new baby to produce milk for that year. Milk would run out after nine months, then another baby would be needed again. No baby meant no milk; no milk meant that they would be turned into meat.

Babies were immediately taken away as soon as they were born so that all the milk meant for them could be squeezed and collected for the consumption of Superiors instead. Mother and child were allowed no chance to be bonded so there would no sadness in their partings; that was what the Superiors said. Mikayla said that she already had had five babies.

"*I remember them all*," she said.

She talked about a lesson of how to love, the type of men she should be interested in. I could relate so much with her at this point that I started to ask her lots of questions enthusiastically. I told her that I had been taught the same thing, but the only difference from mine was the type of men. For Mik, she was only meant to love men with red hair.

In the final year of her life in the estate, Mik had difficulty conceiving, even though she was getting inseminated by the males. No matter how much she tried, she was not getting pregnant. In her desperation, she stripped herself naked and walked around the field to advertise herself. It was a dirty tactic, unapproved by the other girls, but it worked wonderfully.

All of the men, big and small, no matter the personality, came to her. It was a big estate with a thousand girls and fifty studly men at the time. She received the attention of all fifty.

"*It was not rape,*" she said. "*I wanted it. No... I needed it.*"

Even now she said she did not regret it, because not conceiving meant certain death. It was the only way to live. Unfortunately, it still did not work. There was something wrong with her body. Unsurprisingly, she was sent off to a slaughterhouse when the mating season ended and she was still had nothing.

However, the truck flipped over in an accident. There happened to be a couple of Inferior lovers driving behind, and it was then that she was adopted by them. They took pity on her and paid the truck driver to purchase her life. She was moved to a house with a small area in the back where a few other Taurines were raised without getting taken advantage of. The owners were kind and they treated her like a pet. They even gave her the name Milkshake. However, for work-related reasons, they were forced to move house, so she was given to the Inferior hospital as a donation.

"*I didn't even want to think of letting a single stranger have sex with me, but you...fifty men?*" I could not help but make a disgusted face. I did not meant be rude to my friend, but I just could not resist.

"*Probably more than that; fifty was just that year. And of course, I did it many times with each of them, so I don't know. But at the time it was in my best interest to do that. I just wanted to survive.*"

"*No, I am not calling you a slut or anything. I just feel bad for girls who have to live through those kinds of things. I would rather die than to do that.*"

"*You are a strange girl. I thought all Taurines are supposed to always want it. So...have you had one yet? Copulation, I mean.*"

"*I...um...*" I couldn't say it, but I felt my face go all red with embarrassment.

"*You have? With Brun?*" She read me like a book. There was a big smile on her face.

I felt myself go even redder.

"*I am just teasing you. I just wish my experience could be like yours. If they were worth getting shy about, they had to be pretty good. All I can remember is the pain.*"

"*I am sorry for bringing this up.*"

"*Don't worry about it. It was what happened to everyone in our industries, anyway, and nobody is embarrassed about it. It's better to move on. It is, after all, what you do in the present that is more important, and my goal now is just to be a good and happy person.*"

"*I think I will too,*" I finally said and smiled.

Chapter 50: Back Home

"We will take you there." Joanna finally gave in after I had pestered her and Andrew for a week. My request came as extreme shock to everybody when I told them that I wanted to go 'home'. Not Larringtons' estate, or the forest, but the place where I was born. Where my mother was and possibly my father as well. With a help of Hugh, who had analysed the microchip I had inside of me, we found out which the exact name of the estate of my birthplace.

The couple was somewhat reluctant to bring me out of the lab for fear of getting caught, but I reminded them that I had been passed successfully as a Superior girl before.

Not soon after, I found myself sitting in a small black car driving looking across the wide desert once again. Joanna did the research regarding my father and planned the whole trip. We knew who he was, and he owed me an explanation.

The estate where I was born in was named the 'The Estate of Epiphany' located about halfway back towards North Devanta, but in a different direction. I sat in the back while Andrew and Joanna discussed our strategies in front. We came out of the lab without telling anyone else apart from Hugh and Mik, so it was extremely secretive.

During the whole trip, I was so nervous to finally get to see the place I was born. Being just a meat Taurine, it was unlikely that my mother would have survived for eighteen years after giving birth to me.

However, there was a chance to meet my other parent. I was thinking about what I should say to him, and the tension made restless.

At last, after two days, we finally found it. I looked at the area in awe. It was one of the biggest estates in the region and it was nothing like the Larringtons. When we drove up to a large sign scribbling 'The Estate of Epiphany', I vaguely recalled seeing it somewhere in my memory.

The estate was on a flat ground with a large house situated in the distant. Several buildings like the Nest lined both sides of the large central dirt road leading there. However, the place was dead quiet.

262

There was no sign of either brown or blonde lifeforms. I thought that they had to be off working somewhere.

When we were closer to the house, or mansion, to be more accurate, we still could not find a soul. This place looked depressing. There was a large marble fountain, but it was not pouring out any water. Instead, ingrown vines covered most of its barren surface. A massive but disarranged garden was filled with nothing but tall weeds. The mansion itself seemed to be ancient with strange fashion of a few centuries ago. It was painted all white, yet now was stained with rain scald that covered almost the whole building.

Only when we came down of our car and rang the bell did two male Sangas come out. They were in pretty rough clothing and their faces were as unkempt as the garden. The two of them were about the same height. They looked at each other and one sped back up inside the building. After half a minute, a voice could be heard from within the mansion.

"Who is it? What do you want?" It was clearly the voice of an older Superior man who was quite irritated that he had visitors.

"We are here to visit Mr. Wells, sir?" Andrew called back.

"Well... what do you want?" the voice answered.

"I have something to offer you, sir. I know that you might like it, so would you come down here, sir?"

"No, I've got bad legs. You come up here." He then shouted a command to his nearest Sanga to bring us up.

To impersonate a Superior girl, in addition to a brightly colored blond wig on my head, I also had bright blue contact lenses. They were new gifts from Hugh and much better than acting like a blind girl.

I was kind of nervous about my presentation because of the one-piece white dress Jo had chosen for me. It was thin and revealing, as it left a hole on top of my breasts so anyone taller than me could see them if they looked down. It also left the arms, shoulders and most of the legs bare. Apparently, it was a popular type of clothing for young Superior girls, but I had never worn anything like this before.

I stepped inside the unknown building and found it to be just as bad as the outdoors. The building smelt of antiquity, of wetness and of

263

mold. The ceilings was full of spider webs, random objects were lying around, and the floor was full of dust.

When we entered the bedroom, a balding scrawny old man was sitting on a small table next to the window. The room was dark because all the curtains were closed except for the one the man was next to. He scrutinised us with his large eyes. Unlike the other Superiors, he did not have any make-up on his face and the little leftover hair on his head was entirely white. Everything made him looked like a sad pitiful old man rather than a proper Superior.

"*Who are you?*" he asked.

"*My name is George Danlingford. This is my wife Georgia, and my daughter Hazel. I heard that, you, Mr. Wells, were looking for a young woman to marry.*"

"*That's true. Where did you hear that?*" The old man raised his voice and opened up a little.

"*Mrs. Esterdam's auction down in the Raldon last month. A colleague of mine informed me of your wish. Anyway, he told me that Mr. Wells, the very owner of the great Estate of Epiphany, had been looking for a young wife to marry for some time now.*"

"*You came to offer... her?*" he said and pointed at me. His mouth parted slightly as he thoroughly leered across my body with his eyes. I could see his rotting and crooked teeth through his mouth.

"*What do you think of our daughter, sir?*"

"*Boobs are too small, not young enough and not blond enough!*" the old man yelled, and his spit sprayed everywhere.

"*Sir, maybe you will change your mind after you spend some time with her.*" Joanna said "*Come Hazel, come here and talk to Mister Wells.*" I went past everyone else and stopped in front of the old, depressing-looking man and smiled politely.

"*Isn't she beautiful?*" Joanna uttered. Her eyes were full of excitement. "*She is shy with strangers, but at home she likes to talk a lot, I assure you. Once you get to know her, she will be the most loyal thing that will ever happen to you. She is our only fifth child, you see? And we can't take care of her anymore. But we made her work very hard in our estate. Yes! We, too, are estate owners, so she knows how*" *everything works. We trained her to take care of the house and handle the Inferiors. She is especially great with meat Taurines."*

"No, no, not important, I just want to know if she is a second hand or not?"

"Oh! She is definitely a virgin if you want to ask about that. Always hard working, never touched a boy in her life. This one never strays anywhere, you see? Isn't that right, my darling?" My 'mother' looked at me for confirmation.

"Yes, mother." I answered as was rehearsed.

"She will be the most obedient thing for you to use, Mr. Wells. I can't believe how people let their kids get pregnant at thirteen; it's such a disgrace to our beautiful traditions, sir. I miss the times when the obedient women were considered the best of all. We can't find any nowadays, but here she is, the purest girl you will ever find."

When she finished, I was amazed how good Joanna's acting was. She sounded exactly like a very old-fashioned mother with only one wish: to get her daughter married. From her tone of voice to her body language and facial expression, everything was absolutely perfect.

The old grump hesitated but then finally gave in. *"Maybe I should give her a chance."* He said.

"Of course, sir, you have our permission as parents that you can touch her in any place as much as you want. Strip her to nothing if you want a good look. But may I ask for you to stop yourself from breaking her purity. In the case that you change your mind, she will still be a maiden, sir. Unless you decide to marry her of course, then she is yours to do as you wish." Joanna pulled her husband and exited the room with a big smile.

Chapter 51: A Life's Worth

The old man turned to stare at me, looking from the top of my head to the toes, assessing me with a watchful but expressionless glare, like I was merely an object to be inspected. Every so often, I saw a movement in his throat indicating that he had swallowed something. He stood up from his seat then went across the room to lock the door.

"*So you are from an estate?*" he asked casually.

"*Yes, sir,*" I answered. The nervousness had made my voice quiet, and it suited the character of the shy girl perfectly.

"*What do you do at home?*"

"*I help my parents with work. We run a hundred meat Taurine estate.*"

"*So you are poor after all. No wonder you want to marry me. I don't have much right now either, but I think I can work something out. Now that I'm this old, I figured out that money isn't everything.*"

"*I agree, sir. It is better to have love than money.*"

"*Hmm... You speak well. Smarts will get you very far indeed. You know what? I used to be rich, but now I'm not. I'm just living day to day, using my store up until the day I die. It was very sad, because everything is gone.*"

"*What happened, sir? What do you mean, you lost everything?*"

"*One day, they just came in and burnt everything I had to the ground. Now the only thing I have is this house. I have nothing to give you but love. Sorry. But I believe love will overcome everything. Whatever I do, I just can't help myself but holding up in here every day. But I think that is going to change very soon because of you.*"

I remained quiet.

"*You are not up to my specs, but when I look at you closely, you are cuter than I thought.*" He walked to his bed and lay down, then signaled to me. "*Let me see how you perform in bed. I promise not to break your virginity, but I guess everything else goes.*"

It was quicker than I thought. This man wasted no time at all in trying to pretend to like me. I understood now why Joanna and Andrew were against me doing this plan. They told me that this old man had always been broke, yet he always went to bride auctions to look at teenage Superior girls. He never had any money and me coming here was probably the best thing that had happened to him in a decade. Of course, he would decide to take advantage of it, then refuse the deal after.

"*Wait a minute, I need to wash my mouth first. I just had my lunch and I don't feel comfortable putting it on you, sir.*"

"*Yes, of course, my dear. I'll wait, but don't be long.*"

I went into the bathroom and quickly threw away the blonde wig to reveal my abnormal colored hair underneath. Then I took out the contact lenses quickly and washed the makeup away. When I came out, I found a light switch near the entrance and turned it on. The white light instantly illuminated the dim room. "*I'm ready,*" I said.

"*What? Don't turn on the light. Ugh...*" he muttered and turned around. His mouth opened wide in an astonished expression.

"*Here I am, a meat Taurine. I heard you like brown hair.*"

"*You... Why are you dressing up as a meat Taurine? Is this some sort of a fetish?*"

"*No, this is not a cosplay, you idiot. This is the real me. I AM A MEAT TAURINE.*" I approached him on his most vulnerable position on his own bed.

"*I will not have your dirty feet in my house!*" He pulled out a typical electrocutor remote from a bedside drawer.

He pressed the buttons, but the device did not affect me at all since there was no longer a microchip in my body. "*Work, you stupid thing!*" he said before scrambling away haphazardly with very scared eyes as I made a show to slowly pull my knife out. I put it up to the loose skin of his throat.

"*I'll stick this into you, old man, if you so much as trying to call for help.*" I knew that Joanna and Andrew had already dosed the Sangas below with sleeping pills, but I wanted him to be scared of me.

"*Do you remember me?*" I asked coldly.

"*No! I don't know who you are. Just...just... if you want to take my treasure, then go ahead. Take them all, I don't have anything left to live for anyway. But please, spare me,*" he cried.

267

"You think money can solve everything? I just want to ask you a few things, and then I will decide what to do later depending on your answers. And you haven't answered my first question." I put the tip of the knife right on his skin to the point that it drew some blood.

"Maybe, I don't know. I used to own two thousand Taurines. How can I remember you all?"

"You can. Think carefully; maybe it was someone that you brought in here." He reluctantly looked at my face but was clearly too scared to stare into it for too long.

"Mary? No... Mary? Is it you, Mary?" he cried.

"You are close, but not quite. Because that's the name of my mother."

"You...are her daughter? Don't tell me... you are... her first one. The first child ever to receive my magic touch. But... How is it possible that you are here? You should be in North Devanta gaining fame for the Larringtons. I sent you as a gift for that poor bastard Robert." He opened his mouth wide and let out some ugly chuckles to himself.

"I was a gift?" I could not believe my own ears.

"He was an old friend of mine. Of course, friends must help friends. I heard he wasn't doing very well with his business, so I sent you to him. You are the first product of my magic finger. It is nice seeing that my work is still alive, and you are returning to me." He suddenly grinned creepily.

"I am not staying here with you," I shouted at his face, but he seemed to be in his own world right now, and there was no way I could pull him back out.

"Oh! I forgot that you seem to be intelligent for an Inferior. You can even pretend to speak Superior. Hmph... I might actually be hallucinating right now, because only in dreams can an Inferior animal talk to me. Hahaha!" He laughed to himself.

"That's enough! I am your daughter. Don't you even feel any guilt in sending me to certain death?"

"You claim to be my daughter? But you are an Inferior. You cannot be my daughter. I know that the golden god simply doesn't allow such monstrosity to happen."

268

"This doesn't make any sense. You are my father. The DNA confirmed it."

"It's my magic finger, you ignorant girl."

"What the hell are you talking about? Your magic what?"

"It's a blessing from the golden god himself. I was the one who sprinkled the entire meat Taurine estate with my blessing. It was my magic finger. Have you heard of the hand of Midas? The hand that turns anything it touches into gold?"

"No! What?" I was dumbfounded.

"Mine was the only estate in the world to have such divine power. Many of them have a sprinkle of gold in their hair, just like you do. But you are not the very best of mine, since there is only earth in your eyes, but the sky was in theirs." He was talking like a mad person, yet I understood him, and that made me sad.

"Where are they now? Where is every one that used to live here? Where is my mother?"

"They destroyed them, those governmental bastards. They were jealous of me for having so many of the holy Taurines that I sold for ten times the price. They were so jealous that one day they came in, killed, and buried all two thousands of them in the paddock behind this house."

"Then my mother...Mary..."

"Your mother had it better than them because at least she was useful in her death. She was indeed a good Taurine, despite being that old. I assure you that she was extremely good. Because we had a great cook back then too. From roast, to stir fry, to stew, every bit of her was fine as hell."

Chapter 52: Mother

I was back at the seat of Andrew's car staring out vacantly. It was a sad feeling that filled me from the inside. Yet I could not cry. It was because my mother was dead, but at the same time, she had fulfilled her ultimate destiny.

Andrew and Joanna asked me about the details that I had gotten from my father. They said that they understood that it was probably painful to remember, and it was all right if I decided not to. But I insisted that I could, so I began to tell the story of my life in the Estate of Epiphany. I started with my mother first.

I remembered her as a kind woman with large dark brown eyes and messy curly hair. She was the ultimate definition of good, strong and hardworking, but she was always very compliant with everyone. It was as if her sole purpose of existence was to live for the others. She tried to avoid conflicts at all costs as she would give in to anyone, both to her peers and Superiors.

She wanted me to be like her, and every day she made sure I followed her way of life. She told me to listen to the trainers and obey their every command. She told me to never bend the rules even slightly. She told me to always be kind to others and help them even if it is not my business. She told me to lie down and show my belly to everyone. Although I tried, I could never be like her.

The only reminder of her was the locket in my hand. Even that, I knew it was not her writing. She would never be mischievous enough to learn Superior language. When I showed it to my father, he revealed that it was his gift to her.

I used to hate being so different, the slow-growing body of mine, the colour of my hair and name callings by other girls. 'Mongrel' they often shouted at me. Even other adults called me that. My mother never stood up to them; instead, she would affirm to-me that I was a meat Taurine as much as she was and kiss me on my ugly coloured head.

I never understood why she would send me away until now. Back then, she simply said that it was our duty, that we not question the decision of the estate owner. I did what I was told, but always thought that it was actually because she hated me.

Other children were sold to other estates as well, so it was not strange that I was leaving. In fact, on the day of the departure, many other scared children with their mothers huddled together in a waiting enclosure as instructed by a trainer. The truck came and only the children were ushered up a ramp.

However, in the final moments, I was so afraid. I held on to her with the tightest grip of my life and could not even say anything at all. She was reluctant to let go of me until the trainer told her to. I decided to walk away and not look back. When I nearing the point of no return, all of a sudden, she came running and pulled me back.

"Don't go!"sShe cried.

"Stay out!" the trainer shouted.

"No, I will never." She clung on to me even tighter.

"No.3746 let go of your daughter immediately or you will be punished severely," the greater woman commanded.

"Go fuck yourself," my mother swore. It was the only time in my life that I had seen her putting up a fight with anyone, let alone a Superior. The trainer looked at my mum with an angry expression and blew a whistle.

Instantaneously, two Sanga men jumped on her. They tore me away from her with ease and threw me into the truck. It was too extreme of an event for an innocent child to watch her mother being beaten badly, so I turned away, but the voice could not be shut out. The sound of her scream and cries that those brutal Sangas gave her was still fresh in my memories after so many years.

Initially, I thought it was because she disobeyed the order, so she deserved it. After a while, when I was far away from her, I blamed her for being so weak. I blamed the entire population of Inferiors for being so stupid by letting others control them. They did not even so much as to try to fight back.

It was because they made us this way. Since we were indoctrinated since birth, it was no wonder they managed to keep us all tame for all these times. But I now realised that maybe that could be changed. We needed someone who knew the truth and at the same time, brave enough to stand up to them.

Maybe the only person who could do that was me.

Chapter 53: The Shades Between

"What is this called?" I pointed at a drawing on a whiteboard.

"It's a bear." The combined shout of the children echoed in the hall.

"What about this?" I moved to the next one.

"It's a lion."

"Good work, boys and girls." I smiled widely and clapped and they followed my example. *"Who wants to come up here and draw a dog for me?"*

"Me! Me! Me!" Every single one of them put their hands up.

"Hey! What are you two doing? Logan! Sarah!" I yelled at the two kids who were now fighting across the table. They stopped and looked at me.

"What did you do to her? Logan!" I stared at a fair-haired boy who sat behind a brown-haired girl.

"He didn't do anything, Miss. It was my fault," the little girl in front of him said while looking downward.

"Yeah, I didn't do anything." The boy immediately responded but looked away with the lips pressed tightly together. It was obvious that he was lying.

"Logan! Get out of this room and stand outside."

"Why, Miss Cattleya? I said I didn't do it. She just started punching me out of all sudden."

"Yeah, that's right. You can't blame Logan if Sarah was attacking him first." a red-haired girl called Rosy in front of the room chimed in.

"Yeah! It's Sarah's fault. Poor Logan didn't even try to defend himself." A Zebu boy now joined in, and more children supported the Superior child.

"Enough! All of you, be quiet right now, or I will send you all out!" I shouted. The class went immediately quiet and I resumed teaching. I asked the two kids to stay behind when we were finished.

"I saw what happened." I confronted the little boy with perfect facial features. He looked away from me in disobedience.

273

"I don't know what you are talking about, Miss."

"You pinched Sarah's ears again. I have seen it many times. And I saw you punching her back too. Don't lie to me. You are staying in detention this afternoon and that's final." I used a commanding tone on the spoiled child, who gave an annoyed expression before walking away and sat down at his desk. I was relieved that he did not argue further.

I turned towards the little girl, who did not even look up to me once. Her face hung down, looking ashamed of what she did. I grabbed her hand and led her outside the room, out of the earshot of the boy.

"Sarah." I spoke to her in my mother tongue, which she too would understand, then lowered myself down to her level on the floor. "I know it's not your fault that you lashed out at him like that."

"But I couldn't control myself, Missus. I shouldn't have hit him, a Superior and I'm... only an Inferior. It was wrong of me to do that." Behind her messy brown hair, I could see tears silently run down her cheeks.

"No, sometimes, you've got to stand up for yourself, you know? No matter who they are or who you are. If they are bullying you, then you've got to hit them back. This might be strange for me to say, but I am proud of you, Sarah." I gently parted the hair fringe that covered her face with my fingers to wipe away her tears.

"I want you to stay in the detention with me today, but that's not because you have done wrong, but because the rule is the rule." I stood up and opened the door to the classroom for her to get back in.

I might have used 'no violence permitted in class' as an excuse for her detention, but in reality, it was because a certain politic. If Logan's parents found out that I had punished only their child and not an Inferior in this situation, they would probably get upset and take up the matter with me.

I continued running the detention myself until a male Zebu gardener called in. He told me that I had a visitor. Even though he had a very strong Zebu accent, he was able to communicate well enough with me in the Superior language.

He was a humble and a helpful man, and he came around often so the children often shipped me with him. Nevertheless, his manners and his language seemed foreign to me, so I could never think of being with him. Zebus were pretty hard for me to connect with, since I did not know so much about how they think. Sangas and Minis did not talk at all, and most of the time they just acted like wild animals, so it was hard for me to see them as anything but that. It made me feel terrible, though, that this mindset of mine was not so different than that of a typical Superior.

I told him to watch the kids instead of me and left the room. I wondered that maybe it was Mik or Andrew who came. They had often visited once in a while since I started the teaching job in this suburb a year ago. I lived on site alone, which was pretty far from the lab in the center of Felicity, so it was not often that they would come by.

The last time I spoke to Mik was when she received the permission to lead the lab Inferiors to the outside world. As anyone would have guessed, we discovered that they were doing regular jobs on the streets much better than taking complicated lessons in classrooms.

Living here was nice. The location was beautiful, as it was surrounded by trees and peacefulness. Ted, the ex-deputy was now elected as a mayor, so it was much easier to keep this place a secret.

It was my idea, the school, and all these teaching facilities. I wanted to change the world from the ground up, to start teaching them from a young age to change the false views they had held for generations.

One day, I suggested to the Rights group that changing children was much better than trying to change adults. When it was approved, I passed myself as a Superior teacher, and we managed to get every type of children to classes. We taught them to sit alongside each other and play as equals. It was extremely successful when it came to teaching the common language which they learnt to be fluent in no time, but the racial discrimination was undeniably still present.

We purchased some Inferior children from various estates to save their lives, then put them together in my school, which also acted as a boarding house. However, none of them were born here, and all the kids brought with them the experiences of their old life. That was why we could not start on a clean slate.

275

Superior children were a different matter altogether. Their parents were mostly lovers of Inferiors, because they were the only Superiors around that dared to put their children into a classroom full of Inferior animals. Most of them did not stay here and instead went back and forth from home every day. Yet, they were revered in the classroom just as in the real society.

I was walking with happy thoughts that I would see Mik again but stopped short when the surprise hit me. Sitting along the edge of the garden was a six-foot tall man. In his hand was a bunch of white and purple flowers that I had never seen before. He turned around and our eyes met.

"*Brun!*" I cried out.

"*Hi Cat,*" he said casually.

"*What are you doing here?*"

"*I'm here to give you these.*" He handed me the flowers. I gave them a disapproving look and pushed them away.

"Y*ou don't want them?*"

"*Do I want them? Are you seriously asking me this?*" I said angrily.

"*Why not? These are Cattleya flowers...your namesake.*" He pushed the bouquet up to me again. I shook my head and this time did not even touch it. I distanced myself from him, crossed my arms and stared at him coldly.

"*What are you doing here, exactly?*"

All of a sudden, he said something that shock me.

"*I love you.*"

"*That's why I came here,*" he continued. "*I know it's been five years since our time together in the forest, but I have been unable to stop thinking about you. I tried to forget but I just couldn't.*"

"*That's a lie. You never liked me,*" I said flatly.

"*Why do you say that?*"

"*You sold me out to your dad so that you could return to being a Superior again.*"

"*You know that's not true. My dad called Nathaniel and I was just as shocked as you. I am sorry for what happened. I really am. Let me make it up to you however I can,"* he replied. I knew that what he was telling was the truth or else he would not have helped me after that. His statement made me shaky.

"You have done enough. You saved me from the slaughterhouse and you gave me this life. For that, I am grateful. But you..." I felt my heart throbbing from the sadness and once again I felt like the vulnerable little girl I was years ago. *"You ignored me. I didn't think you loved me anymore."*

"Of course I do. I think about you every day. In the morning, at mealtime, at night, Every single day, I would imagine you with your smile sitting beside me and walking with me. But then I would realise that you aren't, and I would get sad. I love you, Cat. You are everything that I have ever wanted."

"Me...Me too. I have always thought about you. But it is still not right." I paused.

"Look at me!" I opened my arms and looked at him straight in the eyes, showing him my new features, the long light blond hair and the sky-blue eyes that this world had decided was the ultimate form of beauty.

"All these are fake," I said. *"But this is who I am now, pretending to be like them. Yet... I agree with them. The world can't be united, Brun. People will always be separated because the stupid do the work, and the smart should rule the world. I like it. I like this life and the privilege that comes with it. But underneath, I am only an Inferior."* I gave my speech. Before he could interrupt, I continued on.

"Do you know what 'ya' means in my language?" I asked him, and he shook his head.

"It means tame. *That's right. My name is 'tamed cattle,' as my mother had named me. Nobody even pronounces it right. It's* cattle-ya, not cattle-lee-ya. *Cattle, the legendary animal known for obedience. They followed each other everywhere and did what the humans told them to do. I'm not those beautiful animals, Brun. My mother wanted me to be like them, but I failed her. Not only that, I have become what I tried to vanquish."*

"You are neither of them, Cat. And you don't have to be."

"That's right. I am a Chimera." I pulled the blond wig off my head out to reveal my true grotesque hair. "Look at me now; can you still love this?"

He reached out and gently took some of my hair in his hand. While he was holding them under the light of the sun, it glowed lightly

"Beautiful," he said. "Look Cat, your hair. It's brown at the root,s but it's blond when I put it up to the sun. You have both colours in one."

"See? It's brown and blond but it's not fully either."

"Actually, it is both, Cat. This colour is called 'ombre'. Ironically, its origin is in the Superior language. You are not a monster, but a living proof that Superiors are wrong. Your existence alone announces that the unity between the races is possible."

"Ombre…"

"Yes, ombre. It means shading," he said. "Even today, underneath this blond dye, my heart is still as brown as ever. I too am neither a Superior nor an Inferior. When I returned to my father, the government took and tortured me. I am damaged goods, Cat. But I never gave in because of you."

"Wait! You were tortured?"

"Well…my body is a bit crooked from that. But I gave in because I wanted to be able to get out of prison as soon as possible to help you. I said whatever they wanted but my heart had never betrayed you."

"I am sorry you had to go through that, and I blamed you. I am truly a monster, am I not?"

"You are not a monster, Cat," he replied. "Because I know you have been working very hard to change this world and you always look so happy when teaching the children." He signaled to the classroom.

"You were spying on me?" I uttered, incredulous in his action.

"Only a few times a week," he replied with laughter and it had an effect on me.

"Yeah, not creepy at all," I remarked sarcastically. Well... it was not too bad if it was Brun, after all. When I was done, we had an awkward silence.

"So, let me ask you again. Will you be my girlfriend, Cat?"

Without speaking another word, I walked towards him with butterflies all inside my belly and a red face from flushing so heavily. I stared at his light blue eyes, and he stared back at me. There was never even a split second that we averted away from each other until the last moment. I closed my eyes, stood on my toes, and kissed him.

Chapter 54: The End of the World

When I was twenty-one years old, Brun and I married each other secretly. There was no ceremony. We simply promised to ourselves to keep each other company, to never look at other men or women, and to stay together until one of us died. Then I moved into Brun's house near the great river surrounding the city. Because of that, I learnt to drive on my own so that I could bring myself to teach the children in the morning. He loved me for the way I was and insisted that I never put any dye over my ombre hair.

Brun always treated me nicely and made me feel like the luckiest girl in the world. Not only did we both like to be surrounded by nature, but we also shared a lot of common interests. If something interested him, I would get interested too. If it was something I had no idea about, I would still support him fully.

When going out together, we often preferred to share our moments quietly, and away from the crowds. Often we found ourselves making out with each other in a quiet corner while busy carnivals and dances were going on. We loved and cherished each other as companions as well as lovers.

Shortly after we were married, another life awoke inside of me. It was a boy and we gave him the name 'Ahredden' which meant 'rescuer'. He was a tiny little thing with a tuft of brown hair. For some reason, the look he had was completely meat Taurine despite being three-quarters Superior, so we pretended that he was a male meat Taurine we had adopted.

Everyone in the Rights group believed it, since he did not look anything Superior. Even the fact that I was Brun's wife was never known to anyone but my favorite superiors and Mikayla. The others thought that I simply lived as a housemaid for Brun and nothing more. Even then, nobody thought it was possible for a Superior to have an offspring with such a union. We decided to have no more babies since it was too risky, but before I could talk about the options, Brun secretly got himself sterilised by a doctor.

The boy grew up very smart. His mind was equal, if not better than, that of a normal Superior child, but he had the physique of a meat Taurine. He was strong, agile, and good at sports. Not long after he joined my youngest class, he quickly became the top student. Despite his achievement, he remained a gentle and kind boy.

Brun would go away for weeks or months at a time. I knew that he had to take care of the Rights group in other cities, and he also owned a business. He was getting more and more famous as time went on as the guy who fought for Inferiors. The law in this country was not as strict as in North Devanta regarding the absolute authority of the Superiors, so he got away with it for a long time. He became a hero to many people, but many more hated him.

When he was gone, I would wait for him at home with Ahredden. There would often be just the two of us in a small house that Brun had bought for us. Our son would often ask where his father was, but there was rarely an answer I could give him.

Due to his work to help protect the Inferiors, Brun also went overseas to the much poorer countries where Inferiors were presumably treated much worse than here. It was one of these trips that finally got him killed. He was pushed over a cliff by a male milk Taurine—because it was a breeding season, they said. But I hardly believed them, as I found the circumstances of his death extremely suspicious.

I tried to remain completely unfazed on the day, but as Ahredden came to ask me where his dad was, I cried my heart out in front of him, and I was sure that he knew what happened then and there. Thereafter, we spent our time comforting each other throughout the night.

Brun's death changed me. I was sometimes depressed and thought about the hopelessness of this world, how we would all remain forever the slaves of the Superior people. However, my boy, who had been drilled by both of us about the unfairness of this system, never gave up on me. He kept telling me that one day, we would achieve it.

Everything changed when I was thirty years of age.

It did not stop raining for the sixth day in a row. Even though the city had been draining very well, the water level of the river was rising rapidly. There was fear within me, a thought that the city would be destroyed one day, but never this soon.

Each day the water was rising higher; every time I looked at the water it rose. All I saw was the impending doom reflecting back, but I had to wait for my love to come back. The city announced an evacuation but he was still traveling so I made my decision to move on without him. I had driven out the city and had no idea how to go to the mountain before, so I chose to go with the city bus.

I had my disguises on, but my son did not, since there was never any need for him to put one on. Everybody knew his features were very a meat Taurine-like, so it was impossible to change him into a Superior. Even so, I decided to join the city people. I thought that many of them would have their Sangas, Zebus or Minis with them, but I was wrong.

Amidst the stormy rain, I quickly parked my car in a public space, exited, and went against the blustery squalls with my son, both of us clad in thick rain jackets and gumboots. The wind was so strong it nearly blew my little boy away. Also, there was water everywhere and it was soaking through even the inside of my jacket with its unpredictable angle. Some corner of the street were already lightly flooded, so it was difficult to walk through. As I approached one of the evacuation staff, I put my son at the side of me to show him clearly to the officer, but he looked at both of us with haughty eyes.

"*Why are you bringing a meat Taurine child with you?*" An officer in uniform asked.

"*He's...*" My son, I wanted to say.

"*Can't you see, Miss? We are in a hurry right now. Look at this bus. What does it say?*" He pointed his finger at the writing.

"*Superior only, no Inferior allowed.*"

"*Let me tell you what, Miss. Even expensive Sangas and Zebus aren't even allowed on, so why do you think you can just waste space for your stupid pet Taurine? You need to leave all your unnecessary belongings or I will have to refuse you the seat.*"

I remained silent despite the immense anger boiling within me. Without answering, I turned around and strode off. The officer insulted me by implying I was a madwoman, but I ignored him. We got back in my car and drove off. I would not beg for Superiors' sympathy since I could just as easily save Ahredden by myself.

"That guy hated me because I'm a meat Taurine?" my son suddenly asked.

"No, he doesn't hate you. He hates me because I have the most beautiful boy." I gritted my teeth. It was painful to know that I was completely helpless to spare my son from unwarranted prejudices. It was stupid of me to even choose to go with the others in the first place.

I knew where I needed to go. I knew which roads would be filled with water and which roads would not. This knowledge was what I had learned from the previous floods. I took my son and brought some essentials with me into our car and I drove off.

We faced some traffic jams as people were all escaping the city at once, but we finally succeeding in exiting Felicity. The final part was incredibly scary because I had to drive past a low area where it had become like a pond. I was glad that I was driving a tall car so the water was not high enough to get to the engine.

The rain was still pouring down without any sign of slowing down. The drops were numerous and massive to the point that they would blind my windshield if I did not turn the wipers up to maximum speed. As I drove, multiple lightning strikes were going on throughout the Plain of Merriment. With each, a terrifying roar of thunder that shook the sky followed. I told Ahredden that it was going to be all right even though I was having some doubts myself. The end was coming, I could feel it, but I had to keep driving until we reach the tall mountain in this area. There, we would wait together for the water level to reduce.

There were many cars on the road, both big and small. Many of them were heading up towards the same hill as us. After two hours later in the slowest lane, we finally made it up to the base of the mountain. The path skyward was treacherous as it was filled with loose soil on excessively wet ground and steep slopes. On the way, I could see an unusual number of meat Taurines on the hills who looked at us strangely. I thought that the weather had made them upset. For some reason, they were hanging around outside in the pouring rain instead of staying indoors.

I was very relieved that we made it up to the highest point that the car could go. The resort on top here boasted a nice view overlooking the Plain of Merriment and the city of Felicity, and it was a popular location for holidays. It was not long after when I could feel the earth rumble. The ground shook violently from side to side. Then suddenly, a massive wave of water came flushing into the plain below. Then Felicity took a massive hit from its own water source.

The sturdy buildings did not appear to be affected, but the streets were immediately filled with torrential liquid. From up here, I could not see the details of its inhabitants, but I thought about possibly thousands of poor Inferiors who were left to their deaths.

A hundred cars of escapees had chosen this mountain as their sanctuary, but none of them dared to go outside their vehicle, because the rain was still mercilessly coming down. About an hour later, strange intimidating steps and the accompanying splashing of water were heard from all directions.

Strong and masculine meat Taurine women appeared. Their dark brown hair fell sloppily because of the heavy pouring rain. Yet none of them was wearing a raincoat. They did not look afraid like any of the Superiors in the cars, but instead, their expressions were ones of anger. There were not one, but hundreds of them, surrounding us. Their hands held various kinds of tools.

"*Get out of your fucking car!*" one of them shouted. Surprisingly, it was Superior language. Instead of heeding the instruction, I locked my automobile. No other car dared comply either. When they saw our defiance, the Taurines sounded their battle cry and attacked. They stormed every one of the cars, including mine, and started smashing. One of them, with a ferocious look in her eyes, kept bashing the windows with a rock until it broke. I could not do anything to stop them, but instead, I held on to my brave son, who only now broke into his first cry of the day.

When the windscreen was gone, they reached over and unlocked the door. After that, we were dragged outside where the wig on my head fell off and was immediately walked over by other Taurines. Both my

284

son and I were thrown on the ground and ordered to sit down with the other Superior women and children.

The other vehicles were assaulted in the same manner. Some Superiors had given up easily while others resisted. People who tried to drive off found themselves stuck when their cars were surrounded by muscular meat Taurine who stabbed all four tires with their knives. Anyone who managed to get through suffered the same fate when the car was deflated by some nail traps that were elaborately placed at the only exit.

One Superior man tried to fight back using his tiny electrocutor. However, it only worked on one Inferior at the time. As they all jumped on him simultaneously, he never had a chance. His head was bashed open with a sledgehammer and his throat was cut open with a scythe. This all happened while his wife could do nothing but scream at the top of her lungs.

Any Superiors who tried to fight back were punched, kicked, stabbed, or bashed to death. Then their bodies would be thrown over the clifftop. Eventually, every single Superior was in the same state as us, sitting down helpless and covered in mud.

When everything quietened down, the aggressive meat Taurines looked silently towards their leader, a female Taurine of small size. From my estimation, she was about the same height and build as me. Unlike any typical meat Taurine, her body was lean and her hair appeared to have a fleck of gold. Her face also hinted of something Superior.

"*Do you know what your sins are, Superiors?*" She spoke with an excellent accent.

"*A talking Taurine?*" one of the Superior women screamed.

"Take care of her," the leader ordered in her original language. Her muscular underlings picked the woman up and threw her over the cliff.

"*Anyone who talks while I am speaking again will die right away.*" This time the reply from Superiors was absolute silence.

"*I am here today to announce that you don't own the world. Not anymore. And it's starting today. I will establish the new ruler of the*

285

earth." Suddenly, something had her attention and she stood on her toes to see the road below.

"Oh! What's is that? A red bus from the city, I see. I think there are about a hundred more people on there, but I don't think we need that many people up here. Go, girls, get rid of it." she ordered.

Her blindly loyal servants rushed down the steep road below without questions. They started blocking off the path of the red bus with their bodies. The driver sounded the horn repeatedly in an attempt to get them off the road, but it was to no avail. Instead of obeying the driver's wish, the women started pushing against the vehicle, grabbing and heaving it while the driver pressed against the accelerator with all his might. The girls managed to overpower it and slip it off the muddy road down to the abyss below.

"I'm glad that's over," the leader said again when her underlings returned with sludge pasted everywhere on their bodies and faces.

"I think we still have too many people here. Food is scarce and we need to conserve it. So let's start with the males. They eat a lot and don't produce anything, so kill them."

Then another struggle began. Screams and shouts were heard everywhere as the Superiors fought against their inescapable massacre. I did not know what was going on. The only thing I did was hold on to my son. Everything was filled with water, mud, and the grey sky. The result was as expected. All male Superiors died with their corpses scattered all over the marshy battlefield. Their wives and children were left to cry over their dead bodies.

At last, the chief of the barbaric female tribe noticed me. She told me to stand up and I did. With the exact same height, we stood eyes to eye. I looked into hers without backing down. If it was my fate to die by the hand of another chimera, then I would have no regret. Her eyes told me that she had learnt all the truth about the world, just as I had. I understood all her reasoning as if they it was my own. I saw myself in her, a creature of sorrow who thought of nothing else but to seek justice for this unfair world.

"You are not a Superior? Your hair is brown, but your eyes are blue?" she asked with a genuine interest in my eyes. I suddenly

286

remembered that my hair would turn completely brown when it was wet. She could not tell that I was partly blond.

"*I am not. This is not my true eye colour. Let me take it off,*" I said, then took out the contact lenses. When I was done, she opened her mouth in genuine interest.

"*So you are a meat Taurine? And your son too?*" she asked.

"Yes, I am and so is he," I answered her in my mother tongue, which got her to smile. It was a warm, welcoming smile, even though I knew that behind that smile was a tremendously cruel person.

"Sister! That's what I want to call you. But...why did you pretend to be them?" She pointed with her head to the group of pitiful sobbing Superiors.

"I...I don't know." I honestly could not think of anything. She hit me in the face with a slap.

"You can't answer me like that, sister. We all depend on honesty here. We are not Superiors. We do not lie, you hear? Now, tell me the truth or I will throw you and your son over the cliff."

"I um...I..." I could not utter a word.

"They brought us here." A clear voice suddenly came from beside me. It was my son. "They were going to use us as an emergency food supply."

"Oh! Poor thing, you must have had it hard, didn't you? But it's all right now, because there will be no more Superiors," the woman said, and patted my son on the head with another sardonic smile before facing me again.

"You have such a cute son, so I'll take him." She signaled to others with her finger.

"No!" I ran after him when a very buff Taurine lifted him with ease came and took him away. Suddenly, I stumbled and hit my face on the ground as I realised that it was my nemesis's leg that tripped me.

"You are lucky to have a smart son, sister. If it weren't for him, you would be down there under the cliff already." She smiled and walked off, leaving me among the corpses of the people who used to be the dominant species.

Epilogue

We cooked and ate Superiors' corpses on the mountain to survive. Throughout our stay, the leader constantly killed a few of them at a time until every single one of them was dead by the time the water reduced two months later. Once the land was inhabitable, I was chased down as soon as possible. The only reason I was left alive was because of my blood.

Even when everything was back to normal, I realised that it seemed that God had truly intended to finish off the Superior race. There was a massive disease that obliterated most of the population, and for some mysterious reason, it only affected them and not the others. In no time, our country suddenly became an empty place filled with abandoned cities and rotting corpses.

The Inferior uprising was not only contained with our little region, but had also spread throughout the continent like a domino effect either during or after the apocalyptic event.

Even though I knew that the world was better off without the cruel race, I didn't think that every one of them was bad. There were good and bad Superiors just like good and bad Taurines. I missed Andrew, Joanna, and Hugh, whose demises I learned of through my friend Mik later on.

However, the person I thought of the most was Ahredden. My son remained in the hands of my nemesis. When I was on the mountain, I often saw her forcing him to slaughter our livestock and instill in him the sick ideology against the previous Superior race. When I was kicked out of the mountain, I never saw him again.

I walked on the Plain of Merriment for days until I came across a settlement. I focused all my energy to help them, the survivors who consisted of Sangas, Zebus, milk or meat Taurines. I put in my physical labor at first but was soon recognised for my knowledge of the world. Even when the Superior race had lost most of their powers, their remnants of technology persisted.

Many of them were still alive, so we recruited them to join the rest of our people, although they were not considered 'Superior' anymore. Their knowledge was probably the most important factor that enabled us to survive and rebuild the new world entirely from scratch. I was their leader and made sure that everybody was treated as equals.

With a lot of effort, a new town was successfully built with the help of many others. I did not have a new husband, even though many tried to get my attention. It was the promise I had given to Brun, a promise I wanted to keep, even though my company was lacking. But one day, I had a surprise visit from Mikayla, whose youthful appearance of a milk Taurine was no more. She told me that our favourite Superiors had already succumbed to the disease. I cried a lot when I heard about them, so Mik decided to stay with me in the village. However, due to her genetic,s she died at the young age of forty.

It was when I was forty-five that I heard about my son again. At that time, he was a young man of seventeen years old. His unique name of 'Ahredden' came up when I did not recognise his face on the news. The headline announced that he had become the new leader of the country which had now divided into about ten different parts with each governed by either Zebus or meat Taurines.

I was so happy, but soon realised that he had become a completely different person. His election campaign was anything but normal, as he openly threatened and killed several of his competitors to become the sole dictator of the new country. The strong hatred ran within his veins and caused him strong prejudice against Superiors. This was evidenced by a crusade he decided to run a few years later, an extermination program against the remaining surviving Superiors. Even the people who had helped greatly with the restoration in the past were mercilessly slaughtered. My town was not an exception, because my nemesis's previous action had 'united' many towns including mine under her rule.

My son selected only the stupidest of Superior children to spare. He raised them in dirty pig pens together, never taught them any language and kept on breeding them. Many years later, I still saw their blue saddened eyes looking at me from within the television. Then the slogan would come: 'Choose S graded meat - S for Superior".

The dictator was a monster incarnate, and I could see no trace of my boy left in him. Instead, he had become what his fake mother had taught him. In that same year after his massive campaign of ethnic cleansing, the chimera woman never heard of again, and it was rumored that Adredden had imprisoned her for life. It was her punishment for being a half Superior.

When I was seventy-two years old, after running away from the lunch table, I woke up to the darkness of the evening. Having snoozed off into my dream world of the past, the feeling of terror in the past was still lingering in my mind. It was so long ago that I had felt any happiness at all. Everyone I cared about was dead, and my boy had turned into a monster.

I sat there, on the bench overlooking the garden outside, feeling so empty. A world without love was not worth living at all, I had realised. I fought so hard, yet nothing had gotten better. The village I had built had become a town then a city yet the world was just as unequal as before.

I decided that it was time to go back inside and join the others for dinner. As expected, there were some leftovers from lunch, but no meat was left, of course, and I was glad about that. So I ate only vegetables as a meal. When I was done, I picked up some letters in my room that I had been thinking of delivering for weeks. Then put them into a mailbox outside.

Those letters were addressed to multiple governmental offices, including the opposition party, Senators, and the House of Representatives, along with other anti-government organisations and other nearby countries. I claimed that I was the dictator's mother, and I attached a few strands of my white hair as proof of my DNA connection to my son. My purpose was to announce that the hypocrite who had been slaughtering thousands of Superiors were, in fact, a three-quarter superior himself.

Every single morning thereafter, I was always the first person to get up and check on the news. My body moved slowly, but I was glad that my brain was still intact so that those letters could finally change the world.

Breakfast time came, and everybody else gradually came into the room to join me. It was only at eight o'clock that the breaking news came up on the screen. I stared at it intensely, as I had done for the past two weeks.

Finally, the envelopes appeared on the news reporter's hands. When she was announcing my accusation to the long-running dictator, all heads in the room turned towards the screen at once. The old people suddenly listened with serious looks on their faces.

They all hated my son, I knew, but I still loved him. That was why it was my responsibility to take him down. However, in the middle of the broadcast, the television became static all of a sudden. It was cut off just before they could announce the result of the DNA test. I was hugely disappointed, but knew that it was he and his goons that had interfered with the broadcast.

Half a minute of complete silence later, the signal came back. However, this time, the presenter was a completely different person. It was an old woman, probably about sixty years old. Her hair was white, but there was no mistake that she used to be a Superior, because her bright blue eyes stood out. In the back of the stage, I could see hazily a little girl of about thirteen years old standing behind her.

The old woman stepped in front of the stage, and the accompanying name tag on the screen showed *"Hayley Cotter"*. My mouth dropped open in surprise before I began to examine her features. Even though she had changed a lot, behind her white hair and sagging skin, I could still see her as a little girl of four years old.

She said that she was broadcasting from another country, because our government was too cowardly to let the media reveal the truth. She condemned them for exterminating the Superior race and for the many monstrous atrocities they had committed against people of all races. The speech lasted for about thirty minutes before she stood down. It was finished except for the final truth that was yet to be revealed. Instead of revealing it herself, she told the teenage girl behind her to walk up to the stage.

Only when the kid came closer could I see her features. She had light brown skin and curly black hair, a little bit like a Sanga, or something in between. It was very hard to tell. However, her eyes were the most striking thing in the whole world. For some reason, they were of different colors. Her right was earth brown while her left was sky blue. She stepped onto the podium and opened an envelope in her hand.

"Positive, I announced it positive!" she shouted, and the whole world seemed to stop moving.

After some time, I heard someone in the crowd below the podium yell back.

"Who is this girl? President Cotter?"

"She's my granddaughter. Her name is…" She patted the little girl on the shoulder then mouthed at her silently *"Tell them."* I read from her lips.

The young female looked at her older relative unsurely, but nodded once before opening her mouth again.

"Cat…Cattleya."

About the author

My name is Shanon Ngampiyaskul. I graduated as a veterinarian from Massey University in New Zealand. During my years of training, I had many opportunities to visit farms and other animal-related industries. One day, I realised that almost nobody can truly understand what it is like to be an animal. Physical pain is easy enough to imagine and has been proven to be something animals can feel. Emotional pain, however, is an entirely different matter. Although I have no political alignment with either meat lovers or haters, I still feel empathy for the poor creatures who have suffered so much for us. That is why I have written this piece to offer an alternative viewpoint from the animal's perspective.

Acknowledgement

Thank you to my very first readers of mine, my mum and her friend, Aunty Pet. Thank you so much for always supporting me while I was writing, attentively following every single chapter as they came out, and correcting me on grammar and plot holes.

Thank you for all the dear readers who have persevered from start to finish, no matter how much heartbreak it may have caused. I hope that this story impacts your perspective on life, even just a tiny bit.

www.ingramcontent.com/pod-product-compliance
Lightning Source LLC
Chambersburg PA
CBHW030031180626
46810CB00001B/317